BITTEN

The Graced Series

BITTEN

Book Two

AMANDA PILLAR

Published by Maatkare Books
www.amandapillar.com

Editor: Pete Kempshall

ISBN: 978-0-6480295-1-9

Cover Design: Ljiljana Romanovic © 2016
Internal Layout: Amanda Pillar © 2016

First Published February 2016

For Liz Grzyb. Wonderful friend and editor extraordinaire.
You'll smash it.

PROLOGUE

The Trsetti tell of a peak, high in the Oberona Mountains; sometimes it is clothed in the white of snow, other times in green and flowers of startling blue. They call it the Old Woman, and on its cliffs, there sits a hut. None of the Trsetti have seen this building in hundreds of years, although there are those who swear the stone house is empty, that no one has lived there for decades. But those who say this are young and do not believe in that which cannot be seen, or touched or heard.

The older Trsetti know better.

In truth, the hut has sat abandoned from time to time, once for centuries. Every now and then, however, it has been occupied. An auburn-haired woman would go there, when she was weary of the world beyond the valley. Indeed, the Traveler, as the Trsetti call her, had been visiting this stone building for as long as they could remember, and their memories were long, stretching far back to times when the purple and yellow-eyed demons fought for control of the world. The blood drinkers and the shape changers. The Traveler, they say, was a blood drinker, yet she never drank from the Trsetti, not even when sustenance was offered freely.

Then one day, she arrived in the valley with a small girl who had eyes so dark Brown they could be Black. She traded for food and essentials, while the girl child stood alone outside the small town, watching the ground at her feet. And when the Traveler was done, she led the child away, disappearing up the Old Woman's trails. It was over a hundred years before the Trsetti laid eyes on either one again.

PART I

Nature is wont to hide herself

CHAPTER ONE

Trsetti village

Fin was running for his life.

Again.

For the third time this month.

His feet beat along the dirt tracks that meandered between the Trsetti huts, his breath coming fast. He swore as a villager leaped out from a gap between dwellings. Spotting Fin, the man released a bloodcurdling shout, his eyes wide and savage. Fin skidded to a stop, met the man's wild stare and grinned. The Trsetti cursed in his native language, raised a club above his head, and swung. With a burst of speed, Fin dodged to the left, sliding around his attacker. He winced at the loud *thunk* of the club on a daub wall. If that had been his skull, it would have cracked like an egg.

Breathing hard, Fin banked right, before bursting from the edge of the village. He ran for the trees, their emerald tops glinting against an azure skyline. Yells and cries followed him, but he didn't look back to see how many villagers were giving chase. The cacophony was enough to let him know that there were too many. Stones thudded into the ground around him; he was lucky the villagers were such bad shots. He ran on. Once he hit the tree line, he'd be safe.

Well, safer.

The yells grew more excited as a rock struck his shoulder, and he bit back a grunt. The sharp burn of fatigue seared his legs, and his lungs ached. The trees beckoned, a green line of safety that promised him a breather, a cool drink of water, and a long and no doubt furious chat with a pissed-off werebear.

While each villager might know the surrounding forests like the backs of their weathered hands, they wouldn't follow him in far, not once they'd seen Byrne. Coming up close to a hulking were would make them think twice about coming near Fin ever again, the superstitious bunch of idiots. That was why he'd gone into town alone. With his Hazel eyes, Fin was surprised they'd even tolerated him. But his pretty face generally smoothed things over.

Yes, he'd survive this day; he'd put gold on it.

He didn't want to think about what Byrne would say when they met up. It wouldn't be flattering toward Fin; then again, it never was. Byrne was grumpy. Being in cold weather in his human form tended to leave him agitated. Bears liked to hibernate, after all. It also didn't help that it was the third time this month that Fin had gotten them kicked out of a town. But that wasn't his fault. Not *entirely*.

How was he meant to know that the Trsetti woman was married?

CHAPTER TWO

The Old Mother

Hannah hadn't spoken to another person in over a year. She couldn't even remember the sound of her own voice. After all, there were only so many conversations one could have with oneself before boredom — or madness — became a serious issue.

She kicked the wooden door shut behind her and walked across the open room. Leaning down, she dropped the bucket of blackberries onto the timber bench that constituted her kitchen table. The pack full of roots she'd carried slung over her shoulder soon joined the bucket on the scarred benchtop. She had enough to eat for a few days yet.

Hannah snorted.

She could go without food for longer than anyone else she knew. Not that she knew many people. Eating food was necessary; it just didn't need to be a daily occurrence for her, not so long as she could hunt animals for blood. But that was the thing with boredom — gathering and eating produce gave her something to do.

Hannah reached her arms high above her head, toward the beams that spanned the ceiling, and stretched out, arching backward as she did so. She held the position for a few seconds before she dropped her arms and looked around the small cabin. The dishes — misshapen pieces of pottery that they were — had been washed, the ceiling was free of cobwebs, and her bed was made. She'd also catalogued her larder and meager collection of books.

The large room, which housed her kitchen and living area, was stone-walled and hung with thick tapestries that were out of place in the small cabin, their richness in stark contrast to the serviceable furniture of the hut. They depicted scenes of vast cities, of death, and of life. Even though they hung on the walls of her home, insulating the interior against the cold, Hannah still wouldn't touch them. Another's hands had woven the cloth; another's memories and impressions were as intertwined in the images as the individual threads. When her mother came to visit, she would beat the dust out of them for Hannah. No, the hangings were too potent for Hannah to handle, even wearing gloves.

She wasn't that desperate for things to do.

In the metal hearth, the fire had died down to coals, so she walked over and began to stoke it. As flames started to flicker and lick at the kindling, she fed the growing blaze some of the wood she'd stocked next to the chimney. Like almost everything else in the cabin — from the battered table, to the chairs, the bed, and even the cutlery — Hannah had made the hearth herself. She'd sold all the other items she'd been given over the years, except for the tapestries. Those she'd kept for her mother.

Once the blaze had settled in, she rose and took off her gloves, dropping them on the kitchen table. She should get some water, so she could wash her face and the roots she'd collected. And she should check on Betty, her goat.

Grabbing a second bucket from near the sink, she headed outside. Turning left, she strode around to the small stable — a shed she had converted. A natural spring ran about two hundred steps from her kitchen window. In the summer it flowed freely, and she used that rather than the pump inside. Like most other things, she'd made the pump herself, and it worked, usually. Most of the time though, it was quicker to head outside for water.

The grassy banks along the stream were so green it almost hurt to look at them. Small yellow and white star-shaped flowers dotted the verdant expanse, and Hannah could hear small animals and insects crawling through the vegetation. Even a few bees buzzed happily from flower to flower. It was still early spring, not really all that warm yet, but up here, on the Old Woman, animals took what opportunities they had.

Hannah bent low and dropped the bucket into the stream; it filled quickly. She reveled in the sensation of the water as it flowed over her hands, chilling her. She almost felt naked, the bare skin of her hands exposed. But there was nothing to contaminate the liquid up here — from mountain to cup, that's how she liked it. Fresh as a daisy, as her mother would say with a smile.

She hauled the bucket out of the stream, then turned and headed toward the stable. She'd fill up Betty's trough for the night, then go back and grab some water for herself. Hopefully the goat's supply wouldn't freeze over; the nights were still cold, but Hannah had insulated the little addendum to her cabin as best she could.

She opened the stable door and smiled when she spotted Betty, although the expression wilted when she spotted the carnage. The goat had chewed through several pieces of scrap leather that Hannah had thought were placed well above her reach. The animal turned and looked at her with large, liquid brown eyes. It was difficult to be annoyed at having her leather collection ruined, when confronted with such a pathetic display.

Hannah emptied the trough, then filled it with fresh water while Betty nibbled on her piece of leather. She dropped the bucket by the door, and collected the other half-chewed pieces. They were beyond salvaging, weak from the gnawing, and would have to be thrown out. Hannah could just leave them for Betty to chew on some more, but she wasn't sure how healthy that was for the silly nanny. Thankfully, it was cow leather, so at least Betty hadn't inadvertently partaken in cannibalism, although she wouldn't put it past the goat to try.

Checking the supply of hay, Hannah determined there would be enough for the night and following day. She would let Betty roam tomorrow, the only problem being tracking the goat down again afterward. The nanny could cover a surprising amount of terrain in a day.

Hannah stroked Betty's head for a few minutes and the goat shut her eyes in bliss. They'd been together for five years now; the animal was a faithful, if cheeky companion. Hannah had traded for her when her old goat, Molly, had died. There were some rare herbs that grew on the slopes of the Old Mother, much prized by the Trsetti women, and they'd more than covered the cost of a goat. Withdrawing her hand slowly, her heart swelled with emotion. It was dangerous to fall in love with her pets — they always died — but she couldn't help it.

After making sure the stable was locked behind her, Hannah headed back to the stream, pail in hand. A thin wail drifted to her on the breeze, like a cat howling. There were few cats on the Old Woman: a cougar or two, but nothing that had ever ventured close to her hut. Not close enough for her to hear, anyway. They could detect that another predator had marked out her territory.

The cry sounded again, thin and weak. If Hannah hadn't been a vampire, she probably wouldn't have been able to hear it.

Maybe it was a person? A child who had gotten lost on the slopes?

Dropping her bucket, she ran in the direction of the sound. It grew weaker as her feet sped over the green-carpeted slopes, but she followed it to the source. Barely panting, she came to a sudden stop, eyes wide at the sight laid out before her.

It was a baby.

CHAPTER THREE

Pinton City

Being short had never really been a problem for Alice Reive. Sure, there was that time when she'd dated Roger Mingly, who'd been six foot two, and with her just five three, kissing had been a bit of an issue. And normally she was fine with her height, or lack of it. But today she was trying to paint the ceiling in her flat, and even though she had climbed to the top of her ladder, the last bit of plaster was just beyond her reach.

Huffing, she held the paintbrush out and tried to stretch that extra couple of inches, but she wasn't in luck. The unpainted patch mocked her with its greenness. Who had ever thought that green was a good color to paint a ceiling. That's what she wanted to know. Admitting defeat — temporarily — she climbed down the ladder and took the paintbrush to the sink. Maybe she should ask one of the guards she worked with if they'd mind lending her a hand. Kyle McInnes and the guard captain Mikael Johnston were tall enough that they could paint that corner with ease. *Probably wouldn't even need a ladder*, Alice thought with a frown. *Bastards.*

As she rinsed the last of the white paint down the drain, a knock sounded. She turned the faucet off and dried her hands before opening the door to her visitor — a small boy in the black cap that identified him as a messenger for the City Guard. Pinton's guards had taken to employing a regular stable of runners, as it made their communication system much more reliable, compared to the previous method of grabbing the nearest street urchin and promising them bronze. Even though most of the messengers they now employed permanently were the same urchins.

But when it came to messages from the guards, Alice knew it could be only one thing.

"They found a body, miss," the boy said without preamble.

Alice sighed. A life cataloguing corpses certainly wasn't how she'd imagined her adulthood would turn out. It was her type of penance or punishment; she wasn't sure which. "Where?"

"Down in King's Park."

Blinking, Alice looked down at the boy. She wasn't sure she'd heard him right. "*Where* did you say?"

"King's Park, miss."

"Let me get my things."

◆

Alice carefully set her black leather bag beside the shrouded body and took a deep breath. She didn't think she'd ever get over the fear of the unknown; the horrible uncertainty that rocked her the moment before she pulled back the cover to reveal the dead face.

Distracting herself, she stole glimpses of the surrounding park. Green grass extended as far as the eye could see, intersected by tracks and flowerbeds. Tall iron structures designed to mimic trees dominated the landscape, covered in thick, flowering vines. And then there were the aristos who had gathered around the guard perimeter to stare at the body. They were dressed like a children's coloring set; pinks, blues, greens, blacks and every other shade in between. All in no doubt extremely expensive fabric — fabric she could only dream of touching, let alone owning.

Humans didn't generally get to visit this area. Oh, they could come into the park and even wander around, but the death stares they'd earn from the vampire aristos generally meant it wasn't worth the bother. Neither was the risk of ending up as a vampire's next meal, or worse, the risk of becoming bit-ridden. One bite was all it took, the drug-like high induced by their saliva second to none. So she'd heard.

Alice didn't believe in tempting fate to find out.

"When was the last time a body was found here?" Alice asked. She glanced over at the crowd of onlookers.

"For a vampire body, around fifty years ago," Dinya answered. The day captain had organized for three guards to stand sentry at the perimeter of the site. Their hands were folded behind their backs, military style. Dinya, meanwhile, hovered close to Alice and the corpse. "Humans are pretty common. Someone gets a bit enthusiastic about lunch or some such. You're lucky it's daytime, otherwise the crowd would be three times this size."

And Alice wouldn't be able to see a thing. Darkness was no blessing for the human population, not in a vampire-run town, and the street lights didn't extend far into aristo parks like this one. "I need to look at the body."

Dinya shrugged. "Figured as much."

"I mean, do you mind if I check it out with these onlookers here? Or you want less of a crowd?" The presence of the aristo audience indicated to Alice that the victim was a vampire. A human body would have barely earned a glance from the bejeweled fribbles.

Dinya looked around the crowd and made her decision. Shoving her whistle into her mouth, she blew a series of ear-piercing blasts. Most of the vampires pressed their hands against their ears; some even had their eyes scrunched shut.

Effective, Alice thought. Perhaps she should invest in a whistle herself. Not that she had a lot to do with vampires, but you couldn't predict the future.

"You lot," Dinya shouted. "Clear out, we need to continue this investigation."

One man in the crowd drew himself up to his full height — which wasn't a lot greater than Alice's. His chin was almost obscured by his collar, and he had the most obnoxious yellow and pink waistcoat/cravat combination she'd ever had the misfortune of seeing.

The aristo spluttered. "What did you just say?"

"Clear out!" Dinya repeated. *Rather tactful for the day captain,* Alice thought.

The vampire took a step closer. "Do you have *any* idea who you're speaking to, human?"

Dinya played with her whistle. The other vampires looked nervous. "I don't care if you're the king himself, which you ain't, cos I've met the man. I have a crime scene and I want it cleared of spectators."

The idiot vampire's expression turned hard. *Oh boy, this isn't going to end well.* Dinya eyed the man off, a faint smile dancing on the edges of her mouth. With the captain's height and musculature, Alice would put money on the human over the vampire any day of the week, no matter that vampires were biologically stronger. And she'd bet that Dinya would enjoy beating some sense into the fool; the woman wasn't known for her tolerance of vampires. That's why she was the day captain.

"I am going to report you to your superior for this—"

Dinya laughed. "I *am* the superior. Your report has been noted and filed under 'I', for 'I couldn't give a fuck.' Now leave."

The aristo's mouth opened, and Dinya's hand dropped to her steel baton. "Do I need to charge you for obstructing an investigation?"

The vampire spluttered something outraged, then turned on his heel and stormed from the park. The remaining onlookers trailed after him, no doubt wishing to dissect the scene in full.

Once they'd left, Alice knelt on the soft grass next to the corpse. The dew from the green blades soaked into her black pants. She held her breath the way she always did when uncovering a corpse. Some small part of her never forgot what it was like to lift that sheet, to see someone you loved lying there, dead and forever gone.

Slowly, Alice pulled back the cover, exposing the victim's face.

The extended fangs and purple eyes — not to mention the long hair and youthful features — clearly marked the dead man as a vampire. No one she knew. No one she'd have ever even met. She didn't deal with dead — or alive — vampires particularly often. The former, because they were long-lived and didn't tend to attract the interest of the city coroner unless there was an accident; the latter, because she was just about as common as you could get. Vampires were generally from aristo families, or were trying to become aristos; they didn't tend to mix with lowly humans like her.

"Do you know who he is?" Alice asked.

Dinya crouched down next to her. "Not yet. One of those fools could have probably identified him for me, but I figure we're better off checking the body out first. Once the aristos work out it's one of their own, we're going to have a hard time keeping custody of the corpse."

Alice threw the sheet off the body. Noting the dead man's dark-blue tailored jacket, white silk shirt and tan linen pants, she came to the same conclusion as the captain. The vampire was an aristo — or at least came from money. Lots of it. The coin spent on clothes like these could have fed, clothed and housed a human family for four months.

Alice began her inspection in earnest, starting with the man's head and working her way down.

"No marks at the neck. Jacket is undone. Shirt is buttoned haphazardly. No signs of struggle — hands aren't cut or bleeding and no foreign matter under the fingernails. No bruising on the abdomen. Body is still in rigor. Minor wound on the anterior." She didn't bother undoing his pants. She'd do that when she stripped the body for an autopsy, if she had a chance to do one. She glanced at his feet, which had been shoved into a pair of unlaced shoes, then turned the body over with a grunt. He was surprisingly heavy.

Looking up, she nodded at Dinya. "Can you help me get his jacket off?"

Together, they cut the jacket off the body. It would have been nearly impossible to get it off otherwise. Underneath the jacket, rusty colored blood stained the back of the silk shirt. She lifted the garment up.

"Staked in the back," she said. "Lividity shows he was laid on his back and left there soon after. That — with the rigor — indicates the victim was killed less than twelve hours ago." Looking around the park, she nodded to herself. "No doubt dumped here afterward. He was dressed rather quickly first."

Murder, then. The reason she'd become a doctor. She'd started out hoping to save people, but had soon realized that she was drawn to helping those it was too late to heal. And so she'd learned all there was to know about dead bodies, and the information they could share. When asked why she'd gone into the death market, she usually said it was because dead people couldn't lie like the living, but that was only part of the reason.

"They picked a rather public place to leave the body," Dinya commented, running a hand over her baton.

"Kill an aristo vampire, dump them in an aristo park? My guess is it's a message, to get someone's attention." While Alice wasn't a guard, there was something to be said about knowing death as well as she did.

Dinya tapped the whistle to her chin, then turned in a slow circle, her brown gaze taking in the park. "Or maybe," the day captain said, "it's a warning."

Chapter Four

Trsetti village

The villagers caught up to Fin just before he reached the camp. One managed to grab his shoulder, throwing him off balance, as another landed a lucky punch, hitting him square in the eye. Pain burst through him, and his eye immediately began to swell. It was going to leave one heck of a bruise come morning.

Ducking another club swung at his head, Fin tried to dart between the towering trees, hoping that Byrne had heard the commotion and was already coming to investigate. When a hand grabbed the back of his leather jacket and jerked him off balance, he realized that he was not going to be quite that lucky. He threw out his arms to try and keep upright, but a villager punched him in the stomach. The air whooshed from his lungs.

Hitting dirt, Fin cried out as pain shot up his chest. *Not the ribs.* He really hoped that he hadn't broken any. Ribs were a bitch to heal.

"That half-demon bastard fucked my wife!"

A boot shot out and smashed him in his aching chest and he heard something crack loudly.

Mother fucker.

Gasping for breath and clutching at his side, Fin curled into a ball. He didn't have enough air to set the man right. The guy's wife had fucked *him.* She'd put an aphrodisiac in his drink, for blood's sake.

Why hadn't Byrne come blasting out of the trees and scared the living daylights out of these backward villagers yet? Maybe he hadn't heard the fight. Or he'd moved the camp. Or maybe he'd just left Fin to fend for himself. It had to happen sooner or later.

"You said he raped your wife?" Another man was speaking now, his voice gravelly and thick. Probably the town's headman; he smoked like he was dying of thirst in a desert, and each cigar was his only source of hydration.

"Not rape. But she swears he seduced her with his foreign ways. His demon eyes."

The. Bitch.

"I thought he had normal eyes."

"Mostly."

"No mercy then. We can't risk other women thinking they can cuckold their husbands. Or fuck demons."

The blows rained down on him again, every villager who'd followed him kicking, punching and spitting on him. *I'm going to die.*

Curled into a protective ball, his hands and arms covering his head, he thought he was hallucinating when a roar shattered the air, and the assault faltered.

"What was that?"

Then came the sound of breaking tree limbs and foliage. And the screaming started.

"Bear! It's a bear!"

Fin wanted to shout in relief, but he could scarcely catch his breath. And what if this wasn't salvation? It could very well be a real bear. His eyes had swollen shut from the beating, and there was no way for him to know.

"Run! We must have woken it up from hibernation."

"Just break this bastard's neck and be done with it."

Hands grabbed him roughly, large rough palms securing a hold on his head. Fin twisted and turned, trying to throw them off.

The hands disappeared.

More screams erupted, and the sound of footsteps pounding on the forest floor reached Fin's ears, among the shouts of rage and terror.

Then one of the most beautiful noises he'd ever heard, a deep, rumbling voice, pierced the forest. "Leave him!"

Byrne.

"Demon!"

"Monster!"

"He seduced my poor wife!"

"Really?" Byrne growled. Fin sensed someone standing over him, heard several loud sniffs. Man, he hated when Byrne did that.

"Then why does he stink of aphrodisiac?"

Fin winced. Of course Byrne would be able to smell that. But he wished he could see the remaining villagers' faces; he was surprised they had lingered long enough to speak with an angry were. Maybe he'd underestimated them.

Or they were just idiots.

"Of *what?*"

"Minar root. It's an aphrodisiac," Byrne repeated.

"Maybe they don't know what the word means either," Fin gasped in his native language. "They're certainly dumb enough not to."

Byrne didn't laugh. "Then tell me a word they will understand."

Fin coughed, blood trickling down his chin. "Sex stimulant? I don't know. Do I look like a fucking dictionary?"

Well, he kind of was. But now was not the time to get into that.

"Someone gave him something to make him horny," Byrne stated.

Fin loved that the guy was straight to the point.

"Liar!"

"What did you call me?" Byrne's voice was soft, but Fin could picture what the bear looked like. Even in his human suit, the towering man could be terrifying. Or he might be in his in-between form. Even worse.

"I—"

"If you want to survive the day, I'd suggest you leave."

"But—"

Almost conversationally, Byrne said, "It's been a while since I had human steak."

The sound of their hurried departure would have made Fin laugh, if he hadn't hurt so much. Minutes passed as Byrne waited to make sure the villagers wouldn't return, and then the were's hands were on him, businesslike, deftly checking Fin's injuries.

"I swear, Fin, you're a magnet for trouble."

"No shit," Fin muttered.

"Can you walk?"

His body said he couldn't, but pride made Fin say, "I can try."

Byrne pretty much had to carry him back to their camp; Fin could barely see anything more than a blurry grayish line. Soon he was warming by a fire, the comforting pain of a blanket spread over his shoulders. He didn't want to think about the bruises he was going to have if even wearing a blanket hurt.

Then Byrne began the long job of patching him up and of telling him how much of an idiot he was. The trouble was, Fin couldn't really argue with him. One, because Byrne was stitching up the worst of his cuts, and the bear wasn't above making it hurt if he thought Fin needed it; and two, because his friend was right. Fin had been an idiot, but he wasn't going to agree with the other man, just on principle.

"What took you so long to find me?" Fin grumbled about halfway through the stitching. He still couldn't see properly, especially as he was holding a deer steak over his eyes. He wasn't exactly sure how this was meant to help the swelling, but Byrne had insisted on it.

"Oh, it didn't take me long. Figured you could do with a bit of roughing up."

Fin choked. "A bit of roughing up? You call this *roughing up*?"

"Well, it got a bit out of hand. Heated up pretty fast. But I stepped in before you got your stupid neck broken, so you should be thanking me."

"Thanking you? You got the shit beaten out of me! Ow!" Fin flinched as Byrne jabbed a needle into his hand.

"You're alive. And I had to threaten to turn people into food. You know how I hate having to do that."

Fin sighed. He knew. When they'd first met, Byrne had made mincemeat out of a bunch of scumbag humans. He'd been picking bits of them out of his teeth for days after. Long pig, he called it.

Thing was, Byrne wasn't really a pork man.

CHAPTER FIVE

Hannah stared at the small, wrinkly infant as it cried weakly, fists raised to the sky. The baby was naked, its eyes shut, its little limbs kicking in protest as the cold licked at it. Hurrying over, she reached down to pick the baby up, but paused, arms outstretched. Standing motionless over the small form, her eyes locked on her gloveless hands.

It's only young, she told herself. *It won't have many memories for you to withstand.*

But still she hesitated. Did that make her a horrible person? Why hadn't she gone back for her gloves first? She growled. She knew better than to forget them.

The baby's skin was developing a blue tinge. Cold, Hannah realized; it was starting to suffer from exposure. She couldn't leave it here, despite her lack of gloves.

Grow a spine.

Okay. Okay, she could do this.

The child was lying on a blanket that had been spread over the damp grass. The material was frayed at the edges, but good quality, with a blue diamond-shaped pattern running over its length. Someone had spent a lot of time weaving the cloth. Hannah sighed. She wore only a long-sleeved shirt and leather vest — she didn't have anything else she could wrap around the babe to keep it warm on the journey back to her cabin. She'd have to grab the blanket. Gritting her teeth, she thrust her hands forward, seized the cloth and wrapped it around the infant as quickly as she could. Just as she'd just tucked the last fold in place, her eyesight vanished and her ability imprisoned her.

Hannah dropped to her knees beside the baby. She dimly felt the impact shudder through her joints. Memories upon memories soaked the material of the blanket. Scenes sped through her mind, so fast she had trouble keeping up with them.

Gnarled hands spinning the wool from which the cloth was woven, the warm smile and faded brown eyes of the weaver. The whispered words of love as the blanket was passed on to the weaver's oldest daughter. Delight and tenderness as the blanket was wrapped around the daughter's first babe. And then anger and angst, as the cloth was draped a final time around a newborn daughter, to be left on the slopes of the Old Mother.

All those memories and more rushed through Hannah.

Gritting her teeth, Hannah sorted through those thoughts and recollections, forcing herself to focus on the blanket's immediate history.

♦

It didn't matter, Ezra thought, a girl child wasn't a curse like her husband's father said. They were not ornaments that adorned houses, taking up space and costing gold to feed. They bred children; created the next generation, then raised that generation so they could inherit property and keep the Trsetti traditions alive.

She was *proud* to have given birth to a daughter.

"It's a *what?*" her husband shouted from the other room. It was clear the midwife had delivered the news, much as Ezra had delivered her babe.

Ezra glanced down at the infant in her arms, its naked wrinkled skin pressed close to hers as it suckled from her breast. Her mother had told her this was the moment that a woman bonded with her child. That it was this initial feeding that cemented the love a mother felt for her baby.

But something didn't feel *right*.

Her head tickled, and her stomach fluttered. Maybe her unease stemmed from her husband's reaction? A plate smashed in the adjacent room, and it was followed by cursing. The timber walls didn't do much toward dampening the sound.

"A *girl*?" That was her father-in-law, voice slurred, presumably from drink. He'd been celebrating the birth of his first grandson all morning. "I didn't pay good money for that woman to give you *girl children*!"

She could hear her husband rumble a reply, but Ezra could not make out the words.

"By the blood, she will give you a son! Even if I have to tie her down to the bed to ensure it!"

Ezra wanted to shout, to scream back through the wall that she hadn't meant for the child to be female. She'd done everything right; had eaten apples and red meat until she'd felt nauseated from the mere smell. Her mother-in-law had assured her that this was the recipe for producing male young. Ezra hadn't even touched a lemon during the pregnancy for fear she'd have a girl.

Now her husband would mount her again and again until she fell pregnant. It didn't matter that she might want a break between babes. That her milk might dry up if she became pregnant too soon. It wouldn't matter to her husband or his father at all. After all, her husband had three deceased sisters, proof of his family's disregard for her sex.

The door smashed open and her husband stood in the threshold. He was breathing heavily, scowling in anger.

"Let me see this child you have given me," he said.

The babe was still feeding, but he plucked it from her breast, supporting his daughter's weak neck with one large palm. Ezra raised her hands uselessly. The newborn cried at the sudden loss of nourishment.

"Demon!"

Ezra shrunk back, thinking the insult had been spat at her. But then she saw her husband's shaking hands, his trembling body. He all but threw the infant back at her.

Awkwardly Ezra took back the baby, the child's cries high-pitched from the rough treatment. She didn't know what to do, what was happening.

"You didn't tell me you had demon blood in you!"

"Demon blood?" Ezra blanched. "I don't know what you are talking about."

"The babe, look at its eyes!"

Ezra looked down, at the squalling infant, at the child she'd nurtured in her womb for nine long months.

Green.

Murky, not yet fully developed, but its eyes were definitely green.

She almost dropped the infant.

"It's not in my family!" Ezra shouted back.

"You dare imply it is in *mine*?"

Ezra stared at her husband, mute rage filling her. Not *his* family: not his father, the perfect headman with his perfect wife who had perfect sons — excluding his dead daughters — whose line had been ruling the Trsetti for generation upon generation.

"Or is this demon the offspring of some other man?"

She wanted to laugh at that claim, but if he thought she had been unfaithful, he would give her back to her family; leave her in shame. No man would marry her after that. "I was a virgin when you took me to bed. I conceived that very night."

Those facts he could not argue with.

Red faced, rage burning in his brown eyes, he jabbed a finger at her. "If you do not get rid of that demon, I will. You have until tomorrow morning." He slammed the door behind him, and the walls rattled from the force.

Ezra shut her eyes, tears burning behind her eyelids, as he shouted to his father and whoever else was in the room that he wanted a divorce. Biting back a sob, Ezra nodded to herself. She'd get rid of the baby. Then maybe her husband wouldn't leave her, wouldn't force her back to her family to be ostracized.

♦

Ezra's fear and anger suffused Hannah. She experienced it all, as Ezra swaddled the infant, then slipped outside her little cottage and walked up the slopes to the Old Woman. It had hurt the new mother to walk, but she'd made the two-hour journey the following morning. She'd unwrapped the infant and then without even a backward glance, left. It would be up to the Old Woman to do what was right.

That is where the blanket's memories ended. Or Ezra's memories, at any rate. The remaining echoes were the babe's, and they spoke of discomfort and hunger.

Shaking from the emotional journey, Hannah picked the infant up and held it close, hugging it to her chest. To be left unwanted out here was heartbreaking. How many children had been similarly discarded over the years? She wondered how many bones she'd find, if she were to walk toward the little town in the valley down below.

She'd always thought the Trsetti were good people, despite being fearful of those who were different. They'd been nothing but honest and hardworking in the little contact she'd had with them. Their fear, well, it had been based on *physical* differences; hair, skin or eye color. Anyone who didn't look like them was a demon. Hannah's mother had told her it was a remnant from a war the villagers could barely remember. Her own differences had made them wary around her, but they had accepted her as her skin was not too much paler than their own, and many villagers had black hair. They'd also thought her eyes were a very dark Brown. Which they weren't.

But Hannah had never guessed they would kill a baby because of its eye color. It was abhorrent. Disgust welled in her and she wanted to march down that slope, right up to Ezra's door and yell at her. Call her out as the murderer she was, as her husband was.

But the baby was hungry and cold and Hannah needed to sort through the rest of the blanket's memories. Hopefully, there was something that showed her how to feed a child who had no mother. No doubt one of the grandmothers had known what to do and their memories were as locked into the blanket as Ezra's.

She hoped they'd been nicer people.

CHAPTER SIX

"So, whose wife did you screw this time?" Byrne asked with a sigh. He kept his hands steady while he worked. Stitching was difficult for him; he was a big man with big hands. It took a lot of concentration to do a proper job of sewing someone up. Especially since Fin wouldn't let him cauterize the wounds.

Chicken.

Fin flinched and with one hand adjusted the raw steak that was dripping red down his cheeks. It looked like he was crying blood. An overly dramatic thing for Byrne to think, but Fin was all about the drama. The more, the better. Go big or go home, that was the human's saying. "Headman's son."

Byrne added the final stitch to Fin's arm, rinsed the needle, and held it over the small fire he'd thrown together to sterilize it. He then packed it away in the first aid kit that was part of their travel gear. Byrne had had plenty of cause to put the medical equipment to good use since he'd met the human. Like now, where he'd had to put in fifty stitches, mostly on Fin's arms, some on his face. Luckily for Fin, the stitches barely intersected the man's intricate tattoos.

Byrne still needed to rinse the cuts clean. Infection wasn't a big concern for weres, but humans could die from septic wounds, and Byrne owed Fin too much to let the idiot get sick over a few measly cuts. Picking up a bottle of spirits from a leather bag near his foot, he quickly — and quietly — unscrewed the lid. The bag was nestled on a bed of pine needles, the greenery scenting the air with crisp, acidic freshness, mingling with Fin's aroma of sex, minar root, blood and dirt, and the normal Fin odor: verbena and lemon.

The tall pine trees created a sense of seclusion, something that reminded Byrne of home, a place he hadn't seen in far too long. But not long enough that he was tempted to return there, either.

Byrne hadn't wanted to shift camps, but had thought it would be the smart thing to do, just in case the stupid humans decided to try and attack them under the cover of night. This area hadn't had a human walk across it in at least a year. He'd have smelled it otherwise.

"Hopefully you didn't sleep with the heir's wife," Byrne said.

"No, her husband was the second son. Apparently." Fin shifted uncomfortably on the ten-yard-long log Byrne had set out next to the fire as a make-shift chair. "The first son's wife was in confinement giving birth to the much-awaited boy-child of his father's dreams."

"Eh, tribesmen. Don't understand them." Byrne had grown up — like most people on the northern continent — in a matrilineal descent structure. There was no doubt that a woman's babe was a woman's babe. The father on the other hand...well, the child may not be his, and there was no way to tell. Not unless there was a Green-eyed human around — a Graced — who could read the mother's mind. Little villages like the one the Trsetti lived in were Graced-free, though. Only Brown-eyed folk lived there.

Graceds, weres and vampires — and even some other humans, if they had the wrong skin or hair color — were demons to the villagers. Monsters.

Those terms meant nothing to anyone with half a brain. There were no such things as monsters or demons. But it did tell Byrne that the person who used those words was ignorant and foolish. But that didn't make them less dangerous. At least the bigger towns and cities didn't follow the same idiocy.

Fin had enough Brown in his eyes that he could usually pass

for a normal human. The Trsetti had noticed, though.

"I hadn't realized that the woman was talking about her sister-in-law; I didn't think she was married," Fin said.

Byrne raised an eyebrow. "So you wouldn't have had sex with the human female if you knew she was married?"

"Probably not."

Byrne doubted that. Fin was generally led about by his brain, but not the one in his head. And he'd been dosed up with an aphrodisiac. The man wouldn't have been focusing on much else aside from what was going on in his pants.

Byrne upended the bottle of vodka over Fin's arm. The human jerked, but the were grabbed Fin's arm, holding it in place. The man's screech was loud enough to make Byrne wince.

"Loud, much?" he muttered.

Panting, Fin tried to snatch his hand back, but couldn't shake loose from Byrne's grip. The human lowered the steak from his swollen eyes. "Just in case you can't work it out, I'm glaring the fuck out of you right now."

Byrne laughed, a burst of surprised sound. "Ooooo, I'm frightened."

"Fuck you."

"You wish."

"Asshole."

"Precious *petal*."

Byrne grabbed Fin's other arm, and poured more of the vodka over his friend's wounds.

"Mother *fucker!*"

"There, there. All done. Such a whiner."

Fin slapped the steak back to his black eyes. "Do you know how much that hurts? I'm not like you; I don't heal this shit up in five minutes."

Byrne grunted. "It's more like two."

"Smartass."

Byrne bandaged Fin's newly stitched wounds. Then, folding a piece of cloth, he soaked it with alcohol and dabbed the material against the scratches on Fin's face. At least the clever bastard had protected his greatest asset when the beating had gone down.

Fin swore in a dozen languages, and shrank from Byrne's ministrations.

"Now Fin, do you really need to use all that bad language?"

The last curse caught Byrne's attention — it was spoken in his native Armonite. Man, he hadn't been back to his birthplace in centuries. "You hope I suck on a horse's penis and choke to death? That's just gross. I'm not into bestiality."

"You *are* a beast."

"True. But I have standards."

"Standards? You'd actually have to have sex with someone to have standards."

Byrne rolled his eyes, not that the human could see the gesture. "Look, I'm not the one who screwed my way through the last three towns."

"All those women were *hot*."

No doubt they were. Byrne had a face like chiseled jet. Fin was pretty as a daisy. Women loved him. And he loved them. Too much, if you asked Byrne, which Fin never did.

"Yeah, and the last one drugged you," Byrne said.

"I was tired."

"So she wanted to give you some help?"

"You could say that."

"Idiot."

"Cocksucker."

"Dick."

"Tickle-brained maggot."

Fin paused, thinking about Byrne's insult. He shifted his head in a strangely bird-like manner.

"Good one."

"Thanks. I try."

CHAPTER SEVEN

Oberona Mountains

Hannah's head ached: a slow throbbing behind her eyes. Raising her free hand, she rubbed her sore orbs, but it didn't ease the pain. Only time, and actually sorting through the mess inside her head, would help.

Hannah stared with resentment at the cloth lying on her bed. Why had Ezra chosen a blanket with so much history woven into its fibers? She'd wrapped a valuable family possession around an infant she hadn't wanted, and then left both to the Old Mother. Maybe it was a way of saying sorry to the poor baby. Hannah could find out, but that would mean picking through the fine layers of memory, and she had a baby to look after.

As it was, she'd be dreaming Ezra and her mother and grandmother's memories for weeks to come. *Maybe it hurts so much because you've been lazy*, her mind whispered. But, she argued with herself, it was hard to practice with her ability, isolated as she was up here. There weren't people or their things to touch.

Liar. What about the tapestries?

Hannah's eyes tracked to the monumental works that hung on her walls. So many more hands had touched those pieces of art. So many more memories drenched the fibers. They would be ten times worse than the blanket; it would overwhelm her for days if she touched them. But what else did she have to do up here? The older she grew, the more control she had. She *should* have been practicing. Her mother would be disappointed in her. But she was afraid. She admitted that. Absorbing memories debilitated her. When she'd been younger, she'd been trapped, paralyzed, in a kind of coma. It had been difficult to determine where she ended and the foreign memories began.

A gurgle drew her attention back to the bed. The baby wiggled her arms free. They were no longer blue-tinged, but Hannah worried the air in the cabin might not be warm enough, despite the fire. She didn't know what a human might need, temperature-wise. Stooping at the hearth, she added more wood and poked the flames back into roaring life.

The baby whimpered softly, and Hannah rushed back to her, making shushing sounds. The whimpers became a wail, and something...tickled inside her head. The baby, Hannah realized, was probably trying to project her need telepathically. But Hannah had strong shields against Greens, against telepaths — she hadn't wanted to risk absorbing someone's memories through an inadvertent mental touch as well as physical contact. It was good to see her defenses hadn't deteriorated through lack of use.

The infant's cries were echoing off the cabin's walls now.

"What do you want, little one?" Hannah asked. Her voice, rusty from lack of use, was raspy and squeaky.

That's what I sound like? I'd better practice speaking.

Running a gentle hand over the baby's head, Hannah made soothing sounds. The physical connection sent rushes of feeling through her, but it wasn't overloading. Hannah was at no risk of a meltdown. Rather, it made her stomach ache with hunger.

What could she feed a baby that should be nursed at its mother's breast?

Picking the infant up, Hannah held her to her chest and began to rock, trying to emanate calm. It didn't work. The little girl was making sucking faces between cries. This close, the screaming hurt Hannah's ears, but what was a little more pain? She forced her aching head to sort through the memories from the blanket. Hopefully, they would provide her with something useful.

As her mind turned inward, the infant's cries faded to nothing.

Hannah searched through the memories that she had dumped like a box of papers in an unused corner of her psyche, rummaging through the recollections with increasing rapidity. She ignored Ezra completely this time; as a new mother, the woman would know nothing of caring for babes who had no access to breast milk. She struck gold with the great-grandmother, Zeda — the woman had been a midwife — and while Hannah would need to dip back into her memories again some time, she had what she needed for now.

She didn't know how much time she spent sorting through the long-dead woman's memories, but when Hannah returned to herself the baby was screaming hysterically. She placed the desperate infant on her bed, then hurried outside to Betty. According to Zeda, goat's milk, a bit of water and some honey should do the trick. It wouldn't be anywhere near as good as breast milk, but Hannah was short of that commodity here on the Old Mother.

Quickly she milked Betty into a glass jar, thankful she had decided against letting the goat roam for the evening, then brought the jar and a piece of unchewed leather back into the cabin. She made a teat out of the boiled leather; if she had had time, she would have re-boiled it, but the baby's screams were deafening, and she was worried the child would exhaust herself. Hannah added the water and honey, and then warmed the glass jar briefly over the fire in a bent metal cup. After testing that the mixture wasn't too hot — on her wrist, like Zeda had done — she filled the teat to halfway. She cut a small hole at the bottom and then held the baby in the crook of her arm, like the memories showed. The infant's head thrashed from side to side, her face wrinkled and furious, her mouth open.

At first, the baby wouldn't take the teat. "Come on, little one, you need to drink."

Desperate, Hannah dabbed her finger in the milk mixture and then inserted it into the babe's mouth. The child sucked greedily and quickly, and Hannah replaced the finger with the teat. But the baby spat it out, so she tried her finger again. Eventually, the babe took the leather teat, and Hannah kept a careful watch on how fast the baby drank. "Good girl, that's it. You were starving, that's all. It's all right."

It was a messy business, with the milk spilling over the baby's mouth and down her neck, but it seemed to work. After an hour, the baby stopped sucking and lay there, quiet and still. Worried that she'd done something wrong, Hannah propped the little one forward, hand under the baby's chin and patted her back. A burp followed, along with half the milk the infant had consumed. But she didn't start crying again, for which Hannah was thankful.

According what Hannah had learned, the babe would be hungry again in a few hours and she'd have to repeat the whole process. A strange feeling like hysteria bubbled through her. Although, now she had an idea about what to do, it shouldn't be so stressful. At least, that's what she told herself.

"Time for a sleep, little one." She laid the baby on the bed and wiped her clean of milk and vomit. Then she put a pot of water to boil over the fire and dropped the leather teat in it to cleanse it. She was going to have to see if she had any more leather that Betty hadn't already nibbled on.

I can do this, Hannah thought, looking back at the baby, who was now sound asleep.

Can you really? her mind asked. *What if something goes wrong? You don't really know the first thing about babies, other than what the blanket told you. And the blanket's owners were bigoted and backward. What happens if the baby needs something special because it's Graced?*

Graced.

Like her. But so unlike her, and so completely defenseless.

You need help.

Yes, she admitted to herself. *I do.*

CHAPTER EIGHT

Pinton City

The corpse looked bleached in the lamps of the underground morgue, the suture marks all the more visible for the whiteness. Alice's autopsy had confirmed that the victim had died from a stake to the heart. Fragments of wood in what was left of the organ had revealed that pretty quickly. Pulling off her leather gloves, she threw them in the bin before washing her hands. Three times.

Alice had always imagined that death clung to the undersides of her fingernails after an autopsy, even though she wore gloves. Fanciful of her, but that didn't erase the fear that if she wasn't careful when she cleaned up after a post-mortem, she might catch something nasty. Although, the risk was higher with the human victims that came through her doors than any were or vampire corpses that she might see. The vampire and were immune systems were so strong they probably killed anything horrible they came into contact with, even after death.

Sometimes, she wondered what it would be like to be that strong, that healthy. To know that even if you were stabbed, you could survive. Although, Alice *had* been stabbed and lived; unlike her mother, who had been knifed fifteen times. But being a were or vampire would negate that fear, an idea that appealed so much she could almost taste it. But it was like cotton candy: sweet, sharp, but fleeting, dissolving in a rush of disappointment. She was human, and she'd lived. Her mother hadn't been so lucky.

"So," a voice said, cutting across her thoughts. "How did the vic die?"

Alice looked up — and up — into the face of Kyle McInnes. He typically worked the night shift, and if he was on duty, that meant she'd been trapped down here for hours.

She pointed at the puncture hole on the corpse's chest. It wasn't as large as the one on the back, but it was pretty obvious nonetheless. "Stake through the heart."

Kyle flashed her a toothy grin. "A woman of few words, I like it."

Rolling her eyes, Alice patted the body dry with a cloth; she'd wiped it down with water after stitching the chest back together. She then walked over to the stone bench that wrapped around the perimeter of the room and picked up her clipboard, scanning the writing.

D.o.D: 7th Day, Fifth Month
Time & location of autopsy: 1600, City Morgue, Pinton
Species: Vampire
Sex: Male
Height: Five foot eleven inches
Weight: 170 pounds
Age: ???
Eye color: Purple (dah, vampire)
Hair color: Chocolate Brown
Skin color: White
Cause of death: Stake Homicide
Distinguishing features: Physically perfect? Hole from stake. No scars or birth marks. NB: do vampires even have *birthmarks?*
General notes: Body was discovered in King's Park. Victim was haphazardly dressed before being dumped in the park. Deceased was discovered by vampire aristocrats who called the City Guard. External examination at the park indicated that there were no signs of struggle. Body was still in rigor; estimated time of death was within the previous 12 hours. Internal examination demonstrated that the deceased had anal sex prior to being staked. Semen present in rectum. No signs of rape. No

noticeable pathology, not that I would have expected any ~~(vampire and all)~~. All organs as to be expected for a vampire: heart larger than human's (with necrotic tissue damage from stake); greater number of blood vessels; larger lungs. Remnant fragments of wood lodged in heart from stake. Area around stake shows signs of total tissue failure.

NB: Brown powder noted on clothing: composition unknown. A type of snuff? Or drug?

She'd listed the various weights of the organs and their respective details on the second and third pages. This was only the tenth vampire she had ever autopsied, so she'd been as detailed as possible. Normally, the aristos wouldn't let coroners near their corpses. Vampire dead were often cremated immediately, with the ashes interred in their family crypts. Any information she could record would help her — and other human doctors and coroners — in the future.

Looking up from the clipboard, Alice realized Kyle hadn't left. The tall city guard was staring at the dead vampire with a look of mild interest on his face. He must have felt her eyes on him, because his warm brown gaze swung back her way. He gave her another charming grin. "So, are you doing much after your shift tonight, sexypants?"

Sexypants?

Alice's clipboard drooped as she raised an eyebrow. "Excuse me?"

His grin grew wider. "Sexypants. Cos you fill those pants out in a really sexy manner."

Alice couldn't help but crack a smile. The guy was as subtle as a baton to the skull. "Does this kind of thing work for you normally?"

Kyle folded his arms across his broad chest, and gave an awkward shrug. It made the material ripple nicely over his shoulders. The bastard knew he was built like a...well, like a city guard. "No one's complained before."

"Well, I'll be the first, then."

"C'mon, sexypants. You know you want me to take you out to breakfast."

Alice shook her head. She'd been thinking of asking this guy over to her *house*? Admittedly, she had just wanted to borrow his height to help paint, but the idiot would probably think that was an invitation straight into her sexy pants. He had his pluses: he was tall, hot and exceedingly well-built, and most human guys Alice knew weren't so comfortable around corpses. The last non-city guard she'd had in the morgue was her ex-boyfriend. He'd ended up vomiting in the waste bin.

But date Kyle McInnes? The man who was more interested in breaking skulls than making friends?

"No, I don't want breakfast." Cutting people up tended to dent her appetite.

Kyle waggled his eyebrows. "I can just give you a bit of dessert."

"Really? You just said that?"

"You're a tough woman, Dr. Reive. I'll win that heart over yet."

"You aren't after my heart."

He slapped a hand to his chest. "You wound me. You really wound me."

Alice set her clipboard down. She was about to kick him out when he suddenly grew serious. "Anything else about the vic, then? Something we can go off to catch the murderer? Dead leeches aren't that common."

"I don't know." Alice ran a hand over her face. "I'll send a full report through this afternoon. All I can tell you is that he was staked — yes, obvious — but he had sex beforehand."

Kyle peered at the corpse's groin. "You can tell that?"

"Disrespectful much?" Alice muttered. "He had sex with another man."

Kyle rocked back on his heels. "Right. Consensual?"

"Appears so."

"Have we got his identity yet?"

"Nope, that's your job."

"Okay, we'll no doubt find out soon. When we do, I'll get my team to check out if the guy was in a relationship. Problem with the aristos though, they're in and out of people's beds all the time.

While I admire the lifestyle, if he doesn't have a long-term partner, it'll be hard to track his lover down."

Alice gave a small smile. "And that's why I just work with corpses."

CHAPTER NINE

Near the Trsetti village

I have the worst hangover in the history of hangovers.

Fin moaned. His blood was pounding a steady and unwelcome beat through his head. It was as if the villagers were still bashing him in the skull with their weapons, fists and feet. With a wince, he tried to roll over and couldn't. Pain shot through every square inch of his body. Even his balls hurt. Had someone managed to land a lucky hit? He thought he'd protected his best assets during the assault. A low groan was torn from his chest as he moved, and that hurt even worse. He stopped trying to roll over and collapsed onto his back. Breathing was definitely an effort. Maybe he should limit his concentration to sucking air into his lungs. It would be a worthy cause: keeping himself alive. Everyone should be thankful he was expending so much effort.

"The prince has awoken," Byrne said.

"Fuck you," Fin managed to gasp. "Why is the bed moving?"

"It's not."

His mattress seemed to be relatively soft — since when did he even *have* a mattress? — but it was also prickly. Like he was lying on a bed of pine needles.

"Feels like it is." Fin raised his arm to rub his head, but the movement pulled on his ribs. More pain, gasping and profanity ensued. He thought he heard Byrne laugh.

Complete and utter asshat.

His ribs must be broken, just what he didn't want to happen. Aside from his skull — or beautiful face — it was probably the worst set of bones to break. At least, it was from his experience.

"You've probably got a concussion," Byrne said.

"Thanks for stating the obvious." Fin's words were more air than sound, but weres had good hearing. And anyway, a concussion might be the least of his worries. Maybe his skull was fractured. It would figure.

"Hey, you're alive, so don't complain." Byrne's voice was almost cheerful.

Fucker.

Fin couldn't see much more than a faint blurry line, but he could sense Byrne had just shrugged. He could hear it in the bear's voice.

The pounding in his head was getting worse, if it could. "Can't you give me something?"

"Give you what?"

"Something for the pain. Surely we have some laudanum..."

The bed creaked, and there came the sound of Byrne rummaging around. "How much do I give a human?"

"Enough so that you don't kill me."

"And that is how much? I could probably drink the whole bottle and have no lasting effects."

Bragger.

How was Fin meant to know the answer? His brain was beating itself to death inside his skull. It wasn't like concentrating was his forte right now.

"A teaspoon?" The whole bottle would be nice, like Byrne suggested, but even in this much pain he didn't want to be dead. He had too much to live for. What, exactly, that 'too much' was, he didn't know right at this very minute. But it would come to him when his brain wasn't committing suicide.

"Will it be enough?" Byrne asked.

"Do I look like a sawbones?" Fin tried to scowl, but that just hurt.

"You look like you've been sawed."

"Fuck you."

"You wish."

"Just give me the bloody painkiller."

"Maybe I should hold off; you seem to be in good spirits."

"If you don't give me the drugs, I'm going to rip off your arm and beat you to death with it." Well, he'd certainly try. And wasn't it all meant to be about the effort or some crap?

A huge hand gently cupped the back of his head. He jolted and moaned. Every. Part. Of. Him. Hurt.

Without waiting for him to stop groaning, Byrne poured the liquid down Fin's throat, choking him.

"What the fuck!?"

"There; I gave you two teaspoons."

The laudanum had better work soon, or he'd perish from pain. "If I die, it's all your fault."

"I didn't sleep with the married woman."

"No, you just let the villagers beat me to within an inch of my life. And then overdosed me with pain killer."

♦

Byrne shook his head and capped the small bottle of laudanum before tucking it away in the first aid kit. The stuff smelled nasty, but Fin was in bad shape, and would probably drink horse piss if it made him feel better. He looked more like pounded meat than a person. Both his eyes were swollen and black, his face mottled with bruises, and the rest of him wasn't much better. Broken ribs, bruised bones. No arm or leg fractures that Byrne had noticed, which was a small bonus.

Maybe he shouldn't have waited so long to come to Fin's rescue. But the human had needed some sense beaten into him, some kind of lesson to keep his pants buttoned. From the gibberish Fin had been spouting just now, though, it seemed like the sense had been knocked *out* of him. What little sense he had, that was.

The laudanum appeared to have kicked in, though. Maybe Byrne had given him a bit much, but he could hear his friend breathing — raspy and rattling, but breathing — so he was still alive.

For once, Byrne could really see the benefits of being a were. Normally, being a werebear at the start of spring, trapped in human form, did not help his temper much. Hibernation — for him — was a thing of the past, and he mourned the loss, but he had responsibilities. Such as not letting the human get murdered.

Self-control, that was the real issue with Fin. The human had little to none when it came to women. He loved them. All of them. Fat, skinny, beautiful, ugly, old, young: Fin managed to charm the lot with little effort. A flash of white teeth and a dimple, and the guy could do whatever he wanted.

Was Byrne...jealous?

No, that was ridiculous. Why was he even thinking such malarkey?

Maybe because Fin had been laid at least three times in the last month, and Byrne hadn't had sex for...years? Had it really been years? Surely not. Months, it had to be. Sitting back on the wagon — avoiding the bed he'd set up for Fin — he clasped his hands behind his head and thought. But those thoughts weren't calming, rather they were frustrating and tinged with embarrassment.

He climbed down from the wagon and began tidying up the campsite. The crisp scent of crushed pine needles was all around him. The smell of home, of early spring and a time for family, but instead, he was out here, looking after a broken human who had as much sense as a gnat.

The fire was close to burning out, and he threw on some more wood, prodding it to life. The distraction didn't work; his embarrassment still churned deep within. He had to acknowledge what he'd been ignoring. It *had* been ages since he'd gotten laid. Three years, if you counted being drugged out of his mind and used. More than a hundred since it had been consensual. He hadn't been with anyone since Fin had saved him.

Maybe he *was* jealous.

And angry. He was certainly that.

Chapter Ten

Oberona Mountains

I can't look after a baby.

It was a mantra, her new one. Normally, it was 'I can't go outside and be near people or their things', but that was going to have to change. No more being afraid of life and the people who lived it.

She was going to have to go to her mother.

The idea locked her muscles in instinctive denial. Her mother lived hundreds of miles away, in the city of Skarva. Hannah hadn't been there for years, but her memories spoke of a place featuring tall stone buildings swathed in coal smoke and the stench of vampires, humans, shit and stagnant water. People had rushed around the city, barreling down streets, not caring if they bumped shoulders with a small child who couldn't bear the slightest touch from a stranger. It had taken her mother years to come to terms with the fact her daughter wouldn't be able to develop the shields she needed if she kept having them shattered by accident.

By the time Hannah reached the tender age of ten, she had learned about love, hate, greed, lust, obsession, apathy and the rest of those tangled emotions and feelings that imbued memories both good and bad. She'd endured them all through inadvertent physical contacts. She didn't think she'd ever been 'innocent', not when she could see everything within people's memories. But she had been naïve.

Sometimes you could only learn through experience.

But her life wasn't about just her anymore; it was about the baby who needed more than she could give. She'd taken on the role of a parent the moment she'd picked the infant up from the ground. Most people had nine months to come to terms with motherhood; Hannah had had mere seconds. But she'd made her choice, and now she would abide by it.

It wasn't the baby's fault that her biological mother had abandoned her shortly after giving birth, and that the only available person to save her was a Graced vampire — a freak of nature if ever there was one — who had more problems than she had answers. Hannah *owed* it to the scrappy piece of humanity to give parenthood her best shot; she couldn't just rely on the memories in the blanket to see her through.

And her mother was a *mother*; she'd raised babes before. Clearly she could help Hannah, or at least, help her find a wet nurse or someone who knew what to do with an abandoned infant. Maybe she could even help Hannah find Graced parents who would adopt the baby. Blues, Greens or Grays would know what to do, how to care for a baby. Because while Hannah was happy to take on the role of a parent in the short term, she wasn't capable of raising a child; she had to acknowledge that.

Leaning down, Hannah checked the little girl and saw she was still asleep, her arms and legs swaddled tight in one of Hannah's blankets. Hannah had even fastened a diaper around the infant, although it had taken a few tries to get it right. At least at this age, there couldn't be too much urine or feces.

Could there?

Hannah ran a gentle finger down the baby's cheek. Soft feelings of contentment travelled along the connection. Perhaps with no real memories to transfer to Hannah, the baby passed feelings on instead.

"You're a strange-looking thing, aren't you?" Hannah murmured.

From her own memories, and those she had absorbed from

others, she understood infants were meant to be cute, but while this baby's skin had an olive tone to it, and sooty lashes above plump cheeks, her lack of hair made her look more like a grumpy old man than a two day old. Hannah had never really thought that grumpy old men were cute, but maybe she could grow accustomed to the idea.

She turned away from the baby, and went back to packing. There wasn't much she could take — she was limited to what she could carry and what she could tie to Betty. And most of that would be cloths and blankets for the baby. And spare leather for teats. And her meagre supply of honey. And fire-making items...

"I guess I won't be taking many clothes with me," Hannah said, more to practice speaking than anything else. Her voice was still hoarse from disuse.

She opened the storage box where she kept clothing — vests, jackets and pants made from leather she had cured after her few hunting trips on the Old Mother. Cloth she made on her own loom, from wool bought down in the valley, and fashioned into underthings and shirts. She fingered the pale material, grateful that no memories lingered in the shirts. If only she had known about the Trsetti sooner, about what they were really like. She would have...

What?

Done nothing? Hidden on the slopes of the Old Mother? Maybe complained to her mother, when the older vampire dropped by during the year?

Sighing, Hannah drew out three shirts and two sets of leather trousers. She was pathetic. What could she really have done? Clearly the villagers feared everyone other than themselves, and if they had discovered she was a vampire, they may have attacked her. After all, they already considered her an eccentric, if one who was solitary. Safe. Harmless.

Weak.

"I am *not* weak."

Shoving her clothing into her satchel, she growled to herself. Clearly, so much 'alone time' was not good for her mental wellbeing. She had talked herself into being a coward. And while her life had no space for heroism — another word for stupidity, according to her mother — she did have room to grow a backbone.

"I am not a coward," she said. And she'd prove it. When morning came, they would leave. Her, Betty and the baby.

The little girl made fussing noises. Hannah looked over at the small, scrunched face. "You are not alone, little one." Reaching down, she picked up the infant and held her close. The baby sighed and curled her fists up tight under her chin.

"*We* are no longer alone."

CHAPTER ELEVEN

Pinton City

Killing was easy.

From all the things he'd heard, it wasn't meant to be, not if you were human. For vampires and weres, it was part of life. But for humans, killing each other was supposed to be anathema. Sometimes, he thought the idea had been bred into humans by the weres and vampires, so that their food source didn't wipe itself out. But killing was as much a part of human nature as it was for any predator; they just pretended that their violence was limited to animals, to food. But that wasn't true. The strong hunted the weak, even in their own kind. Animals regularly destroyed the weakest members of their packs. Why should humans do any different?

The humans he'd talked with had answers, but he found them hard to believe. They seemed to think that by killing someone, you were destroying something precious, unique. Something irreplaceable. After all, taking someone's life was taking their potential: their future, their lineage, their legacy.

Except so few humans actually had anything to *offer*.

Then again, he didn't think many vampires — or weres, not that he knew that many — possessed many worthwhile traits or skills, either. They were there to offset the truly remarkable individuals. The ones worth preserving, like himself. He was a gardener, cultivating the growth and bloom of society.

And he had some pruning to do.

Chapter Twelve

Pinton City

"Did you *see* the way that ass filled those pants?"

Alice turned from the window and looked at her best friend. Talan's eyes were wide open and watching something — or more accurately, someone — on the street. Her black hair was swept up in a neat bun, and her pearlescent skin glowed in the candlelight. Whoever was out there didn't know what they were missing out on.

Tal was as bad as Kyle. Maybe she should set them up? Alice thought about it for a few moments. No, Tal would eat Kyle for breakfast. And not in a good way. Poor guy.

Tal was staring at her, expecting an answer. Alice realized she'd been quiet a little too long. "No, I didn't," Alice said. "But should I care?"

She fiddled with her fork, which had been laid without precision on her cloth napkin. She straightened it. Then she tried to discreetly re-arrange the other utensils and glassware until they had some kind of order. Tal watched her with an amused expression.

They were in a small restaurant that specialized in not having a specialty. It was the kind of thing that Tal loved: something new every time. For Alice, it meant perusing the menu, trying to find something familiar and therefore potentially edible. It wasn't that the food wasn't nice; it was just that Alice was a meat-and-three-veggie kind of gal. She didn't need fancy new culinary experiences to make her week. Tal, however, did, although she hadn't even bothered to read the menu like any other normal person would in a fancy establishment. No, Tal was eyeing off the meat outside.

Alice did have to admit they had great seats. Their table was tucked in the front corner, with a view overlooking the cobblestone street and the ornate metal lamps slowly glowing to yellow life. It was a nice part of town, so the sidewalks were swept clean of dirt, and stone buildings soared toward the sky, their decorative masonry catching the golden sunset. Bright canvases overhung street vendors, who sold wares from exotic fruit to silk shawls, spicy meats to glittering silver jewelry. As it was dusk, the vampires were just starting to head out for their day. Or evening. However it worked. The men were dressed just as finely as the women, with lace, silks and satins, and even some velvet, with gems glittering in the light.

Suddenly, Alice's joy in the sights dimmed. All that wealth, paraded by the aristos, made her feel slightly nauseated. While she made a decent living, there were a lot of humans in Pinton who didn't. The clothes these aristos wore could feed a family for a year, if converted to gold and wages.

Tal leaned forward, her gray eyes glinting with mischief. "You should care about that ass, Ally. When was the last time you got laid?"

Alice picked up the menu and opened it with a flick. "None of your business." If she ignored Tal, would that make her and this stupid conversation disappear?

"It's not healthy, I tell you. A young woman as pretty as you shouldn't be acting like a dying old spinster."

She lowered the menu. "Dying *old* spinster?"

"Look at you. I had to practically beg you to come out with me, a *month in advance*." Tal stabbed a finger on the tablecloth.

"That's how long it took for this restaurant to have an opening. It is 'the place to eat', you know." Alice rolled her eyes.

Tal waved a dismissive hand. "Meaningless details."

"You know I'm not an adventurous eater."

"You're not an adventurous *anything*."

"Just cos I don't have to be out every moment I'm not working—"

"That's not what I'm referring to at all, and you know it. And when are you *not* working?"

Someone tapped on the window. Alice, Tal and the other people sitting at the front of the restaurant turned to look. With a feeling close to relief, Alice recognized the black cap of a City Guard messenger.

"I will be right back." Alice slid from her chair.

"Where do you think you're going?" Tal demanded.

Alice pointed at the young girl, who stood outside hopping from foot to foot.

"Ignore her. We're here for dinner."

Alice dodged away from the table and Tal's glare. "It could be important."

"More important than enjoying a nice meal with your best friend?" Tal's gray eyes narrowed menacingly.

"Leave the guilt trip until we know whether or not I have to stand you up."

Tal humphed and picked up the menu.

Alice hurried outside. "Are you looking for me?" she asked the messenger.

The young girl — probably no more than ten years of age — nodded her head. "Yes, ma'am. They found another one." Dirty blonde hair escaped from underneath the black cap, and the girl tugged on it absently. She had smudges on her cheeks, but otherwise appeared clean enough. Alice could feel the people inside the restaurant, watching their interaction.

She turned her back to the window. "Another what?"

"Body, ma'am."

"There are plenty of those. Can't it wait for me at the morgue?" Sometimes new guards called her out for every corpse they encountered. Alice had learned to only go to the scene when it was murder, potential murder, or suicide.

The girl leaned forward, making Alice bend down. "It's one of *them*," the girl whispered and jerked her head at the other side of the street, where vampires were climbing into a carriage. The tethered horses neighed in protest.

"Right." Alice's blood began to tingle. Two dead vampires in almost as many days; what were the odds?

"So are you coming, ma'am?"

Alice looked down at her dress and heels. She'd even put on some makeup. "I don't have my bag."

"They said someone is getting your spare one from the Guard House."

She sighed. She'd been outmaneuvered by whoever had found the body. They knew she wouldn't be able to pass up another dead vamp. "Let me say goodbye to my friend."

"No need. Your friend is right here."

Alice turned. Tal stood behind her, a shuttered look on her face. Alice hated to disappoint her, had probably done it twenty times too many because of her job. But this was a dead vampire...

"I have to go, Tal."

"They're dead, Ally." Tal's foot began tapping. "It's not like you can save them."

"No, but it's one of *them*."

A line formed between Tal's perfectly arched black eyebrows. "One of who?"

The messenger rubbed her chin, her thumb pointing in the direction of the vampires in their carriage. "One of *them*."

Tal's eyes lit with understanding. "Really? Well, then. I'll forgive you if you tell me all about it later."

"You are the best!"

Tal hugged her. "We're rescheduling; you're going to pay."

"You drive a hard bargain."

"Now get gone."

♦

A whistle greeted her at the crime scene. Looking over at the source, Alice shook her head. Tall and muscular as any were, Kyle loomed under a streetlight, the lamp casting an absurd halo around him. In the shadows a way behind him, someone knelt beside what Alice assumed was the body, taking notes. The darkness obscured their identity, but it had to be another guard. The messenger ran over to Kyle, clearly awaiting payment.

"Alice, I like the new uniform," Kyle said. "I could get behind the whole dress and heels thing for work. It really...works."

Alice snorted. "Witty."

Kyle opened his mouth, preparing another no doubt hilarious comment, only to jump a foot into the air as a pale hand slapped down on his shoulder.

"Seriously, Kyle? Was that the best you could come up with? No wonder why you're still single." The hand gave a squeeze.

Kyle cringed. "By the blood, Elle! Stop sneaking up like that. And don't hit so hard." He rubbed his shoulder.

Alice laughed at Kyle, whining like a baby at a little tap from his partner. Eleanor — Elle — Brown was one of only two vampire city guards in Pinton.

"Alice! Good to see you. I wasn't sure the messenger I sent would find you." Elle smiled, and it was slightly disconcerting. Her teeth were glow-in-the-dark white, with her canines just a little bit too long for comfort.

Alice swallowed. "Hey, Elle. I didn't realize you were back on duty."

They'd been friends of a sort, back when Elle had been human. They'd never caught up outside work, but there'd been an easy camaraderie between them. Alice had always thought they would get along if they ever did socialize outside the Guard House, but life hadn't worked out that way. Elle had been killed — well, everyone had thought she'd been killed. They'd even had a funeral. Weeks later, word had spread that she was still alive and had been Chosen. And staked. And that she was engaged to a were.

It had been no secret that Elle was a racist; she'd been fiercely protective of her kid sister after a vampire had tried to abduct the little girl in a human store years ago. She'd understandably never had time for either weres or vamps. But the rumors had been *true*, and Elle was now firmly enmeshed with *both* non-human races. What's more, it had been her own grandmother who'd been behind Elle's staking. It boggled Alice's mind — and the minds of most of the city guards — but Elle was Elle. She seemed to make her own rules.

"First week back on the job." Elle rubbed the back of her neck and grinned. "I had a hard time convincing Mikael I still wanted to bash heads, now I'm an aristo fribble. And my fiancé, Clay, was being a pain in the ass about it. He's still convinced someone wants to stake me again."

"You think there are people who *don't* want to stake you?" Kyle asked. "I swear, I could produce a list of about ten people off the top of my head who'd be happy to do the deed."

"And I bet you're on the top of the list," Elle said. She narrowed her eyes at him. "I could break you like a twig."

"I know." Kyle grinned. He flicked a glance at Alice. "Is it wrong that I find that hot?"

Elle looked at her fingernails. "I'll mention that to Clay. And by the way, that is gross. You're like my brother. Come on, Alice, I'll show you the body."

"What? No!" Kyle said, following them. "You won't say anything to Clay, will you?"

Elle ignored Kyle. Alice followed the vampire guard to where the corpse had been positioned in the center of a small park — nothing as grand as King's Park, but still public and often frequented by vampire aristos. Someone had covered the cadaver with a shroud.

Alice knelt on the ground, silently apologizing to her dress and her stockings. *This is why you can't have nice things,* she told herself. Taking a deep, fortifying breath, she pulled back the body's covering. She jerked her chin in Kyle's direction. "Is he having a panic attack?"

"Clay is his new best buddy," Elle said. "Kyle threatened him the first time they met and now they get along great. But Clay is a bit...possessive." She grinned.

Alice raised her eyebrows. "And you like that?" A more independent, headstrong woman Alice had never met, and she knew her aunt, Tal, and her friend, Billie. Those three women alone were scary and inspiring enough.

Elle's smile turned softer. "Sometimes. And sometimes I want to kill him for it. But I'm just as bad."

Now that, Alice could believe.

"What's your take on the situation?" Alice asked as she examined the body. Prior to being Chosen, Elle had been good at doing quick crime scene analyses, and while Alice would love to find out more about Elle's adventures — and meet the man who had captured the prickly woman's heart — she did have a job to do.

"Staked through the back," Elle said. "Body was quickly dressed. Recently dumped here — bruising is on the stomach, but the body was found on its back. Body is in rigor."

Alice sat back on her heels, biting her bottom lip. "This is almost exactly the same as the last one. But in a slightly less public location." She glanced up at Kyle. "Did you get an ID on the last body?"

Kyle nodded. "Gerard Thornewood, third or fourth cousin to Baron Sloughmere."

Elle frowned. "Alice, stop biting your lip. I can smell your blood."

Probably not the best course of action when you're right next to the equivalent of a bloodhound. A blush burned Alice's cheeks.

"Ooh, Elle wants to bite the coroner!"

Elle glared at Kyle. "If you don't shut up, I will take a bite out of *you*."

Kyle's mouth snapped shut.

Elle turned to Alice. "Sorry, didn't mean to make you uncomfortable. But I was told to be on my best behavior, and your blood *does* smell tasty." Elle pointed a long finger at Kyle. "If you make another smartass remark, I swear I will beat the ever-living shit out of you."

Kyle held up both hands, palms forward. "I said nothing."

Elle's eyes narrowed. "You were *thinking* it."

"Guy can't help where his mind wanders."

Elle snorted. "I'll ask Dante's sister if she knows of any political connections, dramas and so on, that Thornewood may have been involved in."

Dante Kipling had Chosen Elle, and had recently married a human, which had been so much of a scandal even Alice had heard of it. The announcements had been published in the newspaper, along with a detailed account of the wedding. Dante's sister was a viscountess. Just thinking of all the connections gave Alice a headache.

"You believe it's political?" Alice asked, frowning.

"Who knows with vampires?" Elle shrugged. "He could have slept with the wrong person and this was payback. But that can be political, too."

Alice wondered if Elle realized she still spoke of vampires as if they were something different to her. Something *other*.

"Let's take some more notes and get him to the morgue," Alice said. "I want to try and get an autopsy done before the vampire aristos descend."

Chapter Thirteen

Near the Trsetti village

Fin wasn't in great shape. He'd had to be dosed up on laudanum for the past day so that he could sleep off the worst of the pain. Byrne thought that a bath might do him wonders, but the nearest town was a day's journey away, even when he didn't have an injured human bouncing around in the back of a wagon. The mountains were closer, and snow would be almost as good as a bath, but that would mean a detour and less shelter. Byrne may not have much of a choice in the matter, however; his direction depended on the heading the road took once it emerged from the forest. He had stuck mostly to the woodland since their arrival at the Trsetti village, and he wasn't too sure about the road to the east.

He'd soon find out, he thought.

To make his day even better, their horse shied away whenever Byrne approached. The piebald could smell the difference on him after he came back from saving Fin. It had taken Byrne weeks to get the horse to trust him initially, because of his predator scent. The were always smelled like a bear, but after a shift, it was *intense.* And while he wasn't really interested in horsemeat, the horse didn't understand that. He hadn't shifted in months and typically avoided the horse afterward, figuring it was cruel to frighten the beast for no real reason, but he hadn't had much choice this time. It was save Fin and scare the horse, or keep the horse happy and abandon his friend. Just another thing to chalk up on the invisible tally board of Fin's crimes against Byrne.

After an hour-long struggle with the horse, he managed to hitch it to the wagon. The poor beast's eyes rolled and its flank twitched, but at least it wasn't bucking anymore. Climbing into the back of the cart, he inspected Fin, who was mumbling incoherently under his breath. Probably speaking in his native language, or one of the hundreds Fin seemed to know. Byrne had never met anyone who could pick up and speak as many dialects as this human. It was one of the idiot's truly redeeming features. That, and his kindness.

Checking Fin's temperature by the highly technical method of palm to forehead, Byrne noted he wasn't any hotter than an hour ago. Hopefully a fever wouldn't set in. All Byrne had to combat that was some willow bark tea, and he wasn't sure how effective that would be, despite Fin swearing it was the cure for most ailments.

After checking Fin's bedding was secure, Byrne jumped from the back of the wagon, secured the back panel, and pulled himself up into the seat. Then, grabbing the reins, he clicked the poor horse into motion.

It was time to get out of the Trsetti's forest. They had been lucky over the last two days — the village people hadn't descended on them in vengeful outrage. Byrne figured their fear and bigotry were more powerful deterrents than their ire was an inciter, but he didn't want to chance it. After all, in his drugged and weakened state, Fin would be unable to fight off an attacker. It would take just one hardheaded villager to get past Byrne, and Fin would be dead.

The almost invisible path was edged either side by towering pines. Byrne kept an eye out for irate bears or wolves: the animal kind, not the were. He hadn't smelled any predators since entering the forest, but food was scarce during the dawning spring months, and wolves were especially excellent hunters. They would know to keep downwind. Byrne hoped his own scent would keep them at bay. At least down in the valley below, the snows hadn't covered everything in a thick blanket of white, leaving the prey to settle there. Hopefully the wolves had kept to the valley as a result.

The next town, Brindle, was approximately twenty-five miles away. Normally, the horse and cart would make that journey in a day, but Byrne didn't want to push the horse, which wasn't used to carrying the two of them in the wagon. He also didn't want to risk bumping Fin too much. For really bad breaks, he'd wrap or splint the bone while it healed, but he hadn't bandaged the human's ribs, choosing to let them heal naturally. He'd heard a lot of humans arguing about the benefits of this technique, but Byrne figured if his ribs didn't need it, neither did Fin's. Admittedly, Byrne's bones healed in hours, but the process would be the same, so Fin got the same treatment as he'd give himself. The human was too drugged to argue, anyway. Even so, he didn't want the cart rattling the human's bones into new and interesting shapes.

Slowly, the horse — Baldy, Fin called it — picked her way along the barely-there trail until they hit a more well-used thoroughfare. Byrne's awareness doubled, his hearing and sense of smell becoming more acute. Animals were no longer the main concern; now, it was the human menace. There weren't, or shouldn't be, any other weres out here. And as for vampires...well, Byrne didn't think they'd been out this way for decades. Most of that race tended to mass in cities, with the constant food supply they offered.

Baldy's pace increased on the better trail, and they soon emerged from the forest, where the path forked. One branch headed south-west and into what appeared to be the center of the Trsetti town; the other, which looked distinctly less traveled, would take them north-west and hugged the edge of the Old Mother mountain chain. Byrne could smell the presence of humans in both directions, although the Old Mother's path was probably more of a hunting trail than a road to anywhere in particular. It would be a slightly longer journey and the road wasn't as well maintained, but he couldn't risk going through the town. That would just be asking for Fin's dead body at his feet.

Looking toward the small houses with their thatched roofs, so very far from the world of weres and vampires, Byrne shook his head. It was no wonder the villagers had become insular. Why Fin had thought that sleeping with one of their people was a good idea, he'd never know. Even under the influence of an aphrodisiac, the human should have known better.

Then again, some of those drugs really messed with your mind.

The smell of woodsmoke drifted through the air, as did the sound of voices muttering and talking. Something was happening in the town, but Byrne didn't want to wait around to find out what. If the villagers did decide to come after him and Fin, he wanted to be out of that forest and halfway to Brindle by the time they worked out their quarry had gone.

Turning north-west, Byrne headed along the hunting path. If he bumped into any humans, he was sure his yellow eyes would send them scurrying away.

Demons were demons, after all.

Chapter Fourteen

Oberona Mountains

Hannah tugged on the leash she'd attached to Betty, sighing with impatience. The goat stood placidly next to the side of the gravel track, chewing with single-minded determination on some greenery she had managed to snatch up when Hannah had looked down to check on the infant. Hannah had wrapped a cloth around herself in a large sling and tucked the baby inside, figuring her body heat would help keep the little girl warm. She'd also swaddled the tiny bundle of humanity, and had tied what she thought was an excellent diaper around her.

Hands tucked under her chin, feet snuggled up against her stomach between them both, the baby seemed content enough after her morning feed and vomit. Hannah worried she was probably doing something wrong during the feeding. Was it normal for babies to spew up a portion of everything they ate? She couldn't be certain, though; she only had the blanket's memories to go on.

"Come on, Betty." Hannah gave the leash another tug. At this rate, the baby would be ten years old by the time they made it to the next town. And Hannah could hear a cart in the distance; she didn't want to be caught in the middle of the road, dragging a recalcitrant goat.

She'd chosen this track because it circumvented the Trsetti's town; hopefully the approaching travelers weren't from the village. She could see the small roofs in the distance, surrounded by dirt brown fields and a ring of forest. If the driver of the cart saw her with a young baby with Green eyes...

She wouldn't let them take her back. Not just to be left for dead.

Hannah wondered if she'd even give the baby back if it was Ezra herself, wracked with guilt, coming up the track behind them. But Hannah had sensed the woman's need for self-preservation and her own comfort beyond any feeling of care she had for her daughter. Unless Ezra's husband had suddenly demanded the baby be returned, the woman wouldn't want the infant back.

So no, Hannah wouldn't return the baby, no matter who asked for her.

Tilting her head back, Hannah breathed deeply. That smell on the breeze. Not the horse...was that *bear*?

Raising an eyebrow, she shook her head. Couldn't be. There were no bears anywhere near the Old Mother that she'd ever scented or heard. More likely the other travelers had a bearskin rug or something similar in their luggage.

Betty continued chewing and edged closer to scraggly green shrubs that grew along the side of the dirt track. Hannah gripped the leash. The foliage sprouted on the small embankment that then dropped sharply off the side of the mountain pass. If Betty wasn't careful, she'd fall.

Narrowing her eyes, Hannah glared at the goat. "If I didn't need you for your milk, I'd skin you alive, you cannibal."

Okay, that wasn't fair. It had been cow leather. But Betty just blinked slowly, her jaw working.

Hissing, Hannah pushed against the goat's rump, and managed to get the animal skidding along the path, leaving hoof-grooves behind it. Hannah was a lot stronger than Betty, but didn't want to hurt her.

Dratted animal.

The rumbling of approaching wheels was growing louder. Hannah huffed with impatience. "We don't want to be caught out here, you stupid goat!" Betty kept chewing on her stolen greenery.

"Let's go!"

One of Betty's ears pricked up and she started ambling along. Finally. Hannah gritted her teeth and wrapped the leash around her wrist. This was going to be a disaster. If it was Hannah on her own — even just her and the baby — she could have run for miles, making the nearest town well before dusk. But the baby needed the blasted goat's milk.

The hoof beats and cartwheels increased in volume, while the smell of horse, bear, and pine needles became more intense. Breathing, Hannah frowned. Blood. There was also definitely human blood approaching. Hannah's mouth watered involuntarily and her fangs began to prod downward. Taking a shallow breath, she thought calming thoughts. She had eaten berries and roots yesterday; she didn't *need* to feed on blood for a while yet. Not if she kept up with the human food.

The cart would be in sight any minute.

Without thinking, Hannah clutched the baby tight. The child wailed.

"Ssshh," Hannah whispered.

The baby screamed louder.

"Come on, little one. Ssshh." Hannah jiggled the baby in the sling, recalling Zeda doing something similar in the memories. She turned in a slow circle, searching for a place where she could hide. But the track had a cliff on one side, and granitic rock face on the other. There wasn't a small crevice she could shove the goat or herself into. They were stuck. Something warm and wet soaked through her shirt.

Hannah sniffed.

Urine.

Great.

Sighing, Hannah herded the goat to the side of the track, so the cart wouldn't barrel them down. The smells of pine, blood, bear and horse were much stronger now, mixed with vodka and the odor of two bodies. She lowered her gaze to the track. If she didn't make eye contact with the people in the cart, hopefully they would just ignore her, Betty and the child, and keep going.

Stuck on the track and covered in pee, this wasn't the best start to her journey. Trying to tug Betty closer — who wasn't moving because she'd found another patch of pathetic grass to nibble — Hannah reached for one of the saddle bags. The baby's cries were louder now, more indigent.

The cart wheels behind her came to a stop.

"Having a bit of fun there?" asked a voice in heavily accented Varshian.

Varsh was the nearest big city, but Hannah spoke the language badly. She knew just enough to understand the speaker.

Shielding her eyes against the bright blue sky, she looked up at the cart for the first time and her jaw dropped. Even sitting down, the man in the driving seat was *huge*. She'd hate to see how tall he was standing up.

Now the bear smell made sense.

The driver's skin was a beautiful jet black. His bright yellow eyes were accentuated by long, dark lashes that should have belonged to a woman, and they watched her with something like amusement glinting within their depths.

He was gob-smackingly good-looking. Face chiseled along all the right lines.

But coming into contact with a strange were was dangerous. Her having the wrong colored eyes and stinking like a vampire would only attract unwanted attention. Even though she could admire his attractiveness, she couldn't even *think* about anything more complicated with a were, even if he was the handsomest man she'd seen for over a hundred years. It would just end badly — largely for her.

It wasn't fair.

The baby was screaming in sheer outrage now. Hannah unhooked the sling, and the little girl's wails reduced to whimpering gurgles.

"Do you speak Skarvs?" she asked in Varshian.

The were nodded. "It's better than my Varshian. Did you want me to put the back down so you can change the baby on the panel?" He smiled at her.

Hannah blushed. He could probably smell the urine on her and the baby. Actually, there'd be no probably about it. Being a bear meant there wouldn't be much he couldn't tell from scent alone. But using the cart would make the diaper change much easier, so long as she didn't touch the wagon. She had gloves on, so it *should* be safe.

"That would be great," she said.

The werebear clucked under his tongue and the horse twitched. The smell of fear coiled through the air, but the horse held its spot. The were swung down from his seat, and walked around to the back of the cart.

Hannah was right. He was *huge*.

"Do you think it's safe to do this here?" Hannah asked, tugging Betty along with her. "We won't block anyone?"

The were lowered the back of the wagon. "I can't smell anyone for a mile in either direction. We'll be all right for a while yet. Road is pretty much unused. Wasn't expecting to see anyone else out here, to be honest." He placed a piece of folded material on the panel.

Hannah dropped Betty's leash — the goat was thoroughly consumed with her bounty so wouldn't wander — and laid the baby down.

"Goat giving you problems?" the were asked.

"I'd turn her into stew, if I didn't need her." Which wasn't true, because Hannah did love that stupid goat. But she'd never had to rely on Betty before, and the goat could be quite cantankerous when she felt like it.

The were gave a bark of laughter, then pointed at the cart's bed. "I'd do the same to the human, but I owe him."

Further back in the cart, a supine form lay on a pine-needle mattress, covered by a blanket. From the smell of vodka wafting from him, Hannah assumed he was sleeping off a hangover.

Hannah shook her head in mock sympathy. "The things we tolerate." She unwrapped the wet diaper, and the little girl kicked her legs, face scrunched in anger, but not screaming now.

"Name's Byrne." The were extended a hand for her to shake.

Hannah just stared, diaper hanging from one hand. She was wearing gloves...but touching a living person, even with protection, could be bad. Especially if it was a were or a vampire, who had centuries of memories.

Slowly, Byrne lowered his hand. His gaze locked on hers, head tilting to one side. His yellow eyes narrowed, and then he nodded to himself.

"You both have names?" he asked.

He took a step toward her, slowly, as if expecting her to bolt in fear. But it wasn't him Hannah was afraid of. It was herself.

"Names?" She had to crane her neck up to look at him — and she was six foot tall herself.

"Yeah, what are your names? You and the baby."

Hannah stared at the little girl, naked on the back of the cart. She had completely forgotten that the baby would need a name. Ezra had never bothered to give her one. The sheer enormity — the weight of the decision — almost felled her.

"I'm Hannah Romanov." She paused briefly, eyes closing in something almost like pain. "The baby hasn't got a name yet."

Byrne smiled, an easy expression. "Well, then. Let's get this diaper changed and we'll see about coming up with one."

CHAPTER FIFTEEN

Alice shut the front door behind her, and dropped her shoes on the floor. Her poor feet were screaming in protest. She'd have to remember to leave a spare pair of shoes at the morgue. Not that she showed up at work dressed this way particularly often — if ever. But it had been a long night. The vampire autopsy had shown that the method of murder had been almost identical to the other victim. Stake to the heart. Victim killed elsewhere then brought to the site.

No. They weren't just victims. They had names. But she only knew the first one: Gerard Thornewood.

She mouthed the moniker to herself. He had been a person, until a stake had been shoved through his back. Now he was gone. Someone must have cared for him, would miss him. He'd had sex just before he'd died. Alice wanted to think that the sex and violence hadn't occurred simultaneously, but she doubted it. What better way to distract your victim?

She'd studied the sperm she'd obtained from the latest victim, hoping she could tell if it came from a human, vampire or were, but she didn't really have anything to compare it to, not having been able to study any vampire or were semen since she started her job as coroner. She'd never even gotten to view the three different kinds at university. All the same, she'd popped the collected cells under her microscope and drawn up a reference diagram of the sperm's morphology, just in case.

"I need more samples," she muttered to herself. Bending down, she righted the shoes so they stood side by side under the small entrance table. Left next to right, in the proper order of things.

"Samples of what?"

Alice nearly jumped out of her skin. If she'd been a were, she very well may have. "Tal! What the—?"

An innocent look from cool gray eyes. "What? Did I scare you?"

Looking around her small hallway, Alice threw her keys on the dainty table, then reached out and popped them in the bowl she had there to house them. Why she bothered to even be temporarily messy, she'd never know. "You know you scared me! What are you doing here?" She hadn't meant to sound quite so cranky, but it had been a big day and she just wanted to crawl into her bed, pull up the covers, and pass out.

It was no mystery how Tal had gotten inside — she had a set of spare keys — but she didn't normally abuse the privilege of having access to Alice's home. Especially as she knew Alice had problems with people entering her apartment unexpectedly.

When Tal didn't respond immediately, Alice pulled her watch from her bag. "It's six in the morning!"

Tal shrugged. Her shiny, crow-black hair hung loose over her shoulders. "You said you'd tell me everything about the dead vamp. So I thought I'd wait for you." She turned and headed toward the living area.

"I did say that," Alice muttered. But she was tired. Bone tired. She'd kind of thought that the telling would occur at a later point in time.

Tal stopped in the open plan kitchen and living room and a delicious — and completely out of place — aroma wafted through the air. Alice wavered on her feet. Tal flicked a hand at the bench in front of her. "I thought I'd bring you some dinner, as I doubted that those lug-head guards would actually feed you."

A lump formed in Alice's throat as she stared at the pots Tal had placed on her kitchen counter. No one had ever tried to look after Alice, no one but her Aunt Zara and Tal. And Alice had resisted their care for years, struggling to make it on her own, but it was times like this that Alice knew she was lucky. Even though she had pushed away their help, they still cared enough to ignore her and help anyway.

"I was right, wasn't I? They didn't feed you." Tal's eyebrows set in a frown. "I am going to have words with those idiots."

Alice shook her head. "Suddenly, I'm starving."

Her best friend's expression lightened. "Well, I brought you some stew. It was left over from my dinner."

Alice's face fell. "Didn't you stay at the restaurant?"

Tal's mouth quirked in a half-smile. "Wasn't so much fun to ogle all the passers-by without you there to scowl at me."

"I don't scowl."

Tal laughed and served up two bowls of stew, then cut some slices from a loaf of bread. It smelled absolutely divine.

Alice raised an eyebrow. "You made bread?"

"Are you kidding? I got this on the way over."

"You're eating, too?" Alice asked, grabbing one bowl.

"It's time for breakfast, idiot."

Alice kept her thoughts behind closed lips. Stew wasn't really a breakfast food, but then, Tal had different notions about appropriate cuisine. For Alice, it was technically dinner. So that made it acceptable.

Tal wagged a finger at Alice. "Stop glowering at me."

"I already said I don't scowl."

They sat down on her battered couch. Alice curled her feet up underneath her, but Tal kicked her feet up on the coffee table. She quickly removed them after Alice glared at the offending body parts. Tal knew better, but she always liked to try and push the boundaries, to see if Alice could veer away from her structured existence.

Today was not the day.

"Fussy." Tal scooped up some stew with her bread. But she didn't put her feet back on the table. "So, tell me. What happened with the dead vamp?"

"Two bodies have been found in public parks now. Both dead vamps. Both murdered."

Tal's brows drew together. "That hasn't made the papers. Two? In how many days?"

Alice finished her mouthful. "Three. The Guard wants to keep it quiet to begin with; they're trying to work out who the victims are."

"They don't know yet?"

"They know one."

"Give me all the details."

Alice thought about how Captain Dinya would lecture her for not keeping the information confidential, but Tal knew how to keep her mouth shut. And she had an amazing mind. Tal was a professor of mathematics at Pinton's Royal University, and there were very few people in the entire country who could challenge her intellect. Alice had never met someone who could see patterns the way Tal did. Maybe she could help the case.

When Alice finished, Tal sat, tapping her spoon on the side of the bowl. Fast, slow, then fast. "So you need more samples of sperm? Would you be able to tell the difference between human, vamp and were?"

"I assume so; there's enough physiological differences in general that there should be variances."

Tal pursed her lips. "I can probably get you some samples."

Alice scrunched her nose. "Tal!"

"What? It's not like I haven't slept with a vampire before. And I wouldn't mind adding a were to the mix."

Alice shuddered. "But vampires like to bite." She didn't even want to think about what weres could do to a human during the throes of sex.

Tal shrugged one shoulder, then grinned. "What can I say? I am just that fantastic a best friend. I am willing to do what it takes to help solve this murder."

CHAPTER SIXTEEN

Pinton City

Elle slammed a book down in front of the man who'd forever changed her life.

"What do you call this?"

Dante Kipling glanced down at the volume, its beautiful painted cover gleaming between them, an accusatory text. He then eyed Elle like she had lost what few marbles he'd thought she had, and quickly shifted his paperwork into a pile and pushed it to the edge of the table. Like he was afraid she was about to go on a rampage and destroy everything in sight.

"It's a *book*," Dante spoke slowly.

"She knows it's a book," said Baron Anton Greystoke. He stood in the doorway behind her. Dante's husband had followed her down the hallway, cane clicking while he had lectured her on how Dante's intentions were no doubt utterly noble. While Elle appreciated Anton's loyalty, she could have done without it right now.

Elle was shaking, she was so angry. Now her abilities as a Green had awakened, she could have just slipped into Dante's mind and ripped the thoughts from his stupid brain. But that would be a breach of privacy. Both he and Clay had lectured her about that on more than one occasion. Power corrupts and absolute power...

Yeah, she'd heard enough of that over the last few months.

It wasn't like she didn't know it was a bad thing. Her grandmother had been the best example of the dangers of abusing power that anyone could ever need to keep themselves in check. Personally, Elle thought 'evil' too light a word to describe the dead woman. Shaking her head, she dragged her thoughts back to the moment: Dante was interfering with the one thing that Elle had utterly forbidden him to.

"It's a book on *anatomy*." She was aware that the way she said the word sounded more like 'bestiality', but it was almost as bad. At least in this situation.

Dante tapped the chair next to him, looking pointedly at Anton. He only turned back to Elle once Anton had taken a seat, by which time steam was fairly pouring out of her ears.

"Yes," Dante said. "It is in instructional book on human anatomy."

She bit out each word. "I found it in Emmie's room."

Elle probably shouldn't have been snooping about in her seven-year-old sister's room, but she had been and that was that. Elle's mother, Melissande, and Anton's mother, Beatrice, would no doubt lecture her about her lack of respect for personal boundaries, but this was Emmie. The kid was not allowed to *have* personal boundaries. At least not with Elle.

Dante blinked. She'd come to learn that this was his 'innocent' look. Like a sociopathic vampire who only cared for two people in the world could even understand what 'innocent' meant.

Emmie — or even Elle — was not on his extremely short list of 'cared for' individuals, but Elle did know he was fond of her sister, the strange Teal-eyed stepniece he'd gained through Choosing Elle.

The family relationship was complicated.

"This book is an important educational tool," the vampire said.

"She is *seven years old*," Elle hissed.

"And she is very clever for her age." Dante tapped a long finger against the book's cover. Coming from Dante, that was a massive compliment. The vampire may have the empathy of a gnat, but he *was* a genius. And he'd been studying human anatomy for longer than Elle had been alive.

Elle flicked his hand away, and opened the book to one of its three hundred and seventy-two offensive pages. There, on page two hundred and sixty-five, in detail, was the human circulatory system marked out in beautiful hand-drawn brilliance.

Elle stabbed a finger downward. "This!"

Dante looked at it, as did Anton. Then they both turned to her. Even Anton appeared confused.

"...is the human circulatory system?" Dante finished, one eyebrow raised.

"You are giving her medical texts. I *told* you that we didn't want her to be encouraged to use her...ability. Giving her this is going to make her want to practice. We can't risk it!"

"It is just a book." Anton's tone was placating.

Elle whipped her head round to stare at the human baron. "He is putting her in a risky — *tempting* — situation. She could kill herself from using her healing ability."

There'd never been another born with Emmie's Teal-colored eyes. At least, no one that Elle or her grandmother had heard about. They didn't know what Emmie could do — what her limits were.

Dante stood, placing both hands on the table between them, and leaned forward. "All I am doing is giving her knowledge. She has agreed not to use her ability to heal because it is dangerous for her, and you, if people were to find out. But keeping her in ignorance is also harmful. What if the reason she gets so drained by her use of power is because her body is reacting instinctively? What if she actually knew what was required, and could then direct her gift to fix that specific problem, rather than fixing every tiny health issue a person may have?"

"She only healed my shoulder when I busted it," Elle said.

Dante nodded. "That's because you had an injury her ability could hone in on."

"She promised she won't heal anyone," Elle protested.

"On purpose," Anton commented.

Elle slumped into an empty chair as the two words hit home.

"She's only a kid."

Dante sat slowly, violet eyes locked on her unique purple, Green and Gray irises. "But she has a power she *cannot* control," he said. "She really needs to be in medical school now." He held up a hand as Elle opened her mouth to protest. "But she is too young, I know. That doesn't mean we can't provide a basic level of education that may help her during her accidental healings."

"I don't want her practicing."

Dante pinched the bridge of his nose. "If you were a doctor, would you be able to operate on someone in your first year of medical school?"

Elle frowned. "I don't know. No?"

Dante sighed. "No, you wouldn't. If I had been allowed to go to medical school then I wouldn't have been allowed near a live patient for five years. That would be after I learned all the theory and worked on cadavers. Of course, medical school is too low-brow for an aristo *or* a Kipling, but I had access to slaves."

Elle decided not to read between the lines. And forced herself to not remember how she'd been 'recruited' as a test subject for one of Dante's experiments. "Do you have a point?"

He seemed to realize he'd said something wrong, but the idiot probably didn't know what exactly.

"That she needs to have a thorough working knowledge of the human body *before* she is allowed to practice her healing ability on anyone. That means books. Pictures. More books. Theory. Maybe even access to a cadaver or three."

No doubt under Dante's supervision. Which wasn't necessarily a bad thing, provided the person was already dead. And Elle *did* know the city's coroner.

She wondered how she could convince Alice to let a kid into the morgue.

"I'll think about it," Elle said.

"Give Emmie the book back." Dante sighed. "And stop slamming it around. It was not cheap. I bought it especially for her, and I'm not worth what I used to be. I'm a married man now." The Creep — Elle's favorite nickname for Dante — smiled.

"Ugh." Elle stood and picked up the book. Dante's relationship with Anton was complicated, but he wouldn't do anything to jeopardize it, even if it was something simple like spending too much coin. They were only just learning the boundaries of their marriage, and Dante was discovering that he actually *liked* his husband, which was more than he felt about most people, Elle knew.

Turning for the door, she stopped as she reached the threshold. "By the way, I need to speak to your sister."

"Misty?" Dante's face seemed to get even paler, if that was possible.

"Who else?"

"Do you *have* to speak to her?" The poor vampire looked a little worried. Viscountess Kipling was a difficult woman to like: flighty, vain, and narcissistic. The complete opposite of Dante who was largely emotionless, brilliant and completely unsociable. But then, Misty was on Dante's short list of 'cared fors', even if he didn't realize it. He'd ask his sibling over.

"It's about work."

Anton snorted. "Work? As in City Guard work? Good luck getting Mistique to help you there."

"Just invite her over for a tea or whatever it is you aristos do. I'll ask her then."

Dante shook his head. "Anything that goes wrong, I'm blaming on you."

CHAPTER SEVENTEEN

Oberona Mountains

Byrne watched surreptitiously as the young woman tried —
rather badly — to tie a diaper around the very new infant. Who
didn't have a name. What parent didn't have a name for their cub?
And where was the father? Was she traveling to meet him? She
had no baby bump that he could see, and he couldn't smell any
blood on her, so she wasn't bleeding after giving birth. But
vampires were different, and like weres, tended to heal within
hours of a physical injury. Although this wasn't necessarily an
injury...

He was giving himself a headache.

The little girl was kicking and whimpering and did not seem
at all pleased about the way things were progressing.

"Do you want some help?" Byrne hid his smile behind a hand.
The woman was wearing gloves while changing a diaper. He
didn't want to think about the hygiene issues.

Hannah was muttering under her breath, and while politeness
suggested he not listen in, he couldn't help it. Besides, she knew
he was a were; she should know he had super hearing. But really,
when she said things like, "The stupid memory said this was how
it was done," he couldn't stop himself from leaning a little closer.

Everything about this woman was interesting. It was a good
thing that Fin was almost comatose in the cart, otherwise he'd be
all over the pretty vampire, charming her out of her pants and into

his pine needle bed. The fact she had a cub would probably just be a bonus. Like Byrne, Fin loved kids.

Go figure.

But there was clearly something special about her. She was a vampire, but with her Black eyes, she was also Graced. He could see how someone might think her eyes were a very dark Brown, but his eyesight was excellent; there wasn't even the hint of color to those obsidian depths. The cool, icy leech scent was tempered, too — possibly by the urine staining her shirt — but it was definitely there. A Graced vamp. Byrne had never met one. From what he'd heard, most of them had been killed shortly after the Civil War, and that was before his time.

And the cub — she was also Graced. Green eyes, but completely human, which was unexpected.

"I almost had it!" Hannah's was voice raspy, like a purr. It danced through his head and he almost wished he had Fin's boundless charm. But facts were facts. Byrne clearly wasn't the kind of guy who jumped in and out of women's beds — his sexual dry spell pointed that out all too clearly. And this Hannah wasn't his mate.

Fin would no doubt be laughing his ass off at Byrne if he were well enough. The human thought that the whole idea of 'finding your mate' was absolute fiction, and for vamps, humans and some weres, it was. But for weres who were tenth generation or more, the ability to track your mate by some kind of psychic sense of smell was a very real phenomena. A couple of years ago, Byrne had talked with a wolf he'd known forever: the other were thought the reason later generations of weres had this ability was due to their interbreeding with Graceds. That the psychic ability had mutated in pure were offspring, to the point where all it provided was a clue as to who a were would mate with for life.

But considering Byrne was thousands of years old — not that he'd admitted as much to the idiot human — and he'd never found his perfect partner, he hadn't believed it would happen. After all, finding that mythical person who was 'perfect' for you? The chances were pretty slim.

Maybe he should just settle for Miss Right Now. But he was pretty sure that wasn't going to be the cute, black-haired Graced vampire unsuccessfully tying a diaper around the poor unnamed cub before him.

"There!" Hannah picked the cub up, and the diaper fell off. The vampire's face drooped comically.

"Here," Byrne leaned forward to take the babe from the woman's arms. She stepped back, like he'd pulled a knife on her.

"Don't touch me." Hannah's voice wavered, and he caught the distinct scent of fear on the air.

"I won't. But can I take the cub?"

She clutched the infant to her chest. "Why?"

"So I can eat it."

To his surprise, she snorted a laugh and handed the cub over. She took care to ensure that her gloved hands didn't touch him, Byrne noticed. Curiouser and curiouser.

"I've changed a few nappies in my time," Byrne said, trying to sound conversational. He was so used to spending his time bickering with Fin that he'd almost forgotten how to have a normal discussion.

"You have?" Hannah's eyes went so wide, he couldn't differentiate her pupil from her iris.

"Yeah, I had quite a few cousins, and they had cubs of their own. Had to do my fair share."

Blood, how he missed his family. Especially his sisters, Gina and Ruby. Gina had been pregnant the last time he'd seen her; her cub would be an adult now. But he wasn't ready to go home, to see them, or to answer their questions. They probably just thought he was dead. He'd been missing for over a hundred years after all.

But he didn't want to think about that.

Laying the cub on the blanket he'd set out earlier, he grabbed the fallen diaper and flattened it out. It wasn't the best material, so he folded it in half, into a rectangle and then half again, into a square. It'd have to do for now. No wonder Hannah had a pee patch on her shirt, though.

He waved a hand at her. The cub was looking a little cold in the crisp mountain air. "Now, come here. I'll show you how to get a good fold."

Hannah hustled closer, but not close enough that he might accidentally touch her. "You were getting too fancy. This is a newborn, they just need it simple. So fold the diaper into a triangle. The material is now eight thicknesses, which should be enough to capture the worst of her efforts. Then," he raised the cub's hips by her lifting her feet, "slide the diaper in, and fold the bottom corner up, then the side corners in."

The cub now had a diaper that would stay put. Unlike Hannah's poor efforts.

"Now wait here while I get a pin. Hold it in place."

Hannah gingerly held the diaper down with two fingers, while he grabbed a safety pin from the trusty first aid kit. Fin groaned while he was rustling about.

"Drugs?" the human slurred.

Byrne checked the position of the sun. "In another half an hour."

Another moan.

Byrne returned to the cub, and clipped the pin in place. "This will hold it better than a knot."

Hannah gave a slight smile. "Thank you." She quickly swaddled the infant, but she did that well enough so he offered no more advice. Her technique could use a bit of improvement, but he'd work on it.

"Do you mind watching the baby while I change my shirt?" Hannah asked.

"It will be my pleasure."

Hannah paused, looking at the covered mound in the back of the cart. "Is he a drug addict as well as a drunk?"

While Byrne considered explaining, he decided not to. Fin only stank of alcohol courtesy of Byrne's wound cleaning, but perhaps it would be good for the human to start on the back foot with this pretty woman.

"Just wants something for his headache."

"Right. Okay, I'll get changed now."

Unlike Fin — who admittedly, couldn't move — Byrne turned his back to give the woman some privacy. He heard her scold the goat for some misdeed, and the rustle of clothing. Byrne picked up the cub and tucked the little scrap of nothing under his chin. A sense of peace like he hadn't felt in years descended on him.

And the tickling sensation against his brain? He didn't mind it at all.

"There now, little girl." He rubbed the cub's back and she let out a contented sigh. "We'll find a name for you yet."

CHAPTER EIGHTEEN

Pinton City

How *dare* he?

No one — and he meant *no one* — threatened him. That piece of a fucking *weed*, Pierce Butterworth, wanted to speak of their affair? To tell the one person who could take away everything he'd worked for?

No.

He couldn't let that happen.

And he hadn't.

Gerard — his first vampire kill — had just been fun. Something to practice his skills on. He'd needed to know that he could overpower a leech, that he was able to do the job that needed doing. And he'd succeeded. It had been better than he'd even imagined. Knowing he'd managed to overpower a being stronger than him?

Pure exhilaration.

By the blood, his pulse raced just thinking about it. He'd been in the process of choosing his next victim when Pierce had cornered him in his rooms. Talked about spilling the beans. He'd had to respond. Not with immediate violence, no: with seduction. And since they were at his place, he had all his toys available to him.

He'd made Pierce scream before he'd killed the bastard. And then he'd dumped the body clothed, because he hadn't wanted any of Pierce's belongings left at his house. But given the choice, he would have left the asshole naked as the day he was born, to show the world how truly pathetic he was.

No one threatened him.

No one.

CHAPTER NINETEEN

Alice blinked, not sure she'd heard Elle Brown right. "The Viscountess Kipling is coming *here*?"

Elle nodded, straightening the baton strapped to her side. "It took a bit of convincing, but then the viscountess decided she liked a man in uniform and said she'd come check out the body if she got to try and persuade a guard to have a little 'fun time.'"

Alice looked around the morgue, from the spotlessly clean benches to the bodies covered in thick canvas bags. An aristo in her morgue? Well, the city's morgue. But still...no live noble had graced these doors in the entire time she'd worked here. Dead ones didn't count. And, she thought, regarding the line of red-shrouded cadavers in the second half of the room, there weren't many of those either. Only one body here was non-human — her unknown murder victim for whom she'd used a purple body bag.

Vampires had a different mourning color to humans. The morgue always had spare shrouds on hand, but she'd rarely had to dip into the purple or yellow piles. Weres and vampires had picked hues that matched their eyes. Looking at the single purple covered body, Alice sighed. The other vampire victim had already been sent to the funeral home for cremation.

"And a guard would agree to that?" Alice raised an eyebrow, before putting her clipboard down on the bench. She figured 'fun time' was a euphemism for 'blood donation time.' Although, she wouldn't be surprised if Kyle was keen for the adventure.

"Not likely. But she did say she would try."

"Why is she coming here?" Alice asked. "Can't she just use the sketch that was drawn up?"

"Apparently she needs to see the victim in person. Sketches are so 'yesterday.'"

Alice wasn't even sure she understood the last statement. She pulled out her pocket watch and checked the time. "When is she arriving?"

Elle's cheeks took on a faint pink hue. "Ah, now."

Footsteps sounded in the antechamber to the morgue. "Stepniece, where is this dead body you want me to view?"

Alice looked over at the woman in the doorway. She was alone, which was strange for an aristo. Her silvery blonde hair hung over her shoulders in artificial curls, and her white dress hugged a stunning figure. Tall, slender but with curves in all the right places. Vampires really got the best part of the looks department.

Sometimes, being human sucked.

Elle waved a hand at Alice. "Aunt Misty, this is Doctor Alice Reive, City Coroner."

The viscountess barely glanced at her.

"Alice, this is Viscountess Kipling."

The vampire fluffed her hair.

Alice dropped in a crummy imitation of a curtsy. Turning to Elle, she mouthed, "Stepniece? Aunt?" The guard shook her head. *Not now.*

"Through here," Alice said. She turned to the shrouded corpses. Two could play at the ignoring game.

Reaching the purple-wrapped body, Alice undid the first six buttons on the bag, and lowered the covering, exposing the dead victim's face. Elle and the vampire aristo took up a position on the other side of the body. Elle appeared torn somewhere between amusement, anxiety and annoyance.

The viscountess sniffed. Pale lavender eyes flicked in Alice's direction. "Your morgue stinks."

Alice shrugged, aiming for nonchalant. "They tend to."

It wasn't as if she had a lot of experience talking to aristos. She'd only ever spoken with one, really, and only then because he'd saved her friend Billie's life. Plus, Vere Radcliffe wasn't the typical aristo. He didn't even *look* like a vampire.

She wished Tal were here; as a university professor, she at least had some experience with the nobility.

Something almost like a smile crept across the noblewoman's face at Alice's tart response. "This," the viscountess pointed one disdainful finger at the dead vampire, "is Pierce Butterworth."

Alice kept her face blank. She'd never heard of him. But then, she wouldn't have. Grabbing the clipboard she'd left hanging from the foot of the corpse's gurney, she quickly wrote the man's name on the top of her documentation.

"What else can you tell us?" Elle had her notebook out and was scribbling notes.

The blonde vampire fluffed her hair. "I thought you just wanted him identified."

"Any other information you could provide would also be useful, sister."

Alice jumped, clutching the clipboard to her chest as she spun toward the new voice. She hadn't heard anyone enter. She blinked to see the newcomer was standing right next to her.

The owner of the voice was the prettiest man she'd ever seen. Shiny black hair, sharp jawline, bright violet eyes. Maybe 'pretty' wasn't a good enough description. Alice realized her jaw was hanging open. She shut it with a snap.

Someone snorted.

But really.

"Dante, did you really have to sneak in here?" Elle's voice sounded more amused than chastising.

"I *walked* in here," the male vampire said, clearly affronted. "I don't sneak."

The viscountess looked at him, her expression exasperated. "And you're late."

"Traffic was bad."

"Of course it was."

Elle interrupted what Alice could only assume was a burgeoning squabble. "So, any other information about the dead guy?"

The viscountess looked down her nose at Elle. "You really need to learn how to talk about aristos with more...respect. The 'dead guy' is the third cousin to Baron Whitfield. The man himself didn't have a lot of clout, but he did travel in influential circles. He was something of a poet, and so was often involved in court entertainment."

Elle frowned as she quickly wrote the information down. "Was the other vic," she flicked through her notebook, "Gerard Thornewood, also involved in court?"

The blonde vampire tugged on a curl. "The better question to ask is who *isn't* involved in court. The list would be very short." Her look turned into a glower. "And it would include you two. And your other guard friend's boyfriend."

Other guard friend —

Billie's boyfriend? Vere?

Dante sighed. "Not now, Misty."

Elle flicked a glance at Alice. "Thanks for your help. I'll just grab a bit more information from the viscountess —"

The aristo narrowed her pale eyes. "You mean your 'aunt.'"

"—while you tidy up." Elle turned back to the other female vampire. "I will send a notice to his family. Who would be the best contact?"

Alice buttoned up the shroud. "I can get the death certificate ready now I have the name."

"Great, thanks."

Alice left the three of them to talk over the dead vampire. As she washed her hands, someone tapped on the glass window to her left. The window looked out on the morgue's antechamber and she could see someone standing on the other side. Grabbing a towel, she grinned. "Tal!"

Drying her hands, she strode into the other room. "Hey! What are you doing here?"

Tal smiled and held out a cloth bag. "Brought you some lunch.

I was in the area. Have time for a break?"

"Sure, once my guests leave."

"Guests?"

Alice flicked her head back in the direction of the room she just left. "Viscountess Kipling and, I presume, her brother."

Both of Tal's eyebrows shot upward. "You have aristos in your *morgue*?"

"She did have." Elle had moved into the doorway behind Alice. "We'll head out now." The redhead's eyes locked on Tal. Tal stared straight back, her face slowly forming a friendly smile.

Alice tensed. Something felt off. Like there was some undercurrent she was missing. She didn't think that Tal and Elle even knew each other.

"Elle, this is Professor Talan Silver. Tal, this is the Honorable Elle Brown." Alice hoped she got the rank right. She didn't think that Elle would care about the title, but she had a feeling the viscountess, who insisted upon Elle calling her 'aunt', would.

Elle nodded, her eyes shuttered. "Nice to meet you."

Tal gave her a toothy grin, gray eyes glinting. "Likewise."

"Professor in what?" Dante asked, as he and his sister moved into the room beside Elle.

"Applied mathematics."

The viscountess gave a polite smile. "How fascinating."

Dante gave the viscountess what Alice interpreted as an incredulous stare. Then he turned back to Tal. "It actually is. I'd like to talk to you one day about it, Professor..."

Elle glanced at the both of them. "Let's go. You can pick the professor's brain another time." Then Elle winced, like she'd said something bad.

Alice noticed Dante was looking at Tal with a little too much intensity.

"Stepniece, didn't you promise me something about people in uniforms?" The viscountess ran a hand over her white dress. She paused. "On that note, why are the dead humans in there still full of blood?"

Alice, Tal and Elle stared at the vampire woman.

The viscountess rolled her eyes. "There's perfectly good blood going to waste in those dead bodies. If they were drained the day they died, then the blood could be sold to vampires who couldn't afford slaves. It would also provide funds for the victims' families."

"Aunt..." Elle's voice was a warning.

"What? They're dead. It's not like they need their blood anymore. And there's no nasty little addiction risk if vampires are using newly dead humans for sustenance."

The scary thing was, Alice thought the viscountess' idea was a good one.

Chapter Twenty

Oberona Mountains

Hannah paused at the sight of the huge bear cradling the baby Graced girl. One of his hands dwarfed the infant; only the top of her head and her feet were visible. But the baby seemed content, snuffling into his shirt. And Byrne looked...happy, holding the babe, like she was a missing puzzle piece.

Hannah wished she had the same feeling; the poor baby induced panic in her. She was constantly worried she was doing the wrong thing.

"Where were you heading?" Byrne asked.

She figured there was no harm in telling the truth; the were had helped her so far. "Skarva. My mother lives there."

The bear nodded. "Where's the baby's father?"

Hannah's heart hardened. "What does it matter?"

"Where is he?"

She narrowed her eyes. If the bear thought he was going to hand the little girl back to the Trsetti... "Why?"

"He knock you up and abandon you?"

"*What?*" Hannah's jaw dropped.

Byrne tilted his head to the side. "He knock you up and *you* abandon *him*?"

"No! I mean, she's not mine." Hannah quickly clarified, "Not mine biologically."

Both of the bear's eyebrows rose. He sniffed the baby, then the air. "Then how did you come by her? Did you kill her parents?"

Hannah's gut clenched. The baby was *hers*. At least for now. Ezra and her husband had just provided the raw biological material. "No, but I should have."

The way the were kept looking at her, slow and steady, put Hannah on the defensive. But why? This wasn't her fault. She'd only tried to do the right thing. "Give her back."

Byrne made no move to let the baby go.

"I said, *give her back*."

"Look, something isn't right here. You're a Graced vampire, you have a Graced human baby, and you're traveling all alone. What is going on?"

Hannah's heart stuttered before starting to pound again, painfully. Each beat thudded in her ears. He *knew*. He *knew* there were Graceds and that she was...different. Weres, vampires and humans weren't meant to know that anymore, at least according to her mother.

"I—"

"Don't panic," Byrne said. "I'm not going to dob you in to anyone. Not that anyone would believe me, anyway. Your people did a fantastic job mind-wiping everyone; making them forget there was ever anything different about folks with colored eyes. Now you just have people like the Trsetti who are afraid of *anyone* different."

"O-okay."

Blood, but she felt like an idiot.

Byrne's gaze hardened. "Just, what is happening here?"

She really should have prepared herself better. Thought of a cover story, had a lie easily in place. Her first encounter with people — admittedly, the bear was the first person she'd spoken to other than her mother or the Trsetti traders in *years* — and she had completely blown it. Nothing for it but the truth, she figured.

Looking him in the eyes, she started telling him *almost* everything. "I found the baby on the slopes of the Old Mother. She was naked, on her blanket. No humans in sight. I couldn't hear or see them either. They'd just *left* her there."

A low growl emerged from the bear. The infant whimpered. The sound cut off as Byrne looked down and gently ran a hand up and down the baby's back.

"What were you doing on the Old Mother? How did you find her?"

Hannah swallowed. "I live there. I heard her crying."

She expected a barrage of questions, but instead, the bear continued to rub the baby's back. "Lucky."

"I just...I don't know how they could do it. Just leave their baby to die. I had always liked the Trsetti."

Byrne's hand stopped for a moment, before resuming the gentle movement. "Narrow-minded bigots. We had a run in with them, picked up some injuries, that's why we're heading out."

Hannah looked past Byrne to the man lying in the back of the cart. If Byrne had been injured, he would have healed by now, no doubt. A human, on the other hand...The alcohol might have served a different purpose than her original suspicion. "He came off the worse for wear?"

"He screwed someone's wife. They weren't happy about it."

Hannah scrunched her nose.

"I hadn't gone into town." With his free hand, he pointed at his eyes. "But I had a little run in with them in the forest. They chased Fin there, trying to kill him."

She had no idea what Byrne's temperament was like when attacked, but he *was* a bear. They were rumored to be fearsome. "Did you eat anyone?" She didn't figure it was a rude question. While weres typically didn't consume human flesh, they still *could*. According to her mother, it had once been the only thing they were able to eat.

Byrne rolled his eyes. "Human steak isn't really my thing."

The blankets rustled loudly, and Byrne's companion groaned. "Isn't...a...pork man."

Byrne looked over his shoulder. "Fin, are you conscious?"

"Unfortunately." It was almost drawled. "Why did I hear a baby crying?"

Byrne shook his head. "Because there's a baby crying."

There was silence, the rustling of cloth and more pain-sounds. The man had quite a library of them. "Where'd you find a baby?"

Byrne's mouth quirked. "I saw one on the side of the road."

"*What?*"

"A woman and a baby were traveling down this path."

"Right." The blanket mound fell silent for a second. "Is she hot? The mother, not the baby."

"*What?*" Hannah spluttered.

"No, she's hideous."

Hannah gaped at Byrne. He winked one bright yellow eye.

It was surprising the amount of suspicion packed into blanket man's voice. "You're lying."

"All right. You caught me. She's only mildly attractive."

"*Mildly?*"

Byrne grinned then. "What? I'm honest."

It was a good thing Hannah wasn't particularly vain. The baby started to whimper. Byrne shushed her gently.

"You're making the baby cry, Byrne. I bet it's allergic to your lies." Hannah heard the human's murmur through the blankets, although she didn't think she was meant to. She barked a surprised laugh.

"Help me sit," the blanket man demanded.

Byrne was clearly debating whether or not to return the infant to her. Deciding to hand her back, he quietly said, "We'll talk more later."

The bear pulled aside some of the man's covers and the smell of alcohol grew stronger. "I don't think you should sit up, Fin."

A grunt, then, "Need to piss."

Byrne sighed. "I'll help you up. But wait till I get you out the back of the cart."

Hannah heard a muttered "no shit". Byrne helped the human up, and Hannah's skin tingled at her first sight of him, imagined pain throbbing along her own limbs. Black and purple bruises were spread across his face in a panorama of pain. Both eyes were swollen shut, and his nose looked like it had been broken and reset. Byrne handled the human with excessive care, not that the man realized, she thought. She had the feeling that she was intruding on something private — perhaps she should milk Betty. At least then she could feed the baby, who would no doubt be hungry soon.

Byrne shuffled past with the human, pretty much carrying the man. He was careful to avoid contact with her. Over his shoulder, he said, "Ride with us for a while, we're heading to Skarva, too."

Hannah considered, then nodded at the were. It was a risk, a huge one, but she and the were both had vulnerable humans in their care. She didn't think he'd do them any harm. She could be certain of that assumption, if only she touched him, but she didn't want to risk the inundation, the loss of self. Hannah wouldn't be able to protect the baby if he wanted to take her away and she was lost in his memories.

Life had just gotten more complicated.

CHAPTER TWENTY-ONE

Pinton City

Blood.

It was everywhere. Alice didn't think she'd ever seen so much. Not even that time she'd sneaked over to the blood den on a dare, to watch when vampires drank from willing humans. Alice stared at her hand, like it belonged to someone else; her fingers were smeared in the sticky red substance, coated from touching the doorframe. She stood just inside the door, staring blankly at her fingers like an idiot, unable to move, unable to even really think. The blood was still warm, like it had just been pumped from its source.

She didn't want to take another step, to walk further into the nightmare that awaited her. The smell of iron permeated the air, until she thought she could taste it. She didn't want to see the prone figure on the bed. Something wild and hot welled inside her, and she was torn between screaming and crying. She had no idea tears were snaking their way down her face, not until their salty tang overrode the metal flavor in the air.

Her nightdress hung below her knees, but she suddenly felt naked. Stripped and exposed, as if every shameful and secret thought she'd ever had was on display. Her bare feet squelched as she forced herself further into her mother's bedroom. Her heart pounded a fast, terrified beat. She knew what she would find under the dark-soaked sheets.

"Mom?" her voice came out strangled, tear-choked.

No response. But it had to be her, Alice knew it. Wait, where was her brother? Where was —

"Ashok?"

Movement out of the corner of her eye had her looking sharply to the side. And there was pain, so much of it. It radiated from the center of her chest, a starburst of agony that didn't seem to end. Looking down, she saw the knife handle protruding from her sternum.

And then she saw nothing.

Alice woke with a gasp, hand clutching the blankets to her chest like a shield. Her sternum ached with remembered pain. Absently, she rubbed the scar under her nightdress, picturing it, silvered against her pale brown skin, a needless reminder of something she could never forget. Slowly sitting up, she brushed strands of curly hair from her face. Sweat stuck a few tendrils to her forehead.

She'd been foolish to think she'd grown out of the nightmare completely, just because she hadn't had it for a while. It had been almost nine months since the last time. Just after the attack, she hadn't been able to imagine a time when the nightmare wouldn't haunt her sleep. Every detail of it was so real. The metallic stench. The burst of fear. That night had stripped away her dreams for the future.

It had been such a defining point in her life, the attack. It had occurred just days after her fourteenth birthday. In one fell swoop, she'd lost her mother, her brother. And there had been the pain, pain such as she thought she'd never survive.

After she'd been stabbed, she'd woken up in the local hospital, the sawbones telling her she was lucky to be alive. The City Guard had found her lying on the floor in the blood-soaked bedroom, the knife still in her chest. Days later, she'd been standing unsteadily and against medical advice, in the city morgue — the old one, not hers — next to her predecessor, watching the red shroud being pulled back to reveal her mother's face. Raylene Reive had been stabbed fifteen times — once in the neck, the rest in her torso. Her mother had been so vibrant: her brown spiral curls had seemed to bounce with pure joy, and her smile had been sincerity incarnate. And she'd had lustrous blue eyes that had melted everyone's hearts. But in death, she'd been so still...so empty.

There were no words to describe how Alice had felt that day, or in the days after, when she closed her eyes and saw the shroud being lowered, as if in slow-motion.

Now every time she pulled down the covering of a new corpse in her morgue — or out in the city — she would remember that heart-rending moment, and would dread that under the cloth cover would be someone she knew, someone she loved.

She'd lost Ashok, too. Even now, he was a missing persons cold case. The City Guard had thought that her brother had also been attacked. There'd certainly been enough blood in the bedroom for a second victim. But they'd never found his body. Perhaps he'd crawled off to die. Perhaps he'd been abducted. No one knew.

If not for Tal and Aunt Zara, her paternal aunt, she'd have been completely lost. As it was, she'd spent a good year in a haze, not knowing her head from her butt. Aunt Zara had started calling her Ghost Alice. Yet she'd emerged from her self-enforced cocoon eventually, to a world that was exactly the same as it had been before. It had been shocking to make that discovery — that everything fundamental in a person's life could be ripped away, and yet the world just went *on*. It couldn't care less about her and her losses. It just kept spinning, and people kept on living the lives they had lived before.

Enough memories. Swiveling so that her feet touched the floor, Alice dropped the bedsheet from stiff fingers. She pulled the sweat-soaked nightshirt over her head and threw it in the dirty clothes basket, before walking into her bathroom. It was tiny, but it had a shower, a toilet and a sink. It was all she needed. And right now, she just needed to wash the rancid smell of fear, loss and pain from her skin.

CHAPTER TWENTY-TWO

Oberona Mountains

Byrne had found a woman and a baby. Just wandering around on the slopes of the Old Mother. Did the cart have a sign on it that said "Trouble, please hop aboard"? Fin had to wonder.

Why else would Byrne pick up a woman and a baby?

Then the sound of bleating reached his poor, abused ears.

A woman, baby and a *goat*?

"Did I just hear a goat?" Fin demanded. He wished he could glare at Byrne, but his eyes were too swollen.

The bear grunted. "Does it matter?"

"Everything matters," Fin said darkly. Byrne laid him back down on the pine-needle mattress. Fin had needed to visit the little boys' room — well, the bush next to the path. He hoped the woman hadn't been watching; he wasn't at his finest right now. No doubt his poor cock and balls weren't in their best shape, either. Not that he could see them to verify it.

"Do we have anything to eat?"

"Here," Byrne thrust something at him.

Propping himself up with care, Fin took hold of it. From the feel of it, it was flat bread. A tentative mouthful of soft chewy goodness confirmed it, although it hurt to work his jaw. It didn't have much flavor, but that might be because with his smashed nose, his sense of taste was non-existent. "Where did you get bread from?"

"I made some, while you were unconscious."

Nice.

His face hurt, but it had been a couple of days since Fin had eaten anything. His stomach grumbled even though he finished his bread, and a slight feeling of nausea spread upward into his throat. It was probably all that laudanum. "Water?"

Byrne muttered something suspiciously like, "When did your last slave die off?" but still handed Fin a tin cup of water.

Fin sipped carefully, and then passed the cup back. "What are you talking about? My slave's still alive."

"But *you* may not be for much longer."

"My confidence in you is higher than it was two days ago. Laudanum?" He knew he must have sounded a little like an addict. Byrne passed him a teaspoon of the liquid gold, and Fin swallowed it with a grimace.

"What happened two days ago?"

The unfamiliar voice was low, raspy and sent shivers up Fin's spine. Then again, that could just have been the pain. He wished he could see this woman's face; with that voice, she had to be hot. And even if she wasn't, she could still talk to him in the dark...

Although, maybe he should give up on women for a while. Things clearly weren't working out for him in that area.

Fin waved a stitched hand at his face. "This happened. Cos my *best friend* couldn't be assed saving me on time."

Byrne humphed. "I already explained that."

That sexy voice again. "Well, if you sleep with someone's wife, their husband is bound to be a bit annoyed."

Fin turned his head toward where he thought Byrne was. "You *told* her that?"

He pictured the bear shrugging. "We were sharing."

Fin would have snorted, if he could. "Asshole."

"Prick."

"Dickwad."

"Milk-livered apple-john."

Fin paused. "*Milk-livered*? *Apple-john*? Where are you coming up with these?"

Soft laughter floated through the air. "You are both acting like five year olds."

"But good-looking five year olds," Fin said. Not that she'd be able to see much of his pretty face at the moment, but he thought he should let her know about his excellent looks in advance. It was only fair.

"Let's get moving," Byrne said. "We're not going anywhere, but the daylight is."

"Will we make the next town before dark?" the woman asked.

"Hopefully. Climb in the back. There's room for you and the baby."

There was silence, but after a few seconds, the cart shifted under Fin as someone climbed into the storage area with him. He heard Byrne pull the cover up.

"I tied Betty to the back of the cart; is that okay?" The woman was obviously talking to Byrne, not him. She had to be referring to the stupid goat, since the horse was called Baldy. Fin didn't like goats. They tended to butt people and eat *everything*. Including his shoes. He *liked* his shoes. Luckily his feet — with boots attached — were inside the wagon.

Plus, what kind of a name was Betty? So stereotypical.

"No problem. Can she keep up?"

"Yes, she's just easily distracted." Fin swore he could hear a scowl in her voice.

The cart moved again, from side to side now. Byrne must have been climbing into the driving seat. "Baldy isn't moving too fast, anyway." Then they were off.

"Baldy?" The woman's voice was louder now; she might be next to him.

Byrne's deep voice rolled over them. "You can blame Fin for that one."

"What?" Fin bristled. "It's a dignified name." The horse was a piebald, and he hadn't been about to call her Pie. That was just stupid.

"Baldy? Dignified?"

"Don't judge. Didn't I hear that the baby hasn't got a name?"

Although that could have been the laudanum wearing off.

Some shuffling, then her low, delicious voice. "I only found her yesterday. I haven't had time to think of a name."

"*Found* her?" He had clearly missed out on some juicy information while he had been passed out. Women didn't normally refer to giving birth as 'finding' their baby. And he didn't think he stuffed the translation up. Languages were kind of his thing.

"She was abandoned." The woman's tone didn't invite any further questions.

But Fin had so many...

Byrne spoke over the *clop clop* of hooves. "Baby is Graced. Was left on the slopes of the Old Mother by the Trsetti."

Well, that answered some of his more pressing questions. There was a squeak and a lot of rustling next to him. The woman was probably freaking out that he knew about Graceds, or that he and Byrne talked about them so casually. But she wouldn't be able to see his eye color, so wouldn't know he was a half-blood himself.

Fin pulled the blanket up to his chin. The mountain air was cold. "Graced. Huh. What color?"

There was silence for a few heartbeats. "Green," the woman said.

Fin exhaled. "Maybe that's why my head hurts."

"Your head hurt before we found the baby," Byrne said helpfully.

"True." But baby Greens had trouble controlling their ability. They often sought out the comfort of other minds. The best result was a Green to Green, as the mature Green could send calming thoughts back, but for others, it was like someone was tickling their brains. It was...discomforting. But Fin had pretty strong shields; even his annoying sisters couldn't break through them. And they had tried.

Nosy. No sense of privacy.

It didn't help that Marcia, Fin's eldest sister, was the strongest Blue he'd ever met, and she had an ego to match. No emotion was safe from her empathic abilities. Then there was Naomi, who had

Gray eyes and a serene composure he figured was hard won, considering she was a year younger than Marcia. Plus, you had to be composed when you could demolish buildings with a thought. Privately, he was glad he didn't have telekinesis. Then there was his twin sister, Faith, was a fearsomely powerful Green, and it was proximity to her in the womb that must have led to his developing strong, natural shields. Otherwise her telepathy would have probably turned his brain to mush before he'd been born. His youngest sibling, Petra, was a Brown, and had no ability whatsoever, although they had taught her some shields.

And every one of them gave Fin grief.

Man, he missed them.

Sometimes.

No doubt they would have agreed with Byrne and left him for dead as well. They'd often said he needed a forcible injection of sense.

Into the silence, he said, "What about Finlay?"

The woman made a startled noise. "What?"

"For the baby. Finlay. Clearly, it's a great name."

Byrne laughed sharply.

"Finlay?" The woman repeated. So much skepticism, so few words.

"Fin obviously hasn't strayed too far from home for name ideas," Byrne called back into the wagon.

"Right."

It occurred to Fin that he didn't know what she was called. "What's your name?"

"Hannah."

He raised a hand, as if to touch her arm — where he thought it was — but he heard material swish back away from him. "Nice to meet you?" He hadn't meant to make it a question, but he was surprised by her reaction.

"Don't touch me." She was breathing hard.

"Sorry?"

"Don't. Touch. Me."

"Okay," Fin said. He was confused as shit, but he'd go along with it. Maybe she didn't want dried blood on her or something. Maybe she just didn't like being touched. But he didn't go around forcing himself on women, even accidentally.

"Ever," she added. Just in case he hadn't got the picture the first time.

Fin held his hands up, palms out. "No, I get it. No touching." He thought about wiggling his fingers, but that was probably a bit too much.

He just hoped she wasn't as hot as her voice. Because that rule was really going to suck, otherwise.

CHAPTER TWENTY-THREE

Oberona Mountains

How did a half-comatose man manage to put so much doubt into a single sentence?

She probably shouldn't have been so rude to Fin, but she couldn't risk being touched. Even though they talked about Graceds like they were common knowledge —which went counter to what her mother claimed about the race being a secret — she couldn't trust how the human would react to learning of her ability. She'd never heard of anyone else suffering the way she did. And of the few people who'd found out, some had then deliberately touched her, just to see if they were exempt from her abilities. Or to make her weak.

No one was immune, apart from her mother. Her theory was that their shared bloodline was responsible. Hannah had no idea how that worked, but it did, and for that, she was thankful. She didn't want to know what was in her mother's mind. What's more, her mother was *old*; the amount of memories her mother had, both forgotten and remembered, would overwhelm Hannah. Maybe even kill her.

The last time a stranger had touched her it had been someone who had wanted to take her hostage, so her mother would pay a ransom in the form of titles, money and power. Hannah had been debilitated by the flood of memories and easy to grab, but what her captors hadn't understood was that she absorbed *everything*.

She'd been able to escape using the kidnappers' secret routes and tunnels, and work her way back to her mother. Who had *destroyed* the people responsible.

Hannah had nightmares about that for years. About people becoming tiny pieces of pulverized flesh. A whole family torn to fragments in a few minutes. It was that day she'd understood that while vampires could appear civilized, it was just a veneer. Manners, fancy dresses, they meant nothing when a monster lurked underneath. And her mother *was* a monster. One who could love, and be loved, one could smile and dance and laugh. But there was a barely contained ferocity to her at times, like she'd learned to replicate just enough humanity to hide her true nature.

Tatiana Romanov had earned the nickname the Deadly Duchess after taking her revenge on the kidnappers.

Hannah had thought it was a rather nice euphemism.

Afterward, she'd taken Hannah to the hut on the Old Mother. Hannah had returned to Skarva a few times over the past two centuries, but only rarely, and never for long. Her life had been worse back in the city, if anything. Hannah was the duchess' 'special' daughter, and everyone knew to avoid her like she was a plague-carrier. She'd been surrounded by people she couldn't touch and who refused to even speak to her for fear of being obliterated from existence. It was lonelier being near people and being ignored than just being alone.

"I still think Finlay is a great name," the human said into the silence.

Hannah came back to the present. Fin was covered in blankets up to his chin, and was lying stiff as a board. His face was so battered and swollen she had no idea what he'd look like normally, but the charm fair oozed off him. It was why she'd been so harsh with him about the touching rule. The few playboys who'd known about her ability had all wanted to try and see if they were "resistant".

Byrne half-turned in the driving seat. The sun's journey toward the horizon tinted the sky in the first shades of sunset. "You need to change tack, Fin. Why would Hannah want to call her baby after *you*?"

The blanket moved a little, tucking back into shape, as the cart jiggled it out of place. "Better question is: why *wouldn't* she?"

"Do I have to start listing reasons?" Byrne asked.

"Well, I haven't heard *you* come up with a better suggestion."

"I haven't had a chance; you never shut up. Even when you're half dead you manage to talk endlessly."

"Well, whose fault is it that I'm half dead?"

"We've been *over* this."

"Yeah, well I'm still not convinced about your reasons."

"Do I even have to have a reason? Why is it *my* fault almost an entire town decided to kill you?"

"It's not like you came into the village and saw what happened."

"How could I? I'm a *were*. Those people hate 'demons.'"

"And I had to stick out *my* neck so I could get *us* supplies."

"And did you manage to get any?"

Blessed silence. Then, "It's not my fault she dosed me with minar root."

Hannah shook her head. The baby moved against her and she checked the swaddling. It looked okay. The infant sighed and dribbled a little on her shirt. She didn't pack enough clothing.

It occurred to Hannah that even though she was seated in the cart, she hadn't absorbed the memories of its previous passengers or the person who built it. Perhaps her clothes protected her more than she'd anticipated, or her shields were stronger than she'd assumed. Maybe she *could* live a semi-normal life.

And maybe she'd have better luck wishing on the stars.

Fin and Byrne continued to bicker. But even though accusations were flung about, it all seemed rather amicable; neither one raised their voice, and their tones were still relatively light-hearted, even if the words were not.

"What about Tatiana?" Hannah interjected.

The squabbling stopped, and then Fin demanded, "What about her?"

"As a name," Hannah said.

"Isn't there some famous duchess called that?" Byrne asked. "Slaughtered an entire town or some such?"

"Oh yeah," Fin said. "Bit bloodthirsty for a little one, don't you think?"

Hannah's cheeks grew hot, with embarrassment or irritation, she couldn't quite work out which. That was *her* mother they were talking about, like she was some horror that you dragged out to scare little children. Back in Skarva, that probably *was* the case. By the blood, her mother even scared Hannah at times. But Tatiana was *her* mother. These people had never met her.

"The Deadly Duchess, that's what she's called," Fin announced, pointing a finger in the air.

"That's right," Byrne agreed.

"She's based in Skarva," Fin said.

"That's where we're headed," Byrne added.

Hannah shut her eyes and took a deep breath.

As Fin drew his hand back beneath the blankets, Hannah spotted swirls of black wreathing his wrist and disappearing underneath his bandages. The man had tattoos. Interesting and terrible. If he ever touched her, it would be even worse than usual. Those artists' thoughts would be impressed into the human's very skin. Fin not only carried his own memories, but also those of all the people who'd worked on him.

"Let's avoid the duchess, then," Fin said.

"As if we're even going to be at risk of meeting one of the aristos in that city, let alone a duchess," Byrne countered. "And isn't Skarva run by four dukes? No way we'd meet one of them."

"It could happen. A strange were, arriving on a city's doorstep with a handsome fellow in tow..."

"Handsome fellow? Lucky you don't have a mirror."

"I bet I rock the 'survived a gruesome assault' look." Fin smoothed back his hair, which was awkward considering he was lying prone in a cart.

Byrne looked over his shoulder, one black eyebrow raised. "I cannot believe you just spouted that asinine crap."

"Don't insult the donkey."

"What donkey?"

"Betsy."

"Her name is Betty and she's a goat," Hannah said helpfully.

"That's what I said," Fin all but grunted.

Hannah frowned. "You said—"

Byrne cut across her. "What about Mallory?"

Fin raised his head a little. "What about her? Do we know one?"

Hannah wondered if the laudanum had kicked in. It sure sounded like it had. She could smell the bitter liquid, like it was oozing from the human's pores. "I'm not sure it suits the baby," Hannah said.

"It means 'lucky'," Byrne added.

The cart bumped over a deep rut. Hannah threw her hands out to keep her balance; her palms connected with a backpack and the side of the cart. She braced herself, her whole body tensing in anticipation. But no memories flooded into her mind. She was herself. How? The pack hadn't been hers. She was wearing gloves, but...

Hannah shuddered.

Luck.

She'd just been lucky.

The baby sighed gently, responding to Hannah's body language.

Fin groaned at the rough treatment. "Don't be ridiculous. Mallory's a name for a teenager, not a baby."

Byrne sighed. "Teenagers were babies once."

"But the kid is a baby now. Wait, it's a *girl* baby?" Fin sort of blinked, but with his three-quarters shut eyes, it didn't work well.

"No shit," Byrne said. "Weren't you just suggesting a girl's name earlier?"

"Finlay? Finlay is a boy's name."

"No, it's a girl's name," Byrne countered.

"I thought it was a girl's name," Hannah added.

Fin grumbled.

"Either way," Hannah added, "we're not calling the baby

Finlay." Byrne opened his mouth to speak, but she held up a hand. "Or Mallory."

"Or Tatiana," Fin muttered.

Why was she even allowing them to have a vote in this, she thought. She didn't know them at all.

A few heartbeats of silence descended, and Hannah had never thought quiet could be so welcome. They were funny, these two, and they seemed nice enough, but between them, there never seemed to be a soundless moment.

From his breathing, Fin may have even fallen asleep.

Settling back, Hannah cupped the baby's bald head and smiled. Maybe she had finally had some good fortune. She was on the road, Betty was following along slowly, the baby was alive and well, and she had some traveling companions who would scare off most of the kind of villains who would think to attack a woman and a baby on their own.

"What about Serenity?" So Fin wasn't asleep then.

"What about it?"

If the human's eyes weren't so swollen, Hannah was sure he would be rolling them. "As a name for the baby."

She frowned. "Isn't it a bit...odd?"

"Odd how?"

"Well..."

"She was found through the serendipity of the Old Mother," Fin said. "I thought Serenity was a good comprise."

"What about Serena?" Hannah mused.

"Rena," Fin corrected.

Hannah gently tilted the baby's face to one side, examined the round cheeks, the hairless scalp and the tiny snub nose. "Rena," she tried.

The baby opened her murky Green eyes and looked at her, and then gave Hannah a toothless grin. Hannah couldn't help but smile back.

"Rena, it is."

PART II

The road up and the road down are one and the same

CHAPTER TWENTY-FOUR

As a child, he'd always been lacking in his mother's eyes. She'd pretended that she found nothing amiss, that she loved him as much as a mother should, but he just didn't have the empathy she had for others. He was very good at reading people, though, and he knew part of her hated him.

Despised his *lack*.

Once, when he was ten, he'd buried a dead rabbit in their tiny backyard; he'd killed it by wringing its neck, and then stomping on its back. It had squealed as it died, and the sense of power that had flooded him...the only thing to match it had been one particular death that he'd caused.

He thought he'd done a rather good job of disposing of the corpse, but his mother had sensed his change in mood with unerring accuracy, and had found him as he'd patted the last piece of soil down.

"You should feel remorse for this," she'd said.

"It's just a rabbit," he'd replied. "Food."

She looked at him with such sad eyes. "Well, you didn't kill it so we could eat it, did you?"

Her logic had been irrefutable. "It's just an animal."

"Animals have the right to life, just as we do."

"Not everyone has a right to life," he'd protested. It was something he still *firmly* believed. "They waste it. Just look at Mr.

Johnson; he sits in his apartment all day, eating and shitting, reading newspapers and naughty pamphlets. What kind of life is that?"

She'd gripped his shoulders, shaken him a little. "Language!"

"It's true."

"He may not do much with his life, but you don't get to choose who lives or who doesn't. It's *not* your right. You shouldn't even *think* such a thing."

That had been his mother: constantly telling him how he should think and feel, like these basic parts of him were hers to control. By the blood, he'd hated her and her all-knowing attitude. But part of him had loved her, too. She'd given him life, and that was a gift beyond price.

Over the years, he'd watched other mothers throughout society, seen how each one told their children what they should and shouldn't do, how they should feel, what they should think. Training their children in what was expected of them, reining in their progeny's base instincts, turning them soft. So now he had a special place in his heart for *all* mothers, knowing that his own had not been unique in her demands.

He'd kill them all, except for the fact that they were necessary for the continuation of the species...

But sometimes he let it get to him, and that's how he'd chosen his next victim. She was a mother — her daughter was born hundreds of years ago, but that didn't negate her role as a parent, even though she seemed to think her job was done. Clearly, her offspring needed guidance. Her daughter was an insipid, frustrating bitch. He'd kill her, if she wasn't such a favorite with the king. That would draw too much attention his way and he didn't think the king would like one of his pet aristos slaughtered, even if they deserved it.

But her mother? She gallivanted around the kingdom, fucking her way through servants and aristos alike. She had power, but did nothing with it. She had all but begged him to screw her senseless, even though she knew who he was. Had she no respect? Or was she using what power she thought she had?

Either way, it didn't matter. He'd agreed to a 'rendezvous', wining and dining in a hotel room. Not at the Rutherford, the most prestigious hotel in Pinton, no. He'd told the bitch he couldn't afford that and she'd tittered gleefully, happy to be 'slumming it' with him. No, he'd booked a room at the Myracle Inn — a much less dignified establishment — under an alias, where they would spend the evening, and where he would bring out his 'toys.' He picked up the stake and ran his fingers over the wood, lovingly.

Too bad she wasn't going to enjoy the evening half as much as he was.

Chapter Twenty-Five

Pinton City

It had been a week since the last vampire body had been found. Alice had gone over her notes time and again, and had kept Tal up to date with the investigation, even though she probably shouldn't, but no other leads had emerged. Even Elle Brown's aristocratic ties hadn't provided much intelligence as to the identity of the killer, although, thanks to the newly Chosen vampire, they did know that Pierce Butterworth's family hadn't accepted the death certificate she'd written. They were very unhappy with his 'change in life circumstances.'

As the coroner, it wasn't Alice's job to try and solve the crimes, rather to work out cause of death and provide the relevant documentation to the grieving family. But the inquiry was like a man treading the murky depths of the Thyme, barely keeping his chin above water, and unsolved murders always affected her. There was no denying her dream that she might one day catch the man who'd stabbed her, killed her mother, and either murdered or abducted her brother.

She'd been told by the city guard at the time that it had been a deliberate attack, although she hadn't known anyone who would want to hurt her mom. They'd said sometimes the killer didn't have to know the victim, that murder was all about power. It was a concept Alice had trouble grasping, but she figured that wasn't necessarily a bad thing. What it did mean was that her mother's death could have been totally random — and then Alice would have no chance of finding the truth, or her brother. The likelihood that Ashok was still alive was already slim to none, but she still hoped that one day she'd find him. Too bad hope was such a fickle mistress.

She smoothed a few stray auburn ringlets from her forehead and sighed. Her breath fogged slightly in the cool air. She'd long since grown accustomed to the cool temperatures of the morgue and accepted it was a tradeoff: being perpetually cold was better than having to tolerate the strong odors of decomposition. Besides, the black jacket she wore over her red work shirt and her sturdy shoes kept her warm enough.

She shoved her notes into her leather briefcase, and shut the brass lock with a snap. She wouldn't let her lack of success get to her. Violent death happened in Pinton all the time; she was used to cleaning up after it. Most of the cadavers that entered her morgue were vampire-created: death by exsanguination, or by the occasional rage-driven heart-ripped-from-chest, neck-almost-torn-off method. In a vampire-run city, and in her line of work, Alice had grown accustomed to vampires being the monsters, with humans being the good guys by default. That was the norm.

But she figured this killer had to be human, or maybe another vampire who was on the bottom of the aristo food chain. And that wasn't *normal*.

Argh, it was too hard to say with the information she had. Vampires weren't exactly the most popular people around, at least not in the lower classes. It could be *anyone.*

Except her; she knew she was innocent.

Whoever it was, though, Alice had never known someone with a grudge against vampires to succeed in acting on it like this, not just once but twice.

Time to leave. Alice shut and locked the door to the morgue behind her, and turned toward the stairs. Shrieking, she dropped the briefcase, belatedly watching as it fell to the floor with a clatter. A messenger had come up behind her, without making a sound. The young boy pulled the cap from his head and scuffed a shoe on the stone floor, a blush tinting his cheeks.

"Sorry to startle you, ma'am, but you're needed."

Slowly regaining her composure, Alice crouched down and picked up her bag. The contents rattled. Why was everyone sneaking up on her lately? Hoping nothing in the case was broken, she asked, "What for?"

"There's been another body found. And they said to tell you this one's different."

♦

This one's different, all right, Alice thought.

She was in King's Park again, although closer to the entrance this time. It was one of the more populated areas of the leisure park, and one more likely to be frequented by humans, if they were game enough to enter. Four guards ringed the site where the body had been dumped, on an open expanse of grass next to the gravel footpath that meandered through the park. To the south, large bluestone walls rose up to the sky, marking the boundary of the gardens. A pretty, twisted metal bench was perched on a slight rise to the north; if someone were to sit on it, they would have a perfect view of the deceased.

Long, flaxen hair trailed over wet grass in a discarded swathe of silk, crowning the dead woman in shining glory. Wet blades of grass glinted in the sunlight, fine strands of hair caught on their tips. The victim's head was turned to the side, facing the rolling hill and metal bench, mauve eyes staring sightlessly ahead, cheekbones sharp and jutting. A mint-green nightgown clung to the supine figure, although it was open in the front, baring white breasts and jagged wounds to the blue sky.

"Was her gown opened by anyone here?" Alice asked.

All the other bodies had had their clothing set right somewhat, even though it had been put on after they were killed. Alice knelt down next to the cadaver, the woman's pale skin even whiter in death. The spring sun was high overhead, warming the back of Alice's black jacket. Thankfully, the daylight meant there were few vampires around, although there was a handful of human onlookers surrounding the dump site — those who'd been brave enough to enter the park to ogle a dead vampire. They'd probably talk about this for weeks afterward.

The captain shook her head. "This is getting out of control," Dinya muttered.

Alice nodded. "Three bodies in two weeks."

The knees of her black pants were growing damp quickly, absorbing water from the grass. It had rained earlier, although the body was dry. At least it gave them a time indicator. She examined the body; hands working automatically as she tilted the neck, lifted the wrist, inspected the fingernails. Frowning, she leaned down for a closer look. Was that powder? She turned the hand to catch the sunlight. Yes. She'd have to take a sample of it back at the morgue. The first body had had an unknown substance like this as well. The analysis had been inconclusive so far, although it was organic in nature.

"Multiple stab wounds," Alice said to Dinya. She could count four without having to move the victim's nightgown. There was no bruising on her chest, and the wounds were clean, indicating they may have been done while the vampire had been lying on her back, or standing upright. Facing her attacker. A nervous tingle spread throughout Alice's veins. Was it the differences in the way this victim had been killed? The fact it was clearly more violent? Or maybe it was because this victim was a woman?

"Reckon it's the same killer?" Dinya asked.

Alice sat back on her haunches. "I don't know."

But who else could it be?

Biting her lip, Alice reached forward and covered the victim's chest with the torn nightgown. "I need to do a proper autopsy."

"She died from staking, even I can tell you that." Dinya was matter-of-fact, as always. Alice doubted the captain meant to question her abilities, despite the cynicism of the comment. Dinya's hand moved to rest on her steel baton as she stared at the corpse, and Alice could swear she'd done it without thinking.

Alice stood. "Yes, but I need to see if there are any similarities to the other victims."

"Like being dumped in a public place, poorly dressed?" One of the other guards snorted. Alice glared at the sniggering guard's back.

"Yes, like that. But there are other things I can check. Have her delivered." Alice grabbed her black leather bag. It now seemed like she wouldn't be heading back to her apartment after all. Maybe she could convince Tal to feed her on the way home, after she finished the autopsy.

Dinya nodded, and barked orders at the other guards.

As Alice turned to leave the park, her footsteps crunching on the gravel path, she couldn't stop the unease that spread through her.

Something was off here; she just couldn't work out what it was.

CHAPTER TWENTY-SIX

Skarva City

They'd made it.

Byrne found it hard to believe their little group had survived the journey to the city. Not because of the multitudes of bandits and highwaymen that were out there — they were around, but even they knew to leave a large were and a vampire alone — but because Fin was an even bigger pain in the ass when he was recovering from a beating than he was normally. Byrne hadn't thought that could be possible, but he'd been proven wrong. Once the laudanum doses had been reduced, Hannah and Byrne had been regaled with descriptions of all the many and varied aches and pains that beset recovering humans.

And of course, all of these aches and pains were *Byrne's* fault.

Not Fin's.

Maybe the villagers.

But definitely *Byrne's*.

Byrne now considered himself rather fortunate that he'd never really known what mortality was like. Even when he'd been held prisoner for a hundred years, chained in a dank and disgusting dungeon, he'd never known the types of agony that Fin was supposedly suffering. His friend certainly looked worse for wear, although his face was now a mottled mix of yellow and green bruises, rather than the impressive purple and red mess from the day of the attack.

Before they'd reached the border of Skarva, Fin had hauled himself upright in the back of the cart, which had swayed a little in protest. Byrne had been up the front, driving the buggy, with Baldy morosely plodding away along the dirt road. The horse still hadn't forgiven Byrne for going completely bear. The goat, Betty, had followed behind, desperately trying to nibble on any greenery that survived the track's traffic. She, at least, didn't seem to care there was a human-shaped bear around.

Fin had muttered some drivel about good impressions, and Byrne had heard him opening packs and sorting through them. Hannah was paying no notice to all this, cooing and talking to the cub as if she regularly spent the day ignoring strange men. He'd erected the cover on the wagon, so that the poor little baby could get some shade from the sun. At least she seemed happy.

Byrne had turned to look back into the wagon and seen Fin checking himself out in a little hand mirror he'd stashed somewhere. When Byrne had politely questioned Fin's vanity, the half-Graced man had explained that he'd needed to know how bad the injuries were, and if the damage to his pretty face would scare away the local children. The nitwit had then turned the little square mirror left, then right, squinting his bruised eyes and pursing his lips. He'd even scratched thoughtfully at the sandy colored beard that had set in over the past week.

"I think the green in the bruises really brings out the Hazel in my eyes," the human had said.

Byrne snorted. It was all the response he'd been willing to give.

Fin was Fin.

Unfortunately.

Now they were on the outskirts of town. For the past hour, they'd driven by a series of farms, each with a slightly different crop that stretched out for miles away from the road. Currently, it was straggly wheat, the stalks and heads still green. A small house was perched near the edge of the road, its walls smeared with mud plaster, and the thatched roof in decent condition. The farmers seemed prosperous, which was a good indication of the town's wealth.

The further they ventured toward Skarva, the more traffic appeared. Traders, families and farmers all made their way along the Skarva-Varsh Road, with carts, buggies, horses and donkeys. A couple of black lacquered carriages trundled by, their red curtains swaying behind closed glass windows. Byrne knew they contained vampires — the opulence and the daylight aversion were clues, but the icy smell of leech was the giveaway.

Soon the gravel surface gave way to a cobblestone pavement, and the cart followed the worn ruts toward the city's busier precincts. Towering warehouses led on to smaller, sturdier structures of stone and brick. The wooden window frames and doors looked out onto the main thoroughfare, and the buildings' porches were raised away from the street muck by a series of stairs. And, Byrne acknowledged, the streets were certainly mucky; they were caked with refuse from people's chamber pots, crusted with the grime and dirt that cities tended to accumulate. He wrinkled his nose in protest. Sometimes, having an excellent sense of smell was more of a burden than blessing. Already, he missed the clean, crisp pine smell of the mountains.

Streets branched away from the main thoroughfare, and buildings clustered together more. Soon, houses and stores shared walls, with alleys and mews snaking away behind the structures, providing the occupants with access and some privacy. The one-story buildings became two, then three, and the wealth of the area became apparent as the stench of unwashed streets faded. The cool smell of vampires grew stronger.

Byrne slowed Baldy to a plodding walk as they reached a street market. Vendors lined both sides of the main road, with hawkers yelling their wares, and brightly colored awnings hanging over stall fronts. People from all over the continent were at the market, boasting of their one-of-a-kind products that couldn't be found anywhere else. Except at any other city market.

"So where are we heading?" Byrne asked, keeping his eyes on the road. With her vampire senses she'd hear him, even through the background noise of the traders.

"Into the center of the city," Hannah replied.

Byrne thought they were already there, but apparently not. "Can you direct me?"

Silence, then, "I think so."

The were pulled the cart to a stop, to allow Hannah to climb out and head around to the front. Her fear of touch made her hesitant, carefully exiting the tray and then dodging around passersby. She was about to climb up next to Byrne when she froze, her arm outstretched, gloved hand gripping the edge of the seat's rail.

Byrne looked over and spotted a stranger hovering close to Hannah. Too close. It was a hawker, greed tangible in the man's eyes. The seller's arm was extended, as if to grab Hannah, but Fin's hand had closed around the hawker's wrist. The vendor was glaring down at where Fin gripped him.

"Do not *touch* her." Fin's voice was low and mean, the words spoken like a native Skarvan.

Byrne reined in his surprise.

Fin was often silly, sometimes lascivious, usually jovial, and most of all, friendly. He was rarely nasty; Byrne often forgot the human had it in him to be anything other than pleasant. But Byrne realized then that Fin had adopted Hannah and the cub into their little group as much as Byrne had. They protected their own, even if that care was sometimes a little belated.

Ignoring Fin's grip, the hawker flashed a winning smile at Hannah. He was missing an eyetooth, and his dusky skin had a slight coating of city dust, but his clothing was of good quality and he smelled clean. "But the pretty lady and her baby need to come to my store. Such wonderful blankets."

"The pretty lady isn't interested," Fin countered. Byrne saw his friend's hand tighten on the hawker's arm. How the injured idiot had moved so fast, Byrne couldn't say. Fin was meant to have been dying in a melodramatic fashion, after all.

The smile grew forced, the man persistent. "The pretty lady can speak for herself."

Hannah gave herself a slight shake and then climbed into the cart. "And she isn't interested."

"But—"

Byrne could feel the stares beginning to bore into the back of his head. They were starting to draw unwanted attention. Turning the full brunt of his attention on the hawker, he growled menacingly. "No buts."

And suddenly, the hawker had somewhere else to be.

Byrne nodded at Fin and shuffled across the bench, to allow Hannah space up next to him. She hunched closer to the edge of the seat, but gave Rena a gentle pat on her back as she did so.

"Thank you."

"For what?" Byrne asked, clicking Baldy into movement.

"Not letting him touch me."

"I'd say thank Fin, but we don't need his ego to get any bigger."

Hannah gave a small snort.

"Now," Byrne said. "Where to?"

CHAPTER TWENTY-SEVEN

The new autopsy had provided Alice with much the same results as the others, although more data about vampire physiology was always useful. It was a shame someone had to die for her to obtain it. Three someones now.

The woman had been staked four times in comparison to the one stab wound the other victims had suffered, although only one wound had proved fatal. Three appeared to have been done post mortem. Which meant that she'd been staked once while alive, although hadn't lived long after the wound had been inflicted.

From the recent results of the autopsies, Alice had determined a theory that the older the vampire, the more tolerance they gained to their 'allergy' to wood. Inflammation and necrosis would be greater around the wounds on younger victims, the opposite to humans, in terms of allergic reactions. Humans tended to suffer more extreme reactions with exposure and age. From the conditions of the wounds on her latest subject, the victim had been a reasonably old vampire.

Why the female had been stabbed more than the male victims, though, Alice couldn't say. That was for the guards to work out. Like the killer's other victims, she'd had sex prior to her death. It appeared to have been consensual; no tearing, bruising or damage. She'd also been killed elsewhere; Dinya's report had said there hadn't been much blood left on the ground after they removed the body. Alice set her clipboard down on the stone bench that ran along the three walls of the first half of the morgue. She rested her hands either side of the paperwork, palms pressed down onto the cold, smooth surface. Taking a deep breath, she mentally counted to three. She would help stop this murderer, somehow.

She pulled her jacket on and headed to the other side of the morgue, where she kept the processed cadavers. She'd had the guards put the new vampire body onto a gurney earlier, where she'd covered it in a purple body bag, and now rolled it over to the other corpses, positioning the table at the end of the neat row. The woman had been beautiful. She still was; even the pallor of death couldn't change that. But something about her seemed familiar. Was it the silky tresses that were so pale they almost glowed in the dark, or the aristocratic tilt to her features?

Alice buttoned up the shroud, obscuring the dead woman's legs, the wounds on her chest, then her face. Once the vampire was completely covered, Alice turned her attention to closing up the morgue. There wasn't much more she could do today.

Tal had mentioned something about having organized 'samples' for her research into the potential species of the murderer. Alice figured that she could drop by her friend's apartment and see if she really had managed to obtain the semen she'd promised. Alice crinkled her nose. Back when she'd been at university, she hadn't ever imagined that studying samples of sperm would be a requirement of her job as a coroner. Life was full of surprises.

With the morgue and her office locked up, Alice headed up the stairs and out through the reception area of the Guard House. She waved at Billie, who was staffing the front desk. The vampire city guard waved back at her, a small smile on her face. Alice wondered if the she was still feeling ill. Ever since she'd been Chosen, Billie had been plagued by nausea. She kept mostly to office duty as a result.

Outside, night had fallen. The air was slightly warmer than it had been in the morgue, but the wind had some bite. Buttoning her jacket up, Alice gripped the handle of her black medical bag tightly and began the trek to Tal's. She stuck to Pittbrough Street, rather than take the short-cut, keeping under the glow of the sodium lamps. Public areas generally meant safer places for humans. Her leather shoes tapped softly on the bluestone sidewalk, which was swept and washed clean each evening by the shop owners. This part of town would become popular with the vampire elite in another hour or so, when it was fashionable to be seen out of doors.

Turning left down Marcus Drive, Alice took a deep breath, tasting the coal smoke on the breeze. The cold air burned on its way down to her lungs. The last of winter's clutches were still evident in the evening drafts, but spring was here to stay. It was Alice's favorite time of year, when the plants flowered, babies were born, and things just *renewed*. It was also the season Alice had first woken from her shell-shock, when she'd come to understand that life continued, with or without her.

Tal lived in an apartment complex near the corner of Marcus Drive and Court Road. It was a richer area than where Alice lived, but being a university professor paid better than being a coroner. Reaching the intersection, Alice quickly crossed the road, ducking between carriages that bowled along a little too quickly for safety. Tal's building was made of a blue-gray stone, with white painted features. Its red steel door was shut and locked, so Alice drew out her spare key.

Once inside, Alice shut the door with a click then made her way up the wooden staircase. Tal lived on the third floor, in number 311. It was a prime number, and Tal said it was part of the reason why she'd bought the apartment. Knowing Tal, it was probably the main reason, she just didn't want to own up to it. Tal loved numbers, probably more than she liked most people, although she gave the impression she was a complete extrovert.

Thigh muscles burning slightly from the effort, Alice reached the apartment and knocked on the door. It was a bright, cheery yellow. This month. Tal changed the color of her front door whenever the mood struck her. It drove Alice slightly insane each time. Doors were meant to be painted and then *stay* that color. It's why she'd taken two years to paint the ceiling in her apartment. Even though green was *not* an appropriate color for a ceiling, she'd lived with it because ceilings needed to maintain some sense of permanency.

She was raising her hand to knock a second time when the yellow door opened inward. Tal stood in the doorway, laughing over her shoulder at someone. She was wearing a pretty gray dress that matched her eyes, and her hair was swept up in a neat bun, with her bangs caressing the line of her eyebrows. "Did you hear that King Johan has a new lover?" she said. "That he's actually acknowledged it publicly? Guess there's a first for everything."

How did Tal even *know* that? Maybe the university gossip mill was even better than Alice thought.

A female voice responded from back inside the apartment. "Of course I know. But did *you* know he was a human?"

Human? The king had a *human* lover?

Tal turned toward the doorway, a look of surprise on her face. "Alice!"

"Hi Tal, thought I'd drop by. I didn't realize you had company though. Is it okay if I come in?" Alice shifted from foot to foot.

Tal hesitated for a brief moment, then took a step back. "It's okay, come in."

Something didn't seem right to Alice, though, and her earlier feeling of unease returned. Maybe she was interrupting a date? Normally, Tal would wiggle her eyebrows, and make shooing motions with her hands if she didn't want company. They had that kind of friendship, where temporary rejection was part of the deal. They knew each other well enough to understand that sometimes their company wasn't welcome, but only because the timing was bad. But she didn't indicate that Alice should leave. The door closed quietly behind her and Alice walked into the open lounge room that shared its space with a small kitchen.

Tal's visitor sat on the pale cream couch, composed and calm. She was dressed in an entirely white suit, complete with smart jacket, crisp pants and ruffled shirt. Her lavender eyes narrowed slightly at Alice's appearance, then she smiled, and picked up a glass of red wine — at least, Alice hoped it was red wine.

Viscountess Kipling raised the crystal in a slightly mocking toast. "Why, it's the coroner."

The vampire's pale blonde hair was swept up high on her head, in artfully arranged curls. She looked rather incongruous: a vampire aristo in Tal's lounge room. Tal sat down next to her on the couch.

Alice attempted a slight curtsy — or was it a bow? — and had the feeling she just looked like she was trying to not fall over. "My lady."

"The viscountess just dropped by for a visit," Tal said, slightly awkward. From the scattered remains of cheese and crackers, and the half-empty bottle of wine, Alice guessed that the visit had been planned rather than spontaneous, but simply smiled at the two of them.

Then the viscountess patted her shiny pale hair and Alice forgot why she'd come to Tal's in the first place.

Pale blonde hair.

Beautiful face.

Similar cheekbones.

Suddenly Alice's strange feeling from the park made sense. And without thinking, she blurted, "I think you need to come to the morgue."

CHAPTER TWENTY-EIGHT

Fin's earlier heroism had left him rather shaky. Okay, 'heroism' might be putting it on a bit much, but intervening when the hawker had tried to touch Hannah had caused him considerable discomfort. His ribs were still protesting, a dull ache that spread throughout his chest. But he'd seen the seller reach for the beautiful vampire, and then her look of panic as she realized how close that touch had come.

He wasn't entirely certain what Hannah's problem was, but he knew it was because she was Graced, and a vampire. He'd never seen that eye color before. His sisters would love to meet her, although, he had a feeling they might not approve of her ancestry. Marcia, Faith — and even Naomi — were particular about keeping the bloodlines separate. Even though they had him and Petra as part of the family, he knew they wished that their mother hadn't 'experimented' so much. But at least neither he nor his baby sister had were or vampire blood. Immortal Graceds, while good in theory, did not appeal to his sisters.

Marcia had said it was because an immortal Graced would lose touch with their humanity. "People need to be able to empathize with each other; that's why old vampires and weres are dangerous. They forget how to *feel*." Fin had argued with that, and he still would now. Byrne wasn't exactly a spring chicken, but it was clear to Fin that the bear felt far too deeply. That's why he'd stuck by Fin for the past three years, instead of going home to his family.

In a rare show of agreement, Naomi had stood by Marcia's opinions, but her reason was that vamps and weres could live too long, and inevitably, would go insane. "If they're a Gray, they'd have the capacity to wipe out hundreds in a tantrum."

And Faith, well, Faith just thought that there was a reason their ancestors had wiped the memories of weres and vampires, so that the Graceds would be forgotten. "They could breed new powers; who knows what abilities they'd have? What dangers they could pose."

Hannah was clearly part-Graced and part-vampire, but Fin didn't think she was that fearsome an enemy. After her first outburst, he had gathered that she was afraid of touch the way some people were afraid of spiders or snakes. Phobic. She even avoided accidentally brushing against Fin and Byrne's gear when she rode in the back of the cart; she spent most of her time walking alongside the wagon as a result, with baby Rena in a sling around her front. She'd let Fin and Byrne hold the baby, but only after she unwrapped the cloth around her, and made them re-swaddle Rena with something else. Hannah was pretty closed-mouthed about her past, but Fin could gather that she'd suffered because of her 'sensitivity' and that she'd lived an isolated lifestyle as a result.

Her phobia probably wasn't helped by the fact she was stunningly beautiful. Now Fin's eyes were no longer swollen shut, he'd gotten a good look at the 'mildly attractive' woman. Long straight black hair that would reach her butt if let loose, fine features, sharp nose, pointed chin, large Black eyes. And she filled out her leather pants in a way that made him feel a little like a pervert for noticing, especially considering her aversion to touch. People would just want to be *near* her; it was the unfortunate side effect of being so good-looking. Fin also suffered the same problem. It's why he was so popular with the ladies.

But her social skills would keep anyone intrigued by her looks at a distance. She was prickly. Unlike Fin, who was ridiculously charming. Unfortunately, he kind of liked her attitude. Although, he still didn't approve of the fact that she hadn't even realized she'd need to *name* the baby she'd saved. Like it was normal to just wander around with a nameless infant. He was still a little disappointed they hadn't decided on Finlay like he suggested. It was a good name, with a strong legacy. It could work for a girl, too. Totally.

He wondered if any of his sisters had had kids yet, and if they'd named one after him. Knowing them, they'd probably pick names specifically to avoid sounding like his. They were contrary by nature, especially his twin, Faith. Plus, he wasn't sure if they even knew he was alive. He'd just upped and left. A shattered heart and a messed up mind, and he'd bailed.

Faith had come close to finding him once, but he'd slipped away before she could corner him. While he had a natural mental shield that even her Green abilities couldn't penetrate, she was still his twin; he could sense when she was nearby. They had *the bond*, as Marcia said. He could never tell if she was being sarcastic or not.

"We're here." Hannah's low and raspy voice jerked him back to reality.

Leaning over the edge of the cart, he looked around the street. Traffic was minimal here, even though the road was wide, the cobbles even, and the sidewalks clean. It was as if the humans who lived in Skarva avoided the area. The sky overhead was a deep blue spotted with clouds, but Fin felt like the weather had suddenly grown more ominous. His eyes came to rest on the huge bluestone wall that towered before them, casting a shadow over the cart, then on poor Baldy who looked droopy from her exertions, and more than happy to stop. The stupid goat looked longingly at the closed wrought-iron gates and the stone driveway visible through the metal bars. The drive led toward a manor, which had wide steps spilling onto a porch, where columns provided striped shade. A circular garden at the base of the steps allowed carriages to turn around before heading back to the street. Fin figured that was what Batty-Betsy-Buttercup was mooning over.

Fin's eyes returned to the large bronze crest at the center of each gate: a raven in profile, with thorny rose stems rising in a kind of laurel around it. The ends of the laurel were tipped with stylized roses. He read the words in Skarvs, once, then twice. Looked at the crest again.

Fin's mouth felt awfully dry all of a sudden. "The Duchy of Ravens?" He swung his gaze back to Hannah. Both hands gripped the sides of the cart as he leaned forward toward the driving seat. His knuckles were white, and the stitches stood out against his tanned skin. "Your mother lives at the Raven Duchess' town *estate*?"

Hannah's Black eyes stared at him, and her mouth pinched in an emotion he couldn't decipher. She stepped down from the wagon's seat and re-settled a protesting Rena, before straightening her white shirt around the baby, then smoothing down her thighs like she was removing wrinkles from a dress, rather than dusting off leather pants.

The Raven Duchess. Otherwise affectionately called the Deadly Duchess. Of whom Byrne and Fin had joked when talking of names for the baby. Fin groaned.

Hannah pulled her satchel from the back of the cart. She stared at Betsy-Betty-Batty and sighed. "She's my mother."

Wait.

What?

"Your *mother* is the Raven Duchess?"

"Your *mother* is the Deadly Duchess?"

Byrne's face wore the same stupid look that his did. It wasn't flattering, so Fin tried to school his expression as best he could.

Byrne climbed down off the cart and pointed at the estate. "I can't go in there."

"Someone has to go with her," Fin said. He would have folded his arms across his chest, but knew that would just end in pain. So he glared instead. "And it won't be me."

That hard jaw of Byrne's tightened. "In case you hadn't noticed, I'm a *were*."

"And I'm practically an invalid."

"Oh, so now it suits you to be ill." Byrne snorted.

"I've been almost dead the entire week, *in case you hadn't noticed.*"

"But you're human." The were thought about that for a few seconds. "Mostly. They probably won't try and kill you on sight."

"And you're an idiot. They can't kill a visiting were without cause. Hospitality rules and all that rubbish. Plus, I can't protect someone with broken ribs."

Hannah stepped between the two of them, but still out of arm's reach. Her beautiful features were scrunched in a scowl. "Why does anyone have to go with me? Why do I need protecting?"

"You have a baby, and you're on your own," Fin said.

Hannah gaped at him like he'd lost his marbles. Maybe he had. "People have babies all the time," she said.

"Yes, but you have a human baby and you're walking into a vampire household." Fin spoke slowly. "They may not take it that well."

"Rena is clearly adopted."

"With your eye color, it may not be that clear to some," Byrne said.

"Who is going to know?" asked Hannah, exasperated.

"Your mother," Fin said.

"I don't think my mother would—"

"You do know what her nickname is, right?"

"Yes. You both reminded me a few days ago."

Fin swallowed at the reminder and looked at the ground quickly. Classy of him.

"How about I take the baby and go find accommodation for me, Baldy, the goat and the cart? You and Fin can go in, explain the situation to your mother and see how she takes it."

Hannah's mouth formed into a thin line. At last she nodded. "Fine — but come back here afterward, with Rena."

Fin didn't think that the vampire realized how much she'd grown to trust them until that moment. Or how much she didn't trust her mother.

He hoped it wouldn't take Byrne long to find accommodation, because if he and Hannah had to rely on his combat skills to get them out of a spot of bother, then they were both screwed.

CHAPTER TWENTY-NINE

Hannah handed Rena over to Byrne, careful that her hands didn't touch the were's. Even wearing gloves, she couldn't take the chance of accidental contact. She was so close to being home, so close to having all her problems solved — she couldn't risk falling into a memory-trance now. Even though they were just outside her mother's estate, they weren't in her protection yet. And Tatiana Romanov had enemies, which meant that Hannah had enemies, whether she knew who they were or not. Until she was inside her mother's walls, she had to be cautious.

Slinging her backpack over her shoulder, Hannah took a step toward the large gates. They'd marked the boundary of her world for the first dozen years of her life. She'd been resentful of them at first, but eventually she'd considered them to be the security they were. Too many people didn't care about the personal space of a small, defenseless child, or wanted to take advantage of her difficulty. Now she almost felt nostalgic looking at the metal portals.

Byrne murmured a good-bye, and then climbed up into the cart's seat.

Fin looked back. "You aren't going to wait for us?"

The large man shook his head. "Not unless you think there is going to be an issue."

Hannah sighed. She'd given Rena to Byrne at his request,

because a hidden part of her wasn't entirely sure what her mother's reaction would be. Tatiana liked children, but whether or not she would welcome a stranger's baby into her own home, well, that was up for question. And Hannah wouldn't risk an innocent on that smidgen of doubt.

"Go get the accommodation sorted. Although, I'm sure Mother would let you stay with us, since you helped me return home." Hannah almost managed a smile.

Byrne shifted uncomfortably at the idea. Rena made a gurgling noise, and the were carefully rocked her. For someone so large, he was always so delicate around those smaller than himself. It made her feel safe, in a way Hannah hadn't for almost her entire existence.

Her mother was strong, stronger than probably anyone else alive, but Tatiana had been plagued with moments of irrationality throughout Hannah's life. Maybe it was a result of being so old. Things would just...slip. And although Hannah had never felt truly in danger from her parent, she'd always had the fear that maybe her mother would forget who she was, just for a brief moment, and that would be that.

Hannah wasn't foolish enough to think that Byrne didn't have a mean side, too; he was just as much a bear as a man, and bears were protective of their own. She knew he liked the baby, but what he felt about her was a mystery. Pity, maybe?

"I'll come back here after," Byrne said, then clucked Baldy into protesting movement. Betty followed readily; there'd been no grass here for her to nibble on.

"So what's the plan?" Fin asked as Hannah watched the wagon and the goat depart.

Fin was taller than her, with golden blond hair that was untidy from being slept on for a week. His face was a collection of mottled bruises, although his black eyes were no longer swollen, and his grazes had begun to heal. He'd managed to grow the beginnings of a beard, too, the hair slightly darker than that on his head. She'd heard Byrne and him arguing yesterday about when the stitches on his hands and arms could be removed. Hannah thought Fin had lost that round, although it was hard to keep up.

He seemed like a nice guy, but could she trust him? Because he talked so much, it occurred to her that she might think she knew him better than she really did. True, he'd stopped the peddler from touching her before, which had been one of the nicest things anyone had ever done for her. Didn't that make her life look rather sad?

As she started walking toward the gate, he overtook her, doing a remarkable job of standing upright, considering he'd been at death's door for the past week — at least according to him. He reached the large metal barrier first, and opened the smaller gate that was inset into the right panel. He stepped through, motioning for her to follow, then shut the gate behind her, careful to avoid touching her. Both he and Byrne were always so particular; she'd never known people to take her wishes on board so easily. But then, they knew she was Graced, even if they didn't know what her ability was. They were no doubt smart enough to have worked out it was touch-activated.

Fin followed her up the driveway. His long-sleeved white shirt was wrinkled, and his brown leather vest didn't do much to hide the garment's sorry state. His loose-fitting breeches bagged on him, and the slight odor of alcohol wreathed his body, but despite his disheveled state, he was far too handsome for his own good. No wonder he'd gotten into trouble at the last town. The Trsetti were not known for their tolerance of outsiders, especially ones who'd seduced their women. Although, Fin claimed *he* was seduced. Looking at him, Hannah believed that was equally likely.

She wondered what her mother would think of her traveling companion. Probably nothing too flattering.

Catching her staring, he stopped and quickly ran a hand through his scruffy hair. "Better?"

Considering he still looked like something the cat had dragged in, Hannah nodded. Without a shower, a razor and some new clothes, that was about as good as he was going to get. And it was still better looking than probably half the courtiers who surrounded her mother. "Let's go."

Hannah led the way up the steps and onto the protected porch. Raising her fist to knock on the door, she paused. The wood was old, and was no doubt touched all the time by household staff, and potentially visitors...

Fin reached past her and slammed the knocker down in three rapid strikes. Feeling foolish, Hannah withdrew her fist quickly and fiddled with the strap of her backpack.

"It seems pretty quiet here." Fin shoved his hands in the pockets of his breeches and rocked back on his heels.

Hannah was about to reply when footsteps approached and the door swung inward. A well-dressed man regarded them slowly. He had pale mauve-colored eyes, and his brown hair was slicked back with a pomade that made Hannah's nose wrinkle.

"Can I help you?" The servant's eyes were lingering on Fin, and Hannah wasn't sure she liked the intent in his gaze.

"I am here to see my mother," Hannah said.

The servant whipped his head back toward Hannah. "Your mother?"

A new figure appeared behind the servant, this vampire exuding elegance. He had tied-back black hair, which complemented his smooth skin, and he wore a starched white shirt and a beautiful charcoal-gray dinner suit. Like the servant, he was a little shorter than Hannah. But his eyes were an intense red-violet, the color of a Chosen vampire. Born vampires didn't have such a mix of red and purple.

The newcomer smiled, and stretched out his hands in greeting, before noting her ramrod posture and dropping his arms. "Lady Hannah! My, this is a surprise."

She wracked her brain to remember the man's name. So many memories, so many not her own. But the eyes were a giveaway — her mother didn't keep many Chosen vampires around her. "Mr. Randall, what a pleasure. I was just telling this man that I am here to see my mother." She forced a smile.

"Of course, my lady. Come in." Randall took a step back and indicated the servant do the same.

The large foyer beyond them had white marble floors, with a soaring, vaulted stone ceiling. The plastered walls were lined with tapestries, and two delicate-looking bench chairs sat at either end of the room. The chairs were there for the visitors obliged to wait for the pleasure of the duchess' company, or for those not permitted entry into the drawing rooms or remainder of the house. The duchess had had them added to the foyer after Hannah's 'condition' had grown apparent.

There were three alcoves as well, each holding vases of remarkable age and beauty. One was black, with men and women painted on it in orange, some holding spears, others holding jugs, all wearing strange garments. The second vase was white, and had delicate blue flowers painted all over the surface, while the third was tall and fluted, in a kind of green glass. As a child, Hannah had been curious about them and had touched the black and orange one. She'd only done it once and had been bed-ridden for days, her body helpless while her mind sorted through thousands of years of memories that had been imprinted into the object. Hannah hadn't let her curiosity drive her to the same mistake again.

The large wooden door closed behind her and Fin with a thud. "Where is Mother? Or Montrose?" Hannah asked. Montrose was her mother's most trusted aide. They'd been together for millennia.

"Montrose is on leave," said Randall. "She should be back in a couple of days."

Hannah shifted uncomfortably on her feet. She couldn't hear or smell her mother within the estate; maybe Taliana had left with Montrose? Although that was unusual. Normally one of them stayed at the estate to ensure things were running smoothly.

Randall smiled. "We weren't expecting you back at the estate, Lady Hannah."

"You have already said as much," Fin muttered dryly. He took a step closer to Hannah.

The vampire shot the human a look of contempt. "And who are you?"

"My name is Fin, I'm a *friend* of Hannah's." He crossed his arms over his chest.

Hannah wondered why Fin didn't give his surname. With a start, she realized *she* didn't know it either.

Randall looked incredulous. "A *friend*?"

Hannah didn't like Randall's tone, and wasn't sure she liked the emphasis Fin had placed on the word 'friend', either. "I can have friends."

Aware of his blunder, the vampire said, "Of course you can, my lady."

"So where is my mother?" Hannah tapped her foot, impatient. She suspected her mother was out. Tatiana's hearing was second to none; she'd have heard her daughter arrive and come to greet her in person by now.

"She has gone to Pinton, my lady."

"Pinton?" Hannah repeated.

Fin ran a hand over his beard. "That's another seven days north from here."

"Correct," Randall said.

"Why would she go there?" Hannah wondered.

"To visit your brother."

Hannah gawked.

"My *brother*?"

CHAPTER THIRTY

Pinton City

"I don't see why you all need to be here," Dante muttered.

Anton and Elle followed him out of the Greystoke carriage and onto the street, the driver shutting the door after them. The black lacquered conveyance remained stationary, the horses well-behaved on the busy street. The driver did a quick bobbing bow before climbing back onto the seat and moving the carriage on. He'd be back in an hour. The three of them were left standing out the front of the Kipling town estate, the towering bluestone walls leaving them in shadow.

Dante hadn't been back to his father's residence since he'd married Anton. Well, since he'd been forced to marry Anton. He hadn't had much of a choice in the matter — marry the human or get sent to an insane asylum, or worse. As long as Dante had agreed to one of the options presented, Viktor hadn't cared.

To be fair, Anton hadn't had any choice in the matter, either: marry Dante or lose everything. Thanks to a bad investment, Anton's father had owed Dante's father a substantial amount of coin. Viktor could settle a debt and get rid of his unwanted son in the same plan; it had been an ideal maneuver. Unbeknownst to him, Viktor had actually done Dante a favor, too. Getting away from his parent had been one of the best things that had ever happened to him.

Life had been going surprisingly well ever since.

"The request was sent to me as well," Anton said, his cane clicking against the pavement as he took a step toward the estate.

Dante frowned. "That doesn't explain Elle's presence."

He wasn't sure that Elle meeting his father was a good idea. Sure, they *had* technically met before she'd been Chosen, but she'd been acting like a servant then. Viktor would not appreciate her attitude now she was no longer pretending to be meek or mild. The only insolent person his father seemed to like was Dante's sister, Misty. Everyone else was a problem in Viktor's eyes. And his father eliminated his problems.

The Chosen vampire shrugged. Her long red hair was tied back in a bun, and she was wearing her city guard uniform. "I'm nosy. Sue me."

"Won't you be late for work?" Dante asked.

"My shift doesn't start for another hour and a half."

Dante pinched the bridge of his nose and shut his eyes for a solid three seconds. "This is going to end badly."

Elle slapped him on the back in what Dante guessed was meant to be a show of support. "Come on, don't be such a whiny baby. We'll go in, see your father, work out what he wants, and get out of there. If he's being a total jerk, we'll beat him up a little."

"We can't beat up the earl," Anton said, ever the voice of reason.

"Why not? Dante is his son. Family dispute."

"More like domestic violence. Plus, Dante is his father's social inferior. It would be illegal for him to harm a higher-ranking aristo."

Elle eyed Anton. "You guys really know how to suck the fun out of life, you know?"

"I didn't make the laws," Anton said.

"Let's just get this over with." Dante strode to the door and knocked. A servant in a ridiculous mob-cap answered, bobbing an awkward curtsy at him.

"The Honorable Dante Kipling, Baron Greystoke, and the Honorable Elle Brown here to see Lord Wintermere," Dante announced. He'd decided to keep the meeting formal. After all, his father had requested the presence of Baron Greystoke and the Honorable Dante Kipling. He hadn't asked for his son. No doubt Dante was still in the bad books. When you lived a long time, holding grudges became more of a hobby than anything else.

The servant led them through the warren of stone halls that was the Kipling town estate. They emerged into the exercise yard in the center of the building; the woman was certainly escorting them the long way to his father's study. There had been at least four turns they could have taken that would have had them there by now. Maybe she was new.

As they stood in the empty yard — waiting, Dante assumed, while the servant got her bearings — the sound of yelling reached them, followed by shattering glass. Dante looked up in time to see a body soar from the study window and land with a *thud* on the packed earth floor.

Dante blinked.

Anton gasped.

The servant fainted.

Elle took a step toward the body.

The prone figure wore an expensive suit — now covered in dust — and his left leg had turned at an unnatural angle. Dante recognized him at once.

"Father?"

Viktor Kipling, the Earl of Wintermere simply did *not* plunge out of windows. It was completely out of character. And undignified. Viktor Kipling did not *do* undignified.

A woman appeared at the study window and jumped after him, somersaulting gracefully, her blood red hair streaming behind her, before landing on her feet in the courtyard. She wore leather pants and a long jacket, with a bright red corset underneath and had over-large, very bright, violet eyes. Straightening her jacket sleeves — was that a *tattoo* on her wrist? — she came to stand at his father's feet.

"Did you just call this *man*, 'father'?"

Dante nodded. "Yes?"

He'd always thought the familial connection was rather

obvious; he was the spitting image of his father, after all. But there were more urgent matters at hand. Who was this woman? And why she'd pushed his father out of a window? Although, Dante had to be fair; he'd wanted to do that once or twice himself, so he couldn't really blame her. Viktor could be a total ass.

His father let out a low moan, and then the sound of cracking bone rent the air. The broken leg was healing itself. Although Viktor still hadn't sat up, Dante could feel his father's eyes on him.

The woman took a step toward him. She was about half a foot shorter than Dante, but she had a commanding presence. "You're Dante Daemon Ernest Romanov Kipling?"

"That is my name."

Elle and Anton both moved closer to him. The servant had wisely maintained her faint.

"Don't speak to her any more," his father ordered from his position in the dirt.

The female vampire smiled and sliced a hand through the air. "Ignore that idiot."

Viktor growled, a low, menacing sound, and sat upright. The woman just kept smiling at Dante and it was surprisingly warm. Then she took a sudden step back and stomped down on Viktor's other leg. He let out a scream of agony, and the sound of crunching bone echoed in the courtyard. He collapsed, panting.

The woman held out both hands toward Dante. "It's nice to meet you," she said, her expression genuine.

"I thought you said we couldn't beat him up," Elle hissed in his ear. Dante ignored her and took the other vampire's hands.

"I'm sorry, but what is your name?" Anton asked. Dante's husband had come to stand by his side.

The woman assessed Anton, and Dante felt a frisson of something like fear snake through him. She'd just thrown the Earl of Wintermere from a window and broken his leg...how would she take a human questioning her? Humans were far more fragile. He couldn't let Anton get hurt; husbands were meant to prevent those kinds of things from happening. Dante had read up on it.

She let go of Dante's hands and tilted her head at Anton, her expression cooling. "And you are?"

"Baron Anton Greystoke, Dante's husband. And this," Anton added, ever the gracious one, "is the Honorable Eleanor Brown, Dante's Chosen."

"Ahh, I see."

Dante had no idea what she saw. But he didn't want her attention on those more vulnerable than himself. "And you are?"

She shut her eyes briefly. "Oh, silly me. You wouldn't know, would you?"

Dante had a feeling he must have looked as confused as he felt. And he hadn't really ever felt confusion before Choosing Elle. It was a new experience.

"My name is Tatiana Romanov, Duchess of Ravens, from Skarva." She gave a courtly bow, and Dante found himself repeating the gesture. Anton and Elle followed suit, although Elle's bow wasn't exactly elegant. He was going to have to get Anton to give her more lessons. Or Clay could do it. He seemed to know his way around courtly gestures.

"Nice to meet you, Your Grace," Dante said.

"Her name, Romanov, that's in your name, too." Elle's voice was barely audible, but he heard it nonetheless. So did the other female vampire.

She was searching Dante's expression for something, but whatever it was, she failed to find it. Then she smiled brightly again and re-clasped his hands in a firm grip. "I'm so happy to finally meet you properly. Dante, I am your mother."

CHAPTER THIRTY-ONE

Alice hadn't ever thought she would be walking down the streets of Pinton with a viscountess at her heels. It was an uncomfortable sensation. Viscountess Kipling and Tal walked side by side, so Alice strode along in front, medical bag clasped in a tight grip. Rather than go the shortcut, she retraced her steps back toward the City Guard offices, the three of them walking in silence. After all, what was there to say? Alice had pretty much already said all she was willing to.

Well, she'd more blurted it out: "I think you need to come to the morgue."

The viscountess had looked at her with a frown. "Why?" She'd set her glass of wine on the coffee table with a soft clink.

Alice couldn't make eye contact with her, for more reasons than one. "There's been a new murder."

"Another one?" Tal had asked, sitting upright.

Alice had nodded, feeling rotten. She didn't know what relation the woman in the morgue was to the viscountess, but there was a similarity in their physical appearance. She could be a cousin, aunt, niece...daughter, even. It was hard to tell when vampires aged so slowly. Then again, it could just be coincidence. Alice hoped it was. She knew what it was like to have the shroud drawn back to show someone you loved.

The viscountess had fluffed her hair. "Why do I need to see the body? Is it another aristo?"

Alice had just nodded.

The vampire had scrunched her nose and then sighed. "Your morgue stinks." But she'd stood up nonetheless, grabbed her purse and headed toward the door.

"I want this murderer found," the viscountess said, breaking Alice free from the memory. The streets around them were alive with people, noise and activity. The scent of cooking garlic hung in the air, mixing with the coal smoke that permeated the city. It was the fashionable hour for vampire aristos, and they were out and about. Carriages clattered along the street next to them, while fancily dressed aristos walked down the sides of the road. A few had spotted the viscountess and called out greetings, and she plastered a smile on her face, replying with airy waves. But there was no happiness in her voice as she spoke to Alice and Tal.

"So do I," Alice said.

"Why? Because having a killer run loose makes more work for you?" The vampire's voice was bitter. "Humans aren't exactly the victims here."

"Misty—" Tal began.

They were on a first name basis? Alice mentally kicked herself. The viscountess had been over for wine, *of course* they were on a first name basis. Alice doubted their relationship was professional. But even though Tal might be dating the aristo, and speaking up might damage her friend's relationship, Alice couldn't help herself. "No, who cares about humans? They're just killed here every single day."

There was an awkward moment, then a sigh from behind her. "You're right. I'm sorry. But this is unsettling. Vampires are not usually the victims; they're generally the top of the aristocracy and there's a *reason* for that."

Alice paused, then looked back at the white-clad aristo. "It's shitty to feel like prey, isn't it?"

The viscountess' lavender eyes met Alice's, her expression serious. "I personally don't feel threatened, but I don't like thinking that I'm going to lose friends because of some person who has a grudge against vampires."

Tal took a step between them. "Alice—"

"Don't worry, Tal," Alice said, continuing toward the City Guard building. "I get it. Probably more than anyone could ever know."

Yes, the viscountess was being selfish in her desire for the murderer to be caught. But then, that wasn't unusual. Everyone wanted a killer to be found: because it made them feel safer, because it made them worry less about their friends and family, or because it impacted their lives in some other way. Catching a killer gave people — even complete strangers — closure.

After all, Alice would dearly love to know who had killed her mother, and who had stabbed *her*. But then, you never could get everything you want.

Tal and the viscountess struck up a quiet conversation, and Alice made an effort not to listen in. She stayed in the lead, and was thankful to see the cool stone lines of the City Guard building up ahead. It was made of bluestone and redbrick, with cream render highlighting the windows and doorways. Alice strode up the stairs quickly, aware of Tal and the viscountess coming up slowly behind her.

Opening one of the large wooden double doors, Alice headed inside, nodding at the guard who was on duty at reception. The guard stood behind a large metal desk that spanned the room wall-to-wall. They had had a shift change since Alice had left. This guard's brown and black uniform was slightly rumpled, but he gave Alice a half grin when she walked past, shifting his attention from a human man in expensive-looking civilian clothes: the cit was waving his hands in front of him and complaining loudly. Most guards didn't enjoy getting stuck on desk duty; they were active people. But everyone had to take their turn and be present in case anyone came in to file a complaint or report a crime. Like now.

Alice strode toward a door with the 'City Morgue' brass sign on it. She unlocked it, then turned the light on. A dull pink glow lit the stairwell, warming to yellow as she ventured down the stairs. The air grew perceptibly cooler the further down she went. Reaching the morgue's antechamber, she went through the glass-paneled door, and turned on another light and headed to the end of the examination room. That was one of the benefits of working in a government building: sodium lighting. Her home had lamps; no one in her building could afford gas lights.

Reaching the last body in the room, she began to unbutton its violet shroud while Tal and the viscountess caught up. Looking back, Alice saw the vampire's nose wrinkle in protest. Alice was used to the smell, but it was clearly stronger for vampires. When Tal and the viscountess stood on the other side of the body, Alice opened the covering. Pale flaxen hair spilled out as she pulled back the sides, and the face was exposed.

A gasp echoed through the room.

The viscountess was staring wide-eyed at the body, a fist pressed to her mouth, knuckles white. Her other hand was outstretched, reaching toward the corpse.

Tal gingerly laid a hand on the vampire's shoulder. "Misty?"

The viscountess shuddered, and with shaking hands finished unbuttoning the shroud. Alice stepped back, thankful that she'd properly covered the body with the green nightgown, even if the incisions from the autopsy were still visible.

The viscountess stared at the exposed corpse, and a single tear trickled from her eye before she brushed it aside. Taking a deep breath, she ran a gentle finger down the dead woman's cheek. The tenderness of the gesture nearly brought Alice to tears, and she knew beyond a doubt that this woman belonged to the vampire's family.

Bending down so her forehead touched the dead woman's, the viscountess whispered a soft, "Good-bye, Mother."

Alice's heart jolted in her chest.

Her *mother*.

Memories rushed back to her, threatened to swamp her. But she ground her teeth together and gripped the side of the bench tightly. Across from her, Tal cast her a concerned look, but didn't seem to know who needed help more, Alice or the viscountess.

Straightening, the noblewoman met Alice's gaze, her lavender eyes like flints.

"How did she die?"

Alice looked at Tal, suddenly helpless. This was all too real. She'd just inflicted on someone the same pain that had been inflicted on her. "I'm so sorry."

"Don't spare me the details," the vampire said, ignoring Alice's condolences. "Tell me *everything*. This murder is going to be of interest to the king."

"The *king*?" Alice squeaked.

"This is my mother, Countess Wintermere, Lady Maerylina Kipling." The viscountess stood ramrod straight. "She is a peer of the realm. The king will *have* to become involved now; peers *can't* be murdered, it creates instability."

Alice glanced beseechingly at Tal, who gave a slight shake of her head, which was of no help at all. Alice remembered what it had been like for her, when she'd identified her mother's body...sometimes, having something to focus on other than your own pain was important. It helped keep you going.

So Alice began to speak, "The countess was stabbed four times, although it was the first that proved fatal..."

Chapter Thirty-Two

Fin had a bad feeling about the situation. Sure, he'd felt a little uneasy just strolling into the Deadly Duchess' estate, but who wouldn't? She hadn't earned her reputation by snuggling puppies and hosting tea parties. No, she'd gotten her nickname through the wholesale slaughter of an entire vampire family — grandparents through to grandchildren. Admittedly, those grandkids had been adults, but still. Apparently there'd been so little of them left that they'd only been able to identify the individuals when the duchess had pointed out what body part belonged to whom.

This was supposedly Hannah's *mother*.

Surely Hannah wouldn't have gone running to her parent upon finding Rena, if the woman was a complete psychopath? But then again, Fin didn't really know Hannah all that well. She had her secrets.

And...maybe Hannah was also secretly nuts.

"My *brother*?" She was staring at Mr. Randall with wide, incredulous eyes.

Fin wondered why she looked so shocked. Maybe she'd thought her brother was dead? He guessed he might react the same way if he'd found out that his sisters had come looking for him and that they were in the next room. He repressed the need to glance around to make sure they weren't stashed away nearby somewhere. While the Deadly Duchess was scary, the idea of reuniting with his sisters was even more terrifying. He had a lot of explaining to do.

Randall sniffed haughtily. "Yes, your brother."

"I have a *brother*?" Hannah's mouth was hanging open. Fin wanted to tell her to watch out, that she might swallow a fly, but he doubted there were any flies in this building. It was so pristine, he could see his reflection in the polished floor.

Wait.

"You didn't know you had a *brother*?" Fin asked her, eyebrows raised almost to his hairline. A hairline that hadn't receded one whit, he liked to admit.

Hannah shot him a look that said, 'Clearly, idiot.' He wasn't offended; he liked women with sass. Not that he liked Hannah, not like that. Oh, she was nice, and intimidatingly beautiful. But for one thing she was too intense, and for another she hated being touched. And three, well, her mother was the scary Raven Duchess. Even he had enough sense to not mess with that pedigree, no matter that he found the Deadly Duchess less frightening that the combined wrath of his sisters.

Four to one odds. He could do math.

"Then I guess we had better get on the road tomorrow." Hannah gave Fin a tentative smile. "I will stay here tonight."

"Surely the duchess has a carriage that could take you?" Fin wondered. Not that he wanted to see the back of Hannah or Rena — he'd miss the kid. But surely that would be better for her and the baby? Maybe he and Byrne could follow along behind.

"Of course," Mr. Randall said, but the vampire's expression made the hackles on Fin's neck rise. He wished Byrne were here; the bear would be able to pinpoint the reason for Fin's unease.

Then the vampire lunged forward and grabbed Hannah's arm. She froze, her whole body immobilized in shock. Between clenched teeth, she gritted, "What are you—"

Then she collapsed, her eyes rolling back in her head. Randall caught her as she fell, and her head lolled over his forearm, her long dark hair dangling in a braid down to the shiny marble floor.

Fin rushed forward to grab her, but the servant was there, wrenching his arms back. Pain shot through his ribs, and he dropped to his knees, gasping as fire spread out from his chest. He stared helplessly at Hannah.

He'd come in to protect her, and look how much use he'd been. *None.*

Defeat swamped him. Every single time he needed to protect someone, he failed. Every. Single. Fucking. Time.

That was why his own baby girl was in a grave.

But better not to think on that.

"I'd be really interested to find out how you and Lady Hannah are *friends*," Randall said. Fin realized the vampire was staring at him with cold, flat eyes. "Considering she still seems to be suffering from her 'disability.'"

He'd done it deliberately. Touched Hannah to see if it would harm her. "You're a real bastard," Fin said. "Do you think the duchess will be happy, knowing what you did?"

"Come now, the duchess' daughter suddenly appears after years of self-imposed exile, while the duchess is away? You seriously didn't expect me not to take advantage."

Fin didn't bother to reply. Bad timing, that's all it was. Some opportunistic dick was trying to take advantage of the situation. But they wouldn't be helpless for long, he thought. Byrne would be coming back for them soon, and Fin would put his money on the bear over these primped vampires any day of the week. He just had to make sure that in the meantime he kept himself and Hannah in one piece. Well, two pieces.

"Take them down to the cells," Randall ordered. "I want Lady Hannah to have a think over her temporary change in circumstances."

♦

Fin leaned his head back against the cool stone wall of the cell. Randall the Douchebag really had dumped them down in the dungeon. The air was chill, and the floor was sapping the warmth out of the back of his legs. He'd made sure Hannah had been laid on the prison's single bed. He wasn't entirely sure that was the best idea — what with her sensitivity and her avoiding touching people and things in general — but the bed was made of stone and he'd pulled the mattress off before they'd laid her there. He was now using it to keep the meager warmth in his butt.

It was clear Randall thought Fin had stolen the mattress to make himself more comfortable, at Hannah's expense. The vampire had snickered and muttered as much to the servant, who Fin had pegged as an idiot crony. He didn't bother to correct either of them; let them believe he didn't care for Hannah's safety or comfort. Maybe it would mean they'd think twice about using him or Hannah as collateral.

He wished he wasn't injured, because he sure would have enjoyed punching out their grins.

Without a watch, Fin reckoned Hannah had been out for about three hours. As the minutes ticked by, he grew more worried. Was this normal for her? He'd tried talking to her, shouting, even thought about dumping water on her head, except he didn't have any. The vampires hadn't been back, so Fin assumed that they knew she'd be unconscious for a while. But he wanted her to be alert when they returned; if she was asleep, in a coma, or unconscious — whatever her state was — she'd be completely at their mercy.

There was only one option open to him.

He levered himself to his feet and struggled over to her. His ribs were hurting like a bitch, and he had a feeling he'd set his healing back a week by being wrenched around by that dick of a servant. He was so going to enjoy watching Byrne rip the man a new smile when the bear finally came back for him and Hannah.

Hannah's face was turned to the side, and she was lying on her back, one arm dangling over the stone bench/bed. Standing over her prone form, Fin hovered his hand over her face. *Just do it*, he told himself. His conscience piped up at that moment, accusing him of violating her privacy, calling him all kinds of names. The ones he usually reserved for Byrne.

"She's out cold," he muttered.

But she hates being touched.

And Fin wasn't the kind of guy to go against someone's wishes. But they were stuck here, and she was vulnerable, and there was still no movement from her. She had to wake up, it was the only way she could protect herself.

"I'm sorry," he whispered.

Then he touched her.

Chapter Thirty-Three

Hannah jolted upright, arms flailing. She heard an *oomph* and opened her eyes. It was dark, she couldn't *see*, and the air was cold. Her brain was foggy and she didn't know who was with her.

It's okay, she told herself. Her vision would come back soon, it always did. She heard breathing and a protesting grunt. She recoiled from it, jerking her knees up to her chest and wrapping her arms around them, hands gripping her elbows. Her physical size reduced to something more manageable, she looked around and a fuzzy figure came into focus. *Fin*. He was standing in front of her, a hand cradled to his stubble-covered cheek.

"You hit me," he muttered, rubbing his jaw. He gave her a wounded look. "It *hurt*."

Hannah looked down at her hands, then at his face. She wasn't wearing any gloves.

She didn't have any of Fin's memories, just Randall's. Perhaps the touch had been too quick? Or her mental defenses had been up because she'd been sorting through another set of recollections?

Fin backed away and then sat down on a mattress someone had put on the floor. "The appropriate thing to say in this context is, 'Sorry Fin, of course I didn't mean to hurt you. I understand your best asset is your pretty face.'"

Hannah couldn't help the snort that escaped her. "I'm not

Byrne."

"Unfortunately, you're right."

Hannah glared at him over her knees. "What is that supposed to mean?"

"In case you hadn't noticed, we're trapped in a cell in *your mother's estate*. I'm in no shape to get us out of here, and you can't touch anyone to help me. I should have gone with the baby, Byrne should have stayed. Fuck the politics." He leaned his head back against the wall.

Unease prickled in Hannah, as the memories she'd absorbed from Randall rose to the forefront of her mind. She'd been a fool. Not because she failed to predict her mother might not be here, but because she'd been so trusting of her mother's colleagues.

Fin was right; he was already injured, and from the expression on his face, their captors had probably hurt him some more when they transported him down here. Plus, she'd just smacked him one, and even a gentle tap from a vampire wasn't something to disregard. She'd probably given him a new bruise.

This was all her fault.

"Why did they even keep me alive?" he wondered into the silence.

Hannah flinched and answered from Randall's memories, "They want to use you to make me cooperate."

She didn't admit what they wanted her to cooperate *about*.

"They think you'll give in to whatever they want to save *me*?" Fin shot her an incredulous look.

Hannah bristled. "Why is that a stupid idea? You think I wouldn't want to help you, after everything you've done for Rena and me? You think I'm that selfish?"

"Hannah, we barely know each other. I didn't even know your mother was one of the four founding leaders of Skarva. We *joked* about the Deadly Duchess when you suggested naming Rena after her. You keep yourself to yourself, and I don't blame you. You've obviously got some shit going on with your ability, and no," he held up a hand, the stitches visible even in the dim lighting, "you don't have to tell me what it is. I get it's a secret."

He ran a hand through his hair. "But you don't trust us, well, me, at least. You've spent more time talking to Byrne, and I totally get it. I was half-comatose in the back of a cart after being nearly beaten to a pulp by an entire town 'cos I slept with someone's wife. Not the most stellar way of inducing trust. Then, you arrive home somewhere supposedly safe and within five minutes, someone wants to use you for something. Why would you want to do anything to save someone like me?"

"Someone like you?" Hannah asked. She didn't know what else to say. Most of what he'd said was true, but...

Had his cheeks gone a bit red?

He shut his eyes. "A womanizer, a slut, someone who can't even look after himself, let alone anyone else."

Hannah couldn't help it; she stormed over to where he sat and, as he and Byrne would say, glared the fuck out of him. "What kind of bullshit is that?" She jabbed the air in front of him.

She doubted that Byrne would put up with this self-pity, even though the bear teased the other man enough to make her bored with normal cuss words.

"What?"

"Who cares that you like to have sex?" Hannah slashed a hand through the air. "From what I can see, people enjoy sex. It helps the species keep going. And it's not your fault that you drew the short straw and had to come here to help me, even though you're injured. You *tried*."

Fin looked stunned.

"You don't know everything—"

"I don't need to. You and Byrne have done nothing but help me since you found me on the slopes of the Old Mother. You guys could have turned out to be rapists, or predators, or something, but you weren't. You went out of your way to bring me here to my mother, so that Rena and I could have a chance together. And what have you asked of me?"

She put her hands on her hips and waited.

"I don't know what you're getting at," Fin said finally.

"You have asked me for *nothing*."

He frowned. "Yet."

She rolled her eyes. "Pfft."

"Wait — did you just 'pfft' me?"

"That was the polite version of what I was thinking."

"Why don't you just say what you really think, then?" Fin suggested, wincing as he folded his arms across his chest.

"Fine. You're being a moron."

"A moron?"

"Yes. Just accept that fact that I wouldn't hand you over to be killed by those two assholes."

A grin flashed across his face, transforming the bruised and beaten visage into something stunning. "Aww, you like me."

She caught her breath. Couldn't help it. Now she knew why all those women had fallen into his arms. That smile...it should be illegal. Then she glowered at him. The sly bastard knew what his effect was on women, and he was just trying to distract her. Just because she hadn't had much to do with people, it didn't make her ignorant.

"You and Byrne *are my friends*."

"It's okay," he said. "Most women like me."

She ground her teeth. "This isn't time for jokes."

"You're right. And Hannah, I feel I should be honest with you." His Hazel eyes had a glint in them, but she couldn't tell if it was because he was about to be serious or would continue teasing her.

She raised an eyebrow. "Okay."

"I touched you. When you were sleeping."

"You *what?*"

Chapter Thirty-Four

Skarva City

Byrne headed back into town to find lodging in a were-friendly establishment. It wasn't that Skarva was any less tolerant of weres than any other vampire-controlled city, but he liked to rest his bones somewhere where he didn't have to worry about a silver knife finding its way into his back simply because of what he was. Plus, the bear part of his nature preferred to be amongst other weres, when possible. He liked Fin, but the human just couldn't understand what it was like to be a were, especially a bear trapped in a human skin at the start of spring.

He'd wrapped Rena in a sling across his chest, and the cub was snuffling as she slept against his torso. He rubbed her back, then focused on getting the two of them, Baldy and the pain-in-the-ass goat to an inn. If he remembered correctly, there was a place just off the main road that catered to all kinds of weres. Sure, wolves and cats had trouble getting along at times, but they could do when needed.

Keeping the pace slow, he went back through the market and past the peddler who'd tried to manhandle Hannah. He ignored the man, and the stare that was leveled at the back of his head. Turning left down Market Place — which, funnily enough, didn't have a street market on it — he arrived at the inn. Its iron sign was swinging in the gentle breeze, and the scents of piss, vomit, cooking stew, coal, and about a million other things he preferred not to think about, reached him.

Cities. They always were an assault on the senses.

The sign read 'The Grumpy Bear Inn.' Painted next to the name, a growling bear held a tankard of ale in a clawed grip. He'd forgotten about that. Ah well, too late now to take offense. He pulled his cart to a stop out the front, and a stable boy ran forward to take the reins.

"If you keep it here, there'll be a coin in it for you," Byrne said. The little lad — or girl, it was hard to tell — was a bit grimy, but otherwise healthy, and nodded with a gap-toothed smile.

Climbing down, Byrne avoided getting too close to the poor horse. Baldy still wasn't happy with him. It'd take time.

At the entrance, he had to duck to get under the doorframe. The door swung shut behind him, and the taproom beyond was dim and smoky, but the stench of vomit and piss didn't extend to within the walls. Instead, there was the smell of cigars, ale and crushed herbs; it was almost pleasant. It was also a sign they were used to catering to weres, whose senses were so much more acute than a human's.

Only two people occupied the room: a woman with white-blonde hair and a man with striped blond and brown hair, which was half-covered by a cap. It being midday, the lack of clientele wasn't surprising. Weres were more nocturnal, like their vampire cousins. Not that many people admitted that vampires and weres were related in any way.

Byrne placed his hands on the scarred wooden surface of the bar, and leaned forward a little, careful of the sleeping cub. A woman emerged from the kitchen area, pushing through two half-sized doors that swung shut behind her. She had a dishrag in her hands, and was well over six foot in height, with short brown hair cut into a bob, and yellow eyes that gleamed from her olive skinned face. She looked only about twenty, but that meant nothing.

Sniffing the air discreetly, Byrne frowned as he tried to work out her species. There were other scents in the air: large cat, something vaguely wolf-like, and bear. That would be the other patrons in the taproom and himself. He needed a bath.

"What can I do for you?" the woman asked. She was dressed in a sturdy gown of an intermediate shade of brown, with a stained apron over the top.

"Looking for a room for myself and another, and stabling for my horse and a goat."

The woman raised an eyebrow, then set the dishrag down on the bar between them. "Did you say a goat?"

Byrne nodded.

She pursed her lips. "Odd traveling companion for a bear."

He waved a hand down at the cub strapped to his chest. The woman didn't seem to mind that the child was clearly not his own — the stark skin-color difference made it obvious. She hadn't even seen the eye-color variance yet; if weres tended to have non-were kids, which was crazy rare, they were usually Brown-eyed. Not that most weres understood what the eye colors meant; that's just how things worked.

But then, most weres didn't have the unfortunate experience of being kidnapped and held by an insane group of Graced supremacists for a hundred years, either.

"Ahhh, I see," she said, her expression warming. Weres loved kids. She smiled, bright and toothy, and there was happiness to it, not threat. "Stuck on cub-sitting duty?"

"Not necessarily a bad thing," Byrne said with a half-smile.

"Too true. We have a double room if that will suit? And I'll make sure the animals are looked after properly. Are they out the front?"

Byrne nodded. "How much?"

They haggled for a few moments, since it was expected. Byrne would have paid more for the rooms, but he knew the deal. When both were satisfied that they'd reached a decent bargain, the woman stretched her hand out. "Name's Milly, I own the place. Bought it about five years ago."

He took the offered palm and shook it. "Byrne."

"Nice to meet another bear; they're not usually traveling this time of year."

He grinned fully this time. "Most have better sense than I do."

Milly rumbled a laugh and yelled for one of the stable lads, giving him instructions for the horse and goat. "Take a seat. You can have a drink while I get the room sorted."

Byrne nodded and sat in one of two large leather chairs by the fire, which was just a pile of smoldering embers. The seats looked sturdy enough to hold him — few did — and the dark brown leather creaked as he lowered himself down. A small wooden table had been placed between the chairs, and Milly set a tankard of ale on it before heading back to the bar.

Leaning his head against the chair back, he began absently rubbing Rena's tiny body, his hand dwarfing the infant. She turned her face to the side and let out a contented sigh. She'd probably wake up soon and then scream down the inn in her demand for food and probably a clean diaper. But at least Byrne rather than Hannah was on hand for her. While the vampire had gotten much better at looking after the cub, her diaper-tying skills still left much to be desired. Byrne had lost a few shirts to Rena's 'accidents.'

"Hello, Byrne."

A woman took the empty seat opposite him and crossed her legs, which were clad in tight-fitting tan trousers, overlaid by a strange half-dress like a tunic, made of some fine material. Her skin was whiter than snow, and she had long pale hair that was almost colorless, except for the woven string, beads and bones that decorated the tresses. Then there were the dyed strands, which were blue and green.

She had Pink eyes.

Byrne hadn't *ever* met an albino before, but it made sense they had to exist. Back when he'd been a cub, they'd been killed on sight. Had been for centuries before that. Only his grandfather had argued against the practice. No one had said why they had to die, of course; the reason had been forgotten due to the enforced memory wipe about the Graced. But Byrne knew about the Graced now. And anyone who had eyes other than Brown, yellow and purple — anyone like this woman, like the albinos — were

Graced. And the Graced were more dangerous than anyone he knew.

Apart from Hannah.

And Rena.

And Fin.

Fine, there were a few exceptions. But the fact was, until now he'd always assumed his kind couldn't give birth to a Graced. Yet here was proof they could. Because the woman had the faint smell of a were.

"I'm afraid we haven't met," Byrne said, instinctively clenching his hands into fists.

The were-Graced grinned, and he realized she was striking. Not beautiful, not pretty, but with an appeal that was utterly unique.

"Silly me!" She clapped her hands and Rena made a noise of protest at the sound. The woman looked abashed. "Of course we haven't met," she said, her voice quieter. "Not yet. But we have now, so it's all good."

"Uh, it is?" Byrne was confused, but then, that wasn't unsurprising. He had no idea what Pink eyes meant when it came to psychic talents. But to meet her, and Hannah — two people with eye colors that weren't on the normal Graced list — so close together? He didn't believe in coincidences.

"It is a good thing. Trust me. I know pretty much everything. Can I hold Rena?"

He hadn't mentioned the baby's name since entering the inn. And he had a mental shield, so she shouldn't have been able to pluck the cub's name from his mind.

"I won't hurt her. I like children. I just gained a kid sister-in-law, I'll have you know. She's not a baby, not anymore, of course, but she's still much younger than me. Then again, that isn't particularly hard." She tapped her chin. "But she has the most remarkable eyes. As does my brother's fiancé."

"I'm sorry, I don't even know your name," Byrne said. This woman was clearly not all there...

"It's Ralia, but you can call me Lia. We're going to be friends, you and I. Plus, you already know my brother, so we're practically related."

"I, uh—"

"Come now, let me have a quick cuddle with her. You don't have much time before you need to go and rescue Hannah and Fin."

Byrne handed Rena over; he had no idea what else to do. She didn't seem like the kind of person to hurt a cub, despite her dizzying chatter. Although, to be fair, he doubted her discourse was meaningless. He just didn't understand it.

"Wait — I have to rescue Hannah and Fin?" Byrne was half out of his seat.

She flicked him a glance. "Sit down."

He sat.

Lia hugged Rena close to her chest. She was muttering quietly to the baby, and Byrne had trouble making out the words, even with his hearing. But the smell of almost-wolf was stronger now. The albino must have been born to werewolf parents.

"Hannah and Fin?" he asked again, when he realized Lia was ignoring him.

"Oh yes, they'll need saving." She shot him a quick smile, then cooed at the cub.

"How do you know all this?" Byrne demanded, moving forward to stand. If his friends were in trouble—

Apprehensively Lia looked to the left and right, before tapping the skin just below her right eye. "You know what most are not meant to know, Byrne." Her voice was so quiet he had to lean forward and strain to make out the words. "I know about things before they happen. I know that you'll find your mate sooner than you think; that it was my brother who teased you in the past about the 'psychic sense of smell' that later weres possess. I know that Fin and Hannah are in trouble, but they can hold their own for now. I know that they need the time they have; it's important you don't rescue them too soon, or Fin's future will be at risk. And I know that Rena will have a bright life, brief though it will be."

Byrne's stomach dropped to somewhere underneath his feet.

She was a foreseer. That's what she was saying.

But his mind went to the baby she was holding. "Rena is going to die young?"

"She's got the lifespan of a human. She won't be able to be Chosen or Bitten, you know that."

Relief poured through him, and it was in that moment he realized he loved the little cub, like she was a member of his own family. He clenched his jaw. A week, that's all it had taken for him to adopt the cub into his life. A hundred years of trying not to care about anything, and he'd gone and blown it in seven days.

"Now, we have a couple of hours before you need to get moving," Lia said. "And I need to tell you a few things."

CHAPTER THIRTY-FIVE

Skarva City

"Wow, that sounded creepier than I meant it to," Fin said.

"You touched me?" Hannah blurted, apparently ignoring his comment. She jerked back from him, almost falling on her butt in her haste.

"You were out cold. I didn't know how to wake you up. I'd tried shouting, and talking to you, but I didn't have any other options." Fin gave an awkward half-shrug.

He didn't need to analyze why he'd told Hannah about the touch. He'd told her because he didn't want her to keep thinking that he was some kind of hero, that he was trying to save her when he was just as flawed as anyone else. More so. He could handle it if she admired him for his pretty face, but that was different to liking him for his personality. He wasn't worth it.

"But, I don't have any of your memories," Hannah said. Her arms were hanging loose by her sides, her body slack with surprise.

"Memories?" Fin asked before he could help himself. Not five minutes earlier he'd said she could keep her ability a secret. Wasn't he fantastic at keeping his word?

Hannah just blinked.

"Memories," he said again, more to himself. It all made sense. He stared at her in wonder and horror. She could absorb *memories*. The single most important thing that made a person who they were; their history. Even more intimate than being able to read someone's thoughts. No wonder she avoided touching people, and why she gave Byrne such a wide berth in particular. She could guess how old he was; and the older the were or vampire, the more memories there were to take in. And obviously the transfer left her vulnerable. How many lives had she lived, while she'd been stuck in her solitary existence?

"Which hand did you touch me with?" she asked.

"Uh, my right?" He held up the offending palm. In the dim light, his stitches stood out next to the faint lines of his tattoo. "And I didn't touch you for long. Just a quick pat to your face." He was going to say cheek, but didn't want her to think he'd groped her ass.

She made a funny sound, like a *meep*. "Your tattooed hand!"

"Yes? Is that bad?" He re-crossed his arms, ignoring the pain from his ribs. He deserved a little discomfort.

"They were inked by someone else; that means their memories would be impressed into your skin, too."

"You'd pick up the memories of my tattoo artists as well?"

That sounded — well, horrible, actually.

She rubbed a hand over her face. "Mother calls it clairvoyance."

"Clairvoyance?" he tried out the word. It tasted unfamiliar on his tongue, which was unusual. Fin could pick up languages easier than breathing; he probably had as many foreign words crammed into his skull as Hannah did memories. He'd travelled *a lot* in his short life. Easy to do when you were running away from your past.

"Why would your memories not have been transferred? It doesn't make sense." Hannah paced the cell, but since it was kind of small, she could only walk a few steps before having to turn back and head in the opposite direction.

"Have you been able to pick up on memories from more than one person at a time before?"

She nodded. "The only person I can't absorb memories from is Mother."

Lucky for Hannah. Her mother didn't sound like the nicest lady.

"Maybe..." Fin considered for a moment. "I have a natural mental shield. I hear it's pretty rare. That could be what's protecting me." He couldn't help the fact that it sounded like he was bragging. He was.

Something lit up in her dark eyes. "You do?"

Fin squirmed; he wasn't entirely sure he liked the gleam in her gaze. "Yes?" Argh. He hadn't meant it to sound like a question. But Hannah was doing her intense thing, and it always got him a bit unnerved.

He wasn't going to think of what it would be like if they were together...intimately. All that concentration on him.

No. Don't think like that. That is bad, he told himself. *You're disgusting*, his mind said rather sternly. *She's vulnerable.*

Fin agreed.

She took a couple of steps forward and then halted in front of the mattress. "Touch me!"

Back in the cart, when he'd first heard her voice — that sexy rusty sound — he'd wished her to say those words to him, preferably while her legs were wrapped around his torso. But he hadn't gotten to know her then; to admire her inner strength, her resolve and her commitment to the abandoned baby she'd found. Hannah wasn't just a random woman he wanted to spend a night with.

Plus, women like Hannah didn't mess around with men like him.

"Look, we don't know if my shield will be enough," he said. "I could have just gotten lucky the last time."

If he'd known that she absorbed a person's memories, he probably wouldn't have touched her in the first place, even to help her. He didn't want her to know everything about him. He didn't want *anyone* to have that kind of knowledge about him as a person. Some secrets were best left untouched.

"What can it hurt?" Hannah squatted on her heels and leaned forward, as if to grab his leg.

"I don't want to." He pulled his limbs closer to him, the mattress a barrier between his body and hers. She wouldn't risk touching *that*.

"Trust me," she said, "I don't want to know everything about you, but I *have to know* if there are exceptions to my ability."

He set his jaw in a hard line. "I don't like the idea of being a test subject."

"I seriously think you'll be safe, or I wouldn't do it. I don't exactly *enjoy* knowing everything about someone, you know."

He — just — it was —

She dropped to her knees in front of the mattress, and the pain in her face floored him. "*Please*, Fin. I need to know I won't be alone my entire life. That there's a possibility I can touch someone other than my mother without fear."

"Fuck." His head fell back against the stone wall. And then he did something he never thought he'd do for anyone. He offered his hand and his past.

Hannah closed the distance by reaching out with her arm, and then their palms touched, fingers interlacing. Fin held his breath, and Hannah had her eyes shut tight. He waited, heart pumping once, twice, ten times.

Then Hannah opened her eyes and jerked her arm backward, but without letting go. Fin fell forward, sprawling on top of her.

She's stronger than she looks, he thought, rolling onto his back. Even if she was a vampire with super strength, he'd still be heavy and he didn't want to squash her. Laughing and grinning like a loon, Hannah followed him, straddling his hips.

He doubted she realized what she'd done — the intimacy of the position — she was just so giddy with whatever she had learned. Leaning down, she gave him an awkward hug. Then she kissed him. Just a peck.

But he froze, locked up completely. Once he'd known Hannah had a problem with being touched, he'd never, never in a million years thought they'd be in a cell, him flat on his back, her on top of him, and her soft — really soft — mouth pressing briefly against his.

He pushed at her shoulders. "Hannah, what are you doing?"

"I didn't absorb your memories!"

Then it dawned what she was doing. The joy disappeared from her face and she fell back from him. Her gloveless fingers touched lips she had just pressed to his. "I'm sorry, I was just so happy and I — I don't know what I was thinking."

She'd been starved, that's what she'd been thinking. It didn't take someone with Green eyes to know that she was probably touch-hungry after having lived such an isolated life. But Fin didn't want to be the guy she went to because he was the only one available to her.

The awareness of that made him sit up.

"Byrne has a shield, too," Fin said into the quiet, desperate to ease the tension.

"*What?*"

Fin wasn't going to say how Byrne had learned about his own mental shield; that was the bear's story to tell if he wanted, and Fin doubted he would. Suddenly, he wondered if she would try and kiss Byrne, too. Something dark uncoiled from deep within him, but he pushed the emotion aside.

It wasn't Byrne who she'd tackled to the ground, it was him.

But Byrne isn't here, his mind whispered.

Shut up.

Even his subconscious was a smartass.

How did Byrne put up with him? He could barely stand himself.

But, if Hannah wanted to be with him, he wanted her to want *him*. Not his mental shield. Maybe that was why he'd mentioned Byrne's. So she'd know there was more than one option out there for her. Plus, he couldn't be with her anyway, not like that; he wasn't what someone like her needed. She needed someone stable, who'd stand by her, who'd be with her without fail. It was what she deserved.

Fin just wasn't that kind of guy.

Not anymore.

CHAPTER THIRTY-SIX

Pinton City

"I need to get in contact with the king." The viscountess' voice was low and horribly even. Too calm for someone who had just listened to how her mother had been brutally murdered. But Alice knew what it felt like to hear that particular kind of news; it left a person numb.

To be the one to deliver that information made her skin crawl.

Alice had explained what she could. She couldn't provide details about the motive of the killer or where the countess had been murdered. Alice knew that the viscountess wanted them; she understood that. Alice would have wanted the same thing. By the blood, she *still* wanted to know why someone had stabbed her mother to death in their family home; why they'd taken her brother and why she'd never heard from him again. But wishes were useless. Only facts could tell her the truth. She'd resigned herself to never knowing.

She hoped the viscountess would get the answers that she herself had been denied.

Alice looked at the other woman, seeing the drawn face, the burning eyes. The intensity that was held brutally in check.

"The king?" Alice echoed.

The viscountess slammed a hand against the bench, making her mother's body jump slightly. Alice didn't think the vampire realized. "This cannot be ignored anymore. I brought the previous murders to his attention, but he's been too busy with his new *boyfriend*."

"The City Guard are looking into it," Alice said. "They'll track down whoever did this."

The vampire's lavender eyes blazed. "Not fast enough."

Tal stood awkwardly behind the vehement aristo, her gray eyes wide. "I can go upstairs and ask the guards to send someone to notify the king."

"Tell them to bring him back here."

"Bring him back?" Alice stammered.

Bring the *king* to her morgue?

"Yes, this is now a crime against the kingdom," the viscountess said. "General aristo deaths? That's unfortunate, but there's always more of them. But a countess? That sends a message to the people that cannot be tolerated."

It was more than that; this was the vampire's mother who had been killed. But perhaps the fact that the dead woman was a countess was enough to warrant the king leaving the Crystal Palace to come into the city and its morgue.

Tal turned to leave, but the viscountess gently grabbed her wrist. Their eyes locked, and so quietly Alice could barely hear, the viscountess said, "Thank you."

Tal nodded and then headed up the stairs, her shoulders tense. To get the king.

Alice's life had just gotten far more interesting, and she didn't like it. Tal might be happy to date an aristo, but Alice liked to keep a lengthy distance between them and her. Except for her friend Billie, of course, but that was different. Aristos weren't like ordinary people; their lives were one of privilege and comfort. Folks like Alice only usually saw them from afar; they didn't have dinner with them and they certainly didn't hang around in a *morgue* with them. Her previous conversations with the single aristo she knew had been limited to whether or not her patient would survive. She tried not to look nervous, but what did a commoner say to a peer of the realm?

Best not to say anything.

So Alice quietly sorted through her paperwork, then checked her supplies, leaving the viscountess alone with her mother. Alice wasn't sure how much time had passed, but she was running out of things to tidy. She straightened up the pile of body bags next to the human corpses.

The viscountess spoke into the quiet. "Don't worry, I won't bite."

I must look more panicked than I thought.

Embarrassed, Alice shuffled back to the other side of the morgue, away from the cadavers. She hoped the viscountess would follow her; she wanted to put some distance between the bodies and the noblewoman. Spending too much time with her dead mother might not be healthy. Taking hold of the single stool, Alice used it like a miniature ladder, climbing up to sit on the edge of the stone bench. She'd leave the chair itself to the viscountess.

For a moment she sat, watching her feet as she swung them back and forth. When she looked up, the vampire was standing directly before her; she'd crossed the room so quickly and silently, Alice hadn't even heard her.

Alice stopped swinging her feet. Vampires certainly *did* bite. Maybe the viscountess would, even though she'd said she wouldn't?

But then Alice met the woman's gaze, and all she could feel was sympathy. The aristo's expression spoke to Alice on a level that only someone who'd had a parent murdered could understand.

"Mind if I sit?"

Alice nodded her head at the chair. "I left it for you."

"Leave the vampire with the wooden stool," the viscountess said with what might have been a half-smile.

Alice stiffened. She hadn't thought that providing a seat would be considered an insult, but she should have known better. "I don't have any other kind—"

"It's fine. I'm sure I can manage to sit on a chair and not impale myself." The vampire's voice was dry as sand. Perhaps she was trying to be funny; gallows humor.

The viscountess settled on the stool, somehow managing to look elegant and beautiful, despite her distress. Alice hoped her white clothing wouldn't get dirty; the cleaners didn't like spending a lot of time down in the morgue, and while Alice kept it pretty tidy, she didn't have time to ensure it was spotless.

The vampire's eyes fixed on her, as if she was waiting for Alice to say something.

"I'm sorry for your loss." It was all she could think of. But she meant it.

"Same."

They settled into an uncomfortable silence.

At last the viscountess broke it. "Why did you become a dead-person doctor?"

"Dead-person doctor?" Alice echoed.

The other woman waved a hand around, indicating the morgue.

"A coroner?" Alice asked. The vampire nodded. "You don't really want to know why I became a pathologist." Then, realizing she'd not addressed the aristo properly the whole time she'd been in the morgue, she tacked on, "my lady."

The viscountess rolled her eyes. "I wouldn't have asked if I didn't want to know. And call me Misty."

"I can't call you by your name!" The words burst forth before Alice could stop them.

"You can if I give you permission, which I just did."

Where was Tal? What was taking the other woman so long?

"So, why did you become a pathologist?"

The viscountess was persistent, Alice gave her that. She couldn't know that Alice rarely talked about her reasons why she chose this job; that she usually just gave a flippant answer and left it at that. But Alice didn't think she could brush off the aristo — Misty — like that. Not with her mother lying in the morgue with them.

She took a deep breath. "When I was fourteen, my mother was murdered."

Misty said nothing, but her expression grew thoughtful. Alice suddenly knew her initial impression of the other woman had been completely wrong. She'd thought Misty flighty and a bit naïve; but there was a greater depth to her than possibly anyone else knew. You couldn't face what Misty had and be so composed; not unless you hated the victim or you were completely numb. But Alice hadn't gotten that impression at all.

"I was stabbed too, but only once." Alice settled on the abbreviated version of the story. "I woke up in hospital, lucky to be alive. I decided then that I wanted to help people; to save victims of violence like my mother and me. But there were so few survivors. And so I turned to learning about the dead; taught myself to read a body so that it could give me all the information possible to help solve the murder."

"Have you managed to achieve that?" Misty's head was tilted slightly, as if studying Alice like she was some kind of interesting insect.

"A little," Alice admitted. "I have a theory that this killer is human, but I need to check the sample of sperm I've found in the bodies."

"Sperm?"

"It's all the killer left behind, aside from some skin under the nails, but I can't really use that, not unless we find someone who has some suspicious wounds." Alice shrugged. She didn't mention the powder, because it hadn't been consistent at all the crime scenes. She still wasn't sure what it was.

"What would sperm tell you, though?"

"I think there may be differences between vampire, were and human samples. I need to compare."

The viscountess tapped her chin and frowned. "I see. You remind me of my brother."

Alice wasn't sure if that was a compliment or not.

Then Misty straightened on her chair, turning toward the door of the morgue. A few seconds later, Tal entered the room with a tall man emerging right behind her. He had olive skin, with black hair that was swept away from sharp features. His bright violet eyes searched the room, skipping over Alice to land on Misty.

Alice would have known who he was just from his bearing alone; she didn't need the expensive silk or the arrival of the palace guard behind him to fit all the pieces together.

King Johan had arrived.

Chapter Thirty-Seven

Skarva City

Hannah couldn't believe that she'd kissed Fin.

Well, sort-of kissed him.

Blood rushed to her cheeks and she turned her face to the wall of the cell. What had possessed her? Poor Fin, he'd probably been mortified. He was a ladies man, that was pretty obvious, but he wouldn't want to be accosted by someone like her.

Someone...damaged.

Shutting her eyes, Hannah breathed in deeply. The smell that she'd begun to associate simply as *Fin* filled her senses. Her heart pattered uncomfortably, and she was glad that Fin was human; he wouldn't be able to hear how her body reacted to him. It had been easy to ignore that he was handsome, especially since his face was all battered — although it had been harder to ignore the fact that he was endlessly charming, even when he bickered with Byrne. But he'd just been Fin. Now she knew what his lips felt like. And that changed things.

She was a fool.

Pretending that she wasn't embarrassed right down to her toes, she turned and met Fin's Hazel gaze squarely. "You said Byrne has a mental shield, too?"

A shadow flitted across his normally smiling face, but he nodded.

"What are the odds?" Hannah muttered to herself, wrapping

her arms around her torso. But it explained why her trip with the two men had been so successful, how she'd been able to ride in the cart without absorbing any memories from them. She'd just thought her clothing and her increased mental protections had saved her. But she'd been wrong; it was Fin and Byrne's own natural defenses that had protected *them*.

"Of bumping into two people with natural shields?" Fin ran a hand through his hair. "Pretty low."

Hannah sat down on the stone bed. Her head ached, as it always did when she absorbed someone else's memories, but she was strangely calm. Randall's recollections weren't battering against her mind, swamping her personality now she was awake. She was still Hannah. Somehow, in her comatose state, she'd managed to wrangle what she'd absorbed into something manageable.

Twining her fingers around each other, she considered just how lucky she was, despite being trapped in her mother's dungeon, subject to the whims of her mother's assistant. Now, Hannah had *friends*, something she hadn't thought she'd ever have. Byrne and Fin had simply just accepted her for who she was. She couldn't be touched: okay. She was a bit odd: that was fine. She had a baby that she'd found on the side of a mountain: they'd argue about whose turn it was to feed her. Or what her name should be.

By the blood, she had a daughter.

And a *brother*.

She didn't even know what his name was. Or how to begin processing that information. Her mother had never told Hannah that she had siblings. Ones who were alive, that is. Oh, Hannah knew about the children that had died in the Civil War thousands of years ago, but she hadn't known that Tatiana had more living offspring than just her.

Was that why she'd shipped Hannah off? To enjoy spending time with her other children? Was she *ashamed* of her?

"So, that Randall fellow knew touching you would disable you?" Fin asked, interrupting her degenerating thought process.

Hannah nodded. Fin's bruised face grew taut. "He was a trusted retainer of my mother's," she said. "He knew I was 'special.'"

Not many people knew *why* she was different, only that the duchess' daughter couldn't be touched. Some assumed it was her mother's overprotectiveness, and that alone was enough to ensure Hannah wasn't the subject of unwanted attention.

But Randall had been with Mother for centuries, certainly longer than Hannah had been alive. He'd known about her ability, even if he didn't know what Graceds were. But considering that Hannah had spent so little time at the estate, she'd never had much to do with him. And he'd never shown any inclination to want to hurt her before now. If anything, he'd maintained an aloof distance; probably terrified that an accidental touch would mean his execution.

So why would he risk betraying her mother, and why hurt her now? Tatiana did not take disloyalty lightly, but if Hannah could work out Randall's reasons, then perhaps she could prevent her mother slaughtering too many people in her revenge.

Shutting her eyes, Hannah opened a door in her mind to the memories that had been dumped there. She flicked through Randall's remembrances as if they were the pages in a book, skimming through the few intact memories of his early years.

He'd been a human child, born to merchant parents and raised with love and laughter. But the family aspired to a title, so they'd married Randall to a vampire baronetess. Randall had been happy with the match; the aristo had needed money, and he'd desired the status. She had Chosen Randall, but eventually his wife had wanted offspring, which he hadn't been able to provide. Rather than seek a breeding contract as was normal, she had divorced him.

His position no longer secure, his family's wealth long gone, and his parents long dead, he'd had to seek *employment*.

Randall's disgust at the word seeped through to Hannah, even through the memories. Randall hated having to earn a living.

Enter the Duchess of Ravens.

Randall had settled on the beautiful duchess, one of the founders of Skarva, so he could be aligned with her power. For a while he'd lusted after *her*, too, but the duchess wasn't quite...right, even by vampire standards. Plus, Tatiana didn't do things by halves, and Randall had worked out that if he became her lover, that would be his role until he died — probably by her hands.

So he worked for her instead. She paid well and rewarded those loyal to her. Except the job wasn't enough. He wanted a title, recognition, a position in society; everything that he'd lost.

Hannah opened her eyes and rubbed a hand over her forehead; her skin felt tight and worn. Randall had seen her arrival as a way to bring years of plotting to fruition. And the exact memory of his plans for her had been absorbed along with everything else.

"He wants to marry me," Hannah said into the silence.

Fin was sitting on the mattress again, long limbs akimbo. His head snapped round. "Marry you?"

She fought a frown at the skepticism in his voice. Surely *someone* would want to marry her, one day. Maybe she'd even like to marry them, too. But a marriage born of convenience wasn't for Randall. He'd done that before. It was too risky.

"Marry me," Hannah clarified. "Then quietly 'remove' me. If I die, he'll inherit my title and my wealth, provided the right contracts have been signed. I believe he's off drawing up those very documents now."

"But surely your mother would work it out? That you wouldn't just suddenly form a passion for a staff member, throw caution to the wind, and marry the guy?"

"Eventually. But he thinks he'll be able to lie and say that his touch didn't affect me. Seeing you with me made him realize that I might be immune to people other than my mother. He's never touched me before, so Mother wouldn't know that he was lying."

She took a deep breath. "Then he'll kill me, since I'm the weak link in his plan. He'll hide my death, which he figured would be easy to do, since I don't normally live in town. By the time Mother returns, he'll be able to say that I had gone back to the Old Mother, and then receive word that I'd suffered an 'accident.'"

Fin rubbed his chin. "So you'd marry him, then go straight back to living on the side of a mountain? Not exactly a ringing endorsement of him as a husband. If your mother is as volatile as they say she is, that alone would ring alarm bells."

Hannah held up her hands. "Hey, I didn't say this was *my* plan. He thinks he could just say that we married because I'd grown to care for him, but that I couldn't handle the stress of living in town."

"But he'll happily abandon you to the slopes of the Old Mother, while he frolics around Skarva?"

"He's planning to say that he was tying up loose ends here before joining me. But then before he left, he'd hear word of my 'accident'; from who, I don't know." She gave a twisted smile. "But the idea relies on him being here when I 'die.' That way, Mother won't suspect him. He also thinks that he can kill her if worse came to worst."

Fin shook his head. "Kill the Deadly Duchess?"

"He'd technically be her heir. And he believes that she trusts him."

Fin tapped his fingers on his forearm. "That plan has more holes than my socks do. Plus, the guy's a moron if he thinks he could take on a vampire of her age and win."

Hannah tilted her head to one side. She had no idea how old the general public thought her mother was, but she was curious. "Her age?"

"She has to be, what? Five to six thousand years old? Skarva has been around at least four thousand years and everyone knows she was a founding member."

An involuntary laugh escaped her.

"What? You don't think that's old?"

Hannah looked down at her hands, clasped together in her lap. The truth wasn't technically a secret, but Tatiana didn't like it bandied about. But Fin was her friend, and Hannah had already omitted so many facts about her life...

A frisson of *something* travelled down her spine as she said,

"Mother is a first generation vampire."

"First generation?" His expression went blank.

"Yes."

Then his eyes went wide. *"First generation?"*

"Yes."

Disbelief was etched into his bruised face. "I mean, Byrne's pretty old, but he manages to keep lucid by going bear. At least, that's what he says. Your mother doesn't have the option of just reverting to an animal state. So how on earth is she still sane?"

Hannah snorted. "She isn't."

"Fuck."

That about summed everything up.

CHAPTER THIRTY-EIGHT

The *king* was in her morgue. Right now.

The king. Her morgue. This very instant.

Lightheaded, Alice sat down in the reception area. Her life had been largely uneventful, if one ignored the whole nearly being stabbed to death when she was a teenager. Now she'd met more aristos than she ever had before and even come within touching distance of the freaking *king*.

What was happening to her neatly ordered existence?

Alice and Tal had been politely kicked out of her morgue and, since Dinya's shift was over, the night captain, Mikael Smythe, had been summoned to discuss the murders with the king. The viscountess had been tight-lipped at that point, irritated that it had taken their monarch so long to take action, but she'd nodded quickly at Alice as she'd made her way out of the morgue and up the stone stairwell. Alice couldn't imagine living a life where you could be annoyed that the *king* had taken too long to get around to you.

As for King Johan, well, he had been intimidating, to say the least. He was one of the most handsome men she'd ever seen; and she'd been struck dumb by the viscountess' — Misty's — brother. When it came to unbelievable good looks, the differences between vampires and humans were all too apparent.

Alice wasn't used to spending so much time in the upstairs

section of the City Guard building; and it felt even stranger to have someone else down in her morgue unsupervised. She hoped they didn't fiddle with anything while they were in there. She had all her medical equipment set up just the way she liked it; and there was an order to all the paperwork that made her filing system easy to navigate. And...

Shut up, she told herself.

They had no need to go searching through her things. The notes she'd taken on the countess' death were in a folder hanging off the end of her gurney. And really, she had to let go of her obsession about the morgue. It was probably time that she hired an assistant coroner. She'd held off partly because she didn't like the idea of someone in her space, but there was also the fact that there weren't too many people out there who were interested in dissecting corpses. Most sawbones wanted the glory that came with saving lives, not working out how people died.

She shifted in her seat. The steel benches in the City Guard reception were uncomfortable, had probably been deliberately designed that way so people didn't linger; the Guard didn't really appreciate any extra work, they were already busy enough. Anything that could deter people from loitering was a bonus. Eventually, one of the duty guards took pity on them and brought cushions for her and Tal to sit on. They murmured polite thank yous. The guard nodded and headed behind his large metal desk.

"How'd it go?" Alice asked Tal, turning toward her slightly.

"Not great. The guard didn't want to go to the palace on their own," Tal said. "Apparently the city guards don't have a great relationship with the palace guards, so they figured a request from a guard to summon the king would be ignored. They thought if they sent a university professor, they'd have better luck."

Alice wasn't sure what difference it would have made. A university professor wasn't exactly on king-summoning terms, either. "And did you?"

Tal shook her head. "No. But as I was arguing with the palace guard, a werewolf strode out of the front doors. He took one look at me, then a good sniff — which was a bit rude, to be honest — and suggested that the guard heed my request."

"A werewolf told the palace guard that you should see the king?"

"And not just any werewolf; I think he was your guard friend's boyfriend."

There was something in Tal's tone that Alice couldn't put her finger on. "You mean the wolf was Elle Brown's fiancé?"

"He said that he could vouch for the fact I had been with the viscountess," Tal's cheeks turned pink, "and that if she wanted the king, and the palace guard ignored her request, and it was urgent, well then, that would be their problem."

"So did that get them moving?" Alice asked.

Tal gave a short laugh. "No. So the werewolf just strode back into the palace and returned with the king. He then *left me with the king* and one of the rude guards, because he said — and I quote — 'I have to go make sure that Elle hasn't killed Dante's father.'"

Alice frowned. "Why would Elle want to do that?"

"I didn't exactly ask," Tal said, her expression wry. "But that woman is a liability."

"Tal!"

"What?"

Lowering her voice, Alice leaned closer to her best friend. "Elle is not a liability. Plus, she works here, so watch your voice. I don't understand why you don't like her."

Tal's gray eyes flicked away. "I don't know her."

"Exactly. You're not normally so quick to judge people."

Tal's expression hardened. "I just don't think she's my kind of person, that's all."

"Elle is nice." Sure, the newly Chosen vampire had been slightly standoffish with Alice back when they worked together, but Elle had been standoffish with everyone except Kyle, from what Alice had seen. It hadn't been anything personal. She and Elle had been friends, of a sort.

And then after Elle had been Chosen, her grandmother had tried to kill her, simply because she was now a vampire and had fallen in love with a were. You couldn't get much more damaging than that. Imagine having to grow up with someone so horrible they couldn't handle their grandchild's choices? It wasn't like Elle had run around murdering people for fun. Anyway, most families were happy when someone was Chosen or Bitten; their memories and their family lines would live on for thousands of years. It was odd that someone had hated the idea so much; especially when Elle's grandmother had been in business with half the vampires in Pinton.

"I'm sure Elle is bloody wonderful, but that doesn't mean I have to become friends with her," Tal said quietly.

"If you want to have a relationship with the viscountess, you may have to reconsider that," Alice whispered. "Misty is Elle's 'aunt', after all."

"Misty?" Tal raised one delicately arched eyebrow.

"She gave me leave to call her by her first name." Alice didn't mean to sound so defensive, but she couldn't help herself.

"Look, I'll cross that bridge when I come to it." Tal shifted on her cushion. "For now, Misty and I are just...well, we've been on a couple of dates. I'm not sure what we are."

They fell into a slightly uncomfortable silence. Alice was curious about Tal's relationship with the viscountess, even though she hated to admit it. Alice disliked it when Tal pried into *her* personal life in too much detail. Especially when she'd just started dating someone — you never knew which direction it might take; it could be over before it even really started. Like when Alice had dated Roger Mingly, who'd been a terrible kisser, even without their height difference issue. Tal always got so excited whenever Alice went on a single outing with a guy.

It drove her nuts.

But Alice did want to know more about this new relationship. A vampire and a human; more than that, an aristo and a commoner, even if Tal was a well-placed one.

The large city clock struck ten in the evening, the chimes audible in the foyer. Still early as far as the vampire night was concerned, but Alice hadn't really been sleeping well. Fatigue was weighing her down.

Not long after the bells sounded, Kyle McInnes strolled in from the street, wearing a large coat over his guard uniform to block out the evening chill. His gaze swept the reception area and came to rest on Alice and Tal.

He gave a bright grin and then walked over to the two of them. "Why, if it isn't the lovely coroner and her friend. Did you get lost? Do you need me to help you down to the morgue?"

Alice rolled her eyes, she couldn't help it. "I have been temporarily banned from the morgue."

Kyle rubbed a large hand over his face. "So? You run the morgue. Unban yourself."

"If it were only so easy..." Alice said with a small smile. She wasn't sure if she should admit that the king, a palace guard, a viscountess and the night captain were having a meeting down there.

A moment later, Elle came through the doors dressed in her guard uniform, but without the jacket. Maybe being a vampire meant she didn't feel the cold as much anymore. She stopped beside Kyle and glowered at him. "Are you tormenting Alice again? Because if you are..."

"Tormenting?" Kyle placed a hand on his heart. "You wound me, Elle. You really do." He turned to Alice. "Tell her I am not annoying you. I was just offering my assistance to keep the ladies from dying of boredom."

Tal chuckled, but it sounded forced to Alice. "Do you even know my name?"

A slightly panicked look spread across Kyle's features. "Alice's pretty friend?"

"Oh, you're a right charmer, you are," Tal said, real amusement apparent.

Elle snorted. "Pretty friend? That's the best you could do? Seriously, you wonder why you're still single."

Kyle held his hands up in a silent surrender.

Elle suddenly snapped alert. "Why is the king here?" Her attention then focused on Tal. "And why do you smell strongly of my aunt?"

Tal gaped at her.

Kyle laughed. "And you say I'm tactless."

Chapter Thirty-Nine

This Randall guy was a complete dick. And an utter idiot. Fin reckoned the vampire should just throw himself off a cliff and be done with it. Might even be less messy than what Hannah's mother would do to him when she found out what he'd done. Randall had really thought that he could make Hannah dance to his tune with just a few touches? Sure, she was almost pathologically afraid of physical contact, but the damage had been done and she seemed fine now.

Maybe a second touch wouldn't affect her? He'd have to ask.

Footsteps echoed from outside the cell. Hannah stared in their direction, her Black eyes cold, and her lush mouth set in a hard line. Fin had to work hard to forget that those lips had been pressed to his not long ago.

She'd just overreacted.

Anyway, Hannah wasn't for him. She had a baby. She was the daughter of a *first generation* vampire. And she was part-vampire, part-Graced. His sisters would have conniptions. *He* would have conniptions; he'd be walking into an instant family. He didn't even want to know what the duchess would think of him. Plus, their relationship would be doomed anyway; he would die long before Hannah did.

He was contemplating this way too much.

Because the simple fact was, there was no relationship. There was no Hannah and Fin. Or Hannah, Fin and Rena. Or Hannah, Fin, Rena and then Byrne as an uncle.

It was crazy how much the idea appealed to him.

He thrust his hands through his hair. He was stuck in a fucking dungeon as prisoner. Not only that, but he was trapped with a vampire who couldn't touch people, *and* he was still injured. Byrne — their one good chance of survival, even in an estate filled with vampires — didn't even know they were in trouble.

There was no way Fin was going to walk out of this one alive, so he was an utter idiot for worrying about a future that wouldn't even exist.

The footsteps outside grew closer; there was arguing now, too. There seemed to be a few voices debating with Randall. For some reason, no one was rushing down to save Hannah or Fin's asses, though.

And what fine asses they were.

Do not *think about Hannah's butt.*

Other thoughts. Okay, different thoughts. He concentrated on his feet. They were positioned at the end of his legs — the normal place for feet, he admitted — and the left was higher than the other because he'd crossed his legs at the ankle.

There. Feet.

Much better than thinking about a certain vampire's butt.

Fuck.

She should never have kissed him. Here he was in a doomed situation, and all he could think about was her. And how he shouldn't have pushed her away.

He was a fool.

Focus on the voices, he thought. *That will distract you.* So he did, because he was desperate.

"I still think this is a bad idea," someone was saying. "You should have checked with us first. We didn't have to go along with this plan. We could have picked something else."

"Wait for Montrose to return," came another voice.

"It was too good an opportunity to waste." Randall's voice rose in pitch. "We could take over this duchy."

"You mean *you're* going to take over the duchy. None of us would be married to the bitch."

"You're going to get everyone killed," said the second speaker. "Anyone who didn't stop you is going to be seen as an accomplice, and guilty by association. You do realize that?"

"The duchess won't ever have to know that her daughter wasn't willing," Randall replied.

"You really believe that the duchess is going to think that her precious little freak offspring would have fallen in love with you and married you? Only to move straight back to that stupid mountain?"

At least one person had some sense. Fin had thought the same thing.

"She can't handle being around people, even Tatiana says that."

"Tatiana is the only one who can touch her."

"She was with that *human*."

Hey! Fin bristled. *I'm more than just 'that' human. I'm at least a 'the.'*

"You're risking a lot on a bunch of assumptions! That human may not have touched her at all."

"Nice to see they're rushing to free us," Fin muttered.

Hannah shot a look his way. "Now that I'm stuck in here, and one of them touched me, they're worried they are all going to get killed by my mother. The last time someone kidnapped me and held me for ransom, she wiped out the *entire* family."

Fin let out a low whistle. "Then they're morons for not releasing you straight away."

"I know."

By now Randall was at the bottom of the stairs. Through the bars, Fin could see only one person had finished the journey with him: Douchebag from the entryway.

Fin wanted to punch them both in the face. At least once. Probably more than that.

Okay, definitely more than that.

"So, I see you're awake," Randall said.

Hannah stood up, but kept an arm's length from the gaps in the bars, presumably in case Randall reached in to touch her again. Maybe she was sensitive every time. That would suck.

"No thanks to you," Hannah said.

"Look, if you just agree to help me, I'll let you go. No harm done."

Fin snorted.

Hannah laughed, the rusty sound making him want to curl his toes. But he was a guy, and guys didn't curl their toes at the sound of a woman's laughter. Fin stood up.

"Do you think I'm an idiot?" Hannah asked.

"All you have to do is sign some paperwork, and you're free to go."

"Free?" Hannah shook her head. "I wouldn't define being dead as the same thing as being free."

"No one ever said anything about killing you." Randall flashed his even white teeth. Fin gathered the guy was handsome, but all he could see was the calculation in the vampire's red-purple eyes. He didn't think the man's good looks were working on Hannah, either.

Both Randall and Douchebag were ignoring Fin completely, all their attention on Hannah. He was more than happy to be a wall decoration for now. He'd act if one of them stepped foot inside the cell. Not that he was sure he could take on a vampire, but he knew a thing or two about hand to hand combat. It had been one of his and Byrne's favorite pastimes: Fin trying not to die while Byrne got himself back into shape.

"What did my mother tell you about my ability?" Hannah asked.

"That you absorb people's memories," Randall said.

Douchebag took a step away from the cell. "Memories? What the fuck? You didn't say she was some kind of *real* freak."

Randall looked back at the servant. "She's in the cell, she can't touch you."

Hannah locked gazes with the servant, who slunk back to the far side of the hallway. "I don't just take some memories. I take *all* of them. Everything you've ever thought about or done, everything that's left a lasting enough impression on your personality; those things are absorbed. So I know all about your plan, I know all about your pathetic past. And aside from that, I may be a freak, but I'm *not* stupid. There is no way you'd do this to me and let me live. Because if I even breathed a word to my mother that you touched me, you're dead."

She shrugged. "You're all dead."

"Kill her now, and just forge her signature," Douchebag growled.

Randall slapped him so fast, that if Fin hadn't heard the crack, he might have thought he'd imagined it.

"The document has to have her scent on it; and her scent has to be all over the estate, or the duchess won't believe Hannah was here long enough to do it."

"And what's to stop me from just leaving?" Hannah asked.

Randall stepped closer to the cell bars. If he expected Hannah to flinch or step back, he was disappointed. Randall pointed at Fin. "Him."

"Him?" Hannah echoed.

"Me?" Fin said.

"We'll let him go if you do everything we say."

"Oh, so now *I'm* going to survive? Before Hannah was going to be the one to live." Fin rolled his eyes. "Make up your fucking minds. Your plan is so bullshit I can smell the stink from here."

Randall's face flushed pink, which Fin assumed was the leech equivalent of red-cheeked rage. "Who the fuck are you to talk to me like that?"

Fin laughed, because it would make the vampire even angrier. "I can talk to you however I bloody well want."

"You're just a pathetic piece of meat."

Fin pouted. "Oh, you really hurt my feelings with that one."

"I wouldn't keep arguing with him," Hannah said to Randall. "He can literally do that all day long."

Fin nodded. "It's a talent."

Randall unlocked the door and gestured at Hannah. "Get out."

She planted her feet. "No."

"Get out, or I'll kill him."

Fin sniffed. "You could try."

"Get. Out."

"No."

"I will give you one more chance—"

Something about Hannah's answering smile was off. "Make me."

Randall darted forward and grabbed Hannah's arm. Nothing happened. He looked at her, mouth gone slack. "What?"

Hannah's face turned hard. She formed her hand into a flat blade, and then slammed it forward, into Randall's stomach. His shirt tore with the force. Hannah angled her arm upward and Randall's eyes bulged in his head. He screamed and thrashed to get away, but she had locked her other hand on his shoulder.

"See, I've already taken all your memories." Her voice was almost conversational, like she shoved her hand into someone's gut on a regular basis. Who knows, maybe she did. "You haven't accumulated enough new ones to debilitate me in the few hours you've been away."

Randall gasped. "But—"

Shit, Fin's mouth was hanging agape, but he didn't care. He'd had no idea that Hannah was so strong, even for a vampire. To punch through someone's stomach...to hold them in place while they fought to get free...

"This punishment is far kinder than anything Mother would have dealt you," Hannah said, and Fin had the awful feeling she was speaking the truth.

Then she pulled her hand back.

In her gore-coated palm she held Randall's still-pumping heart. Blood pulsed from the wound and Randall stared at her hand before slowly collapsing to the floor.

Douchebag was pressed against the wall, face a mask of surprised horror. Fin sprang forward, over the spreading puddle of blood. He grabbed the arm of the servant and threw him into the cell. The vampire was too stunned to struggle.

Hannah just stood there, heart in her hand, blood splattered on her shirt. Frozen in shock.

Fin waved a hand at her face. "Come on, Hannah. We need to get moving. Before the others realize what's happened."

She held the heart out to him.

Thanks, but I don't want it.

"I killed him."

Fin kept his face blank and nodded. "Great work, let's move!"

Sensing she wasn't really with him, Fin seized her arm and dragged her from the cell, slamming the door shut and engaging the lock behind them. Adrenaline surged through him, and he shut his eyes, willing his heartbeat to steady. He needed to come up with a plan. He'd had no idea Hannah was capable of something like this. She was staring now, first at him, then at the heart in her palm.

He had a feeling she'd had no idea she was capable of that, either.

Then, from somewhere upstairs, he heard screaming. And a roar.

Fin gave Hannah a gentle shake. "I think Byrne's here."

Chapter Forty

Skarva City

Byrne was going to have to go full bear soon, if the odds didn't improve. Six to one against him. Against humans, that was a no-brainer. He'd easily take on six and walk away with barely a scratch. Well, maybe a few scratches. But six vampires? One were? Even with his height, musculature and strength, they weren't good statistics. Plus, if he had to go bear, in a room full of leeches, it would leave him vulnerable. He could shift quickly, but there was always that moment where he was in that pain-filled state of not-human and not-yet-bear. All someone needed was a silver knife or even a good grip around his head and that was it. Bye bye, Byrne.

Three years ago, he would have welcomed that end.

But not anymore.

The thought startled him, and sensing his distraction, a vampire rushed him with a growl. Byrne slashed out a clawed hand. It tore the man's chest, stripes of blood appearing instantaneously. The force of the blow threw the screaming vampire into the wall. The plaster cracked and the bloodsucker slid down onto the marble floor. The wound would heal quickly. On a nearby pedestal, a vase wobbled.

Five vampires moved toward Byrne; three men and two women. They were arguing, yelling instructions that contradicted each other. All had that icy stink Byrne associated with leeches, except Hannah. Her scent was somehow muted and not really unpleasant.

The vampires all wore extremely well-tailored clothing, and looked to be in perfect health. Whatever people said about the Deadly Duchess, she took care of her own. Although, it appeared that now they'd turned on her, kidnapping her daughter within her own estate. Byrne couldn't see how an insult like that would go unpunished.

He kept his back to the double front doors as the remaining five vampires converged on him. The one he'd knocked into the wall stayed down. Maybe he'd broken the leech's spine. Three leapt at the same time, and Byrne batted two of them out of the air with clawed hands. One got through his guard, and kicked him in the gut. Air rushed out of his chest, but he stayed upright, relaxing his diaphragm through the pain and need for air. But the vampire threw him off balance, and the bloody leech punched him in the face. The crunch of his nose breaking sounded around the high-ceilinged foyer, and tears sprang to his eyes.

It *hurt*.

Roaring, Byrne wrenched the leech's neck at an awkward angle, snapping it. Blood trickled down his face from his nose, ran over his lips. The metallic taste infiltrated his mouth as the vampire collapsed boneless to the floor. The bastard wasn't dead, but at least he was out of the game. His purple eyes watched Byrne, rage clouding their depths.

Byrne grinned, a blood-smeared baring of teeth. "Oops."

He drew the wooden knife that he'd stashed in his waistband, and held it out in front of him, guard up. "You know what this is," he said to the four remaining vampires, his deep voice loud.

That made the other four pause.

"The next person who attacks me is going to get stabbed with it, so I would reconsider your actions and just bring Hannah and Fin to me."

Four sets of eyes focused on the knife.

"We already told you, Lady Hannah isn't here." This came from the vampire collapsed on the floor next to him.

"And I already told you, her scent is fresh." His voice dropped to a growl. "That means *she's still here.*"

If anything had happened to her or even Fin...especially Fin, since it was Byrne who'd made the human come here...

One of the two women spoke. "Look, we don't want to hurt you. If you just go, then we can forget this ever happened."

Forget this ever happened. Hah. Byrne had been let into the foyer under the pretense of an older were coming to greet an older vampire. Rank and title didn't matter in these situations; vamps and weres who'd seen a few millennia were expected to call on each other when in town. It was a leftover of the Civil War days, when entering your territory probably meant an act of aggression, rather than just a social visit.

Normally Byrne ignored the unofficial protocol, but had used it to his advantage this time. After he'd entered the building and casually asked after Hannah and Fin, the attendant had said no one by those names was here. He'd have to wait to speak to some Randall guy. Byrne had called the attendant out as a liar. Only an idiot would say that someone wasn't there when they clearly were; especially considering that weres had sharper senses of smell than leeches. And *no one* had a sense of smell like a bear.

The attendant hadn't taken his accusation kindly, and then five other vampires had descended on the foyer, violence clearly on their minds.

The downside was that Byrne hadn't been expecting to walk into a fight. Lia had just said Hannah and Fin would need help getting away, but that it would be fairly easy. She'd said that if Byrne showed up at the right time — that time being when she'd told him to head over to the estate — then Fin and Hannah would have freed themselves and be ready to go. Hopefully they got their asses here soon.

Because Lia hadn't mentioned anything about those six to one odds or getting his nose broken, although to be fair, the nose was already healing.

The door behind Byrne banged open, slamming into him and sending him stumbling forward. Half-turning to face the newcomer, he dropped his guard, and one of the female vampires leapt on his back, wrapping an arm around his throat, as if to either choke him or snap his neck. But she wasn't as strong as him, so there was little chance she'd succeed in her plan. Byrne just pried her arm away.

The door slammed shut with a bang, then a female voice shouted, "What is going on here?!"

The woman on Byrne's back stopped struggling, and the other vampires halted in place, stock still. Even the one on the ground next to Byrne, who couldn't move due to his broken neck, looked panicked.

Byrne turned slowly to see exactly who'd just come through that door.

A tall woman with deep brown skin and bleached blonde hair glared around the entryway. Her mauve gaze locked with Byrne's and she frowned. "Who the fuck are you?"

From deep in the building came the sound of running footsteps; someone was heading toward the entryway, rather than away, Byrne guessed. He sure hoped it was Hannah and Fin.

"Name's Byrne." Still holding his attacker's arm away from his throat, and with his other fist clenched around the knife, he couldn't offer a hand to shake. He gave a helpless little shrug instead.

The newcomer levelled her gaze on the blade. "You do know it's all kinds of illegal to bring wooden weapons into a vampire estate?"

Byrne slammed his head back, and the woman behind him let out a whoosh of air as his skull connected with her face. More crunching. At least it wasn't his nose his time. She dropped from his back, hands clinging to her smashed features. He'd feel bad, but then, he didn't.

Before he'd been captured and imprisoned all those years ago, Byrne had strongly believed that a man should never hit a woman. Not under any circumstances. But a century of being tortured had changed him, and now if someone attacked him, then they got back what they gave. Sex, gender, they were immaterial. If they left him alone, he'd leave them alone. Still, he'd never hurt a woman who hadn't attacked him first though, that rule remained.

"Well, it's not exactly polite to attack a visiting were, either," Byrne muttered.

"They wouldn't just attack you without reason."

"I was here looking for some friends."

"Friends?" Her tone indicated she thought it was surprising that he could even have friends.

Bitch.

"Friends. Their names are Hannah and Fin. These leeches say they aren't here, but I *can smell them.*"

The woman's brows furrowed. "Hannah? As in Lady Hannah?"

"I just dropped her off a few hours ago..."

Incredulity spread across her face. "*Here?*"

"Yes. I can smell her. She's still here, but they say she left."

The woman glowered at the vampires in the foyer, who'd begun edging toward the doors. "Lady Hannah was here and *no one thought to send me a message?*"

The man on the floor groaned. "You were on leave. Plus, she left already. Randall took care of it."

"Randall? Took care of it? What does that even mean? Why would Lady Hannah come here only to leave right away?" No one answered, or met the vampire's gaze. Byrne thought she was rather impressive in her building rage. "Then why does the bear say she's still here?"

The woman with the broken nose glared over her hand. "I don't know. She left to go find the duchess."

"Lady Hannah came all the way from the Oberona Mountains only to leave the same day?"

By now the footsteps were so close that even the vampires noticed. The blonde woman whipped her head toward the sound, and Byrne followed her gaze. Hannah and Fin came rushing around a corner. Fin was clutching his ribs, and he skidded to a stop upon seeing Byrne surrounded by vampires. Hannah slowed as well, half-hiding behind the human. Byrne stared.

Was Hannah holding a *heart*?

The blonde vampire took a half step forward, face alive with surprise. "Lady Hannah?"

Hannah stepped around Fin. "Montrose?"

The shock vanished from the vampire's mauve eyes and she gave Byrne a black look. "If *someone* would like to tell me what is happening here, I'd be much obliged."

"Don't ask me," Byrne said. "I came here looking for those two," he pointed at Hannah and Fin — why the woman was holding a heart when she couldn't stand to be touched by anyone was a bit of a puzzle — "only to be attacked by these six."

Montrose sighed, and it was a long-suffering sound. "At least tell me whose heart that is?"

"Mr. Randall's," Hannah said, holding out the organ, as if offering it to the other vampire.

CHAPTER FORTY-ONE

The drawing room was large, with a fireplace at one end, and a coffee table, sofas and an arrangement of aesthetically pleasing chairs, all in various shades of gold and cream, offset from the grate. Settled on one of the sofas, Dante crossed his legs and regarded the pianoforte at the other end of the room. He winced. He'd spent the better part of a century here trying to master the bloody thing; but when one had little ability to comprehend emotion, it was difficult to produce something that relied so heavily on experiencing the turmoil of music.

In the past — before he'd been banished from the estate — Dante would visit with his father in the study. Now, the room was drafty from the broken window and his *mother* sat opposite him, staring at Dante with a kind of fascination that made him feel — what he interpreted as, anyway — slightly edgy. He'd never felt that emotion before, so he wasn't really sure how he was meant to react.

Anton shared the small sofa with him, fiddling with his cane where it rested across his knees. Maybe he felt the same way? Was one meant to fidget when they felt edgy?

Feelings were so annoying. If Dante had known that Choosing Elle would have resulted in him becoming more emotional, he might have thought twice about the procedure. Too late now, though.

Viktor sat in a wing chair off to the side, half-turned toward the door, a sullen look on his face. Dante was surprised his father wasn't screaming about how there would be repercussions for all this; how he would make Tatiana pay for what she'd done to him. But something held him in check, maybe the fear of having to admit to his king that the mother of his child was dissatisfied with his parenting. Viktor never liked to be thought of as lacking in anything.

Curiously Dante examined Viktor's re-broken leg, which was resting on an ottoman while it healed. Dante would *never* have dared to hurt his father like that. He kind of admired Tatiana for doing so.

Viktor Kipling *was* an asshole.

Tatiana leveled a cold glare at his father. "I am extremely displeased with how you have fulfilled our breeding contract." She held up a finger. "You had care of him until he was no longer a minor. As soon as he reached his majority, you exiled him from the house," she raised another finger, "and married him to a human. You also allowed his Chosen to nearly be cremated." A third finger joined the other two.

Viktor ignored the first two accusations. "The girl's heart wasn't beating. It was a reasonable assumption that she was dead."

Dante snorted. He couldn't help himself. Viktor scowled at him, but for once, Dante didn't wonder about what his father thought of him. While Viktor still held some paperwork that limited the choices and actions his son could do and make, Dante now had a mother who might actually care about his fate. A mother who clearly outranked his father in social status.

It was a startling revelation. Dante had always assumed that his mother had signed the breeding contract, produced the required offspring, and then not thought about him since.

"I told you at the time Elle was still alive," Dante said to his father. "You just couldn't hear her heartbeat."

"Oh yes, with your 'special' senses." His father made a mocking gesture with his fingers as he said the word 'special.'

Tatiana groaned. "You are an even bigger fool than I remember. As the son of a first generation vampire, his senses can be expected to be far superior than those of a mutt such as yourself."

Viktor spluttered. "First generation? *Mutt*?"

Dante wasn't sure which statement outraged his father the most.

Did Tatiana just say *first generation*?

"First generation?" Anton said, giving voice to Dante's thoughts.

Tatiana's bright, over-sized violet eyes settled on Dante. "Yes. Haven't you ever noticed that you're faster, stronger, and have better senses than all the other vampires around you?"

"Well, yes. But they just said I was sensitive and delicate and—"

"Enough." Viktor frowned, then addressed Tatiana. "Maybe you should have mentioned your background before we signed the breeding contract."

"If you couldn't work it out then why should I have told you? You had all the evidence, but you chose to ignore it, thinking that your abilities were greater than they are." Tatiana shoved her long braid over her shoulder.

"I wouldn't have dismissed Dante's oddities so easily, for one."

Tatiana glowered. "You shouldn't have anyway. That's called *being a good parent*. Something you seem to know little about. Children are not just *things* that you own."

"That's exactly what they are. And isn't it a bit hypocritical to judge *me* about my parenting skills?"

"What is that supposed to mean?" Beside Dante, Anton winced.

"All your other children are dead. You said so. That's why you agreed to the contract."

"All my children *except* Dante and his sister are dead, yes. You know, *your other daughter*. Or did you forget about her?" Tatiana met Dante's curious stare. "My other children died thousands of years ago. Your great-great-great-great-great grandfather wouldn't have even been alive then. They were casualties of a war that was lost eons ago. Plus, I didn't sell them into marriage for the sake of a few coins."

Clearly his matrimonial status annoyed Tatiana, although Dante didn't want his mother to think that he was upset by it. Marrying Anton had been a good thing. Despite his father meaning it as a punishment, it had been a reward. Dante was no longer under his father's heavy-handed control, he was living with people who actually *liked* him, and he was in a sort-of relationship — if you counted kissing a few times a relationship. Dante hadn't ever wanted to be in a relationship with anyone. Ever. But with Anton it was different. It had meaning. At least to him. Dante hoped it did to Anton, too.

From what Dante had observed in the last couple of hours, his mother and father didn't particularly enjoy each other's company. He wondered how they'd ever managed to fulfil the breeding contract. Wait — that was something he wasn't meant to wonder. At least, he was pretty sure that's what Elle would tell him if she was here, listening into his thoughts, which she did a little too frequently for his liking. It didn't matter how many times he or that werewolf boyfriend of hers told her that she shouldn't eavesdrop on Dante's thoughts. She did it anyway. "It just happened," was her favorite excuse.

It was about as believable as someone 'accidentally' losing their virginity. *Oh, I tripped*, Dante thought with an internal snigger.

"Then where *is* my other daughter? Why didn't you bring her here to meet me?" Viktor asked, face smoothing into a mask.

"She is traveling," Tatiana responded.

"So? You should have brought her with you to meet me."

Tatiana snorted. "You're the last person I'd want her to meet."

"I'm her *father*."

"You provided the biological material required for her conception. That is as much of an influence on her life as you'll ever have."

Anton coughed, and Dante turned to make sure he was okay. But the human's brandy-colored eyes held an odd expression Dante couldn't decipher. It was probably a reaction to the social situation, Dante decided. Anton was much more responsive to these things.

The front door slammed shut, and Dante and Tatiana's heads turned toward the sound. Dante heard the butler giving directions, and then two sets of footsteps began approaching the drawing room. And one set of paws.

The door opened and his sister Misty stood in the portal. She was wearing a white suit, and her hair was swept up high. Normally bubbly and vital, Misty seemed flat. Dante made to stand, but something about his sister's expression held him back. Elle hovered in the background behind Misty, and a large brindle wolf with yellow eyes lurked protectively nearby.

Why was Clay here, too?

"Mistique," Viktor said, "why have you brought these...*people*...here?"

Dante couldn't understand why his father was shocked by Elle's arrival; she had been here not long ago, although Clay hadn't been with her last time. He'd waited for her outside the estate, pacing the sidewalk and causing the local vampires to cross to the other side of the street. Clay hadn't come in, because weres didn't typically enter vampire estates without formal invitation, even if they were checking up on their errant fiancé. Which made Dante wonder why Misty had allowed the wolf to follow her — her hatred of weres was rather legendary.

Misty ignored their father's irritation. "Father, I need to speak with you privately."

Viktor slashed a hand through the air. "Just spit it out, I'm in no mood for theatrics."

Folding her arms, Misty glared at the people in the room. Her eyes lingered on Viktor's raised leg, then came to rest on Tatiana, a curious gleam entering her gaze before her lavender eyes clouded over with some other emotion. "Father—"

"Just bloody well say it!"

"Mother — the countess — has been murdered."

Elle stepped forward, her hand suspended uselessly over Misty's shoulder — no matter how much Misty had adopted the Chosen vampire, they were still unequal in the eyes of society, and that meant Elle wouldn't dare touch her. But Elle seemed to offer a silent kind of comfort, which told Dante Misty was telling the truth. Elle wasn't one for useless shows of sentimentality.

Viktor barked a laugh. "That is ridiculous. Maerylina is at the country estate."

Misty shook her head. "Mother is lying in the city morgue."

"Come now, you shouldn't believe everything these...people have to say." Viktor's eyes lingered on Elle in her city guard uniform as he spoke.

Dante didn't know why Viktor hated Elle so much; she hadn't done anything to his father, not that he was aware of. Tatiana had stomped on Viktor's leg and thrown him out a window, and Viktor wasn't showing her nearly as much disdain as he did Dante's Chosen.

"I could pretend to take offense at that, but considering it was the viscountess who identified the body..." Elle's wry voice trailed into silence.

Viktor's eyebrows flew high up on his forehead as he stared at his favorite child. "You were at the city morgue?"

"I have been helping with the investigations into the vampire murders. I told you about the killings." Misty raised a hand and patted her hair, her gaze flittering over to Dante.

"I forbid it!"

"I've already done it," Misty said. His sister normally laughed at their father's antics, but covertly. Misty was sly. It was how she managed to get around their father so often. "Plus, if I hadn't been involved, then we wouldn't know the countess was lying on a slab in that morgue. She was *murdered*, Father. Your wife was killed by some lowlife, and you just sit there and forbid me from assisting in finding her killer?"

"Think of the family's reputation!"

"Because Mother being murdered won't have affected that?"

Viktor's cheeks acquired the rosy hue of what Dante presumed was rage or annoyance. "Are you sure it wasn't just an accident?"

"She was staked four times," Elle said. "I don't think that really classifies as an accident."

Tatiana snorted. All eyes turned toward her and she held up a hand. "Excuse me, I don't mean to laugh at your loss." She nodded at Misty, but ignored Viktor's spluttering. "However, I think this has become a family matter that no longer involves me. I would like to spend more time with my son, so we shall take our leave."

Misty frowned. "Your son?"

"Dante," Tatiana said as she stood. She brushed down her clothing and met Misty's stare. "I waited until he reached his majority, as per the breeding contract. But I find myself extremely displeased with how your father has been handling his upbringing. Consider Dante now my concern."

Viktor waved a finger at Tatiana, wildly. "You did this! You killed my wife in some kind of petty act of retaliation."

"Oh please. If I wanted to take out my anger on you, I would throw you from a window and break your leg a few times. I wouldn't murder your wife, who has nothing to do with me, or with Dante. From what I've heard, she's barely even interacted with my son, and while I find that to be neglectful parenting, it isn't half so bad as your fathering skills."

A sweet smile spread slowly across Tatiana's face. "However, if I hear you're the reason any harm has befallen Dante, I will kill you. I will rip you apart limb by limb and then I will feed your heart to wild dogs. And before you say that I can't harm you, I can. This wouldn't be considered a political incident between Skarva and Pinton, because we have a pre-existing contract, which I will claim you have failed to fulfil, since one of the clauses is to raise any offspring to adulthood and to care for their safety and wellbeing."

Tatiana tilted her head to the side. "Plus, I am one of the four rulers of Skarva. Do you really think your king is going to go to war over a mere earl? I assume there are plenty of other vampires waiting to take on your title."

Viktor hissed at that.

"Do I make myself clear?"

Dante's father swallowed. "Crystal."

CHAPTER FORTY-TWO

Hannah didn't know what to do.

It wasn't every day that she tore someone's heart out of their chest. In fact, it wasn't *any* day that she did that. She'd never killed a person before. Oh, she'd seen it done in the memories she'd taken; vampires didn't tend to live violence-free existences. She'd experienced the rush of excitement, fear, angst, terror, joy at those remembered deaths — exactly as if she'd felt them at the time.

But now she was just stunned.

She didn't know what to feel.

Aside from sticky.

"Hannah?" Fin asked.

Shaking herself, Hannah focused. The heart was a weight in her hand, the blood cooling. Maybe she should put it down? But then that would leave blood in the foyer, and her mother was very particular about the marble floors. Looking away from the organ, she saw Byrne, two vampires on the ground next to him. Three of the other four retainers stood awkwardly in the foyer's white marble expanse, stances wide, eyes darting. Montrose was just inside the door, her intimidating figure looming near Byrne. She looked disapproving, which made Hannah bite her lip.

Montrose had never touched Hannah — the woman wasn't an idiot, and unlike Randall, was actually loyal to her mother — but Hannah didn't need to have the other woman's memories to know that Montrose was a daunting individual. She was able to express her displeasure with a kind of verbal skill that left most people a jibbering mess. Even as precocious and wary child, Hannah had never mucked around for the older vampire. Montrose looked at Hannah, her pale mauve eyes dropping to the organ in Hannah's hand.

"Mr. Randall's heart?" Montrose repeated.

Hannah nodded. And then the other vampires registered what had happened. The ones still upright ran for the exits, their movements panicked and fast. Byrne reached out and seized one by the back of the neck, and Montrose kicked another who tried to duck behind her.

Fin threw his arms out, clotheslining two vampires as they tried to run by. Their heads jolted back, and they crumpled to the floor, twitching. Fin let out an 'oomph' at the impact, then shook his arms out. "That hurt," he muttered. He reached down and stabbed two sharp pieces of wood into the vampires' necks; it would keep them immobile for a little while.

Where had he kept those? And why was he carrying weapons to attack vampires?

Fin looked at her. "What? I like to be prepared."

Montrose grabbed a woman who attempted to slide past, and with a quick twist of her arms, broke her neck. Breaking another vampire's neck was near impossible, unless you were a *lot* stronger. Clearly Montrose had enormous physical power; and not a lot of sympathy for people she deemed untrustworthy. But at least the vampire with the broken neck wasn't dead.

"Will someone please explain to me what is going on here?" Montrose demanded, stepping over one of the fallen vampires.

"How about we lock these guys up in the basement, then we can talk?" Fin suggested. He slid a glance at her. "Also, Hannah needs to do something with that heart. It's gross."

◆

Hannah, Byrne and Fin followed Montrose to her office. It was on the same level as the duchess', but a few doors down. The room had floor-to-ceiling iron shelves, which were lined with books on every subject matter Hannah could think of. She'd spent hours as a child, just standing and looking at the book spines, because she wouldn't dare touch them. Sometimes Montrose would read one to her, but she had a tendency to pick the educational tomes.

Hannah wasn't really sure what Montrose thought of her, but the older woman had never been cruel. And someone as old as Montrose wouldn't be exactly...right in the mind. But she did hold one philosophy in common with her employer: adults were fair game, but children were sacred. Hannah was aware that her mother had lost children earlier in her life — it was hard for her to think of them as her brothers and sisters, since they'd been born and died thousands of years ago — but she didn't know if Montrose had ever been a parent. She wasn't exactly keen on asking, either.

While even Hannah had heard plenty of stories about the tall, dark-skinned woman's extracurricular activities, they'd never affected how she did her job, or her loyalty to Tatiana. And she and the duchess had been together for years; the two women had to be friends of a sort, but Hannah had never really thought of her mother as having 'friends.' That was probably childish oversight on her part — most people had friends. Hannah had been the exception to the norm, at least until she'd met Byrne and Fin.

"Everyone, sit." Montrose walked around behind her large metal desk and pulled out the heavy leather chair. She lowered herself into the padded seat, and placed her clasped hands on the desk's surface. When the trio didn't move, she raised her eyebrows at them.

Byrne and Fin turned questioning looks on Hannah. They were hesitating because of *her*, even though poor Fin looked like he could do with a seat. He was wavering slightly on his feet, and his bruises looked sickly in the yellow light of the office. There was also a new purple one blooming on his jawline, and Hannah had the sinking suspicion she'd been responsible for it.

Guilt slammed her. Fin had also helped drag the vampires down to the cells, while she'd just stood there holding Randall's heart. Fin had only taken one — Montrose and Byrne had taken two each, with Montrose returning for the final traitor — but Fin was a human and she a vampire. She should have helped, but she couldn't. So she'd just watched, holding onto the organ like a fool. It was only when Montrose had offered to take the heart and throw it away, that Hannah had let go of it.

Montrose gestured toward the two chairs positioned opposite her, indicating Fin and Byrne should take one each.

"What about Hannah?" Fin asked, his body wavering.

"What about her?" Montrose turned to look at Hannah.

"She needs a seat, too."

Montrose looked put upon. "Hannah is a vampire and can stand for hours. However, she has a special chair behind that door." The vampire pointed a long finger at a closet to the right of her desk. "If you open it, she can retrieve the seat herself."

Fin walked over, opened the door and grabbed the chair. He grunted a little at the weight of the metal seat, and Hannah stepped forward to help. He met her gaze and shook his head. "I've got it."

"But you're hurt."

"I said I've got it."

"But I don't have broken ribs. Give it to me."

"No."

Hissing in impatience, Hannah shoved forward and wrestled the chair from the protesting Fin. She accidentally brushed hands with him, and jolted away out of habit, but nothing happened. Taking a deep breath, she held his annoyed Hazel glare. "You need to be careful of your injuries. You're human."

"I'm fine."

"It's heavy."

"I'm *fine*."

"Really? That wasn't what you were saying yesterday."

Byrne snorted.

Montrose stood, anger flashing in her eyes. "What are you doing? Why did you touch that chair?"

Fin let out a low growl, which was impressive for a human.

Hannah darted forward and stole the chair, taking it back to the desk and placing it between the two larger leather seats. Byrne and Montrose frowned at her and the idiotic human. Pride. It was a harmful emotion.

Fin took a seat in one of the wingbacks. He let out a low groan. "I was helping Hannah out." He looked like he was pouting.

"She can't sit on that now," Montrose said. She turned a glare on Hannah who was about to take a seat. "You can't sit on that!"

Hannah froze, halfway down to the seat.

"You said you'd been traveling with her." Montrose jabbed a long finger at Fin. "How can you not know she can't use things touched by other people?"

Hannah let her butt drop the rest of the way down to the chair. Montrose's eyes went wide, but when Hannah didn't collapse, she too sat down and eyed the young vampire thoughtfully.

Byrne took the other wingback, his large body making the furniture look small, stretched his long legs out in front of him, and folded his arms across his chest. Even though she wasn't sure if she could touch him, Hannah was still glad for his presence. Byrne made her feel calm. He was solid like the earth, and just as dependable.

Hannah's chair was a spindly affair, made from wrought iron. It wasn't the prettiest, but her mother had made it for her, with Hannah assisting. It's how she learned how to make her own hearth and tools. The seat cushion had terrible embroidery of a bird and flowers on it; it had been the best Hannah could do at the time. She never really did have the patience for needlework. Neither did her mother, for that matter. Hannah was bigger now than when she'd made the chair, so she felt a bit like a giant trying to settle on human-size furniture.

Maybe that's how Byrne felt normally.

"Fin has a natural mental shield that prevents the memory transfer," Hannah said.

Montrose ran a hand over her face. "Do you know the statistics of you meeting someone with a natural mental shield?"

"Pretty low," Hannah admitted, shifting uncomfortably in her seat.

"Beyond 'pretty low.' You took a risk by touching him — he could have taken advantage of the situation."

"Hey!"

"What?"

"No!"

Hannah wasn't sure which protest came from whom. "Fin and Byrne have done nothing but help me and Rena," Hannah said. "I only touched Fin because he mentioned he had the shield and I wanted to see if he was immune. He didn't want to touch me."

It was embarrassing admitting that last part, like she was diseased and he hadn't wanted to catch her illness.

Montrose peered at Fin. "Who's Rena? How did you know about the shield, anyway, human? You're not Graced — well, not one hundred percent."

Surprise flitted across Fin's face when she used the word 'Graced.' "I was born into a Graced family. I'd ask how you know about the Graced, since vampires and weres aren't meant to know, but I suppose having Hannah around would have made it pretty obvious."

Montrose barked a laugh. "I've been around for a long time, and your people have tried to wipe my memory on a number of occasions, but it doesn't...take...for some reason. It lasts for a while, but then everything comes back eventually." Montrose's expression settled into something that Hannah couldn't interpret — wryness, annoyance, amusement...anger?

"But how does the bear know about the Graced?" Montrose asked Byrne.

Hannah looked from Fin to Byrne. She'd never really thought about that; she just assumed Fin had spilled the beans to Byrne about his ancestry. But Fin wasn't really a blabbermouth; he talked a lot, and most of that about himself, but he'd never really discussed being Graced, not unless it related to Hannah or Rena.

"He just does," Fin said, chin jutting out slightly.

Montrose leaned forward. "That is not an explanation."

"It's as good as you're going to get."

"Does the bear not speak for himself?"

"He does," Fin said, "but he doesn't need to explain himself to you."

Montrose let out a sigh and looked at Hannah. "Is he always like this?"

"Usually it's funnier when he argues," Hannah admitted. Fin glared at her.

"I was held captive for one hundred years by a group of radical Graceds." Byrne's deep voice cut through the conversation. Shock zapped through Hannah. He'd been *kidnapped*?

"Byrne—"

"It's fine, Fin. Hannah would have found out eventually," Byrne said "They could read my emotions and throw me around a room easily enough, but when they tried to read my mind, it didn't work. They just figured that I had some natural ability to deflect telepathy. Eventually when they tried to wipe my memory and nothing happened, they realized I have a mental shield; it just doesn't protect me against Grays or Blues."

Hannah couldn't stop staring at the huge were. He'd been held prisoner for a century? Hannah couldn't imagine it. He was so vital and strong and well, large. It would be hard to hold someone like him captive for that length of time. And it would have meant that *generations* of Graceds had done this to him, not just one set of crazy people.

"Shields don't protect you from Blues and Grays; at least, mine doesn't either," Fin said. "Mine works against my twin, Faith, who is a Green, but not my other sisters. I guess mine developed because of having to share a womb with a telepath."

"I'm so sorry, Byrne," Hannah said as she mulled over Fin's words. His shield only protected him from telepaths, which meant that while she didn't have Green eyes, her ability must be related to it, somehow.

Byrne gave an awkward shrug. "It happened. I'm free, thanks to this idiot human. And now I know about the Graced. I would never have had any idea about them, if they hadn't taken me. Such is life."

Montrose rested her chin on her hand. "So we're in a bit of a mess here. For some reason, this human can touch you without your ability triggering. While useful, it does not particularly clarify why you ripped out Randall's heart. He's been with the duchess for a very long time and I don't think she'll be too happy that you killed one of her employees."

"He touched Hannah," Fin said.

"Explain."

CHAPTER FORTY-THREE

Pinton City

Alice knocked on the door of her aunt's apartment. Aunt Zara lived in a one-bedroom flat on the outskirts of the city. The building was a five-minute walk from the Thyme River, which was unfortunately smelly in this part of town. On the opposite bank were the warehouses that housed the city's tanners and dyers, with the overflow from their industries causing the river's stench. It was strange that the reek of the river bothered Alice, considering she spent a considerable amount of time around corpses; but she was used to the smell of decaying flesh, not urine mixed with chemicals.

Aunt Zara's apartment block overlooked an alley, the buildings that surrounded it crafted from heavy bluestone, with the mortar crumbling in places. The glass in the small windows was bubbly and uneven, but expensive enough that metal bars coated in thin mesh were used to prevent kids from breaking them with thrown rocks.

The door opened to reveal Aunt Zara, her brown hair tousled and her eyes slightly bloodshot. She was wearing a pair of pajama pants with a loose nightgown over the top, and a smear of blue paint marked her pale, aquiline nose. "Alice?"

"Hey Aunty Z." Alice gave her a small smile.

"This is a surprise! Come in." Zara stepped aside. Alice squeezed by her and inside the apartment.

The best way to describe Aunt Zara's flat was 'chaotic.' Alice's home was the opposite: neatly ordered, everything had its place, and everything was squeaky clean. Except for the tiny patch of green on her ceiling, her apartment was perfect, although she would fix that when she could. She hadn't admitted to Tal that the green spot was annoying her, because she knew her friend would tease her about it. But it irritated her anyway.

For organized Alice, stepping into Aunt Zara's house was an almost painful experience. It was only bearable because she didn't have to live there anymore. The lounge and kitchen area was open plan, and covered in junk. Well, it wasn't junk to her aunt, but it was junk to Alice. Scarves, shawls, cushions, cups, plates, blankets, paper, letters, books; you name it, all scattered over the couch and coffee table, and even the kitchen bench. The debris was brightly colored and vibrant, which made the room feel a little like a box of paints, and slightly claustrophobic. But it reflected her aunt, who was warm, funny, a bit haphazard, and definitely strong in personality.

And she was an artist. Alice didn't really have a creative bone in her body, but Zara could paint, as well as make the most beautiful mosaics. In between commissions, she worked at some of the local schools, to encourage the poorer kids to try their hand at art. Alice wasn't too sure how successful her aunt was in her endeavors, but Zara loved sharing her passion. She'd tried to get Alice involved once, but it was a lost cause. Alice had been willing to sketch out the human body, its nerves and connective tissues, and bones, but that had been about it. It meant she'd had the best skeletal drawings of any medical student when she was at university, but she had no time for still-life portraits or landscapes.

Zara skirted Alice and headed into the kitchen. She grabbed the teapot off a hook, filled it with water and put it on the wood stove. "What brings you here?"

"Just wanted to see you," Alice said, taking care not to knock the unstable pile of tesserae which sat near the edge of the kitchen bench.

Aunt Zara rifled through tins on the counter, looking for tea. "Pfft."

"Pfft?"

"You never come to visit to just see me. My apartment generally keeps you away."

A blush heated Alice's cheeks, but her darker skin thankfully hid her embarrassment. "I don't know what you mean."

"Of course you don't," her aunt said, looking up through brown bangs. "That's why you didn't spend hours each week running around after me tidying the place up when you lived here."

"You were busy—"

The kettle let out a whistle. Aunt Zara grabbed a random tea towel and then the kettle handle, lifting it off the stove. She poured the water into a bright red teapot. "Hush."

"But—"

"I understand why you did it," Zara said, popping the kettle onto a wooden board. She brought two mugs over to the coffee table, and shoved some sketches to the side to make room. Alice winced as bits of paper fell to the floor.

Aunt Zara collected the teapot and then sat down on the couch. "Sit."

Doing as she was told, Alice found herself surrounded by cushions and rugs — and was that a book on were/vampire romances by her hip? She waited for her aunt to pour the tea, but instead, her aunt quietly said, "You never were like this, before your mother died."

Alice looked at her aunt sharply. "Mother was murdered."

Zara nodded. "Yes, she was. But you were never so obsessed with cleanliness, or with counting things and having things in their exact spot, not until after she died. Even when your father passed, you didn't do it."

Father. Alice hadn't really thought about him in years, which made her feel guilty; she thought of her mother far more often. But John Reive had died when Alice was three years old. He'd been working on the construction of a bridge when a support beam had collapsed, killing him instantly. She didn't know the finer points, but those details had never really mattered to her. He'd died at work, leaving her mother, brother and Alice alone. She'd never really known a life that was different. Aunt Zara had stuck by them, and helped out whenever she could, because Alice's mother hadn't had any of her own blood relatives in Pinton.

And then eleven years later, Raylene Reive had been murdered.

"I was very young when Father died," Alice said into the quiet.

Aunt Zara poured the tea into the two mugs. "True. But I always thought that your need for control was inspired by your mother's murder. And the attack on you."

Alice frowned, taking one of the mugs and holding it between her palms. "I'm not controlling." At least, she didn't think she was. She just liked things done certain ways. Was that a crime?

"No, you don't like to control *people*," Aunt Zara said. "You like to control your environment, where you can."

"I don't see how that's a problem," Alice said.

"It's not a problem." Zara sighed. "Look, I'm just trying to say that I understand — at least, I think I understand — why you have to have things...ordered. But I wasn't sure if you realized it was a result of your mother's death."

Alice was silent. She *hadn't* ever thought about when her obsessive behavior kicked in, just that it had, and that she'd needed to moderate it. To have some control over her life. It probably *was* a reaction to finding her mother killed, to being stabbed herself. Trying to regain power when it had been taken away from her so completely. It hurt to understand that her need for control had punished her aunt — someone who thrived on chaos and freedom — without even knowing it.

"I'm sorry," Alice blurted, reaching a hand out.

"Don't worry, I understand. But you can see why I think that your coming to visit my very disorganized home is out of character." Zara gave Alice a smile and then a hug. The warmth of the embrace made Alice feel like she was home; that she was loved. And she hadn't known how much she missed that sensation, of just being accepted for who she was.

"Work has been hard lately," Alice admitted, pulling away.

"Why?" Aunt Zara didn't necessarily approve of Alice's career choice, but she'd never spoken against it, either. Maybe she'd understood that Alice was trying to find peace with herself by working with the dead.

"Please don't tell anyone — I probably shouldn't tell you — but there've been some murders of vampires."

Zara rubbed at the bit of blue paint on her nose. "I've heard something along those lines. Word of aristo deaths travels quickly, even if they don't want it to. But why is that tough? They're vampires; a few less in the world can't be a bad thing. Too much work, is it?"

"They're still people, Aunt Z."

"True, but they're people with a thin veneer of civilization. You forget that most of my clients are aristo vamps, and I see what goes on in their estates, even at the palace."

Alice hadn't thought about that. Suddenly, she wondered what things her aunt *had* witnessed on her journeys. She opened her mouth, but her aunt raised a hand.

"I don't want to talk about it. If word got out, then they'd be able to work out who said what. And I like being alive."

Alice blew out a breath of air. "It's just...they're being murdered. Staked. It brings back memories, that's all."

There, she'd finally admitted it. She hadn't said anything to Tal, but Tal was now involved far deeper than Alice had ever thought she'd be. And she didn't want Tal worrying about her; the professor had other concerns.

Zara reached over and took Alice's hand, squeezing it. "You survived what happened to you. You're strong. You'll help stop this killer."

"I just wish they'd found Mother's murderer. Maybe then this wouldn't affect me so badly."

"We all wish they'd found her killer."

"And that we knew what happened to Ashok." Dead, alive, a

slave, or free. She had no idea.

"Some things are better lost than found." Aunt Zara let go of Alice's hand and sipped her tea.

Alice nearly dropped her mug. "Are you saying you'd prefer Ashok to stay missing?"

Zara wouldn't meet Alice's gaze, and she was quiet for a full minute. "There was something...not right with Ashok."

Alice wanted to stand up and yell that there had been nothing wrong with her brother. But Aunt Zara wasn't that kind of person. She was thoughtful, considerate and she'd never badmouth a family member, not unless there was a strong reason. And come to think of it, over the years, Zara had never really talked about Ashok much. He'd been her nephew just as much as Alice was her niece, but she hadn't really mourned his loss the way she mourned for her dead sister-in-law.

"What do you mean, 'not right'?" Alice asked.

"Your mother always used to say he didn't really think of people as if they were *people*. At least, that's what she thought. Ashok thought of people as things he could either own or use. He didn't have much time for you, so he largely pretended you didn't exist. I'd heard him even say he was an only child, back when you were ten and he was fourteen."

"That doesn't make him a bad person. And you don't know that he thought like that," Alice argued.

"No, but it does make him unstable. And they never found him after your mother was killed and you were stabbed. And I know the City Guard looked."

"I just...what are you saying?"

Aunt Zara pressed her lips together.

No.

Alice wouldn't believe it. Aunt Zara couldn't really think that it had been Ashok who'd hurt their mother. Even if he had had some problems, Alice couldn't see him ever wanting to hurt her, or their mother, who had been laughter and sunshine. Sure, Aunt Zara was right that Ashok had ignored her a lot, but she was four years younger than him; most older siblings didn't want anything to do with their annoying kid sisters or brothers.

Aunt Zara gave Alice a narrow look, but didn't say anything further. "So how is Talan going?"

She was clearly trying to change the topic and Alice let her. She didn't want to think about what her aunt had implied.

"Well, I think she's dating an aristo vampire."

"Talan?" Aunt Zara's jaw dropped. "Is dating a *vampire*?"

"Well, you know how Tal isn't too discriminating; if she likes the person, she likes the person."

"But a vampire?"

If she was honest, Alice also found it odd. Tal had had flings with vampires before, but she mostly dated humans. Then again, Alice didn't know everyone Tal had ever seen or slept with, nor did she want to.

"A vampire. An aristo."

"Dating? As in, in a relationship?"

Alice thought back to Tal's interactions with the viscountess; yes, they were heading into a relationship, even if they hadn't acknowledged it yet.

"Wait until Talan's mother finds out."

"No! You can't tell her."

"Why not?"

"Because you would be the worst aunty on the planet, ever."

"Really?"

"Really."

"Hrm."

"And Tal would kill me."

Aunt Zara burst out laughing, and Alice chuckled too. Suddenly the world seemed a little bit brighter.

CHAPTER FORTY-FOUR

"So Randall touched you — that sounds perverted, but let's move on — put you in the cells, tried to convince you to *marry* him, then admitted he was going to kill you both?" Montrose's dark eyebrows were nearly at her hairline as she ticked off the list of events.

"That about sums it up," Fin said, crossing his ankles. The heavy metal desk was between the three of them and the disbelieving vampire, and Fin was glad of it. Not that he doubted Montrose could leap the desk in a second and attack them if she chose, but it gave him a false peace of mind he wasn't going to argue with. He didn't trust Montrose — was that her first name or her last name? — and he didn't know what the woman felt about Hannah, or how loyal she was to Tatiana. Sure, Hannah seemed to trust her, but then, Hannah hadn't expected Randall to attack them, either.

He avoided Hannah's eyes, simply because he didn't know what to say to her. "I'm sorry you ripped a guy's heart out of his chest," just didn't have the right ring to it. To be fair, he didn't know what to think. He'd never seen anything like that before, and he'd seen some pretty fucked up shit.

But Fin hadn't believed Hannah would be capable of something like that, which told him how much of an idiot he was. Hannah was a vampire, no matter that she rescued babies off the sides of mountains. Well, one baby off the side of one mountain, but whatever. She might seem human, but she wasn't.

Montrose shook her head in disbelief. "I don't understand what he thought he could gain."

"He thought that he would inherit my fortune with me dead," Hannah said, "and that if Mother suspected anything, he could kill her, then he would inherit the duchy, too."

Montrose gave a humorless laugh. "He thought he could *kill* Tatiana Romanov?"

"I didn't say he had a good plan," Hannah said.

"Kill Tatiana..." Montrose shook her head in something like wonder.

Byrne let out a low whistle. "I leave you guys alone for a few hours and you descend into utter chaos."

"It wasn't my fault!" Fin snapped.

Byrne turned his steady yellow gaze on him. "I didn't say it was."

"You implied that it was Hannah's and my fault. We can't help it that we were attacked."

"You're overreacting."

"You're—"

"Enough!" Montrose's voice lashed out. She was rubbing her temples. "You three are giving me a headache."

"Vampires don't get headaches," Fin said. Then he tapped his chin. "At least, I don't think they do. You don't get headaches, do you, Byrne?" Weres and vampires had similar healing abilities, so Fin reckoned the same rules should apply.

"I have had a constant headache since the moment I met you."

Fin stuck his tongue out. "Oh, funny."

"How did you travel with these two and *not* kill them?" Montrose asked Hannah. It occurred to Fin the older vampire was serious. He shifted uncomfortably on the chair.

Hannah sighed. "I had the baby to care for."

Montrose's face went curiously blank. "Baby? Is this Rena?"

"Yeah, Hannah's a mother," Fin added with a grin. So he wanted to mess with the vampire a little. Sue him.

"You had a *baby*? How did you even get close enough..." Montrose turned her mauve eyes on Fin, the stare turning incredulous. "You? You're the father?"

"Me?" Fin squeaked.

Byrne laughed, the sound booming through the room. He slapped a hand on his thigh. "This is fantastic."

Fin glared. "Byrne!"

"I found the baby," Hannah said, ignoring the two of them.

"You *found* a baby? So it's not yours? You can't just take babies. Where are its parents?"

"No, the Trsetti had abandoned her to the Old Mother. I found her on the slopes, and brought her here." Hannah's jaw set. "I'm not taking her back."

"She's ours," Fin added. To his side, Byrne nodded.

Hannah gave them both an odd look. Fin didn't care that she'd technically been the one to find the little girl; Fin and Byrne had known Rena almost as long as Hannah. The baby was theirs.

"So, you brought the infant here. With these two," Montrose said. "What are you planning on doing next? You have a plan, I hope."

"Well, I was thinking of getting Mother's help, but she isn't here. Randall said she's visiting my brother, but that's ridiculous."

"Ridiculous?"

Hannah clasped her hands together, the skin stretching taut over her knuckles. "That she's visiting my brother. I mean, all my siblings are dead, right?"

Man, this is going to be tough, Fin thought. He had four sisters, and they were hard enough to deal with at the best of times, although he did love them. Usually. But to not know you even had any brothers or sisters, and then for it to be sprung on you? Some people wouldn't care, but someone like Hannah — who'd been isolated nearly her whole life — would. She'd care a lot.

Montrose glanced at Fin and Byrne, before letting her gaze rest on Hannah.

Oh boy, Hannah really does have a missing brother.

"It's not ridiculous..." Montrose said.

"Randall wasn't lying? I have a brother?"

Montrose sighed. "You have a brother."

"Why didn't Mother tell me? Why didn't *anyone* tell me?" Hannah stood up, and went to slam her hands down on the desk but stopped and wrenched her arms back angrily.

"Your mother signed a breeding contract with an earl in Pinton. If a male child was born of their union, the earl would have custody of the infant until it reached its majority. Tatiana was planning on staying in Pinton until the babe grew of age, but she didn't expect there to be two children."

"Two?" Hannah repeated.

"As in twins?" Fin asked.

Montrose shot him a dark look. He ignored it. Well, pretended to, anyway. He was pretty glad Byrne was in the room, even though the were had barely spoken. But Byrne didn't really need to. His presence alone spoke volumes.

"As in twins, yes. And when you were born and Tatiana saw your eye color...she abandoned her plans to oversee Dante's childhood and moved back here."

"I have a twin brother. Wait — he's *normal*?" Hannah's beautiful face went slack, then tight with anger.

"Well, normal might be exaggerating things. I've been keeping tabs on him over the years, and he's a bit eccentric. But he had purple eyes, and no obvious Graced abilities. He recently got himself into a bit of trouble, so your mother went to check things out now he has reached his majority."

"A bit of trouble? Eccentric?"

"He seems to be a psychopath or sociopath, from the reports, although he doesn't go around killing people...often. He is apparently very intelligent and is interested in human anatomy. He has another sister from his father's side, and was recently married to a human baron. And he just Chose his first human."

Fin listened attentively to the report. It was clinical and to the point, and he was sure that reflected Montrose's personality, rather than anything else in particular. "So you're saying he's like the duchess?"

Montrose whipped her head around to glare at him. "What did you just say?"

"Montrose—" Hannah said.

"This human just called your mother a psychopath."

"I could have meant that she was very intelligent," Fin said.

"Do *not* take me for a fool."

"I would never," Fin agreed. He may be a smartass, but he wasn't stupid.

Byrne snorted.

"Well," Hannah rubbed a hand over the back of her neck as she sat back down in her chair. "Mother is both."

"Hmmph. You can't allow outsiders to speak of her with disrespect."

"I don't think Fin and Byrne are outsiders anymore," Hannah muttered. "Byrne, where's Rena?"

"Yeah, where is she?" Fin asked, leaning around Hannah to glare at his friend. "You can't just leave babies by themselves!"

"She's back at the inn. I left her with a...friend's sister, who also happened to be in town."

Fin wanted to question Byrne more about that, but didn't get the chance.

"Okay, so first thing's first," Montrose held up a hand. "Get the baby and bring it back here. I will organize things for your journey, because I presume you are going to still go after your mother?"

Hannah looked at Montrose. Did Fin detect a hopeful gleam in her eyes? "Do you know how to look after babies?"

Montrose snorted. "That can be your mother's problem. I'm no babysitter."

Hannah looked uncertain. "I guess I should meet my brother. Dante, you said his name was?"

"Dante Daemon Ernest Romanov Kipling."

"Right. Why didn't Mother ever tell me about him?"

Montrose looked to the bookshelves. "That is something you'll have to ask her."

Byrne stood. "I'll get the baby. If I come back here and

anything has happened to these two, I will hold you responsible." The large were pointed a finger at Montrose. "I have had a shit day and I should be hibernating, so don't piss me off." With that, he turned on his heel and headed for the door.

Succinct as always. Fin liked that about the bear.

"Are you angry?" he asked Hannah. He would be, if he was her. Kidnapped by her mother's retainers, held in a cell, touched against her will, all to find out that she had a *twin brother* she never knew anything about.

She met his gaze, her Black eyes unreadable. "Furious."

PART III

Nothing endures but change

CHAPTER FORTY-FIVE

Pinton-Skarva Road

They'd been back on the road for five days. They had two horses now, since Hannah had insisted on keeping their semi-covered wagon, rather than riding in the nicely sprung carriage that Montrose had offered. And so Montrose had insisted they take another horse. Byrne had kind of hoped they'd get the nice ride, since it would give his butt a bit of a break. But Hannah had worried about touching anything in the carriage, so that was a no.

At least poor Baldy got time to rest now; she was only harnessed to the wagon for half a day, and could then plod alongside for the other half, flicking her tail in irritation whenever the stupid goat got too close. The new chestnut mare, Foxtrot, didn't like Byrne much more than Baldy did, but now that Fin was up and about, he could make the human harness the horses each day. Saved Byrne from feeling like a complete dick, chasing the beasts around and scaring them.

The gravel road this far out of Pinton was littered with potholes and lined with large oak trees, so the cart ride was bumpy, since they didn't have much room to maneuver around them. There wasn't much traffic, so Byrne directed the horses down the center of the road for the most part. He could smell that they were approaching a small town on the outskirts of a large vampire estate. The icy-cool odor of vampires hung in the air, indicating that there were a number of them congregated together. With so many around, it was unlikely that they'd have were-friendly establishments a day's ride away from Pinton, and Byrne doubted he'd be sleeping in an inn when they got to the town.

The journey from Skarva had felt like six bloody weeks, with Fin's stupid non-stop chattering. The human was talking more than he normally did, like he was trying to cover something up, but Byrne hadn't been able to work out what that was. The only time he shut up was when Rena was sleeping restlessly.

Hannah was no different; perhaps a little quieter than normal, but then, she didn't say much at the best of times. That's why he preferred her as a traveling companion. She knew when to keep her trap shut.

Still, he reckoned Hannah should probably talk about what had happened to her at her mother's estate. Being attacked and then ripping a guy's heart of his chest weren't things that happened to people like Hannah very often. But then, he was hardly one to preach about sharing. He hadn't told anyone about the things that had happened to him while he'd been imprisoned for a hundred years, and he'd been set free three years ago. Hypocrite extraordinaire.

Well, Fin knew a bit about it, but that was only because the human had freed him. He'd seen Byrne chained to a wall, drugged with regular doses of soluble silver to keep him weak. Seen how one of the women in particular treated him...Bile surged to the back of Byrne's throat. She'd thought that Fin had wanted to join them, be part of their sick little fantasy world, where they wanted to create the ultimate Graced.

But Fin wasn't like that.

Byrne hadn't known that at first, because the human had played along, acted like he was into torture and the idea of immortal Graceds. As a result, Byrne had wanted to tear Fin's throat out just as much as he had the bitches who held him prisoner. For a week, Fin had danced to their tunes, but he'd never actually hurt Byrne, claiming he got off on watching the 'experiments', rather than doing them himself.

Byrne could still remember the smell of the place: pain, blood, sweat, death, and silver, all intertwined with the odor of lust. Not his, though. Never his. The were hadn't thought he'd ever be able to look Fin in the face again, not after what the human had seen happen. But then Fin had showed up downstairs in the dungeon with a set of keys. He'd jangled them against the bars of his cell, then given Byrne that cocky grin, the one he'd wanted to rip off the human's face.

"Freedom is within your grasp," Fin had said. "But there's one condition."

"Fuck off."

"I'm not lying to you, I will set you free."

Byrne had shut his eyes, convinced this was another prank. Another 'test.' But he'd learned his lesson. Play along, at least as much as he could tolerate. And right then, Fin hadn't actually been doing anything to him. "Okay, what's the condition?"

"That you don't kill me, or hurt me."

Opening his eyes, he'd stared at the human, at the pretty golden blond hair and those Hazel eyes. "Since you aren't going to let me go, I don't really see why I should agree to that."

Fin had opened the cell door, and Byrne had strained against the chains, silver wires digging into his flesh. Then the human had stepped inside. Byrne had partially changed in response, even with the silver burning his wrists and legs, even with the silver burning him from the inside out. But he'd been so weak, he'd only managed claws and fangs.

"I will let you go, but you can't hurt me. I'm going to get you out of here." Fin had been standing close to him by then, too close. Byrne had been able to smell his aftershave, which had a hint of sandalwood and something else, something like verbena. He didn't stink of rot or decay, or even anger, like some of the humans there.

"Fine, if you let me go, I won't hurt you."

Then Fin had done the stupidest thing in his short life that far. He'd unlocked the shackles holding Byrne. At first, the were hadn't believed what had happened. One hundred fucking years of being chained in the cell — they hadn't dared move him after they got him inside — and with a flick of the wrists from some pretty boy, he'd been freed.

He'd grabbed Fin by the throat, hauling him into the air. Even poisoned by silver, he'd still been stronger than the human. Gasping, legs swinging, Fin had gripped Byrne's arm in an attempt to stop himself from choking.

"You said...you...wouldn't...hurt me."

Byrne had grunted. "I lied."

But something in the human's eyes had stopped him from squeezing the life out of him, even though he'd wanted to. Although sometimes even now he wished he had, but that was more to stop Fin's blathering than anything else.

"As long as you don't stop me, you can live." Byrne had lowered Fin to the ground. Well, lowered, dropped, it was much the same thing.

"Stop you from what?" Fin had asked, crouching on the ground and rubbing his throat.

There'd been footsteps, and then a gasp as his tormentor had arrived and seen what Fin had done. Her Green eyes had focused on Fin, but he hadn't been affected by whatever mind games she was trying to play.

"What have you done?!" she shrieked.

But Fin hadn't been listening. "Stop you from what?" he'd asked Byrne again.

Byrne had smiled then, grinned for the first time in a hundred years. "From killing every person here."

◆

"Yo, Byrne, did you hear a word I just said?"

Byrne turned in his seat and met the annoyed gaze of his human buddy. "No."

He was still meant to be driving the cart, but Foxtrot hadn't seemed to notice his inattention. The horse was still walking along, tail swishing, heading straight down the road. There wasn't any other traffic, so it wasn't like Byrne had to concentrate, thank goodness. But still, he shouldn't let his mind wander so much.

"I didn't think so. You had this feral grin on your face." Fin leaned over the back of the cart's seat, lowering his voice. "Were you thinking about your escape again? You always grin like that when you think about killing all those people."

Byrne frowned.

"Killing who what now?" Hannah called from the back of the cart. She had Rena tucked in a sling around her, makeshift leather teat held in one hand.

"Can't keep your fucking mouth shut, can you, Fin?" Byrne growled.

"What?" Fin shrugged. "I whispered."

"And she's the daughter of a first generation vampire. You're gonna have to do better than that."

"Gee. Relax. It's all good." Fin returned to the back of the cart again. "She won't care that you killed a bunch of people."

With a growl, Byrne turned his attention back to the road.

"I won't care that he killed *a bunch* of people?"

"Fin!"

"What? You told her about your being held prisoner. She'll understand."

"I killed *one person*, Fin. *One.*" Hannah's voice rose a little as she spoke. She was getting annoyed at the human, too.

Good.

"And I didn't say you did the wrong thing," Fin said. "I just didn't think that you'd care that Byrne killed the people who held him captive for a century. Hypocrisy isn't pretty."

Byrne could literally *hear* the blasted human shrug.

"You said a bunch of humans," Hannah replied. "And I *care* that I killed someone!"

Suddenly Byrne understood what Fin was doing. That sly little prick. He was trying to force Hannah into talking about what had happened to her, by using Byrne's history as bait.

"I didn't say that Byrne didn't care that he killed a bunch of humans."

"Well, they were Graceds," Byrne said. He clicked Foxtrot along; at the back of the cart, the goat gave a bleat of protest at the slight increase in speed. "And no, I didn't really care that I killed them. Still kinda happy about it."

"Byrne!" Hannah cried, shocked.

"What? They held me captive for a century. They did horrible things to me, to say the least. I only wish I could have gone back in time and killed the fuckers who took me in the first place."

Rena wailed. The conversation had distracted Hannah, and the baby still needed feeding.

"Here, give her to me," Fin said and plucked the baby from Hannah's grip. He cooed at the little girl and then all but wrested the teat from Hannah's hand.

Hannah glowered at Fin. "Don't touch me!"

"Sorry sweetie, but that rule doesn't apply to me anymore." The shit-eating grin was back. Byrne let out a whistle.

"Why you little—"

"Come on, 'little' is not an adjective that should be used to describe me, in *any* way shape or form." Fin held the teat for Rena, who protested for a little longer, then realized that the food was there for the taking. The human clucked.

Byrne imagined he could see steam pouring from Hannah's ears. He turned back to the roadway.

"How have you *not* killed him by now?" Hannah demanded.

He pursed his lips, pretended to think about it for a bit. "Sheer willpower."

"Thanks. So it's okay to talk about killing me — your savior, for *both* of you — but killing that stupid dick is something to be upset about?" Fin sounded like he was pouting.

"You're annoying," Hannah said.

"So? Randall was an idiot."

"Just because he was an idiot doesn't excuse me killing him."

"But me being annoying is reason enough?"

"Argh!"

From the back of the cart came the noise of something being thrown. It had to be Hannah lobbing something at Fin. Fin was holding a baby, after all.

"If you're going to throw clothing," the human muttered, "make it your bra or underwear or something. Vomit covered shirts are a tad disgusting."

"You never know when to give up, do you?" Byrne asked.

"What? She's the one throwing her clothes at me. I'm only providing suggestions as to how that could be improved."

"You are *such* a sleaze," Hannah growled.

"I can't help it if I'm that attractive to women. And some men too, I might add. I'm a panty-dropper for all genders."

"And modest, too," Byrne said with a nod.

"Modesty has nothing to do with it."

"Can you just be serious for five minutes?" Hannah demanded.

"Sure."

And then there was silence for an instant. It broke when Fin opened his bloody mouth again.

"Fine. You want serious? Yes, you killed that guy, but he was going to murder us both. You *know* he was. He betrayed your mother, and guess what? She wouldn't have let the bastard live. And you were right, when you said that what you'd done to him was far kinder than what your mother would do. So in the end, you probably saved him a lot of pain. Imagine what Montrose is doing to those poor fuckers down in the cells. You think she's going to be offering them puppies to cuddle? If they're lucky, she won't torture them until your mother returns."

Hannah swallowed. "But *I* killed him."

"If he hadn't made a stupid decision to put his life on the line for personal ambition, then he would still be alive. But he didn't. *He* made the choice to come after you."

Byrne kept his eyes on the road, but he wished he could see Hannah's face. It was a rare event indeed, when Fin spoke the truth, but when he did, he sure didn't hold back. Byrne had needed to hear some hard truths himself once or twice. Fin may be a flirt and act like a bit of a ninnyhammer, but he was sharp. Even Byrne forgot that from time to time.

"And you're both fucking vampires," Fin went on. "What do you think happens when vamps piss each other off?

"They kill each other," Hannah said softly.

Fin lifted Rena up and patted her on the back. "And what did he do to you?"

"He kidnapped me."

"And do you think *any other vampire,* or were, would let him live after that?"

"No..."

Then Rena burped, and the smell of milk vomit wafted through the air.

Fin sighed. "I need a new shirt."

CHAPTER FORTY-SIX

Hannah found herself watching as Fin pulled off his vomit-stained shirt. Her mouth went dry as she took in the hard planes of his shoulders and then, when he turned, her eyes trailed down his smooth abdominal muscles and to the golden line of hair that travelled to his waistband. His tattoo — all swirling lines — covered his whole arm and the top of his right pec.

Fin's voice penetrated her thoughts. "It is a pretty good view, I admit it."

Cheeks pinkening, Hannah quickly looked down at Rena. Fin had handed the baby back to her, and Rena had heaved a sigh and then shut her eyes, milk leaking out the side of her mouth. Hannah wiped it away with the shirt she'd thrown at Fin.

Up front, Byrne snorted derisively at Fin's comment, and Hannah hoped the bear hadn't heard her heartbeat accelerate, too. For the past five days, she'd tried to avoid the thought of being able to touch Fin, or possibly Byrne. The idea that there was someone she could have physical contact with and not have to worry about it, someone she could touch and not be terrified of losing herself, or of learning far too much about them...

It changed things.

She wished it didn't, but it did. Before, she'd been able to ignore Fin's charming, annoying self, because she knew nothing could ever come of it. Hannah could simply admire the pretty face that was emerging from the bruising, appreciate the way his muscles moved when he tended to tiny Rena, and enjoy his sense of humor, even if she pretended otherwise. But now there was *possibility*, and that scared her.

Sure, she'd had sex before; it had been awkward and messy but still kind of fun. Except the downside had been knowing everything about her partner. At the time, she'd been fifty, and living back in Skarva with her mother, testing her ability. She'd spotted the handsome human on the other side of the room and had been instantly smitten. He'd been wearing a gorgeous navy blue suit, with crimson waistcoat and snowy white cravat. His black hair had been swept back off his brow with a pomade that smelled like oranges. She'd been wearing a high-waisted pale green gown, but no corset — she'd made the gown herself, but hadn't wanted to make the stays as well. At the time, it had been fashionable for young women to faint when speaking to handsome men, so when Evan — that had been his name — had clasped her hand to politely say hello, clearly unaware of the taboo of touching the duchess' daughter, no one had commented when she'd passed out. Him being human, and only twenty-two, his memories had been easy enough for her to deal with. She'd known he thought her pretty, and that he wished to get to know her better.

Later, in her room, his life had unfolded before her eyes. He was a nice man, interested in securing himself a good future, but he wasn't ambitious. And he hadn't known who she was. That had been one of his greatest appeals, aside from the fact that he was so handsome he'd made her heart all fluttery.

She'd been naïve back then.

They'd started seeing each other secretly. Hannah knew her mother wouldn't approve — more because Tatiana was overprotective, than because she'd have any real objections to Evan. He was human, of merchant stock, and had money. There was nothing to disapprove of, aside from his mortality, which might one day be fixed, given that he had lovely, chocolate Brown eyes. Every time they touched, she'd absorbed the new memories he'd made since their last meeting. It had been flattering at first. And heady. Evan thought her beautiful, smart, the most wonderful woman around. He didn't necessarily tell her these things; oh, he'd flatter her, but he played it cool. He hadn't wanted to come across as too needy. Too bad for him that she knew what he really thought about her; how much he treasured the stolen kisses and cuddles.

She'd thought him handsome, clever and funny. But looking back, she wasn't sure how much of her infatuation had been caused by knowing how he viewed her. Knowing someone was half in love with you changed how you felt about them.

After a month, they progressed their relationship, moving on from stolen caresses, cuddles, or kisses. Hidden in one of the rooms at the Duchess of Roses' estate, with her mother absent, Hannah and Evan had made love. She already knew about the mechanics of it, but it hadn't quite lived up to her expectations. But then, whose first time really did? She'd seen enough in people's memories to understand that much.

But afterward, Evan had lied to her.

He'd told her she was his first lover, and that he wanted to spend the rest of his life with her. Oh, she knew he'd wanted to marry her then, but Hannah had known for a fact that he hadn't been a virgin. When Evan was fifteen, he'd had sex with the local barmaid. And when he was sixteen, the seamstress' daughter. In fact, he'd slept with a new girl from his town almost every other year. He'd date them for a while, but he never promised them anything more, and he liked to think they'd understood. But Hannah had seen his memories and the looks on the girls' faces, and she didn't think they had.

To say Hannah hadn't cared when she'd discovered his...proclivity...would be a lie. Having the memory of all those other times with other girls flash through her mind had caused jealousy to rear its ugly head. She knew exactly how soft their skin was, how sweet they smelled, but also that he hadn't felt the same way about those other girls as he did with Hannah. And so she'd told herself to move past it. *She* was the woman he was falling in love with, not that barmaid with the generous bosom, or the seamstress' daughter with the large hips, or the squire's daughter with the rounded butt. But it didn't help that each one of those girls had something that Hannah was all too aware she was lacking.

Curves.

Evan hadn't known about her ability, just that she was 'delicate', and so she hadn't been able to call him on his lies. Because how else could she have known? He'd fumbled and pretended to not really know what he was doing when they'd first made love, and she'd thought that kind of sweet. He quickly dropped the act, though, the longer they dated, growing more confident. But as one month turned into two, Hannah witnessed his infatuation with her changing.

In her room at night, she'd see how he found her a little too skinny when he clasped her waist, or how her breasts didn't overflow his hands when he caressed them. She'd see his memories, as he compared her to his other lovers: how she didn't please him like the other girls had. But those other girls had all been slightly desperate, willing to do whatever they could to keep him. They'd seen him as their way to advance in the world, and he'd seen them as fun. So whenever he'd asked them to do something, they had generally done it. Or he'd leave them.

That's why he'd left so many broken hearts behind.

With Hannah, he didn't dare do that, and she could see the lack of power bothered him. Soon, it was obvious that she was physically *much* stronger than him, too. Once, he'd wanted to play-wrestle with her, and she hadn't known she should pretend to be weak to please him. She'd won. Easily. He was human, she was a vampire; she hadn't been able to understand how he'd been foolish enough to think that it would be an even match, even if he was male and she female.

That memory in particular had burned. His pride had been stung, even though he never admitted it to her, and had laughed the incident away. In person, Evan was always kind and caring and solicitous. He never said a bad word to her, acted loving and like she'd hung the moon herself. But she knew what he thought, and it ate at her. Nibbled away her self-confidence, until she hadn't known what to do. She didn't want to be like the other girls, the ones who'd made him happy until they didn't. She wanted to be Hannah. And it was then she realized she could *never be* Hannah with him: the vampire daughter of Tatiana Romanov, a girl who couldn't touch people or things.

Evan had grown suspicious of why she wore the same three dresses over and over. He'd thought she might be a little simple-minded or eccentric, since her mother clearly had the money to dress her well. He picked apart her behavior in his mind, until she grew so paranoid her mother stepped in.

And things never ended well when the Deadly Duchess got involved.

Evan had survived, but only because Hannah had ended their relationship. She didn't think he'd minded too much in the end, especially when he found himself the focus of her mother's attention. Within a year, he'd married a rich human aristo woman who had an abundant chest, large hips and generous behind, and they'd produced several offspring. Now, now he was just bones in the dirt.

Hannah sighed. Wasn't that just like her life? Sad. The only man she'd ever half-fallen in love with was long dead, and she was still alone. Alone and pondering a man who was completely wrong for her.

She studied Fin out of the corner of her eyes, hoping not to get caught — the bastard always seemed to know when she was staring. Mentally she ticked off the pros and cons of a relationship with him:

Pros
He had a mental shield
He was *nice* to her
He was clever, even though he pretended otherwise
He was very ~~pretty~~ handsome
He had nice straight teeth

He was good with babies
He was funny
He had soft lips

Cons
He talked way too much
He could be really annoying
He broke too easily
He snored
His favorite topic of conversation was himself
He currently had a beard
He might not actually like her

Hrm. Should the beard go in the pro column? She'd have a think on it.

What are you doing?

Are you an idiot? Maybe you didn't pay attention to the last item in the cons section?

Her argumentative mind had a point, Hannah conceded. She had no idea if Fin would even *want* to be with her physically. He'd pushed her away when she'd kissed him in the cells. Maybe it was because the timing had been terrible — it had been — but maybe it was because he didn't think of Hannah like that. She was tall and gangly and had strange eyes. Sure, she knew Evan had found her pretty, but when you wanted to sleep with someone, you generally needed to find them attractive.

A voice spoke next to her ear, soft and breathy. "Hannah, why are you staring at me?"

Hannah jolted and was seized with concern that she'd squeezed Rena, accidentally hurting the baby. But the child slept soundly in her swaddling, her little snub nose slightly red in the cool air. Hannah rubbed it gently with her gloved finger.

Fin had come up in the back of the wagon to sit next to her. Warmth radiated from him, and she found herself wanting to just lean against him. Feel some of his heat, without absorbing anything else.

"I was thinking, I wasn't staring at you," Hannah replied automatically. How did he always *know*?

"I wouldn't blame you if you were..." His breath smelled like mint. Where did he get mint leaves?

"Give it a rest."

"What were you thinking about? You were frowning, and it was kinda scary. That's why I moved out of your line of sight." He grinned then, and it was charming. How he'd managed not to lose a tooth in the recent beatings, she didn't know. Just lucky, she guessed.

"I do not look scary when I frown." This close, the bruise she'd given him on his cheek looked awful.

Gingerly, she reached out and touched the discoloration that showed through the blond hair on his jaw. Hissing, Fin jerked his head back.

"Sorry," Hannah said.

"You weren't thinking about *that* were you?" Fin rubbed a hand over his other cheek awkwardly.

Hannah resettled Rena, resting the baby against her chest. Maybe that would keep her little nose warm. "Thinking about what?"

"The cells."

"Uhh—"

"Don't feel bad for hitting me. I did touch you to wake you up. You were just quicker than I thought."

"Okay."

"Okay, what?"

"I won't feel bad then."

Byrne gave a short, sharp laugh; even though they spoke quietly, he could still hear them. "I don't think it was bothering her that much," he rumbled.

"Then what else...oh." Fin looked down at his feet, actually stared at them quite intently.

"What?"

"Nothing."

"It can't be nothing. You never have nothing to say," Hannah said.

"I said nothing."

"Hannah's right. You always have some bullshit to blather about," Byrne said from the driver's seat.

"I do not."

"Do too."

"So what was it?" Hannah asked.

"I can't remember now," Fin said, still looking at his feet. Maybe he needed to buy a new pair of boots? "All your accusations made me forget."

CHAPTER FORTY-SEVEN

Pinton City

Alice rubbed her eyes. Time to get back on track. The killer hadn't struck for five days now, and she worried that meant another body would be discovered soon. After all, the killer had barely waited between the first victim and the second. She'd spent the time trying to find a clue — any clue. Maybe there was something about the bodies of the victims that she'd missed, something that could tell her more about the killer.

Looking down at the notes on each of the murder victims, she began flicking through the pages. Comparing things like age, height, weight, position of body when found. State of body, number of wounds. Some of the guards had argued that the countess had been killed by a different individual, because she had more stab wounds than the others, but Alice wasn't so sure. The trauma induced by each staking had been similar, implying to her that the killer had used the same amount of force.

Alice also had the theory that the murderer had delivered the 'death blow' first — the heart strike — otherwise, the countess would have fought back. That would have left the killer with a lot of physical damage; even decadent aristos knew how to hurt people, if push came to shove. If the murderer was a vampire — and she had a hunch they weren't — then they would have recovered quickly from the attack. But if they were human, then their wounds would have been apparent and that could have raised suspicions, depending on their standing within society. To avoid that, they would have had to kill or incapacitate the countess first, then deliver the other blows.

The woman's other wounds had bled — there was visible clotting — but the allergic reaction at these sites had been less severe when compared to the one at the heart. Most vampires could heal from a stake wound to the torso, unless the heart was compromised. Alice had read of some rare cases in medical journals where death had been caused through exposure of any internal organ to wood, but they were definitely not the standard.

So like the other victims, the countess had died from a stake to the heart, but she'd also been subject to three other wounds after the heart had been targeted. Why?

And then there was the dust found on two of the victims. Under magnification, it looked like plant cells. She needed to get her hands on some more textbooks, to identify the exact cell type. It was very possible the powder was snuff. But could the dust have been from contamination of some kind — maybe the transport method?

"Knock knock," a voice said, interrupting her thoughts.

Looking up, Alice smiled at Tal, who stood in the doorway. She was wearing a bright yellow skirt, and a white shirt with a flow of delicate ruffles that hid the buttons at the front of the garment. Over the shirt, she wore a gray jacket, which matched her eyes. Tal gave her a large smile in return; after all the drama of the last few days, Alice hadn't expected that kind of reaction. She knew that Tal had been spending quite a bit of time with the viscountess — Tal had blown her off from their usual third-day dinner date — and Alice had figured it had to be tough for Tal, helping someone through the grieving process.

After all, she had been through it herself.

"You're making these visits rather regularly nowadays," she said. Tal would occasionally come visit Alice at work, but usually to collect her for dinner, or a catch up and a coffee or tea. Not just for a chat.

Her friend stepped further into the room, then held up a paper bag. "I come bearing samples."

"Samples?"

"Semen samples," Tal said, depositing the bag next to Alice's notes with a flourish.

"You managed to get all three?" Alice moved her notes aside, keeping them carefully piled in chronological order. Once she knew more about the crimes, she might find a different system for them, but for now, this would have to do. Alice then ensured the piles of paperwork were all evenly stacked. She could feel Tal watching her, but her friend didn't say anything.

Tal shrugged, tapping her fingers absentmindedly on the stone bench as Alice stood on tiptoes to take a microscope off a shelf. "I could only get two of the three; human and vampire. I thought you might be able to ask your friend, Elle, if her fiancé or whatever he is, would agree to provide a were sample."

Alice snorted. "I can just imagine how that conversation would go. I like not having a black eye."

She didn't know how Elle would really react, but Alice couldn't picture approaching the city guard with that request and not insulting her or her fiancé.

Opening the bag, Alice saw two glass jars sitting side by side. One had 'human' scrawled on a label on the cap, the other had 'vampire.' The writing wasn't Tal's. "How'd you manage to get these, anyway? And how old are they?"

Tal stole Alice's seat, her skirts swooshing around her gently as she did so. "I was told they were done this morning; it's what Professor Monteray recommended."

"Professor Monteray?"

"He's the new medical professor at the university, apparently transferred over from Varsh, thick accent," Tal said.

That's right, Alice, recalled, he was new to the university. Professor Retman had been in charge of the medical school when she'd attended, but that was a few years ago now. She should probably maintain her ties with the university, but she worked with the dead, not with live patients, so didn't need to know about the latest advances in surgery.

"His focus is on surgical procedures, I think, and doesn't have much time for clinical analysis," Tal went on. "That's what one of his students told me, anyway. When I spoke to him, he spent a lot of time talking about how he is trying to ensure that patients don't die during the operating procedure. I didn't dare enquire as to what he was operating on them *for*.

"I asked him if he would be able to obtain some samples for me, for an experiment you were running. He'd heard of you, and so was willing to get me what you needed, provided you let him know if there were any worthwhile results."

"How'd he get the vampire sample? I presume a student?" Alice asked, although, there couldn't be too many vampire medical students. Aside from their wood allergy, vampires didn't tend to get sick, and so didn't really enroll in medicine as a career. That didn't mean it didn't happen, just that it was rare.

"He doesn't have any vampire students," Tal answered. "His research assistant provided the human sample, and well, the vampire sample is his."

The professor was a vampire? Huh. She hadn't realized that. With the microscope set up, Alice opened a drawer, and selected two glass pipettes and four slides. The slides were cold, she hoped that didn't matter. She opened the jar labeled 'vampire', used the pipette to draw out a sample, then dripped three drops of the semen onto the glass slide and diluted it with distilled water.

Alice paused as she picked up the glass slide, but then quickly placed it under the microscope. She focused the lens, and squinted down the eyepiece, concentrating. The shape of this vampire sperm was different to the specimen she'd examined from the last autopsy. Well, all three autopsies; the samples had been the same from all the victims. But that had just meant that it was someone from the same species — potentially — committing the crimes, not necessarily the same person.

This was different.

The head of each sperm cell on the slide was larger, and ended in a pointed tip, compared to the oval shape of the other sample she'd drawn. The mid connecting piece was thicker, and the tail longer — definitely different to the sperm she had recorded from the murder victims. She reached for a pencil and paper and sketched what she saw down the eyepiece. When she was done, she removed the slide, then repeated the process for the jar with the 'human' label. Aunt Zara's drawing lessons were still useful.

"So?" Tal asked, when at last Alice lifted her head from the microscope.

"They are definitely different." She opened up a file and took out a sheet of paper. "This is a drawing of the sample I got from the murder victims," she said.

Tal stared at the picture of the cell. "Okay."

"That matches the human sample provided to me by Professor Monteray. This is the vampire sample he gave me." She handed over the new sketch. Alice tried not to think about the fact that the sample belonged to the head of the medicine school at the university.

Tal studied it. "All right. So do you still need the were sample?"

Alice shook her head. "I don't think so, not when the human sample here matches so closely to the ones from the victims. Normally, I'd need a much larger sample size than this, but we're pressed for time. Besides, what if the were samples all vary?"

"What do you mean?"

"Like different sperm for wolves, leopards, bears..."

"Maybe that should be a student's thesis with the university."

"You could suggest it to the professor."

"No," Tal said, sliding off the chair. "But you could."

"Hah. But at least we know one thing," Alice said.

"Yes?"

"Unless were cells are identical to human's, which I seriously doubt, the killer is human."

"So now the guards just need to find a human who lives in Pinton, and who happens to have a grudge against vampire aristos."

"That won't be difficult *at all*," Alice said with a sigh.

CHAPTER FORTY-EIGHT

Whiteoak Hamlet

Byrne and Fin hauled the last of their gear into the room they'd rented at the inn. Well, technically it was Byrne who was doing most of the hauling. He was loaded down with canvas bags, while Fin was puffed just from climbing the stone staircase, and was secretly hoping for a steaming hipbath. To think, a staircase was too much for him. But then, he did have broken ribs.

Stupid Trsetti.

Stupid Byrne.

And maybe, stupid Fin. It might have been a little bit his fault, too. But he'd never admit that to the bloody were.

The inn wasn't bad — actually, it was pretty good for a small town; it was clean, tidy and had decent bed linen — but it only had one person behind the bar. Still, it was a quiet night, the air cold and crisp, laced with a strong scent of woodsmoke, so the taproom wasn't too busy. Maybe he wouldn't be completely out of luck; a hipbath might be possible.

"Why did I have to carry all the bags?" Byrne asked, bending to avoid the doorframe as he stepped into their room.

"Because I have broken ribs?" Fin said. Plus, he was carrying Rena, all swaddled up in a basket. He set her down a few feet away from the hearth on the woven floor rug, and then knelt down with a groan to set the fire. Rena would need the warmth; on other nights, they'd made a special lean-to for her, and had built a campfire. Fin had taken to sleeping with the baby tucked under his arm, but getting her a proper bath and an enclosed room would be better. She was only two weeks old, and had already travelled further than most adults in their entire lives. Not as much as Fin, but then, few people had.

Most weren't running away from their past.

Byrne set their gear down, then crouched next to Rena and rubbed a big hand over her belly. "What are we going to do when Hannah finds her mother?"

Fin encouraged the kindling into flame, then sat back. He dusted off his hands before poking at the growing flames. "What do you mean?"

Byrne's face was all hard lines, but his eyes were concerned as he looked at the baby. Hannah had decided to stay in the wagon, still worried about touching anything, but she had seen the sense in Rena staying the night inside with Fin and Byrne.

"Hannah and Rena won't need us anymore."

Fin snorted, but he was apprehensive about the same thing. The two of them had become part of their group, and even though it had only been two weeks since they met, he couldn't picture a time when they wouldn't all be traveling together. He didn't want to leave Rena. Or Hannah, but that was more complicated.

"As if she could do without us," he said.

"She has a *first generation* vampire for a mother," Byrne said. "She will have all the support she could need."

"Yes, but we have mental shields. We can help her with the baby. Only her mother can touch her, you know that."

"I don't think I could handle being around vampires all the time," Byrne muttered.

"Hannah might not want to live with her mother. Look what happened when she went to visit." Fin stood, a hand pressed to his ribs. "I'm going to go down and order a bath for me and Rena. Want one?"

Byrne shook his head. "There's a brook out back, I'll use that."

Fin winced. "You'll freeze your balls off."

"Hah! I'm not a weak human."

"Whatever." Shaking his head, Fin opened the wooden door — odd to find one so near a vampire estate — and headed down the stairs. There were only two patrons left in the taproom, and they were huddled near the fire. Both wore long shirts and coats, and had Brown eyes. Locals, Fin guessed. The room smelled of tobacco smoke and onions.

Heading over to the bar, Fin nodded at the innkeeper.

"I was wondering if I could get a hipbath? For me and the baby? And a meal?"

The innkeeper eyed him for a moment, then nodded. He was a bit shorter than Fin, and had ruddy, shiny cheeks. "It'll cost extra. That were won't fit in the bath."

"No problem."

The innkeeper toddled off to put together some food for them; Fin hung around to wait by the bar.

There didn't seem to be a barmaid, but that was probably a good thing. He didn't need a woman fawning over the baby or him. And he didn't want Byrne to have any more reason to be annoyed at him. Plus, Fin didn't want to get them kicked out of a fourth town in a bit over a month. He could only imagine what Byrne would have to say to that. Or Hannah.

He grimaced. Thinking of Hannah would not help him win any points with Byrne, either. Not that Byrne would *know* he was thinking about the vampire, but the were had a way of sensing when Fin was doing something he shouldn't. And Fin shouldn't be thinking about Hannah in any way other than as a friend. He shouldn't be picturing the way her legs looked in her leather pants, or how her breasts stretched her shirt, or how her lips felt against his...

The innkeeper banged a tray of food down on the counter, the plates and tankards rattling. Fin snapped out of his bad thoughts about Hannah and set off up to the room.

By the time he arrived, a bronze hipbath had already been set up, although it was empty. Maybe the innkeeper did have a helper after all.

Byrne had stripped off his shirt, and was doing pushups in the middle of the room. Rena was in the basket in front of him, making sleep noises. Fin stepped around the were and put the tray on the small table next to the window. He eyed the uncooked steaks on one side of the plate, grateful the blood seeping across the dinnerware hadn't reached his cooked steak and potatoes. He preferred his meat well done.

Pulling out the only chair, Fin sat down and then dug into his food, sipping on the ale as he did so. Byrne's food wasn't going to go cold while he was exercising — show off — but his was.

A knock on the door heralded the arrival of the innkeeper and buckets of steaming water. He dumped the bucket's contents into the hipbath, then disappeared down the stairs. Three trips later, Fin was polishing off his food and the bath was full.

Byrne stood up, chest glistening with sweat, and dipped his finger in the water. "Feels okay."

Fin nodded, and hauled himself out of the chair. He picked up the swaddled baby, took her over to the bath and began to unwrap the material from around her. The movement woke her and she blinked open sleepy Green eyes. As her little body was exposed to the cold air, she kicked her legs in protest and screamed.

Wincing, Byrne put his fingers in his ears. "She certainly has a set of lungs on her."

Fin quickly put her in the water, which made her scrunch her face in protest and kick her legs and wave her arms even more vigorously. Her crying didn't stop, either. Cradling her head, Fin quickly grabbed a cloth and soap and began washing her down. He made quick work of it and lifted the baby out, passing her to Byrne, who had a waiting towel. The were gently dried Rena, while Fin got a new diaper ready.

Together, they soon had her re-swaddled and back into the basket. Whimpering, but content now that she was no longer so exposed, she settled fast.

"Bath time for me," Fin said. "At least she didn't pee in the water."

Byrne nodded. "I'll go out to the brook. Back soon."

Then Fin was alone — properly alone — with Rena. Crouching

down, he ran a gentle hand over her bald head. "I had a daughter once," he told her. Rena made a gurgling noise.

Stripping off his shirt, he examined his yellowing bruises and the thin line of scabs that ran up his arms. Byrne had taken out the stitches a few days ago, and the wounds were healing nicely.

Shucking his pants, he stepped into the bath. There wasn't really room for him to sit, so he squatted, rubbing soap over his chest.

"My daughter's name was Calenda," he said to the murmuring infant. "Her mother died giving birth to her." His voice lowered as rinsed the soap off. "I killed them both."

Rena blew a bubble.

"Don't try and be nice," he said to the baby. "If I hadn't gotten Karly pregnant, then she would never have died bringing our little girl into the world." And his Callie wouldn't have died, either.

He never even got to see her take a breath.

She'd been so small and fragile, her tiny body cold in his hands. The midwife and the sawbones had tried to take her from him, begged him to leave the room, so they could prepare both Karly and Callie's bodies, but Fin couldn't leave them. He'd sat in that room, with its coppery stench of blood and pungent scent of fear, his baby in his arms, her Brown eyes shut to the world forever. It was only when Marcia had found him that the stupor had passed.

Fin had buried the two of them, along with his heart, and then left town. He hadn't seen his sisters or family since. He couldn't look them in the eyes, knowing he'd see pity. And worse, acceptance. Fin didn't deserve that.

Finished in the bath, he stepped out and dried himself off. He was buttoning up his shirt when Byrne strode back in, skin goose-pimpled, but looking clean and fresh. The bear opened one of their bags and pulled out a shirt. "You should go and check on Hannah."

"You didn't?" Fin asked.

"I was half naked."

Fin eyed the man's physique with a slightly jealous eye. Byrne had way too many muscles for just one person. It wasn't fair. "I'm sure she wouldn't have minded."

"Don't be an ass."

"You're the prude."

"Just shut up and go and check on her. Wear a coat, it's cold."

"She's a vampire, I'm sure she's fine." Truth was, he didn't trust himself if he was alone with her. And he didn't trust her, either.

"Just do it. I'll go milk the stupid goat and feed Rena."

"Why don't you check on Hannah then, too?"

"Share the duties, that's the deal. Go."

"Fine."

If Fin protested too much, Byrne would detect that he had 'issues' with the vampire. So he pulled a woolen jumper on and then a coat, and headed out the door.

He told himself that it wasn't a big deal. He was an adult. Hannah was an adult. There was no reason to be worried about approaching the woman at night, with no one else around.

Stepping outside, the frigid air was like a slap in the face. One Fin sorely needed. Muttering to himself, he turned right at the inn, then headed down the dirt track that led into and out of the hamlet. Hannah was camped a five minute walk from the inn, far enough away that no one could stumble on her.

In the moonlight, he could see reasonably well, and recognized the cart trail that headed east after about four hundred yards. Turning right again, he set off along it, rubbing his hands together for warmth. Oak trees lined the sides of the track, and he could hear critters scampering in the undergrowth. Even though it was spring, it was still a bit cold for a human.

The top on the wagon was up, and Fin started whistling as he approached, so Hannah would know it was him. After seeing her rip a guy's heart from his chest, he wasn't going to take any chances.

"Fin?"

"Just checking to see if you're okay," he said, stopping at the rear of the cart.

Hannah pushed aside the canvas with a stick. "It's cold, you shouldn't be outside."

"It's fine," Fin said, moving from foot to foot.

"You're human."

Fin rolled his eyes. "I am aware of this fact."

"Humans get cold."

"You're observant."

She jabbed a long, gloved finger at him. "So you're cold."

"I didn't say that."

"Get in the wagon." Hannah pushed the canvas open further.

"I don't think that's a good idea."

Hannah leaned forward. "Get in the wagon."

"It's okay. I just came back to check on you. You seem fine. I'll go now." Fin quickly took a step back. Then two.

But Hannah was fast. Quicker than he could see, she was dragging him inside the wagon.

"My ribs!"

This was a bad idea.

A very bad idea.

CHAPTER FORTY-NINE

Pinton City

"That was my mother!"

He shouldn't be in the king's bedroom at this time of the day, but so be it. Shoving the snuff box into his jacket pocket, he sidled to the doorway. He had a reason to be here, if anyone found him, but he didn't want to take too many chances, especially since the king would be in to eat his lunch at any moment. Despite that, he couldn't stop himself from stopping to listen in on the conversation in the adjacent room. Eavesdropping was such poor behavior, but sometimes lowering one's standards was important. He just hoped neither vampire heard him standing there. Things could get awkward if they did.

"I'm sorry, Misty," the king said in a soothing voice. "I know it was your mother, and the City Guard is doing all it can..."

He could picture the scene: King Johan resplendent in black silk, his hair in a queue. Misty opposite him, dressed in tacky white, her hair over her shoulders. She'd no doubt be playing with those stupid blonde curls, maybe stomping a foot in annoyance on the priceless red and black woven carpet.

That bloody bitch had been throwing a tantrum ever since her mother's body had been found. You'd think that she would have finally realized what a favor he'd done for her — for the kingdom. She no longer had to be embarrassed about her mother's antics, about her inadequacy as a peer of the realm. But no. It was still 'poor me, my mom is dead.'

She was as useless as her mother.

"The murderer is still out there. It's not good enough, and you need to make it known that this is unacceptable."

"Misty—"

"The guards are under-resourced to deal with this! I want the bloody fiend to know that we are looking for him, and that when he's found, there will be no mercy."

No mercy?

That was a tad overdramatic. But he did like to hear that the City Guard was ill-equipped to deal with finding him.

"Look, I'll arrange for a meeting with the night captain." King Johan was placating her. Good. "We'll work out a plan of action. Of course, this murder cannot be allowed to go unpunished."

He drew back. *Cannot be allowed to go unpunished?*

Did the king not understand what he was doing? How important his work was?

Did Johan not *see* his value?

The snuff box was heavy in his jacket pocket; he patted it gently. Maybe the king needed a more emphatic lesson in humility.

Chapter Fifty

Fin lay on his back in the cart bed, his coat open and jumper askew, revealing the taut muscles of his stomach above the waistband of his trousers.

"Hmph."

"Are you okay?" Hannah asked. Perhaps he'd been hurt by being dragged into the cart. She patted him down, checking for injuries. She tried not to think about what her hands were touching as she worked her way over his arms and then his torso and chest. Ignored how firm the planes of his body were...

"I'm fine," Fin said, grabbing her hands, holding them away from him. His voice was slightly pained.

"But you hmphed." Hannah let him keep hold of her hands, embarrassingly pleased to have contact with another person.

With Fin.

"You dragged me into the back of a cart. It was a hmph of surprise." Fin let go of her hands and then propped himself up on his elbows with a wince. This close she could make out flecks of Green in his Hazel eyes, even in the dim light of the covered cart. Having a first generation vampire as a mother did have some benefits. But, how much could Fin see of her?

"You were cold," Hannah said, a little defensive. She didn't want to let Fin get sick. After he'd spent the past two weeks bemoaning how easy it was for humans to get hurt, she hadn't wanted to take the risk. And maybe she'd wanted a little company. She'd grown used to having Rena, Fin and Byrne around. She didn't like being left alone in the cart, but she hadn't been comfortable asking them to stay with her. Fin needed a bed, and Rena needed warmth. Strange how she hadn't really cared about being alone while she lived on the Old Mother, but a couple of weeks with her new friends, and she was leery about solitude.

You're a vampire. You can protect yourself, you don't need people to look after you.

But I don't want to be looked after. I just don't want to be alone.

How sad is that?

"I should probably get back..." Fin sat up, scooting his butt backward, putting space between them. He felt around the back of the cart, as if searching for something — he must be almost blind in the darkness.

She pulled her blanket over her shoulders, wrapping it around her. "There's a lantern behind you."

"I don't need a lantern, I'll be fine when I climb out. I'll be able to see by the moonlight." His words were fast and clipped.

Frowning, Hannah took hold of her 'touching' stick to scoop up the lamp; she might be able to get it going for him. How she'd manage to do it without touching the components, she wasn't sure, but it'd work out. She had almost hooked the handle, when his surprisingly warm body made contact with hers. Hannah dropped the stick in surprise, and Fin flung his hands out for balance. His palms made contact with her upper torso and stayed there.

They were on her breasts.

He didn't move.

Heat burned its way up from their point of contact, her breasts growing heavy and tight. The warmth spread to her neck and cheeks, and she was thankful she hadn't got the lamp going, or Fin would see her full-body blush.

Fin, however, was frozen with his arms outstretched. The contact was making her body tingle, awkwardness fading into something more pleasurable. She was grateful Byrne wasn't here, or he'd know within seconds she was lusting after Fin. No one had a sense of smell like a bear.

"Hannah, what am I touching?" Fin's voice was more like a squeak than the deep baritone she was used to.

He had to know what he was touching, and she probably should have moved his hands away by now, but she didn't want to. It felt good, even if he was just sitting there like a rock. It was still much better than what it had been like when she'd dated Evan.

"You're touching my breasts."

"Breasts?" He squeezed gently and yelped. Throwing himself back, he landed with a clatter on the lantern and some bags.

The loss of warmth was immediate. He was rubbing his hands together, shaking them, and Hannah wasn't sure what he was trying to do. Rub away the feel of her?

"It can't have been that bad," she snapped. Shutting her jaw with a click, she berated herself; she shouldn't have said anything. He fell. He was trying to steady himself. He hadn't deliberately set out to grope her. Just because she happened to like it, didn't mean that was his intention. Which it clearly wasn't, from his hand wringing and scrunched-up face. How did he manage to be so handsome even when he looked like that; mouth puckered, forehead creased in a frown, nose pinched?

Fin paid no attention to her snarky comment, though. "I'm sorry, Hannah."

"Why?" Surely he'd touched lots of breasts before without having a panic attack.

He dropped his hands, staring at them in the dark. "I touched your boobs."

"Boobs?"

"Breasts."

"Right." Hannah wasn't too sure what was wrong, but Fin was upset. Maybe he hadn't liked touching her?

"So I'm sorry."

Hannah shrugged. "I'm not."

His eyes searched for her in the darkness. "*What?*"

"I said I'm not sorry." She smiled ruefully to herself, knowing Fin couldn't see it. "Most action I've had in a long time."

Fin spluttered. "Action?"

"I mean, I know you got laid only a couple of weeks ago, but it's been a bit longer for me." Try one hundred and fifty years longer. Not that she was going to admit that to him.

"Laid?"

"Yes, had sex." Was his brain not be functioning properly? Perhaps he was still feeling guilty about touching her? Shame.

"Sex."

There he went with the one word answers again.

Hannah reached out for him, but didn't quite make contact. "Are you okay?"

Fin shoved a hand through his messy blond hair. "You shouldn't say those words."

"What words?"

"Sex. Laid. Action."

Hannah folded her arms across her chest. "Why not? You and Byrne do."

"Because..." His voice trailed off and he tugged at the collar of his jumper uncomfortably.

"I'm listening." If she'd been standing, she would have been tapping her foot impatiently. As it was, all she could do was glare at Fin.

"You just can't."

"That is not a reason."

Then he mumbled, "It gives people ideas."

"What ideas?"

"Bad ones."

Hannah threw her arms up. "Fin, you make no sense!"

"I had better get moving."

But he just sat there, rubbing the palms of his hands on his thighs. And then it dawned on Hannah: maybe his bad thoughts were about *her*.

Be bold, she told herself.

But I'm scared.

What if Fin rejected her again? The first time, she'd only managed to move past her embarrassment because he hadn't been expecting it, and they'd been in a dungeon. Kissing her back would have been a terrible idea on his part. But some part of her had grown attached to the fantasy that she, Fin, Rena and Byrne would continue traveling together as a family. That they wouldn't separate when she found her mother. That she and Fin would be Rena's parents and Byrne the doting uncle. Not that she'd ever told Fin and Byrne that.

She *liked* Fin.

Dropping the blanket by her side, she leaned forward and gently placed her hands on either side of Fin's face.

"Hannah?"

Then she was pressing her lips to his. They were warm and soft, and his beard was slightly tickly against her face. Hannah thought he was going to push her away again, and sadness began to coil through her, and she pulled back. As their lips parted, Fin groaned.

Hands coming up to her shoulders, he slanted his mouth over hers and kissed her back. Her blood instantly grew hot, burning through her, and warmth coiled low within her belly. Her lips parted, and his tongue swept inside, teasing her with quick, gentle flicks. He tasted of mint and potato, and it was the strangest and most erotic thing she'd ever savored.

Winding her arms around his neck, Hannah pressed forward, her chest against his. A hiss of pleasure left her, the press of his body delicious, the hardness of his muscles against her almost indescribable, so starved was her body of another's contact. But it was Fin, and she doubted anyone else would feel so wonderful. Hard where she was soft, and so bloody *warm*.

Fin pulled away with a moan, his heartbeat pounding loud in her ears. She was surprised that hers was almost as fast. Fin rested his forehead against hers, and his breath came in short pants, mingling with her exhalations.

"This is a really bad idea, Hannah."

Hannah ran a palm down his back, her fingers sensitive as they swept over his shoulder blades and down toward his butt. "It doesn't feel like a bad idea."

In fact, it felt rather amazing.

"That is why it's a really bad idea."

Since when was Fin the voice of reason?

"It's not like we have to get married, Fin. We're adults."

"You have a baby, you're a vampire. I'm human. It's just not going to work."

"It doesn't have to work forever." Why did she get the feeling that she was lying? And mostly to herself? "It just has to work now."

"Hannah—"

She kissed him again. Sliding backward, she tugged at his coat. When he didn't help her, she pulled her shirt off over her head, then grabbed one of his hands and pressed it to a breast. The cold air made her nipple pebble, and Fin gave a low groan.

"Fuck, Hannah—"

He kissed her again, less controlled, more animalistic. Like he was starving, just for her. She wanted to push him back, to climb all over him, but she was worried about hurting his ribs. So she lay back, drawing Fin down on top of her. He didn't resist, and was soon sprawled over her. His weight felt wonderful, like he'd been designed to fit against her and no one else.

Her hands were greedy, hungry to touch as much of him as possible. Rearing up, Fin threw off his jacket, jumper and shirt, and then he was leaning down, the skin of his torso burning as it came into contact with her breasts and stomach. His chest hair created slight friction against her skin and she arched into the contact.

She thought she might explode from the wonder of just *feeling* him. Nothing else. No memories, no invasive ideas. Just skin on skin. Her and Fin.

Finally though, his hands began to explore her with the same intensity as hers on him. She moaned as they closed over her breasts again, and this time, he didn't just leave them there; this time he knew exactly what he was doing. He trailed kisses down her face, neck, and her jaw clenched as his mouth found her nipple. Her breath left her in a whoosh. Sliding her hand down, she encircled the long length of his erection, and his body jerked. He was so big she wondered how he'd fit.

"Hannah."

"Fin?"

She stroked her palm over him, and his eyes rolled back. Then his hand was sliding over her stomach, tautening the muscles. His clever fingers delved beneath the waistband of her pants, and cupped her. Her whole body turned to liquid, and she relaxed into his touch. Panting, her hand still stroking him, she unbuttoned his trousers while one long finger slowly slid inside her.

Fin stilled. *Fuck.*

"Fin?"

"You're so tight."

Then he shut his eyes and slowly pulled his hand away. Sweat beaded on his forehead. "Fin?"

"Hannah, we have to stop. I don't think—"

She stroked his cheek. "It's okay, Fin. I trust you."

"You shouldn't."

"I do anyway."

He stared at her for what felt like an age, before awkwardly removing his pants. When he crawled over to her, it was the sexiest thing she'd ever seen. Everything about Fin was sexy, though. Hannah quickly discarded her trousers, too.

"Hannah—"

Then he was over her, her legs parting to cradle his hips, his hands stroking her skin. But she needed to feel him. To be with him.

His head lowered to hers, face strained. "Are you sure?"

Lifting her hips up, she hissed as the head of his penis touched her. "Yes."

Even that felt amazing.

Slowly he pushed into her, stretching her. Resting his weight on his elbows, he placed one palm under her head, the other clasping one of her hands. Their fingers twined together. Hannah breathed in, tasting the scent of *Fin*: verbena and lemon. She had never felt so precious, so cared for.

Then he was fully within her.

Hannah felt strangely complete; her body intertwined with Fin's, their hearts beating madly within their chests, together.

"Are you okay?" Fin whispered.

She wasn't. Somehow, a large part of her heart wasn't hers anymore. But right now, she didn't care.

"I'm perfect."

CHAPTER FIFTY-ONE

"What's that?"

Looking up — and up — from her paperwork, Alice met Kyle's curious gaze.

"My notes on the autopsies."

He gave her a bright grin as she gathered her paperwork together. He was persistent, that's for sure. Too bad he wasn't her type. Not that she really had a type. But those were just details.

Kyle rubbed his chin, and then picked up a glass slide from the wooden tray where she'd stacked them. She wasn't sure how long the samples would last, so she was checking them every hour or two while she was at the morgue, to determine how long the cells stayed active.

"What are you doing?" He turned the slide over in his fingers.

Alice shoved back a curl that had escaped her bun. "Trying to identify the killer's species."

Kyle held the slide up to his eye level. "What's on these?"

"Sperm."

Kyle glanced at the glass rectangle in his hand, as if he was holding a spider. "As in *seed*?"

"As in seed," Alice repeated.

Kyle quickly replaced the slide, then wiped his hands on his pants, looking around. For a faucet? "Where did you get that from?"

"My friend, Tal."

Kyle frowned. "Tal is a woman. Women don't make seed."

Good to see he knew basic biology. "No, but she got some donated to her from the university's medical school."

"Right. Donated." He made a fist and pumped it up and down in the air, a curious and yet confused look on his face.

Alice nodded, stifling a laugh. "Donated."

"Your job is weird, Alice. You know that?"

"Says the guy who beats people up for a living."

Kyle's fingers rose to his chin again, then he thought better of it and shoved his hands in his pockets. "It's a tough job, but someone has to do it."

"So what brings you down here?" Alice asked.

The large man sighed. "Another body. Elle is bringing it in. After you look at it, Captain Mikael wants to have a chat about the vampire murders."

Alice's heart pounded. "Another vampire?"

"No, this one is human. Killed in a domestic argument, we think."

Relief poured through her. And then she felt sick. She was *comforted* that a human was dead rather than a vampire? That a human had been killed by someone they loved? She was getting too involved in this murder case. Too invested.

What was it about these victims that called to her?

◆

Clutching the handle of her black medical bag, Alice strode up the stone staircase. She pushed open the door at the top and entered the reception area of the City Guard headquarters, where Captain Mikael was waiting for her, dressed in the formal attire of the City Guard: black pants, jacket and cravat, with a white shirt. Medals were pinned on his chest.

Alice checked her own clothing; black pants, red shirt and black jacket. She wasn't dressed anywhere near as formally. "Are you going somewhere after our chat?"

Mikael frowned. "*We're* going somewhere *for* our chat."

"What?"

"Didn't Guard McInnes mention you were meant to attend a meeting about the vampire murders?"

Alice shuffled sideways. "He said we were to have a chat."

Captain Mikael sighed and ran a hand over his closely cropped hair. "We're going to the Crystal Palace."

Alice's bag dropped to the floor with a clatter. "*What?*"

Mikael gave her a humorless smile, his teeth white against his dark skin. "Missed that part of the message, then?"

"Yes," she growled.

"How about we go via your place, so you can pop on something a little more formal?"

"Is there time?" Alice asked.

"No, but the king may be more offended that you didn't dress for the occasion than if you're late."

The two of them walked out of the guard house. Alice didn't know the captain very well, but she'd heard good things about him. He was one of those strong, silent types, and Alice had to admit, something about that was appealing. But Mikael was a good decade or two older than her, and there was an aloofness to him that made her slightly uneasy. But she knew that nothing bad would happen to her while in his company, even surrounded by vampires.

From the edge of the pavement, Mikael hailed a two-person hackney. "What's your address?"

Alice gave him the number on Glove Road and climbed into the cab, taking the second seat while the captain spoke to the driver. Alice couldn't normally afford to catch a hackney, so she peered out the open window into the streets, admiring them from her slightly raised position. Mikael got into the cab, and Alice squished over further in the scratchy but clean seat, to allow the guard captain's large body to fit. Then the driver pulled himself up onto the back of the vehicle and clicked the horses into motion.

They rode in silence, Alice clutching her bag on her lap. As she watched the streets whiz by, her thoughts ran wildly through the potential outfits that were suitable for a meeting with the king.

Sure, she had met him before, but she'd been on duty in the morgue. He could hardly have expected her to be dressed for that occasion.

The cab pulled up out the front of her apartment block, and Alice jumped out then dashed up the stairs, through the entry door and up to her apartment. She slammed the dark blue door shut behind her, and dropped her medical bag on the small table inside the entry. Then she hurried into her room, pulling off her jacket and then her shirt. She dropped them onto the made bed. She wished she could fold them, but there was no time.

Opening the door of her standalone closet, Alice stared at the five dresses she owned, running her fingers across the soft, slippery materials. One was the knee-length number she'd worn when she went out to dinner with Tal; another was a bright yellow sunny dress with a wide skirt, designed for warm weather, not the cool nights of spring. There was really only one option: her burnt-orange gown. She'd only worn it once, for her graduation. It had been a gift from her aunt, and had probably cost her four months' worth of commissions. As a result, Alice had been terrified to wear the outfit.

Her pants joined the rest of her clothing on the bed. After pulling on her stays as quickly as possible, Alice reverently removed the gown from its place at the end of her closet, where the other garments wouldn't crush it. She unlaced the dress and stepped into it. It had inbuilt petticoats, and slid on easily. Thank goodness that she hadn't put on much weight since she graduated.

The dress laced up the side, rather than the back, and while it took a bit of contorting, she managed to fasten it. Alice hoped that Captain Mikael wasn't too impatient. She pulled a pair of high-heeled shoes from the bottom of the wardrobe and slipped them on, then stopped quickly in front of a mirror. It only showed her torso and up, but she was astonished at how her breasts seemed to spill over the top of the gown. Maybe she had grown a bit, but in places she hadn't really thought about.

She didn't have much jewelry, but opted for a black pearl

necklace that her mother had owned. It would do. She then undid her hair, spilling it over her shoulders in rambunctious curls. There wasn't much more she could do with it. Feeling awkward in her high heels and silk gown, she grabbed the only reticule she owned — it was dark gray and happened to match her pearls — shoved her keys inside it, then slipped out the door and dashed down the stairs, like a damsel in a novel.

When she reached the street, she carefully lifted her skirts to avoid getting dust on her hem. This area of town didn't get its sidewalks washed down every day. As she got back into the cab, Mikael let out a low whistle. Blushing, she fiddled with her reticule.

"Only dress I owned that was fancy enough."

He gave her a bright grin. "Well, it's worth the wait."

"I hope the king doesn't mind."

Fifteen minutes later the hackney pulled up in front of the Crystal Palace. A footman ran down the marble stairs and hovered next to the cab, as there was no door to open. He held out his hand for Alice to climb down; as she took it, she met his pale lavender gaze with a start. The man was a vampire.

Almost dropping his hand, Alice lighted on the ground, Mikael close behind her.

"We have an appointment with the king," Mikael said, straightening to his full height. He towered over the servant, and Alice. The footman nodded and led them up the staircase and into the white marble foyer of the palace. Alice was amazed. A crimson rug, lined with filaments of gold thread, ran along the center of the foyer. Her eyes were drawn to a massive chandelier, which hung low overhead, and craning her neck upward, she stared at its glittering, fragile crystals.

A hand touched her shoulder, and Alice started. "We need to go to the king," Captain Mikael said.

Nodding, Alice followed the large guard, her eyes shifting from his shoulders to the recessed niches, which housed vases so unusual she couldn't think of who might have created them. By the time she arrived at the king's reception chamber, Alice was overwhelmed.

She and Mikael stepped inside, to find the king wasn't alone. The viscountess, her brother, Elle Brown, and a tall, wickedly handsome man with long, pale-brown hair were also in the room. The chamber had soaring ceilings, with gilded wallpaper, and a large metal table and matching chairs with delicate legs and red velvet cushions. An empty fireplace stood at one end, and large windows overlooked lush gardens. Elle and the handsome man were talking quietly, Elle in a blood-red dress that took Alice's breath away. She hadn't ever seen the city guard wearing anything other than trousers before. The man she was talking to glanced at Alice with bright yellow eyes; it had to be Elle's fiancé.

Too bad now wasn't the right time to ask him for a semen sample.

To the side of the room, the king was talking to a man — human? — with brown curly hair and skin a few shades darker than her own. The king's face was pinched, as if he was in pain. But vampires didn't really suffer pain, not unless they had an injury. Maybe he was just bored? The man the king conversed with was stiff, like he was annoyed with the conversation. But the human nodded, his back to Alice, and moved his hands. He then pocketed something and he wiped his nose. Shortly after, he left the room through a side door, without glancing at any of the occupants. Alice wondered if he was the king's mysterious lover, the one Tal and Misty had discussed.

Turning toward them all, the king linked his hands in front of him. Then he smiled, and it was devastating. Alice's knees went slightly weak.

"Let's sit."

Chapter Fifty-Two

Whiteoak Hamlet

Fin took a quick — very quick — bath in the stream behind the inn before he headed inside. Shivering and without a shirt, but with his slightly damp jumper covering his torso, he climbed the stairs to the room he shared with Byrne. His shirt was actually soaking wet in his hand, and Fin hoped Byrne wouldn't ask too many questions about it. He couldn't really feel his balls; the water had nearly frozen them off. Cold droplets fell from his overlong hair, trickling uncomfortable paths down the back of his neck. Maybe he should have followed Byrne's stream-bath idea *before* he'd gone to check on Hannah. Then Fin wouldn't have had enough feeling left in his junk to act on his impulses.

Although even that might not have stopped him.

It had been *Hannah*.

He'd made an effort not to pay too much attention to her since the bruising around his eyes had lost its swelling. He didn't think he'd seen a more beautiful woman. Ever. And he'd seen plenty of good-looking ladies, both with clothes and without. No doubt his sisters would say he'd seen too many, but they weren't here to bother him about his lifestyle choices. That's why he'd left. Well, no. That wasn't the entire reason. His sisters had been supportive of him and Karly, even though the two of them hadn't been much more than teenagers.

He just wished they hadn't been so accepting.

He and Hannah hadn't discussed him sleeping there in the back of the wagon cart with her; she hadn't asked and he hadn't offered. After they'd snuggled for a few minutes, he'd hightailed it back to the inn, as if his ass was on fire. Something like panic had sat heavily inside his stomach, as he lay there after they'd joined. She'd looped her arm loosely over his torso, mindful of his ribs; she was always careful of him, because she thought him fragile. *Him.* Fin Castle. *Fragile.* He'd just gotten beaten up by a whole friggin' town, and he'd survived. Sure, Byrne had helped him out a little, but Fin had sort of walked away from the thrashing.

He was totally hardcore.

Still, Fin had laid there, the hard wooden slats of the wagon pressed against his back, hearing Hannah breathing, and he hadn't wanted to move — hadn't wanted to spoil the moment. It had been dark, and even though he hadn't been able to see Hannah, he had truly *seen* her. He'd wanted to stay, but that urge was what had made him leave.

Normally, after sharing a pleasant interlude with a lovely woman, Fin would give the lady a smile and some sweet words. Then he'd skedaddle. But this wasn't just any woman. This was Hannah. And he'd done the unthinkable.

Well, he amended, it had certainly been thinkable. That was why he'd managed to get himself in that situation. Calling himself a few choice swearwords in a language Byrne wouldn't understand, Fin ran a hand through his hair and then opened the door to their room.

"You were gone a while," Byrne said.

Fin couldn't meet the bear's gaze. He'd never been ashamed of himself before, not when it came to women. Sure, he'd hated himself, but that was because of what happened with Karly. If he'd been able to keep it in his pants, then Karly and Callie wouldn't have died. Then again, Callie would never have been conceived and his life would be very different.

However, something awfully like shame was settling over him right now.

"How's Rena?" Fin asked, shutting the door behind him. He crouched down over Rena's basket, close to the fire and discretely laid his shirt out in front of the hearth to dry. It would be wrinkled as fuck, but whatever.

The baby was swaddled, her little bald head the only thing visible. Her eyes were shut, and she made little grumbling noises. Fin couldn't help but think that if his daughter had survived, he might have had a moment like this with her. But he couldn't change the past, no matter how much he wanted to.

A chill spread through him.

He hadn't worn a sheath when he was with Hannah. Hadn't even thought about it. She could get pregnant. *Pregnant.* He couldn't go through that again. Not the fear, the pain, the dread. He wasn't normally so stupid. Not since Karly.

She's a vampire, you're a human, it won't happen.

But she is Graced, and you are half-Graced...

No, she was a vampire. And vampires didn't get pregnant except to other vampires. The risk was low. He shouldn't worry. There was no way Hannah could be pregnant. Not from him.

"You just gonna squat there?" Byrne asked.

Startled, Fin ran a gentle finger over Rena's downy head, and then stood up. He got into bed and rolled to face the wall. The sheets were clean and fresh, and he hoped that any bed bugs would decide to nibble on Byrne rather than himself. He slowed his breathing, pretending to fall asleep; he didn't want Byrne asking questions, because he didn't believe in lying to the were. Byrne had had enough deception in his life, he didn't need Fin to add to it.

◆

Byrne wanted to ask why Fin smelled of water from the stream, but the human was pretending to sleep. His friend was lying on the opposite side to his injured ribs, the blanket pulled up to his chin, his damp hair a dark burnished gold. Normally, Fin was more than happy to share his misadventures, but he'd clearly not wanted to discuss his dip in the stream.

Mayhap Hannah had dunked him in the creek for getting a bit too handsy? Byrne smiled at the thought. Although, to be fair, Fin only propositioned the woman in a joking manner every couple of days, which was the equivalent of him not hitting on the vampire at all. Hannah also had no trouble ignoring all Fin's sleazy comments. But if she hadn't dunked Fin in the stream, why had he taken a swim? Maybe he fell in?

Perhaps Byrne shouldn't have sent Fin out to check on her. The human was weak-willed at the best of times when it came to women, led around by his cock more than his brain. But Byrne had thought Fin respected Hannah enough to leave her be.

Maybe you're just jealous.

Rolling onto his back, Byrne tucked his hands under the back of his head and stared up at the plastered ceiling. He wished that he could respond to the annoying voice in his head with a negative, but he had a sneaking suspicion it was right. Byrne resented Fin's easy way with women, but he wasn't a 'bang 'em and leave 'em' kind of guy like the human.

It wasn't like Fin ever questioned Byrne's choice to keep to himself. Sure, he gave him shit about it from time to time, but that was fine. The human had seen the dank cell in which Byrne had been kept, and had spoken with those who had kept him prisoner, so he had a fair idea of what had been done to Byrne in that bloody place.

It was too late for the were to wish it otherwise.

CHAPTER FIFTY-THREE

Elle had never imagined that she'd be sitting at a table at the Crystal Palace with the king, a viscountess, her fiancé, Dante — AKA, the Creep — the coroner and Captain Mikael.

Then again, she'd never imagined she'd be Chosen, never mind survive the process. Graceds weren't meant to. That's what she'd been always taught. But if you had Hazel eyes, apparently that meant you could break all the rules. And she liked breaking rules, unless she was on guard duty. Then she had to enforce them.

"What can you tell me about this killer?" the king asked into the quiet.

Elle said nothing. She wasn't even the primary guard on the murder investigation. In fact, she was only here because Misty wanted her to be, and because she wanted a reason to get out of the house. Dante's mother had been visiting when the request arrived, and the duchess made Elle's skin crawl. Not because she'd tried to kill Elle yet — although she didn't think that it was completely off the cards — but because there was something so alien about the woman it set Elle's nerves firing. Even Clay had refused to shift out of his wolf shape whenever she was over. And that make her edgy, too.

Oh, and Mikael, had said that he didn't believe in taking one for the team without having someone else to suffer with him.

There was no way Dinya was going to go — she didn't particularly like vampires all that much — and they would never send Kyle to the palace, even if he had been working on the case with Alice. Bulls and china shops and all that.

So that just left her.

Elle studied the monarch. He was normally so attractive that even she got a little tongue-tied around him, which was saying something because she got to have sex with Clay on a regular basis. And Clay was hotter than hot. But now...

'Does the king seem unwell to you?' Elle thought the question at her fiancé. His yellow gaze remained where it was focused on Dante. They seemed to be having a staring contest.

Again.

Morons.

Elle sighed. Dante and Clay were having dominance issues at the moment. Clay was clearly an alpha wolf, but he was also a loner, so that didn't really matter normally. He didn't need to be in charge when in a group of people, because he rarely stuck around groups long enough for it to be an issue. But Dante — even though he was odd, deranged, and a bit sociopathic — was also a dominant personality. They'd been competing to see who was the more 'alpha' since they'd met.

At first, it had just been a little physical fighting, which she could totally get behind. Now it had progressed to mind games. It wasn't winning them any favors with her. After all, anyone with half a brain could work out *she* was the queen fucking bee when it came to the three of them.

'He did look peaky when he was talking to his boyfriend. Jerk-something-or-other.' Clay's mental voice was like his speaking one: low, rough and sexy.

There was no jealousy in Clay's dismissive comment; he was glad the monarch had focused his lovesick eyes on someone else. The were had just decided the object of the king's lust was a dick. *'Guy's name is Lance,'* she thought at him.

'Lance?'

'Yes.'

'That's a stupid name.'

'Be sure to tell his parents then.'

'Maybe I will.'

Elle smothered a snort.

Captain Mikael cleared his throat. "The killer appears to be a human male, although we cannot be one hundred percent sure."

King Johan — or King Jo, as Elle called him — linked his hands together on the metal table. He was wearing a shiny black suit, and his dark hair was smoothed back from his forehead, but left out and long. Vampire hair grew fast, but seemed to stop once it had reached its natural length. For King Jo, that was around his butt. For Elle, it was about the same. Unfortunately. She missed her short, copper-colored hair. Since she'd been Chosen it was dark red and far too long. She actually had to *do* her hair in the morning, rather than just run her fingers through it and call it ready.

Elle's eyes swept around the table. Dante didn't return her gaze, but he would have been aware of her look. He kept staring at Clay. Captain Mikael was looking rather dashing in his formal suit, and next to him Alice the coroner was wearing a burnt orange gown that showed all her amazing — and maybe a little envy-inducing — curves. Misty was wearing a lilac-colored dress that was all clean lines. Not a ruffle or piece of lace to be seen. Very elegant for the viscountess. She rarely wore anything other than white, but as purple was mourning for vampires, the viscountess had changed her wardrobe.

"What makes you think the killer is male? Or human, for that matter?" the king asked.

"The sperm."

All the attention in the room switched to Alice.

'Did she just say 'sperm'?' Dante's mind voice was slightly warmer in tone than his speaking one. But he was curious. And for someone who hadn't really felt emotions before he Chose her, that was interesting.

'Yes.'

Then Clay thought at her. *'Are you and Dante chatting?'*

'Yes. Now I can't concentrate on what people are actually saying, so shut it.'

Clay sat back in his chair. *'Hah. Means I win this round.'*

'How? You were talking to me before. Technically that would be a win for him, then.'

'Humph. Stalemate then.'

Just like every other time.

Alice's face flushed, but she spoke clearly. "I think the murderer is a male, because all the victims had consensual sex prior to being murdered, and semen was left behind. I also believe the killer to be a human because I studied the samples left in all the victims. I don't have a were sample to compare to, but I did check it against vampire and human. It's a perfect match for the human. I would ideally need a larger sample size to be one hundred percent confident, but at this stage, I feel I am correct."

The king thought about this for a moment. "Right."

Dante sat up straighter in his chair. "What kind of magnification did you require to see the sperm cells? I've never actually thought to study that particular body fluid." He rubbed his chin. "I've only ever looked at blood—"

From below the table came the sound of a foot meeting a shin.

Dante turned to his sister. "What?"

"Now is not the time for a medical debate," Misty told her brother. "You can discuss this with Coroner Alice later."

Coroner Alice. Not Doctor Reive, as was her real title. It was funny, Elle thought, how aristos liked to make everything 'Sir this' and 'Lady that.' Even Alice's job position worked.

But Elle had to admit she was impressed by Alice's work. She'd always liked the coroner, but hadn't really made any effort to further their friendship beyond a professional one. When you were trying to make sure that your special younger sister was kept out of your psychotic grandmother's way, you didn't tend to get involved in extra relationships. It had made for a lonely life, and it was only now that Elle had inherited a crazy family that she could appreciate that.

"So the killer is human and male. What else?" The king

surveyed the rest of the table.

Alice bit her lip and sat back, as if her knowledge had been exhausted.

"We believe they are somehow linked to the aristocracy," Mikael said. "They had to have access to their victims."

Elle nodded. "They are either an aristo or someone associated, like a paid consort, singer, or entertainer."

"Well, there are very few aristo human families," the king said. He nodded at Dante. "Your husband's family is one of the ten."

Ten human aristo families. Elle hadn't thought the numbers so low. But it made sense. Pinton and its surrounding towns were largely vampire run, after all. The were representation was probably similar.

"So, we can possibly eliminate the aristos? Depending on who is in town at the moment." That was from Dante.

"We will need to investigate it further. We have already reviewed the Greystoke family, as they agreed to our questioning without too much fuss." Mikael nodded at Dante.

The king was frowning, but what had he expected? Of course Elle was going to use all the resources she had at hand. And every aristo connection counted. Not that she'd had any at the beginning of the year, but it was funny how things could change so quickly.

Dante's voice whispered into her mind. *'Did you see Anton before you left?'*

When she'd first been Chosen, Elle had been able to slip into Dante's mind with ease, but it had all been at her instigation. Now, their bond had changed. Oh, she could still sneak into his mind, but she was trying to avoid doing that. However, he could now start telepathic conversations with her. He couldn't reach *her* mind, but then she had a mental shield and he didn't.

She wondered how it would work if *both* the Chooser and Chosen had shields, but that was something to ponder at another time, when she wasn't sitting in a meeting with the king and trying to work out who was killing aristos.

'I saw him just before I left. Emmie was holding his hand.'

Which had been odd, come to think of it. The two of them had been walking down the main hallway. Anton had been holding his cane with one hand, and Emmie's nut brown palm with the other. Emmie regularly walked around hand in hand with Darla, Anton's younger sister, but not Anton himself. Elle would have to ask her sister what she'd been up to. The young girl wasn't meant to use her healing gift, and Elle was aware that Emmie had wanted to 'fix' Anton on more than one occasion.

Dante's mental voice was thoughtful. *'I hope she wasn't trying to heal his leg. I believe that would be far in excess of what her gift is capable of at the moment.'*

Elle sent a mental nod of assent. Then she focused on the meeting. Having people being able to talk to you telepathically sure made things complicated.

Especially when you were meant to be concentrating on the matter at hand.

CHAPTER FIFTY-FOUR

The outskirts of Pinton

Two days later, Fin found himself staring at the back of Hannah's head as she sat up at the front of the cart, talking softly with Byrne. He couldn't hear what they were saying, which annoyed him. They could be talking about something super interesting, like when they'd arrive at Pinton, or how good-looking he was. But for some strange reason, he doubted they'd be talking about him. Fin was a fantastic subject for conversation, but they did need to discuss other things. He didn't want to become a boring topic.

He was on Rena duty, sitting in the back of the cart with the canvas up. It wasn't really a duty at all; she was sleeping after vomiting on him, and he was enjoying the down time. But everything in the wagon reminded him of what he and Hannah had done. And that was a bad thing.

And staring at Hannah wasn't helping the situation in his trousers, either, although he couldn't help but admire the shape of her back...

The morning after he and Hannah had been together, Fin had felt hugely awkward, which was unusual. She'd smiled upon seeing him and Byrne, and held her arms out. He'd almost stepped forward to complete the embrace, but then he spotted she was wiggling her hands; she was waiting for Rena to be handed over.

Byrne had passed the baby to the vampire, then stopped, his

back going ramrod straight. The were's nostrils had flared, and Fin *knew* that Byrne had figured out what had happened in the back of the wagon. No other animal had a sense of smell like a bear, and Hannah obviously hadn't gotten rid of the evidence well enough. Although, why she would be even thinking of hiding it...he didn't know.

He just wanted to keep it a secret.

Part of the reason was because he didn't want Byrne beating him up for daring to touch Hannah; another part was because this wasn't about Byrne, or Rena. This was about Fin and Hannah.

Byrne hadn't really spoken to him since that morning, just glowered a lot, and humphed. But they didn't really need to talk to set up and break down camp; they'd done it so many times that it was habit. Byrne had made sure he slept next to the cart, though, so that Fin was on the other side of the fire. Did he think he was protecting Hannah from Fin? Too bad Byrne didn't know that Fin was probably the one that needed protecting. Hannah had dragged *him* into the back of the cart, after all. Not the other way around.

"I'm going to pull over for a few minutes," Byrne said. "Nature calls."

The cart trundled to the side of the unpaved road and then stopped. No other travelers seemed to be out, so there was no traffic to avoid. Baldy was in the harness, and Foxtrot flicked her tail in protest at stopping. The stupid goat, however, seemed to be in her element, quickly finding some grass.

Byrne climbed down from the driver's seat and levelled a yellow glare at Fin, as if to tell him to behave. The bear was just wandering off to find a tree and soil it; like Fin had *time* for seduction. Any worthwhile seduction, anyway. A thirty second romp with Hannah would only frustrate him.

After Byrne disappeared behind the oak trees lining the road, Fin scooted forward in the back of the cart, cradling Rena to his chest. The movement hurt, but all movement tended to hurt after you got the shit kicked out of you. Twice. "Hannah."

She swiveled in her seat, and looked at him with those

impossible-to-read Black eyes. "Fin."

"I didn't wear a sheath," he blurted.

"A what?"

A blush stole up his cheeks. And he didn't blush. Ever. "A sheath."

"Why would you have worn a sheath? You weren't carrying a sword."

Raising a hand to his forehead, he rubbed it. She didn't know what a prophylactic was. Great. Just great.

"It's for my *other* sword."

Now she just looked confused. "Your other sword? Do you even own *one* sword?"

Lowering his voice, he hissed. "My penis."

"Your penis has a sword?"

"By the blood. The sheath is for my penis. So when I have sex, my seed doesn't get inside you and you don't risk getting pregnant."

"Oooooh."

"That's all you've got to say?"

"Well, you're a human, Fin. I'm a vampire."

"You're Graced. I'm half-Graced." How was he even managing to speak, the way his jaw was clenching together? He was going to have a headache, he knew it. One was already forming at his temples.

"But I'm still a vampire. I wouldn't worry."

"Hannah—"

"I'm coming back," Byrne's voice rumbled from the trees, "and if you two are making out, I swear I will punch you in the face, Fin."

"I'm not making out with anyone," Fin called back. Then he muttered, "Unfortunately."

Hannah gave him another of her inscrutable looks. Then she turned to Byrne. "What if I was making out with him?"

Byrne took his seat on the cart. "You wouldn't be that stupid."

"Hrrm."

Byrne shot an incredulous look at Hannah, and then Fin.

"Seriously?"

"Seriously, what?" Fin asked, even though he knew he shouldn't. This conversation shouldn't even be happening right now.

"*You* jumped *him*?"

"And what's so hard to believe about that?" Fin demanded, before he could stop himself. Idiot.

"You're *you*."

Fin waved a hand in the air, encompassing himself. "And who wouldn't want all this?"

"Well, since you're so irresistible, keep yourself away. I do not want to put up with you two doing gross shit when I am around. It's bad enough I can still fucking smell it."

Hannah's cheeks went a little pink. "You can?"

"Yes. Now, let's change topics. We're only a few hours out of Pinton, and I want the nausea to wear off before we get there."

Fin shuffled back in the cart, further away from the were. He wasn't sure if Byrne was irate or amused and he didn't want to risk being hauled out of the cart to have some sense shaken into him. It had happened before. More than once. It was too bad Byrne hadn't seemed to work out that the technique wasn't achieving the desired result.

Fin was still a fool.

CHAPTER FIFTY-FIVE

Another body had been found.

Male, and naked as the day he'd been born, it was now lying on the steel bench in the morgue — Alice had gone out to the crime scene to retrieve it, but there'd been nothing to learn from the site.

This victim had been left in the chrysanthemum podium, one of the elaborate gardens of the Crystal Palace. Alice hadn't barely gotten to see any of the floral displays when she was there, and she'd heard murmurs of how stunningly beautiful this one was. But her mind had been on the location of the dump site. It was a strange coincidence that the body had been found at the palace, considering their meeting had been held there the night before.

The killer must be someone who worked in the palace, otherwise, how would they have known about the meeting?

Alice inspected the body — one stake wound was visible and the corpse was in rigor — before pulling on her gloves. She stared at the surgical equipment lined up on the metal tray next to the body. It didn't really feel worthwhile, doing an autopsy now. It was pretty obvious how the vampire male had died. But Alice liked to ensure everything was done by the book.

"So, this is annoying."

Alice whipped her head around. Elle was jammed in the doorway, pressed up next to the vampire who'd Chosen her, and her eyes dark with irritation. Behind them both, Kyle loomed.

Elle was in her guard uniform, her hair tied back in a bun, while Dante was still horribly attractive in his afternoon aristo finery. Alice looked away from them before her heart bounced right out of her chest. It was embarrassing how being around these vampires made her feel.

It wasn't fair that they were so pretty.

"Well, if you stepped out the way, then we wouldn't be crammed in the doorway, now would we?" That calm voice had to be Dante. Alice couldn't picture anyone else talking to Elle in that way. Kyle certainly wouldn't. He valued still being able to walk.

"Fuck off."

"So mature."

"Will you guys just bloody move?" Kyle must have shoved them then, because the two vampires burst into the room. Elle glowered at her partner, whereas Dante simply flicked the sleeves of his crisp white shirt and straightened up.

"Do that again, and we'll see how quickly your hand will heal after I break it." Elle put both fists on her hips.

"Just because you're a vampire now, with super strength, doesn't mean you can go around threatening your partner."

"What? This isn't a new thing. I used to threaten you *before* I got Chosen."

"Yes, but it wasn't a *real* threat then."

Elle opened her mouth to say something, but Dante snapped, "Stop being a jerk. You have been in a *mood* all day. Kyle was just expediting the situation."

"But—"

Alice decided to interrupt. "What can I do for you, Elle?"

Maybe being Chosen turned the part of one's brain that governed social awareness to mush. Maybe when she did this autopsy, Alice would pay more attention to the brain tissue to see if there were any macroscopic differences between vampires and humans...

Elle took a deep breath and then smiled, closing the distance between her and Alice. "I brought Dante to try and identify the body. His husband, the baron, is otherwise occupied and Misty is with the king."

"I told you I wouldn't be much use," Dante muttered.

"You certainly haven't been so far," Elle snapped back.

Alice waved a hand at the corpse. "By all means."

As she grabbed her notes she heard Dante cross the room to stand beside her — which meant he was being polite, since she hadn't heard him move at all the last time. But then she realized he was reading over her shoulder. For a moment, she forgot that he was a vampire, an aristo, and someone she should be afraid of. Reading over someone's shoulder was *rude*.

"Do you mind if I read your notes?" Dante asked. He grabbed the clipboard from her and began scanning the information she'd written there.

Alice stood confused, hands empty in the air. What was she meant to do now?

Elle was walking around the body, inspecting it closely when something grabbed her attention. Alice hadn't noticed anything odd about the inside of the man's elbow, but Elle sure was pondering it. Then the vampire sniffed. "Dante, you're meant to be identifying the victim. You're not meant to be stealing Alice's notes."

The tall vampire held up a hand, telling Elle to wait.

"So, anything different from this victim to the others?" Kyle asked her, apparently oblivious to the bickering between the other two.

"No. Apart from the fact this one was found naked."

Kyle rocked back on his heels. "Huh."

"That would indicate an increasing level of derision toward his victims," Dante announced, handing Alice the clipboard.

"What?" Kyle said.

"Well, he used to clothe them. Putting clothes on people protects their modesty. But Misty's mother was left in a half-undressed state. Combine that with the additional stake wounds, I suspect that some other emotion was driving the killer during his attack on the countess."

Alice studied the vampire, but she couldn't pinpoint any emotion emanating from him. This was his stepmother he was talking about, but he seemed disinterested, aside from recounting the facts of her murder.

"They weren't particularly close," Elle said.

"Sorry?" Alice said.

"Dante and the countess. They weren't particularly close. That's why he doesn't seem too torn up about it."

Dante gave her a bland look.

Heat rushed up to Alice's cheeks. Had she accidentally said her thoughts aloud? Working on her own quite a lot meant that she *sometimes* muttered things while she was thinking. Normal human hearing wouldn't pick up on it, but a vampire might. She didn't think she'd said anything, though.

"Moving on from my lack of familial relationship with my stepmother, shall I continue?"

"By all means," Kyle said.

"So I suspected that the killer had either a certain antipathy toward the countess, or women in general."

"That's a big assumption," Elle said.

"Yes, but there were two male victims and one female. The male victims were both clothed and stabbed once. The female victim was only partially clothed and stabbed multiple times. Even though the stake wound to the heart would have caused catastrophic cardiovascular failure, the killer persisted in injuring his victim."

"But this victim was found naked." Elle pulled herself up onto the stone bench.

"True. I think when he fails to dress them after he kills them, it's a sign of disrespect. I could be wrong." Dante gave an elegant shrug. "It's not like human psychology is a strong point of mine."

"Interesting." Kyle was rubbing his chin with his thumb and index finger. "But it still doesn't tell us who the killer is."

Dante leaned forward then and sniffed the air above the cadaver. "Well, the victim is wearing a specific cologne, if that helps."

Elle shook her head. "Not unless the killer was wearing it, too."

"Well, I can't smell another type of cologne on him. So either the killer doesn't wear one, or it's the same."

"There's cologne?" Alice asked. She bent over the body and sniffed, but detected nothing aside from the odor of death.

"It's a vampire cologne," Dante explained. "They're made so they don't overpower our sense of smell, but so they're still noticeable."

"Huh. The were ones are even less detectable."

"Stronger senses of smell," Kyle added. *That's right*, she thought. Kyle was buddy-buddy with Elle's fiancé now.

"Maybe I should help Coroner Alice with her autopsy," Dante suggested.

Alice clutched her clipboard to her chest. "What?"

"Well, I might be able to notice things that she can't, with my better vision and superior sense of smell."

A little huff escaped her.

"I can't give you permission for that," Elle said.

Kyle shook his head as well. "It's up to Alice."

Three sets of eyes focused on her. Great, she thought, just great. But even though it galled her to admit it, Dante had a point. He might notice something that she couldn't.

"Do you know what an autopsy involves?" Alice asked him. She gathered he had medical training of some kind, but some people — even relatively impassive ones — could find dissecting a body a bit too gruesome.

Dante let out a short laugh. "This wouldn't be my first. Well, it would be my first legal one."

Legal one?

Alice decided she didn't want to know.

Elle jumped off the bench to stand beside the vampire. "Alice is very particular with how she does her work. You do what she says, when she says it. And try to keep the creep factor under control. Plus, try and identify the body if you can."

Dante raised one dark eyebrow. "Creep factor?"

"Yeah, try and be a little less...*you*."

CHAPTER FIFTY-SIX

Thank fuck they had finally reached the city.

The stench of the place pervaded his senses; the odor of urine from the dye warehouses that ringed the southern side of the river mixed with the sting of blood and death from the tanners and butchers. Coal smoke permeated everything, a heavy, itchy overlay. And then there was the scent of vampires. That prickle of half-frozen blood that got beneath his skin. Funny how he didn't mind how Hannah smelled; she was like frozen strawberries. It went surprisingly well with Fin's verbena and lemon.

The pair of them were like produce.

Byrne wasn't sure he could have handled sitting in the cart with the two of them for much longer. Not because they were being all lovey-dovey — the opposite, in fact. They were acting disgustingly normal. What ate at him was that they'd done something that could ruin the little family they'd built.

Whoa, slow down there.

But it was true.

Even though he spent more time wanting to throttle Fin than not, he still loved the idiot like a brother. And Hannah had managed to win him over the moment she'd tied that terrible diaper on Rena. Any woman who took time from fighting against her own demons to save a baby deserved any help he could give. The fact that she also happened to be a nice person who could tolerate Fin's blather was a bonus.

Well, she more than just tolerates it, he thought.

Oh, shut up.

Byrne had been to Pinton before, but a long time ago; passing through when he'd been a bit younger, before he'd been held prisoner. The dialect here was very similar to Skarvs, and so far he'd had no trouble making do.

Fin sat next to him in the front of the cart, eyes scanning the cobblestone roadway ahead. They'd left the top on the wagon, so passersby would have trouble reaching in to touch Hannah, for whatever reason. Their experience with the hawker had taught them all to be cautious. The cart also provided protection from the wind for Rena. Hannah, stashed away in the back of the cart, was cradling Rena in her lap, bobbing the cub up and down.

"So where are we meant to be going?" Hannah asked.

Montrose had given them an address of an inn where the duchess would be staying. She had explained that Tatiana had chosen not to reside at the palace — even though she technically could expect the king's hospitality, being one of the four rulers of Skarva. But because Tatiana was technically in town on family matters, rather than on a political visit, she'd wanted to keep some distance between her and the other monarch.

"Rutherford Hotel, Pittbrough Street," Byrne said.

Foxtrot was in the harness, with Baldy and the goat following behind the cart. They crossed the stone and steel bridge over the river, with Foxtrot giving the horses passing in the opposite direction a disdainful flick of her tail.

On the other side of the river, Pinton came alive. Shiny carriages and brightly colored hackneys trundled by, with people hustling and bustling along the sidewalks in a purposeful manner. Humans and vampires were dressed in a range of attire, from worn calico to silk shirts and linen trousers.

Fin leaned out the side of the cart and read a street sign.

"We're on Bridge Road."

"Reckon Pittbrough Street is further up?" Byrne asked.

Fin studied the streets as they passed, something that

happened at an unfortunately slow rate. Traffic had picked up quite a lot on this side of the river, and Byrne could detect a street market further up the road; the smell of cloth, metal and hot food among the myriad other odors to reach him. The afternoon sunlight glinted off the glass windows of the three- and four-story buildings that lined the streets.

"Yeah, town seems to be laid out in a grid pattern."

Which was unlike Skarva, with its streets twisting in on themselves once you moved away from the commercial areas. More defensible, that way.

At last they reached the intersection of Pittbrough Street and Bridge Road. The street here was quite wide, which would have allowed for a steady flow of traffic, but for the market that lined both curbs. Small stalls with brightly covered awnings were crammed together in front of hulking bluestone walls to the north, and a row of large buildings to the south.

Byrne was taking shallow breaths, to keep his senses from being overwhelmed, but without warning his every nerve ending came to life.

Something smelled absolutely amazing.

Without meaning to, Byrne inhaled deeply, and the warm, dark scent of chocolate and sin reached him. Tinged with a strange dash of formaldehyde.

"Byrne!"

Byrne shook himself. Fin was staring at him like he'd gone nuts. Shouting reached him next — while he'd daydreamed, he'd been sitting in the cart, blocking all the traffic from Bridge Road turning onto Pittbrough Street.

Fin nudged him in the shoulder. "Get moving."

Flicking the reins, Byrne clicked Foxtrot into motion. But his body was thrumming with tension.

"Give those to me," Fin said, grabbing the reins from him. Too stunned and shaken to protest, Byrne handed them over.

Hannah moved forward from the back of the wagon. "What's going on?"

"Byrne's temporarily lost his mind," Fin muttered.

With Fin driving the cart down Pittbrough Street, Byrne was able to look around. They were passing a building with 'City Guard' carved in large letters over the top of the double doors, and the *smell* seemed to be thick around the structure.

A woman emerged and walked down the stairs, and all the air left Byrne's lungs.

She was a tiny thing, barely five foot five, but she had the most amazing curly auburn hair, which crowned a face he could only see in profile. Her skin was a light brown, and her nose straight, with full lips.

Fin poked him. "Dude, you are staring."

Byrne didn't care. He couldn't take his eyes away. "Who is she?"

"As if I know. But I *can* tell you I haven't slept with her."

A low growl rose from deep within Byrne's chest, completely unbidden. He glared at Fin.

Fin gave him an easy grin. "Thought that might get your attention."

Byrne turned back to find the woman, but she'd gone.

"Fuck."

"What is going on?" Hannah demanded, obviously sick of waiting for Byrne to explain himself. Or for Fin to stop being a dick.

She would have to wait a while for the latter, Byrne thought.

"I think Byrne just got his first hard-on in, like, ever," Fin said. "Cover it up, man, you don't want to make the rest of us look bad."

"What?"

Byrne's cheeks warmed. The stupid human was right. He crossed one leg at his knee.

Hannah leaned forward from the back of the wagon, but Fin put a palm across her eyes.

"No looking." His normally jovial face was hard, despite his light tone. "I don't need you to think my charming self is in any way inferior, because I'm not."

He only dropped his hand when she sat back.

That's when it dawned on Byrne. Fin *liked* Hannah. Not the normal way Fin liked women, but in a far more serious manner. The human was jealous of Hannah seeing Byrne's state, even though it had nothing to do with the vampire, and was thankfully reducing as the delicious smell grew fainter. Not that Byrne thought Hannah had been sneaking forward for a peek. She was probably just a bit confused, as most people were around Byrne and Fin.

It was then Fin pulled the wagon to a stop. Taking a deep breath, he turned to look at Byrne and then Hannah. "We're here."

Chapter Fifty-Seven

Hannah's skin tingled with nerves. She hadn't seen Tatiana in around five years. It wasn't because she was being ignored by her mother, it was just that Tatiana sometimes forgot how time travelled. When you were as old as her, days blended into years, and years into centuries.

Hannah didn't know what had happened when Byrne froze on the corner of Pittbrough Street, but she knew his heartbeat had accelerated, and he had given off this strange scent, almost like a predator warning people away from his territory. But Byrne hadn't been to Pinton for over a hundred years, so she had no idea what territory he could have here.

Fin had ducked inside the Rutherford Hotel to see if her mother was there, and now Hannah could smell him approaching, even before the wagon cover was swished aside. "She's here, although reception is refusing to give us her room number. I thought you might have some luck?"

Nodding, Hannah scooted forward and climbed out the back of the cart, careful of Rena. As the thick leather soles of her boots came into contact with the cobbles, she was glad that her footwear protected her from picking up inadvertent memories. Imagine how many thousands of people had walked this street before.

Leaving Byrne in the wagon, Hannah stepped up onto the sidewalk and dodged a couple of humans who rushed by, then climbed the small set of stairs to the hotel. Tatiana would be able to smell Hannah the moment she entered the building; if she was here, she'd come to investigate.

The foyer was resplendent in creams, blues and golds. Looking around, Hannah's eyes widened at the ostentatious display of wealth. A steel desk lined one wall, with large gilt-framed paintings hanging behind it. On the opposite wall a fireplace stood empty, with cream and blue upholstered chairs set around it. Small metal tables dotted the space, topped with vases of lush flowers. Through the center of the room a rug carpeted the walkway, leading to a flight of large marble stairs.

It was exactly the kind of place her mother would stay.

Walking over to the reception area, Hannah met the gaze of a Brown-eyed human. He was dressed in a blue and black uniform, and had a sneer of disinterest on his unremarkable face. Careful to not come too close to the desk, Hannah patted Rena on the back — the baby was in her normal sling — like she was an excuse to keep her distance. "I would like the room number of the Duchess Tatiana Romanov."

The receptionist's sneer grew. "As I told your *companion*, we do not hand out the room numbers of our guests."

Hannah frowned; she didn't like the way he spoke about Fin, who stood at her side, protectively. "Excuse me?"

"We do not hand out the room numbers of our guests."

Not typically a violent person, Hannah itched to wipe the expression from the idiot's face. "And if that is the case, then why are you unable to let one of your guests know that they have visitors?"

"Visitors?" The man let out a bark of laughter.

"Visitors," Hannah repeated.

Incredulity laced the man's words. "You two are visitors for the *duchess*?"

"I am her daughter, Lady Hannah Romanov. And this is my esteemed friend, Mr. Fin...uh—"

"Castle," Fin supplied.

Funny how she hadn't even known his surname. But it suited him. Fin Castle. She rolled the words around in her mind.

"*You* are the duchess' daughter? You aren't a vampire."

Hannah blinked. She was getting cheek from a hotel worker? About her race?

"If you can't tell a vampire when you see one, maybe you should pick a different line of work," Fin suggested.

And then a new voice entered the mix. "*Hannah?*"

"Mother?"

In her peripheral vision, Hannah saw the human blanch, but her attention was all on Tatiana, who was *there*, at the top of the marble staircase. She was wearing a pair of black pants, shiny knee-high boots, and white shirt, her long hair unbound down her back. Ever since Hannah had been little, her mother's hair had been a dark red, but Montrose said it used to be auburn. The older Tatiana got, the more bloody her hair grew in hue.

Tatiana came down the stairs and cupped Hannah's cheeks in her cool hands, her eyes roving over her daughter's face. "Hannah, what are you doing here?"

Then she registered the presence of Fin and Rena, and lowered her voice. "I think you had better come upstairs."

"Another traveling *companion* is out the front with our wagon and animals. Is it possible for one of your hotel staff to see to it while we visit the duchess?" Fin's voice was smooth and oily. Hannah bit back a grin.

The receptionist opened his mouth to protest, but Tatiana waved a hand through the air. "See to it. And give the other one my room number so they can meet us there."

Then she grabbed Hannah's arm and towed her up the staircase and down a long hallway. Fin followed behind.

Soon, they arrived at her mother's suite. Tatiana shut the door and then turned to the two of them. Tatiana ran a hand quickly across her brow, and then sat down on one of the chairs within the sitting area of the suite. She looked almost...fragile. Through a half-open door, Hannah could see an elaborate bedroom. "How long has it been since I last saw you?" Her bright gaze was locked on Rena.

"Five years."

"Five *years*? I'm sorry, Hannah. I hadn't thought it was that long. It is terribly remiss of me not to have seen you sooner," she said sadly.

Hannah didn't know what to say — she hadn't expected this. "That's okay, Mother."

"But...why did you not send me word of you having a child?" Wide violet eyes held Hannah's gaze, bewildered.

Mother thinks that Rena is mine.

"I do not mind that you have had a baby with a...human," Tatiana went on. "I am happy that you found someone you could..."

She thinks that Rena is mine and Fin's.

It shocked Hannah to discover that her mother's misconception didn't make her panic at all. She *liked* the idea of her and Fin as a family.

"Mother, Rena is not my baby."

"Then she is yours?" Tatiana addressed Fin, who was hovering near the door. He looked quite uncomfortable, which was unusual for him.

"No, not mine. Well, not by birth, anyway." Fin was babbling. "She's ours now."

Tatiana shook her head. "I'm afraid you've lost me."

"I found Rena abandoned on the slopes of the Old Mother. She was left on a blanket, naked."

Frowning, Tatiana leaned forward. "By the Trsetti?"

Hannah nodded, then turned Rena within the sling, so her mother could see the baby's face and eye color.

"Huh. I forgot they were superstitious about people with colored eyes. Any color. They tolerate me because I've been visiting that mountain for longer than their culture can remember. Anyone else, well, they're not too welcome."

"Tell me about it," Fin muttered.

Tatiana ignored him. "So you found the baby?"

"But I didn't really know what to do," Hannah confessed. "Luckily the blanket she was lying on gave me some hints and tips about feeding a baby without a mother, but that was about it. So I started traveling to Skarva."

"With the human?"

"No," Hannah admitted. "I found him and his friend on the slopes of the Old Mother. The Trsetti had also taken exception to Fin."

Tatiana nodded, as if the puzzle pieces were slowly fitting together. "Hence the bruises. But his Hazel eyes shouldn't have bothered them too much."

"His eye color wasn't the problem," Hannah said.

Fin glared at her. "What happened in the village has nothing to do with you finding Rena."

"You slept with someone, didn't you?" Tatiana asked, shaking her head.

"Why does everyone assume that about me?" Fin glowered.

Hannah wanted to blurt, 'because it's true', but it would hurt Fin's feelings. And she didn't want to do that. "Either way, I bumped into Fin and Byrne and they helped me get to Skarva."

"And you arrived there to find me gone."

Fin snickered. "Well, we arrived there to have someone touch Hannah and then kidnap her, but sure." He yelped when Hannah punched him in the arm. He rubbed his bicep. "I'm human, Hannah! And I've just been beaten up *twice* in two weeks; go easy."

"Humans are fragile, Hannah. Be nicer to your...lover."

Hannah shifted uncomfortably and Fin's jaw dropped.

Their surprise amused Tatiana. "Please. You both smell like each other far too much to just be friends. Now, what is this about you getting kidnapped and *touched*?"

And so Hannah told the story of Randall and how he had planned on using her to secure his place in Skarvan society. By the end, Tatiana was prowling the room, and her expression made even Hannah uneasy. Rena had started to wail, picking up on the tension. That, or she was hungry.

The crying gave Tatiana pause. The ancient vampire then came over and gently lifted the babe from Hannah's arms. "Sshh." Within moments, Rena settled.

Homicidal one moment, babysitter the next.

"How'd you do that?" Fin peered at Rena over Tatiana's shoulder, like this woman hadn't been ready to seek out Randall's corpse and rip off its head a few seconds ago.

"It's all in the hold," Tatiana replied. "This is not the first time I've held a baby."

"Well, I gathered that since you have Hannah and her brother."

Silence.

Tatiana turned sad eyes on Hannah. "You know about Dante?"

"Randall mentioned it." She tried to be casual, but she couldn't keep the hurt from her face. "Why didn't you tell me?"

Tatiana sighed. "Tell me the rest of your story first."

Chapter Fifty-Eight

Throughout Hannah's tale of what had happened in Skarva, Tatiana sat still as a stone, except for occasionally rubbing Rena's back. Hannah had stood for the whole story, because where could she sit without exposing herself to the memories of those who'd used the chairs before?

Fin studied Tatiana, the Deadly Duchess, legend and all-around terror for people young and old. She was as beautiful as her daughter, but in different ways. Hannah was tall and lithe, while her mother was statuesque and curvy. They had the same face shape, but Tatiana's chin was a little more pointed, and her eyes a bit larger.

At first, he hadn't been sure that letting the duchess hold the baby was a good idea — what with her visibly swapping from enraged to calm in a heartbeat. But while he'd only been in the room about thirty minutes, Tatiana had worked wonders with the infant. Maybe being about a million years old made you an expert with kids.

Who knew?

"So Randall is dead?" Tatiana asked rhetorically.

Fin nodded. "She ripped his heart out; it was pretty gross."

Tatiana snorted. "You picked the wrong family to get involved in if you think a little heart extraction is disturbing."

Fin forced a smile, like the woman was joking, but he knew she wasn't.

"*Mother.*"

"What? Better he knows what he's in for early on. Humans don't live forever, and if he wants to spend the time he has with you, then he should know that we are a little...different to modern vampires. That's all."

"I think he's gathered that I am different."

Tatiana looked at him. "So you *know?*"

"He knows. And he has a mental shield."

Deciding that he needed to rest his legs, Fin sat in one of the expensive chairs. Funny how getting beaten up ruined your stamina.

"Interesting."

So Tatiana Romanov thought he was interesting. Fin wasn't sure he liked that.

Thankfully, a knock sounded on the door to the suite. "Enter!"

Byrne stepped inside, shutting the door behind him. Fin didn't know what had been up with the were on the roadway near the City Guard building, but it was something significant. Maybe it had something to do with his special mate-detecting nose? He would have to try and pry the information out of the huge man later. Now they had other issues.

It was Tatiana's turn to look surprised now. "*Trace?*"

Byrne met her gaze with his yellow eyes. "Name's Byrne."

Succinct, as always.

"Didn't you have a relative called Trace?" Fin asked. One night, early after Fin had hauled Byrne's ass out of the prison, they'd talked about their families. Byrne had told him about his two sisters, Gina and Ruby, and Fin had rattled off about the four pains-in-the-butt he called his siblings. Byrne's parents hadn't been too involved in his upbringing, at least not as a cub. He'd been raised in a clan, with his great-great-great (and so on) grandfather overseeing his early years.

Byrne shot Fin an undecipherable look. "My grandpa, yeah."

"Your *grandfather?*"

"Yeah. Well, there's a few 'greats' in there."

Tatiana looked pensive for a moment, and Fin wondered what

it would be like to have lived for so long that you had to physically sort through your memories. At least, that's what he assumed she was doing. Then she clicked her fingers. "I knew that bastard wasn't dead!"

"You know Byrne's grandpa?" Hannah asked.

"Knew. Was at war with. Had my neck broken by. Much the same," Tatiana said, but there was an almost dreamy quality to her expression. Weird. And a bit creepy, considering the were apparently broke her neck.

"It was a very long time ago." Something wicked flashed in her over-sized violet eyes. "When you next see your grandfather, please pass on my greetings. And that I would dearly love to see him again."

Byrne shifted on his feet. "Sure, as long as you don't plan on snapping his neck if you do manage to catch up with him."

Fin held his breath; would Tatiana take offense? But she trilled a laugh. "It was so long ago. I've let that grudge go."

That just made Fin wonder what other grudges she still held.

"Mother," Hannah said a little uncomfortably, "you said once I had told you about what happened at your estate that you would talk about my brother."

Tatiana's face grew curiously blank and then she heaved out a sigh. "I assume both your friends know about your special...talent?"

Fin and Byrne nodded.

"Dante was born with violet eyes. He was older than you by a few minutes, but he seemed like a normal vampire baby. You, on the other hand, had Black eyes from the moment you were born. I couldn't take the risk that your father would see them and realize you were different. I kept you and Dante with me for two months, before I handed your brother over. Luckily, your father wasn't interested in seeing his second daughter, just the long-awaited boy child.

"I didn't entirely trust your father with Dante, but I didn't have much of a choice. We had signed a breeding contract, where if we had a son, your father would get custody. I had planned on staying in Pinton while your brother was a youngster, but I didn't know what abilities your eyes gave you. Even my memory holds no knowledge of a Black-eyed Graced.

"I knew that if your father discovered you had abilities, whatever they might be, he would use you. And so I moved back to Skarva. I didn't tell you about Dante because I thought it would keep you safe — keep you home. I didn't want you rushing off to your father and your brother, where who knows what could've happened."

"But you could have told me about him!"

"Would you have been willing not to meet him?" Tatiana asked.

Hannah didn't respond. And they all knew why. She might be a loner, but that wasn't by choice. If she could have had more people in her life, she would have. Look at how she embraced him and Byrne, Fin thought.

"And your father, well, he is just as bad as I suspected," Tatiana continued. "He recently sold your brother off in marriage — even though Dante had reached his majority in Pinton law. Your brother also recently Chose someone and your father ordered that she be cremated before she had a chance to wake up from the transformation. The man is a liability, with no concern for the wellbeing of his children.

"Do you know, I was there the other day when his other daughter arrived home to tell him that the countess — his mate — had been murdered. And all he cared about was the social scandal!"

"Other daughter?" Hannah asked.

Tatiana nodded. "His oldest child."

"That would make her your sister, too," Fin said.

Hannah's father sounded like a dick. If Tatiana Romanov disliked him — this being the woman who admitted that heart extraction by hand wasn't abnormal in their family — that didn't instill a great deal of confidence in him. The guy must be a total asshole.

"Can I meet him?" Hannah asked.

Tatiana frowned. "Your father? I would prefer not."

"No, Dante."

Tatiana sighed. "I guess it can be arranged. You're here, after all."

"I'm here," Hannah said with a slow smile. It made Fin's insides feel all warm and gooey. Man, he was pathetic.

Chapter Fifty-Nine

Dante had invited the coroner over to dinner. She'd stammered a list of excuses why she couldn't possibly come, of course, but he'd simply ignored them. He'd told her to bring her friend — the one he suspected was dating Misty — and that he would see them at the Greystoke townhouse at ten that night. He'd send a carriage for them.

Then he'd gone home to tell Anton and his mother-in-law, Lady Beatrice, about their dinner plans. The countess had flown into a bit of a flap, but she excelled at these kinds of things. And she was surprisingly happy that Dante had actually bothered to invite someone over.

Anton, on the other hand, was stunned. "*You* invited the city's coroner over for dinner?"

Dante nodded. They were in the Rose room; the various pink and red hues of the parlor had somehow become comfortingly familiar to him. Normally you'd find at least Darla — Anton's sister — here, but she was apparently out visiting a friend and the room was unusually quiet. Elle was at work, and Clay was sleeping in the backyard, still in his furry coat. He was annoyed at Dante, but hadn't explained why. The vampire figured it was hard to talk when you had a wolf jaw, so he'd wait. If Elle was here she could have just asked him, but she always worked at the most inconvenient times.

"She seemed quite nice. And she let me help her do an autopsy.

I am thinking of asking her if she needs an assistant."

While he'd been working with the small human woman, it had occurred to Dante that he could enjoy doing a job like hers. He liked human anatomy, and had spent half his life studying it and human blood. And now he didn't have any short-term goals. Aside from being a good husband, which was still a work in progress. Assisting in the coroner's office would give him purpose.

His father would have a fit, but Dante was less afraid of his parent now that Tatiana — his mother — had made herself known. He was still a little in awe of her. Throwing his father out of a window had been pure genius.

But getting back to the matter at hand; working in a morgue would also provide Dante with ready access to cadavers for when Emmie would be ready to start her medical training. He was planning ahead, giving Elle less chance to argue against his recommendation.

"You do realize that the coroner might not feel comfortable coming to an aristo's house for dinner?" Anton said.

Dante's face was blank. "She knows me now, and she already knew Elle. Plus, I said to bring her friend. Oh, and I asked Misty to come, too."

Anton's expression fell slightly, but then he gave Dante a smile. "Okay."

Something tightened in Dante's chest. He knew that Anton wasn't crazy about Misty — she could be pretty difficult when she set her mind to it, or even when she wasn't really trying — but she was Dante's sister and he got along better with her nowadays. And so Anton tried to get along with her too, even though she made it hard.

Dante thought Misty believed Anton wasn't good enough for him, which was stupid. If anything, it was the other way around. But Misty was Misty. Once she made her mind up, it was hard to persuade her otherwise.

Dante had grown so used to living in houses surrounded by people, that he didn't think much of the sound of approaching footsteps. The butler appeared in the doorway of the Rose room and cleared his throat.

"The Duchess of Ravens is here to see you, sir."

Nodding, Dante indicated that his mother should be shown in. His mother. It was still an odd concept. He'd never thought of Countess Maerylina as a parent, more an adult who paid him attention from time to time. And yet, she'd been more involved in his life than this strange woman. It was a shame Dante didn't really mourn the countess' loss. Oh, he felt bad for his sister, but not for himself. Then again, death — in some form or another — had surrounded him from a young age. Maybe he was desensitized to it?

A few seconds later footsteps and quiet voices reached his ears. Did his mother have other visitors with her? And why did the smell of bear precede the visitors?

Then Tatiana was walking through the doorway, a wide smile on her face. She held both hands out as she greeted Dante, and he realized he was meant to take them. Standing, he offered his own in return.

Tatiana squeezed his palms, stepped back and swept an arm toward the doorway. Three other people filed into the room, each one looking slightly awkward, as if unsure of their welcome. They smelled of bear, dust, oaks and coal smoke; they must have been traveling. Of the three, only one was human, and Dante noted with interest that it was a male with Hazel eyes. The other man was a were — a bear, Dante gathered — who made even Clay look small, and the final newcomer was a woman who smelled like a vampire, but who had the darkest purple eyes he had ever seen. They looked black.

Anton had stood up and was approaching the trio, hand outstretched for the female vampire to take it. "Hello, my name is Lord Greystoke. I presume you are Tatiana's daughter?"

The woman stared at Anton's hand, as if it were a snake. Dante took a step forward, offended on behalf of his husband. But then Anton's words sank in. Why would Anton assume that the new vampire was Tatiana's daughter? Dante assessed her, took in her long black hair, pale skin and tall figure. She looked more like his father than Tatiana.

And then it clicked.

Could this be his missing twin sister?

Oh, Misty was going to love this.

Not.

Losing her mother, only to have a new sibling arrive. He couldn't imagine this going well.

Anton's smile withered as the woman still failed to move. His hand had begun to droop when the Hazel-eyed human stepped forward and shook it, a bit too vigorously. Tattoos wreathed the man's hand, as did a series of small, newly healed scars. His face was covered with fading bruises, but the bright smile he gave Anton made his husband falter. Dante narrowed his eyes. Could this other human be handsome? Was being blond, tall and muscular appealing? Is that what made Anton react? Dante wasn't sure he liked this new human with his interesting Hazel eyes.

"Name's Fin Castle, nice to meet you." No accent. The man spoke Pintonese flawlessly. "This is Lady Hannah Romanov, and the big hulking fellow over there is Byrne."

No surname. Just Byrne.

The description of the were was rather apt. The man had needed to bend to get in the room, and was standing slightly hunched within the doorway, since the others had failed to move aside and let him enter properly. Something small was strapped to the were's front.

"Is that a baby?" Dante asked, ignoring the introductions.

Five sets of eyes stared at him and everyone took a step forward. And then a wolf barged its way through the door. It avoided brushing up against anyone, its movements quick. Stopping in front of Dante, the wolf yapped.

Dante sighed. "What is your problem, Clay?"

Another yap.

Dante pinched the bridge of his nose between his thumb and

forefinger. "In case you missed it, I don't speak wolf."

Clay's muzzle dropped open, but Anton turned back to address him. "If you want to participate, go and change shape then come back."

With a bright yellow glare, Clay slunk from the room. He gave the bear a sniff on the way through, earning a scowl from the other were. Was it impolite for them to sniff each other?

"He was probably checking who had invaded his territory," Tatiana offered, as if reading Dante's thoughts.

"So whose baby is that?" Dante asked, not too intrigued about were politics when there were other matters at hand. After all, he could easily grill Clay later. Dante was unable to see the face of the baby, but its skin tone indicated that it was not the bear's. And it smelled human. Which meant that it wouldn't be Hannah's, as she was a vampire, even with her very dark purple eyes.

"It is Hannah's adopted daughter," Tatiana said.

There was a tickling sensation at the corner of Dante's mind. He never would have been able to detect it before he'd Chosen Elle, but he knew now when someone was trying to read his thoughts. No one in the room had Green eyes, aside from the human male, who had Green in his Hazel — so Dante concluded it must be the baby.

This raised a number of questions about Graced development that Dante was keen to explore.

Tatiana flicked a hand through the air. "Dante, I would like you to meet your sister."

So Anton had been correct.

Hannah tilted her head in acknowledgement. That was not normal behavior. Dante moved closer to her, and she stepped back, careful to avoid bumping into anything. He was now close enough to see that her eyes were not purple. They *were* Black.

Then, before his brain could stop it from happening, he blurted, "Are you Graced?"

The room went eerily quiet.

"Graced?" Hannah repeated.

"I—uh—"

"How do you know about the Graced?" the Hazel-eyed human asked.

Dante gave a little shrug. "I Chose one."

Fin shook his head. "Impossible, Graceds don't survive being Chosen or Bitten."

"They do if they're Hazel."

Fin appeared to want to say more, but Dante turned away from him to his new sister.

Well, old sister.

Same-age sister.

Sister.

"So, what can you do?" He took another step closer, but Hannah edged away, toward the human.

Clay strode into the room then, dressed in his human skin and a pair of trousers and a shirt. He had bare feet. "Byrne! What are you doing in town?" he said, giving the bear a slap on the back and grinning. "And with a baby! Your sister has been all over the countryside trying to find you, I'll have you know."

So they did know each other.

Byrne's good humor faded. "You've seen Gina?"

"Wasn't Gina, it was Ruby. She's been through Gorke a few times looking for you. Her and her mate."

"Mate?" The were's eyebrows raised.

"Yeah, some big cat decided she smelled right and that she was his. She happened to agree with his assessment. You later-generation weres do it strangely, let me tell you. A bear and a tiger. Odd mix." Clay shook his head. Dante wasn't too good at the social situation thing, but he could see this news appeared to sadden Byrne, and that the human, Fin, was staring at him rather intently as a result.

Tatiana, however, was fixated on Clay. She hissed. "*You.*"

Clay gave an easy shrug. "Me?"

Tatiana glowered at both of the weres. "You're the alpha of *that clan* Trace belonged to."

Dante had no idea what clan she was talking about. Or who Trace was. Odd name.

Clay thought a moment. "Not me, that'd be my uncle, Wolf."

Fin sniggered. "Your uncle was called Wolf? Original."

"His name was Wolfgang." The look Clay gave the human added an unspoken 'ass' to the end of the sentence.

Tatiana nodded, but she didn't look too happy. "What are the chances of meeting two descendants of that time?" Her voice was low, thoughtful.

Dante and Anton stared at Clay, who sighed. "It was a really long time ago. I was just a teenager."

That meant it was so long ago as to be almost legendary. And while that was fascinating, Dante had other things to deal with.

"Apparently, I have a twin sister who is Graced." Dante said. "Anyone care to explain to me what is going on?"

CHAPTER SIXTY

Alice eyed the black and white tiled entry foyer of the Greystoke townhouse in awe. Every aristo place she'd been in since becoming involved in the vampire murder case was opulent. Would she ever get used to this?

Tal stood next to her, dressed in a stunning black gown that hugged her figure, one that Alice hadn't seen before. Her best friend loved to shop, unlike Alice, who mostly enjoyed going out to buy medical equipment. But Tal's outfit made Alice feel a little self-conscious, because Alice was wearing the same dress she'd worn a couple of weeks ago, when the second body had been found. It wasn't floor length, but she didn't want to wear the orange gown again and there weren't too many other options left in her wardrobe to choose from.

Footsteps accompanied by a clacking sound approached and a handsome human male appeared. He was dressed in a charcoal suit, with a snowy white shirt and blue cravat. He was also using a cane, the source of the clicking. Alice wondered what had happened to his leg. "Welcome, I am Lord Greystoke."

Alice dropped into an awkward curtsy, Tal sweeping into a more elegant one beside her. "Pleased to meet you, I am Doctor Alice Reive, and this is Professor Talan Silver."

It was strange using her title, but Alice figured that when with aristos, do as they do. And she'd earned it, after all. Six years of medical school at the university, plus a year as a doctor in the city hospital before working as an assistant to the former coroner. It's just that she wasn't all that fussed by it. Even the guards didn't call her doctor — it wasn't like she was a sawbones for living people, after all.

The baron tilted his head in acknowledgment, and then motioned for them to follow him further into the house. Alice and Tal nodded subtly at each other then trailed after the human. "We have a few unexpected guests here this evening, so you will have to excuse the somewhat haphazard organization that has taken place."

Alice didn't know what that implied, but if it meant this wouldn't be too much of a formal affair, she was happy. She wasn't sure she could do formal.

They soon emerged into a room decorated in a series of pinks and reds, and trimmed with gold. One of the chairs alone would be worth more than all the furniture in Alice's house. She hoped her gawking wasn't too obvious.

The room wasn't devoid of people, though.

The baron's husband, Dante, was there, standing in a corner talking with a woman who looked remarkably like him; tall and lithe with long black hair and dark colored eyes. Next to her was a blond man who was a bit too pretty for his own good, and a woman with dark red hair and flashing violet eyes. They were having an intense conversation and didn't really look up when Alice and Tal entered.

Tal muttered something under her breath that Alice didn't catch. It didn't sound too complimentary, though. Suddenly Alice could tell someone was staring at her. Beside the empty fireplace, was the tallest man she'd ever clapped eyes on, and she'd thought that Kyle and Captain Mikael were vertically gifted. He was also horribly handsome, with beautiful dark black skin and a full mouth that begged for attention. She didn't normally look at mouths and think they needed kissing; well, she hadn't for a while, at any rate, but this one... His bright yellow eyes were locked on her, and a blush rose in her cheeks.

He'd caught her staring.

The man took a deep breath, and then he started toward her, as if drawn. He was wearing tan pants and a brown shirt more suited to traveling, rather than a drawing room, but they were right on him. And there was some kind of sling around his torso, but she couldn't keep her eyes off his face.

Forcing herself to look around the room, Alice wondered what she should do. She'd never met a were before. What was the protocol?

"He's coming this way," Tal said, moving to stand slightly in front of Alice. Was she being protective? Tal's gray eyes flashed at the were as he stopped in front of them.

"What brings a were to these parts of town?" Tal asked, her tone almost rude.

Alice straightened. *"Tal."*

"Just visiting," the were said, his voice deep and gravelly. It sent a pleasant shiver down her spine.

Another were had followed him over, and this one was also tall, but not as towering as the dark-skinned man. He had brown hair that looked like it had been combed by fingers, and a bright glint in his yellow eyes.

The second were spoke. "You must be Elle's friend, the coroner."

Alice nodded. "And you're Clay?"

The were gave her an easy grin. "Glad to see she's mentioned me. Hopefully everything she's said is good, because that would mean she's lying, otherwise."

She laughed, but Tal only gave the two men a tight smile. Alice hadn't been aware that her friend had issues with weres; not when she'd joked about wanting to sleep with one to just see what it was like.

The taller of the weres leaned forward, gently clasping one of Alice's hands in his, and raising the back of her hand to his lips. "Name's Byrne, it is a pleasure to meet you." His voice was warm and deep, and it did strange things to Alice's insides.

Fighting another blush, she smiled. "Nice to meet you, Byrne. I'm Alice."

That was when she spotted that the sling around the man held a baby.

A rush of emotion zapped through her, and she drooped a little, until she saw that the baby had olive skin, paler than her own. This infant was unlikely to have been the were's. Maybe he was minding it for the couple on the other side of the room?

Not that it mattered if he had a baby. He could be married or with someone for all she knew. But she didn't want him to be unavailable, and that startled her.

"Doctor Reive," Tal said, sidling closer to Alice and bringing her thoughts back to the room.

"Doctor?" The were let go of her hand, and the loss crumpled something inside Alice.

She nodded. "I'm the city coroner. This is Talan Silver, she's a professor of applied mathematics at the Royal University."

"A professor?" That was from Clay.

"Yes," Tal said without altering that strange smile.

Clay's yellow gaze was piercing. Something was off about this exchange — Tal's behavior, Clay's response — but Alice couldn't tell what. Besides, there was the fact that the handsome were was making her heart beat a little too fast.

Then, from the other side of the room came a startled, "*What?*"

Dante nodded. "Touch the latest victim in the murder case."

The red-headed vampire had crossed her arms over her chest and was shaking her head firmly. The blond man was glaring at Dante. "No, absolutely not."

"Hannah is her own person, she can answer for herself," Dante said, loud enough that Alice could hear it.

"And she'll say no," the blond man said. He glowered at Dante.

The woman in question — Hannah, Alice presumed — opened her mouth to speak. "I—I—"

Then the human took another step forward, jabbing his finger on Dante's chest. He was either very brave, or very foolish. The vampire could break his neck in seconds. "You don't know what you're asking. No."

Hannah shoved the blond man aside, standing in front of him, concern etched on her face. "Fin, you have to be careful. He's a vampire."

"I *know* he's a vampire."

"You can't go around poking vampires. They might not take it well."

"He wasn't going to bite me cos I poked him with a finger." Fin squinted at Dante. "Were you?"

"Thought hadn't occurred to me, but I wouldn't rule it out."

Hannah stomped a foot. "See? They're dangerous."

"He said he hadn't even considered it."

"If you don't shut up, I will bite the both of you." That came from the red-headed vampire. Her overlarge violet eyes flashed. Fin shut his mouth with a snap. So he had the sense not to bait that woman, whoever she was.

Alice found her attention drifting back to Byrne. His towering height was impressive, if slightly impractical for the things that had suddenly sprung to mind. And that was even assuming he'd be interested in someone like her. Human. Short. Mortal.

Then, without really thinking about it, Alice blurted, "How are you at painting?"

CHAPTER SIXTY-ONE

The doctor — Alice — smelled amazing. It was the same rich scent he'd picked up outside the City Guard building: chocolate and sin, with a hint of formaldehyde, but the fact that she was the city coroner explained that strange tang. And just being near her was drugging his senses.

Would it be rude to throw her over his shoulder and hightail it out of here?

Probably.

Almost certainly.

And that wasn't how Byrne behaved. He was the calm one, the centered one. Fin did crazy shit like that — and usually got away with it. Although, Byrne had to admit, he'd like to see the human try something like that with Hannah. She'd probably tell him off for risking his poor human hide. As it was, she was lecturing him on poking her brother in the chest.

Hannah's brother.

There were physical similarities that made it clear the two were related, but the male vampire had Tatiana's bright violet eyes, rather than his sister's mysterious Black. The vampire — Dante — knew about the Graced, but how or why Byrne wasn't quite sure. Just saying that he 'Chose' one felt like only half the explanation.

Tatiana let out an exasperated sigh. "If you don't shut up, I will bite the both of you."

Hannah shoved Fin further back behind her, putting herself firmly between her brother and her mother. She must *really* like

Fin, Byrne thought. To risk being exposed to touch by Dante, to take on her mother's wrath. She might not even know it herself yet, but she cared for the stupid human a lot. Just like Byrne cared for him. Probably more, since she'd gone ahead and banged the idiot.

Byrne could admit to himself he'd been morosely jealous about the two of them, until he'd caught hold of that amazing scent. It had taken all his willpower earlier in the day to not leap out of the cart and chase after the woman who produced it, but he'd managed. Somehow.

But what else could he have done? Followed her home and acted like some crazy stalker. "You smell like my mate," was a line that might have gotten a door or three slammed in his face.

You smell like my mate.

Byrne froze.

It hadn't really occurred to him until that moment that this was what was happening. That Alice the coroner — that the woman standing in front of him right now — might be his ideal partner. But he'd never reacted this way to a scent before. Sure, he'd picked up on plenty of nice smells, but this was something else. Every particle of his being was humming, and all he wanted to do was hold her hand and just *talk* to her.

Okay. Maybe not just talk.

But he wanted to be with her. And to get her away from everyone else.

His heavy gaze alighted on the human woman. The other human — the Graced one with Gray eyes — was glaring at him, but he didn't care. Alice was even more beautiful than he'd thought from the street. Her curly auburn hair framed her heart-shaped face, and her wide Brown eyes were the color of autumn leaves. Although, she *was* tiny; she barely even came to his sternum. He was worried he'd break her just by being in the same room.

You are fine with Rena, his mind said. *Alice is an adult, even though she's human. Don't panic.*

He kept kind of panicking.

Alice blurted, "How are you at painting?"

Taken aback, Byrne stared down at the woman he hoped was destined to be his mate. Did he hear her right? "Painting?"

"Painting." Her cheeks flushed a warm rose color. "I have a spot at home that I can't reach. It needs painting."

"You could just use a ladder," her friend said.

Alice hunched her shoulders slightly. "Even with a ladder, I can't reach."

Byrne didn't care that she was interested in him painting her ceiling. He was more keen on the fact that she'd considered inviting him to her house. An unfamiliar wicked gleam entered his gaze. He leaned down and rumbled, "I would love to come and paint your ceiling."

Man, did that sound like a bizarre come-on line. Fin was going to give him grief for that. Then again, Fin was still over in the corner arguing with Hannah that while he *might* have implied that humans were fairly breakable, as a general rule they weren't, and he didn't need her trying to wrap him in cotton wool. Hannah looked like she was pondering where she could get that much cotton wool.

Alice's warm eyes brightened. "Really?"

He gave her a grin, and it felt strangely easy. Maybe some of Fin's charm had transferred to him. "We'll make it a date."

"I'm not sure that is a good idea," the Gray-eyed woman said.

"Why not?" That was from Clay. "The woman needs her ceiling taken care of. And Byrne is clearly the man to do it."

Now if there weren't a whole bunch of double meaning behind that statement, Byrne would be shocked. He'd forgotten how much of a rascal Clay was. And the man was millennia older than Byrne. He'd been around when Byrne's grandfather, Trace, had been in his prime. Although, having been a second-generation were, Trace was always going to be in his prime. If he was still alive. Byrne didn't know, since he hadn't seen his family for over a century.

"You just met him," the mathematics professor said to Alice. "Maybe you should ask Kyle to help you."

Byrne couldn't help the low growl that rolled through him. He didn't know who this Kyle was, but he didn't like the idea of the man going over and painting Alice's ceiling. He assumed there really was a ceiling in need of paint. Either way, he didn't like the idea.

Alice was his.

Well, she would be his, once she got to know him. And he her. And they discovered that they liked each other. And that...

Oh, shut up. You're worse than Fin says you are.

He didn't like that his mind had a point.

Or that it was saying Fin was right.

"*Kyle?*" Clay asked. "Trust me, I know Kyle *and* my man, Byrne. You don't want Kyle going over to Alice's house."

"Is the man a predator?" Byrne asked.

Clay nearly choked on his own saliva. "No, he's just a bit of a...ladies man."

Byrne was unimpressed. "Did you meet Fin?"

Fin, who could woo entire towns without even trying. Although Alice hadn't seemed too stunned by the human's pretty face. Which was a miracle in itself.

"You mean that guy?" Clay pointed at Fin, who was still debating with Hannah about the merits of being allowed to argue with whomever he pleased. "The one struggling over there?"

"Hannah has a unique way of looking at things," Byrne said. Rena was beginning to stir, and he rubbed his palm over her back, before gently lifting the cub from her sling.

"Whose pup is that?" Clay asked. He studied the cub with bright eyes. "She's got Green eyes." Clay then looked over at Hannah and Fin. "Those two manage to have a pup?"

Byrne shrugged. Tatiana had apparently wondered the same thing, which meant to Byrne that there was a possibility that Hannah and Fin *could* have cubs, if they were lucky. He wondered if the two of them comprehended that yet. He wasn't sure that Fin would cope well with that discovery. Fin loved kids, but Byrne knew he'd had some bad luck with them in the past.

"No, Hannah found the baby abandoned," Byrne said.

"Abandoned?" Talan asked.

"The local townspeople near where Hannah lived fear anyone who looks a little different. They took one look at the cub's Green eyes and left her out there to die."

Alice put a hand to her mouth. "How could they? People with colored eyes are no different to anyone else!"

Byrne glared at Tal. Her serene expression hardened when she caught his accusatory look.

So pretty Alice had no idea her friend could move things with her mind?

"Hannah saved the cub," Byrne said, "and bumped into Fin and me on the road. The human had just had the shit kicked out of him by a group of townspeople, so he wasn't doing so well at the time. Hence she's a little overprotective. She's worried that humans break too easily, what with having a human baby and a human boyfriend now."

Dante whipped his head around. "Did you just say boyfriend?"

"I did," Byrne said, taking great pleasure in seeing Fin pale. Hannah looked a little whiter than usual herself.

"They're practically married," he added, just for fun.

"That baby can't be more than a month old," Talan said. "So you're implying these two are engaged after knowing each other for a *month*?"

Clay shrugged. "Hey, when you know, you know. I convinced my darling Elle that she wanted to marry me in less time than that."

A snort came from the doorway. Standing next to the human with the cane, and a little girl with bright Teal-colored eyes was a vampire, her own irises a strange mix of purple, Green and Gray.

So this must be the vampire that Dante had Chosen.

"I don't recall you giving me too much of a chance to refuse your proposal," she said, moving into the room, the little girl coming after her. The child had nut-brown skin and brown hair, and smiled shyly at everyone.

The vampire wrapped an arm around Clay's middle.

Suddenly, the room felt a little too crowded for Byrne. He backed away to the edge of the parlor, and he stood there, cuddling Rena. He wasn't used to this many people. Or being surrounded by so many Graced folks. It brought back some unpleasant memories.

"Are you okay?" Alice had followed him, no matter that her friend was glaring at them both.

"Sure."

"You don't look it."

He gave a weak smile. "Been some time since I've had this many people in a room with me. Been traveling for a while."

For three years, actually. And before that he'd been locked in a cell for a century.

Alice reached out a hand — to touch the cub, he assumed — but she patted his arm instead. The contact electrified him. Standing on her tiptoes, her eyes alive with humor, she whispered, "I'm used to spending time with corpses, so this is a bit odd for me, too."

Byrne might just have fallen a little in love.

CHAPTER SIXTY-TWO

Fin couldn't believe it. Byrne had announced to everyone in the room that Hannah was his girlfriend. And she hadn't argued. Not that she would want to, since it was Fin she was supposed to be dating, after all. But *girlfriend*?

There was no way that whatever it was that Fin and Hannah had going was so simple as to be girlfriend and boyfriend. Plus, it made the two of them sound like they were fifteen, which certainly wasn't the case. Fin was thirty, and who knew how old Hannah was.

Actually, that was a good point.

"How old are you?" Fin asked, looking at his 'girlfriend.'

She was pretty hot. So that part was okay.

Hannah glared at him. Was it bad that he found that sexy? In fact, everything she did was sexy. He'd thought that after they'd slept together, things would calm down for him in that department. But they hadn't. Sleeping with her had only made things worse. He now knew what it was like to be with her, and it just made him want more. But he didn't know if she was keen to be with him again, although the fact that she hadn't protested at being called his girlfriend was a good sign.

Maybe he should stop dwelling on that.

"I'm over two hundred years old," Hannah said eventually.

"Well, I assume you are two hundred and four," chipped in her annoying brother, "since that is my age, and I'm told we're twins."

There was something about Dante that set Fin's teeth on edge. Maybe it was the fact that he was about as emotional as a brick. Then again, maybe it was because he'd asked Hannah to touch a fucking dead guy. Hence Fin's poking Dante in the chest.

"Two hundred and four? Where does the time go," Tatiana mused, shaking her head. "Dante was born first, in case you were wondering. So that makes him older."

"Huh. I'm totally dating a cougar," Fin said.

"Cougar? I'm not a were, Fin."

As if he didn't know that.

"Duh. Cougar — they're older women who like to date younger men."

Tatiana let out a bark of surprised laughter. "Every man on the planet is younger than me. What does that make me?"

Fin thought fast. "One of a kind?"

He couldn't imagine anyone having balls enough to climb into bed with Hannah's mother. He knew her father had managed it somehow, and frankly, Fin was surprised the bastard was still alive.

Tatiana tapped him on the arm. It hurt. He had a feeling it was meant to be a light touch.

"Mother! Be careful!" Hannah said. "Did you not just hear me saying how fragile he is?"

"For the millionth time, I'm not fragile," Fin growled. He was glad he was wearing a long-sleeved shirt, so she couldn't see the mark that had no doubt been left behind by her mother's 'gentle' contact.

"Are your ribs still broken?" Hannah demanded.

Fin bit his lip. "A little."

"Then you have to be careful."

"Broken ribs don't mean my arm is broken."

Tatiana sighed. "Hannah, ease up."

"Mother?"

"If you are in a relationship with this human, then you can't mollycoddle him. Either you take him on as a partner, or you don't. Although, you *could* make him a vampire. Then you wouldn't have to worry about him being breakable."

"Humans do break a little too easily," Dante said, as if to help.

Fin frowned.

Dante added, "Not that I've broken too many."

The man with the walking stick approached then. Anton. Dante's husband. Fin couldn't picture an odder combination. Anton actually seemed *nice.*

"Too many?" he said.

A vague shame entered Dante's expression. "Maybe a couple."

"I probably wouldn't survive being Chosen," Fin said. He didn't want to wake up one night having Hannah nibbling on his neck, trying to Choose him. Hazel-eyed Graceds often had immunity to the euphoria-inducing drug in vampire saliva. So it would probably just hurt. And then he'd die.

"See her?" Dante pointed at the newly arrived vampire, who was now standing with a little girl and her arm wrapped around the were called Clay.

"Yes?"

"She had Hazel eyes, too."

Fin glanced at Anton, who nodded, as if he knew all about Graceds. But how could all these people know? No one in Fin's home town had had any idea. He looked more closely at the woman. She was definitely a vampire, she had purple eyes, but within their depths were flecks of Green and Gray. More interestingly, the eyes of the little girl standing with her were bright Teal.

Oh, his sisters would freak the fuck out if they ever met these two. Hannah would be bad enough with her Black eyes, but a Graced who had managed to become a vampire? And a child with a new eye color? His twin, Faith, would be the worst, purist as she was.

Turning back to Dante, Hannah, Anton and Tatiana, he sighed. "But my ability isn't entirely latent."

Hannah frowned. "What do you mean?"

Fin hesitated. In for a penny... "I can speak pretty much any language you've ever heard of, provided I can listen to it for a few minutes."

Tatiana snorted. "Really?"

"Really."

She rattled out a sentence in Varsh, then swapped to Skarvs, then another tongue and another. Fin responded in kind, every time. Dozens of languages. He knew all of them because of a quirk in his eye color — she because she'd been alive so long that she'd had to learn them all the hard way. At last she switched to something he'd never heard before, and no matter how long she spoke, he couldn't pick it up.

It sounded ancient.

"Hrm," Tatiana said at last. She then spoke in Pintonite, which was similar enough to Skarvs that even people who didn't speak it could follow without too many problems. "I think you couldn't learn that one because I have a mental shield, too. I inherited it from my parents. They were Graced. That's why Hannah is Graced. There was always a chance any offspring I had might be. I always expected to just have a Green, Grey or Blue, though. I was surprised that she had a new color, but assumed it was because she is also a vampire."

Dante listened, appearing fascinated by the whole thing. A little too fascinated, if one were to ask Fin, which no one had.

"So you knew you could have a mortal child?" Dante asked.

"The odds were there. They were low, but they were there."

"Perhaps it's time to move into the dining room," Anton said with a strained smile. "Mother has been working hard on ensuring there is enough food for everyone."

Tatiana swept an arm out graciously. "Of course."

As they filed out, Hannah was careful to avoid contact with anyone, even her brother. He'd admitted he didn't have a mental shield, and Fin wasn't sure exactly how he knew that, but the vampire knew enough about Graceds that it wasn't worth pursuing that line of enquiry too far.

A blonde woman was waiting for them in the hallway. She wore a lavender pantsuit, and her long pale hair hung loose down her back. "Dante! You said it was urgent I attend? I didn't realize you were having so many guests over..."

Dante hesitated. "Misty, I thought you might want to come over and meet our sister."

So, Fin thought, this was the child from their father's first alliance. She flicked her hair over her shoulder, but despite her bright, slightly vapid smile, her eyes were hard.

"Our sister?"

Dante nodded. "This is Hannah."

"Lady Hannah Romanov," Tatiana corrected.

Misty's gaze flicked from Dante to Hannah and then back again. Fin stepped in closer to Hannah, lending her silent support. If this Misty rejected her...Dante seemed more interested in Hannah's gift, rather than in Hannah herself. Fin didn't want to see another such reaction.

"And I'm Lady Mistique Kipling, Viscountess of Kipling." The blonde vampire swept forward, hands outstretched to hug Hannah.

But Hannah stepped back, away from her new sister. Or old sister. However it worked. "Nice to meet you." She smiled, but her action had been clearly perceived as a rejection.

"Really?"

Dante put a hand on Misty's arm. "Don't take it personally. She can't touch anyone except her mother and the human."

Her pale lavender eyes swept over Fin. "How convenient."

"She has a...disability," Tatiana said.

"Really." Not a question this time.

"She can read the memories of anyone she touches," Dante explained. "Except for those who have a natural defense against it."

"Dante!" exclaimed several people at once.

Misty laughed, incredulous. "Really?"

Must be her favorite word, Fin thought. *Or maybe she just has a limited vocabulary?*

"It's true," Hannah said, surprising Fin. "I'm sorry, but it's true."

He took her hand and she gently squeezed his in response.

Misty's eyes dropped to their clasped palms. "You can seriously only touch that human and your mother?"

Hannah nodded. "And the baby, for now."

"Baby?"

"It's a long story," Fin said.

"Well, I'm sure we will have time." Misty smiled, and this time it seemed more genuine.

As they resumed walking to the dining room, Dante said, "I still think you should touch the latest victim."

"Excuse me?" Misty asked.

"Well, if Hannah can pick up memories, then if she were to touch the latest victim in the vampire killings, she might find out who the murderer is."

CHAPTER SIXTY-THREE

Hannah was alone. Sitting in the back of the cart, her forearms resting on her knees, all she had for company were her spinning thoughts. Fin and Byrne had been offered rooms at the Greystoke townhouse, and they'd taken Rena inside for her evening bath. Tatiana had wanted Hannah to return to the hotel with her, but Hannah couldn't sleep in the hired room, not with all the things in there made by others. And they'd had the cart brought around to the Greystoke property, complete with Betty, Foxtrot and Baldy. At least Hannah knew she could sleep in there.

Reluctantly, her mother had left her in the stables, promising to return early the following day.

What had her life become?

She'd finally seen her mother, had her burgeoning relationship with Fin outed, met her twin brother, her half-sister, and had her secret exposed to a group of people she'd never seen before this evening. In a month, she'd gone from living in isolation on a mountain, to having a family and — dare she say it — a lover.

Poor Fin.

He'd looked almost offended when Byrne had announced that he was Hannah's boyfriend. She'd have to talk to him and let him know that she was okay with it, if he didn't want to continue whatever it was that they had. It might just kill her to do it, but she would. Dropping her head into her hands, she let out a sobbing laugh. How had she managed to be so stupid as to fall in love with the human?

And why had she only come to terms with it now?

"Hello?"

A small face appeared above the cart's rear tray. It was the little girl from the dinner. Her nut-brown skin had a smear of dust on it, and half her hair had fallen out of its ponytail, but her bright, blue-green eyes were cheerful in the yellow lamplight.

"Can I come in? Your goat is trying to eat my ribbon."

Hannah darted forward and thrust her head out of the wagon. "Betty!"

The goat turned soulful brown eyes on Hannah, her lips still at work nibbling the girl's sash.

"Sure," Hannah said. "But you can't touch me."

Sliding back, Hannah made room for the child. She clambered abroad, quietly berating Betty who refused to release her end of the ribbon.

"Does your sister know you're here?" Hannah had gathered that the half-Graced woman Dante had Chosen was the girl's older sister.

Scrunching her face up, the girl shook her head. "She thinks I'm in bed."

"Maybe you should go back then?" Hannah said uneasily.

"Elle ruins all my fun. Anyway, you won't hurt me, because you can't touch me." The child's logic was reasonably sound, although Hannah had learned that she would fight through the memories to kill if she had someone worth protecting, other than herself. She wasn't worth it. But Fin, Rena and Byrne were.

"My name is Hannah," she said, embarrassed to note that she didn't know the child's name. There had been so many new faces, it had been hard to keep track.

"I know. I'm Emmie."

"Just Emmie?" Hannah asked with a smile.

The child frowned. "Esmeralda, but I hate it."

"I see. Emmie it is."

Emmie sat, her legs folded under her. Fiddling with the chewed end of her ribbon, she looked at Hannah, her Teal eyes bright. "How does it feel to be different?"

So the child had heard about Hannah's ability. Hannah didn't think that anyone could have missed it.

"It's difficult," Hannah said. She could have lied, but then, what would be the point? Hannah had eyes in her head, and she could see that Emmie's bright irises weren't normal.

"Does it get less difficult?" Emmie asked.

"It would depend on your ability, I think," Hannah said. "I don't have a strong natural mental shield, so I absorb other people's memories. However, I think that if I were to practice more, it might help. But I have lived almost entirely alone my whole life as a result."

"At least I can be around people," the girl said.

"That would be nicer."

"But you aren't alone anymore. You have your human. The pretty one."

Hannah let out a surprised laugh. Fin wasn't even here and he had a lingering effect on a female. Sure, this one was a child, but even she'd spotted his good looks.

"He is rather pretty," she agreed.

"I think he knows it, though," Emmie said.

Hannah leaned forward, lowering her voice to a mock whisper. "I think he does, too."

Emmie grinned, but the expression faded. "Can I touch you?"

"I just said that I can't touch people—"

"—who don't have natural shields. I do."

"You do?"

"I think it's to do with my ability," Emmie said, reaching out a hand. "Me and Elle both have one. I don't know why Elle does, but then, our Gran was a very strong Green. Maybe it was a defensive thing."

Hesitantly Hannah stretched out her palm. At the contact with the girl, her skin tingled, and warmth spread throughout her body, centering on her stomach. But nothing else happened. No memories, no crash of having her own personality overlaid by someone else's. It was just Hannah and Emmie. Two separate people.

Letting go, Hannah smiled. "Nothing."

Emmie nodded, as if that's exactly what she'd expected. "Well, you're a vampire."

"Half a vampire."

Emmie shook her head. "You're pretty much whole vampire, just a tiny bit of Graced." She held her fingers an inch apart, to show how small the percentage was.

Then it all clicked. "You could tell that just by touching me?"

"I'm not meant to talk about it."

Hannah nodded. She could understand that, better than anyone else. Perhaps that's why Emmie had sought her out.

"That's okay," Hannah said.

Emmie leaned closer, looking from side to side, as if checking to make sure they were alone. "I can heal people."

"That's—"

"Dangerous," Emmie finished.

"Amazing," Hannah said instead. "I wish I had something like that."

Emmie's eyes went wide. "You do?"

Hannah took Emmie's hand again. The girl's skin contrasted against hers. Physical contact was still surreal to her. "I can't touch anyone, except for a handful of rare individuals. You can touch *everyone*. And make them better. I would *love* to have your ability."

The young girl looked thoughtful. "I never thought of it like that."

"Your ability is a gift, mine is a curse."

Emmie nodded at her. "Well, you have a baby. That is a good thing."

Hannah smiled. That was true.

CHAPTER SIXTY-FOUR

Walking down the halls of the Crystal Palace, toward the king's chambers, he heard hushed talking.

"It's unbelievable, but she really thinks it's true. Her mother didn't deny it, either."

He frowned, silently moving closer to the end of the hallway. It split into a T-intersection, and the talker — that bloody bitch, Misty — was on either side. Pausing about three yards from the end, he stood next to a stone statue of a naked man. Its private parts were covered by a fig leaf, which had always made him think the poor lad hadn't been very well-endowed.

"It could be true." That was King Johan's voice. He'd recognize it anywhere.

Misty's voice rose incredulously. "That she can steal people's memories?"

Steal people's memories?

For once, he found himself in agreement with the airhead; that was ridiculous.

"If she thinks she can, and the Duchess of Ravens believes it, I'd be inclined to believe it, too."

"Johan, be serious."

He scowled at the disrespect Misty's casual manner of address showed the king, but he wasn't about to announce his presence and defend the monarch. It wasn't his place, for one.

Wait, did she say the Duchess of Ravens? That woman was

terrifying. He'd seen her at a distance when she'd visited the palace, and she'd sent a shudder down his spine. He wouldn't want her anywhere near him — and he'd managed to successfully kill four vampires now. Imagine being her child. He almost felt sorry for the daughter.

"I am serious," said King Johan.

"So there's some validity to my brother's idea?"

"That she should touch the newest corpse to learn the identity of the killer? Why not?"

Cold fear flushed through him. He might think the lot of these people fools, but if there was a vampire in Pinton who could touch the dead and see their memories, then that vampire would have to die.

Nothing could interfere with his work.

CHAPTER SIXTY-FIVE

The carriage had deposited them outside Tal's place, on the corner of Court Road and Marcus Drive. The journey there had been passed in uncomfortable silence, and Alice couldn't stand it anymore.

"What's wrong?"

"Apart from you practically inviting that *were* over to your bed?" Tal snapped.

"*What?*"

"I mean, you're normally so sensible, despite the fact you don't date much. But a *were?*"

"Tal! I asked if he wouldn't mind painting my ceiling. You're acting like I proposed to him."

"As if he even believed you want him to paint your ceiling. I don't."

"You are constantly trying to get me to date people, and when I show the slightest bit of interest in someone, you get angry." Hurt welled deep within her. Tal was one of the two people who had stood by her no matter what, and now she was judging her? Because she'd been stupid enough to ask a stranger over to her apartment.

Stupid or brave?

Not that Alice had actually believed the were would want to come over to her apartment or even date her. She'd just blurted out the first thing that had popped into her mind, and she really did need to get rid of that patch of green.

"Weres are dangerous."

"You're dating a *vampire!*" Alice cried in exasperation.

"I can handle myself." Tal's expression was fierce.

"You're human, just like me. Why can you handle a vampire any better than me?"

"I just can," Tal said bluntly.

"Fine. You go ahead and date whoever you want, and feel free to judge me because I simply asked someone for a favor. Get off your high horse, Tal! I have supported you in every decision you make, no matter that I worry about you. You could at least give me the same courtesy." With that, Alice strode away, not bothering to look back to see if her friend was following. If Tal called after her, she was too angry to hear.

She crossed Court Road and stormed down the sidewalk toward her street. Suddenly there was someone in her way and she almost slammed face-first into them. Looking up, and up, she realized it was the were from the dinner party.

In the street.

Right in front of her.

"Uh—"

Byrne ran a hand over his closely cropped hair, a sheepish expression on his face. "I just wanted to make sure you got home okay, and then I saw you have your...talk...with your friend."

Heat worked its way into her cheeks. Would she forever be blushing around him? It was embarrassing. "Thanks, I think."

"I know it's a bit stalkerish, at least, that's what Fin would tell me if I had bothered to ask his opinion. But you're human, and this is a vampire town." His nostrils flared, as if he could scent the vampires in the very air.

Fin was the blond-haired human. Right. His friend.

But even though he was a strange were who'd just shown up outside her doorstep, she didn't mind. He'd done it to protect her.

Because you're weak.

She ignored the voice in her head — Byrne was being chivalrous, and there was a sore shortage of that kind of sentiment in her world.

Her exhalations were forming into mist; they couldn't just keep standing in the street. She gave Byrne what she hoped was a winning smile. "Would you like to come up for a cup of tea?"

His answering grin was swift, and it stole a little of her breath away. "I'd love to."

Side-stepping the huge were, Alice headed toward her apartment building, opened the entry and then climbed the stairs. Byrne had to duck to get in the door, but it didn't bother him as far as she could tell. She unlocked her front door, dropped her keys in the bowl on the side table, and then indicated that he should follow her inside. They emerged into the lounge room and kitchen area, and Alice was glad suddenly for the stupidly tall ceiling. At least it meant Byrne could stand comfortably.

As she filled the kettle with water and popped it on the stove, Byrne's sexily deep voice rumbled through the apartment. "I see what you mean by the painting thing."

He was gazing up at that taunting patch of green on her ceiling. "Whoever paints a ceiling green?" she grumbled.

He laughed, and then gingerly sat down on her couch. There was just enough room for her to squeeze in next to him...or she could sit on the chair opposite. She had a feeling she'd been squeezing her way onto that couch.

What had gotten into her?

♦

Byrne had high-tailed it out of the dinner. His skin had been itchy, as if his bear wanted out, and he couldn't stand to be around others. Even Clay, a were he'd known since he was a cub, was grating him. It had to be because of the little slip of a human woman, with her pretty hair and autumn-leaf eyes, and a figure to die for. Literally; it might kill him if he never got to touch her.

How pathetic was he?

And so he'd followed the carriage, seen Alice and Talan fighting; he'd even heard the words, from his semi-hidden position down the road. They'd been arguing about *him*.

It was clear that Alice had no idea her friend was Graced, so

Byrne could understand her hurt to learn her friend thought she was too weak to be with a were. That she was stupid for even wanting to spend time with him.

As if he would ever hurt her.

But then Alice had invited him upstairs, and he'd almost toppled over from surprise. He'd followed her, because he wasn't an idiot, no matter what Fin said when it came to Byrne and women. It was just that until now he hadn't found one who had captured his interest so thoroughly. Inside her apartment, it smelled even more strongly of chocolate and sin, to the point that when he took a seat on the couch, he had to grab one of her bright orange cushions to hold over his lap.

The kettle whistled and Alice poured the water into a pot. They made small talk, his nerves ensuring he wouldn't remember much of it later, as she gently placed two teacups on the small coffee table before him. He was sure that she would take the seat opposite, but she surprised him by squishing herself into the small space next to him.

"Do you have a surname?" Alice asked.

Suddenly self-conscious, he ran his fingers over the smooth fibers on the cushion. "Torben. Byrne Torben. I don't really use it much."

Alice held out her hand, and without thinking, he shook it. "Nice to meet you Byrne Torben."

He let go, but reluctantly. The feel of her skin against his was electrifying. Even his bear rumbled with pleasure.

"I really did mean it, about the painting thing," Alice said, concentrating on the teacup in her hands.

Byrne grinned. "I gathered." Her house was neat as a pin, everything placed with the utmost care. He was worried that he might accidentally knock something and ruin the order she had so painstakingly imposed. "But I hope you don't plan on having me paint it now."

She gave a slightly nervous laugh. "Oh, no."

Then she leaned forward, and placed a hand on his chest. Before he could think, she was pressing her red lips to his.

Every muscle in his body locked up. She tasted amazing, but too quickly other thoughts assaulted his senses — the memories of other mouths pressed to his, other hands touching his chest.

Sensing his unease, Alice backed off with a soft, sad little smile.

Feeling her warmth so close, having her scent wrap around him, he couldn't pretend that this was just fun, not when he was dreading that sex would be almost as traumatic as it would be pleasurable, at least the first time.

"I want to be honest here," Byrne said.

"Okay. Was it really that bad?"

"No! No..."

"You didn't kiss me back, so..."

Byrne shut his eyes and ran a hand over his face. "It's not you. It's nothing to do with you."

Alice raised an eyebrow. "We're already having this conversation?"

"No. I mean, yes. I mean no. Not that kind of conversation." Oh, how he wished he had Fin's way with words.

Alice bit her lip.

Then, with all the suave charm he was known for, he blurted, "I think you're my mate."

The stunned silence stretched out. "Your mate? What does that even mean?"

"Clay says it's like weres have a psychic sense of smell. When we find someone who smells so utterly irresistible, they're your mate. You're destined to be together."

"You believe in destiny?"

"I hoped that I'd one day find someone for me. I just wasn't sure the 'psychic smell' would work."

"So I smell?" Alice sniffed her armpit.

Byrne couldn't help but chuckle. "You smell *amazing*."

Her eyes took on a slightly wicked gleam. "Like what?"

"Chocolate and sin."

"Sin has a smell?" Alice asked.

"Apparently."

Then she leaned forward, and breathed in deeply. "What are

you doing?"

"Smelling you."

"And?"

"Honey and cloves," she said, a little wonderingly. "You smell like cookies. I like cookies."

Byrne grinned. "Aren't I lucky then?"

CHAPTER SIXTY-SIX

"You're a nuisance, you know that?"

The bloody goat just stared at Fin with her odd slit-pupil eyes, her chewed-through leash in her mouth. He'd been coming over to the stable to see Hannah and found the beast wandering loose outside. Taking hold of the mangled leather, he pulled the goat back under cover.

There were voices, coming from the wagon. He'd thought that Hannah would be alone.

He peered into the back of the cart, knowing that Hannah had already heard him enter the stables. She was sitting in the back of the wagon, with a little girl. Not Rena; Elle — of all people — had snaffled the baby and disappeared with Lady Beatrice, the Baron's mother. Even though the half-Graced vampire clearly loved her own little sister, Fin hadn't really pictured her being fond of other people's babies. But she'd cooed all over the infant, her werewolf fiancé looking a little uncomfortable at the display.

Fin had felt sorry for the were. But only a little bit.

Elle's sister had long brown hair and brown skin, but her Teal eyes were startling. Maybe it wasn't surprising that she'd sought out Hannah, the only other person Fin had met with eyes a color that no one else had.

"Hello," Fin said, leaning on the edge of the wagon.

The little girl spun around, but stayed polite. "Hello."

Fin met Hannah's gaze over the girl's head. She smiled at him, and he grinned back, stupidly happy. Ah, he was in so much trouble.

"Are you meant to be here?" he asked Emmie. "I thought I heard your sister muttering about you being in bed and that's how she could get away with snuggling Rena without your mother finding out."

"What? Elle took Rena?" Emmie's curious gaze latched onto him.

"I'm just reporting on what I saw."

Emmie scooted out the back of the wagon. "Mom has been teasing her that Elle is clucky. I have to see this." Turning back to Hannah, Emmie waved. "Bye!" Then, with a swish of her skirts, she was scampering across the stables, stopping briefly to scold Bettina / Barry / Betty and wave a ribbon at the creature.

Fin climbed into the cart and sat next to Hannah. She gave him another small smile, and this one felt special, as if it was just for him.

"She's like me," Hannah said slowly.

"Like you?" Fin asked.

"Not the same, but special."

He didn't ask. If there was one thing he'd learnt from living with talented sisters, it was that being special was something better left hidden. Especially from him. He didn't want to accidentally get the girl in trouble one day, if his sisters asked too many questions. It's not that he thought they'd harm a child, but he hadn't seen them in years, and he didn't know how they'd react to a new color. A new type of Graced.

Hannah lay down in the back of the cart, and pulled her blanket up to her chin. "Is it wrong that I'm jealous of her?"

"Jealous?"

"That she has something wonderful, and I have *this*." So much bitterness in one word.

Fin shook his head. "What you can do is amazing, too."

"Really? What good has it done me?"

"You were able to work out how to feed Rena and keep her alive. If not for your ability, would you have had any idea what to do? Would you have known that she'd be in danger if you'd brought her back to the Trsetti?"

Hannah mumbled something into her blanket. Lying down on his back, Fin scooped an arm under her neck, then looped her arm over his chest. She resisted for a moment, then wrapped herself around him, still careful of his ribs.

"But I would have been lost without you and Byrne. I couldn't even tie a diaper."

She still struggled, but he wasn't about to mention that. He didn't want her to throw him out of the cart. He was enjoying her snuggling into his side, although he would never admit it to Byrne. Fucking bear. He'd just vanished after the meal had finished, which was totally unlike him. Fin might have been worried if not for the fact that he was a huge black bear.

Well, maybe he was a bit worried.

Just a little.

"I just wish I could do something good," Hannah said.

Fin ran a hand over her silky black hair. "Don't talk like that. You're fantastic, Hannah. You saved Rena's life. You saved *my* life. You're not the one who fucks everything up, that's me."

And he'd been doing it ever since he was seventeen. You'd think he would have learned his lesson by now, but nope. Still a dickhead.

"So what, you had sex with the wrong woman. Byrne said she drugged you."

Well, that might have been true. There had been an aphrodisiac, but the woman had told him it was in there. He'd thought she was joking — or just flirting a bit — but no, it had been true. His cock and balls had bloody *hurt* with need.

Fin sighed. "That's not it."

"Fin—"

"No, really." Without warning, the words spilled from him, about Karly and Callie, and the shame and pain he had carried for over ten years. About his weakness. Hannah would know, finally know what a waste of space he was.

"We were only seventeen and I wanted her so badly. We had sex, and she got pregnant. I was so scared about it, but she was happy. Ecstatic, even. And then, nine months later, the labor started." His breath was sawing in and out of his chest. "It was horrible. There was blood everywhere, and then Callie came out, the cord was around her neck, and she was blue. My little girl was born dead. And Karly went not long after. The perfect baby she'd been so happy to have, killed her.

"*I* killed her."

And then Hannah was leaning over him, her Black eyes fierce. Tears had wound their way down her cheeks, and she smeared one of them away angrily before placing her hands on his cheeks, a touch to anchor him. To anchor her.

"You *did not kill her.*"

"If I hadn't had sex..."

"Did you force her?"

Horror filled him. "What? *No.*"

"Then you did not kill her. She chose to have sex with you. She wanted the baby. It was just horrible, horrible what happened. But it isn't your fault."

"My daughter is *dead.*"

Hannah nodded, her gaze serious. "But it is not your fault. No one will ever replace Callie, but now you have a family that needs you. Rena needs you. I need you. And you are not to blame."

Part of him wanted to believe her, but another knew that it wasn't so simple. He was selfish enough to be happy that she didn't hate him for his mistakes, though. That she wanted to be with him anyway.

"If you want to be with me, Hannah, I won't let you go. I want you to know that. You're stuck with my sorry aging ass."

She gave him a wicked grin. "I like your ass, so that's okay."

He leered. "Who *wouldn't* like my ass?"

Laughing, she gently tapped him on the shoulder. "I love you."

Her words turned him hard as a rock. In more ways than one. But the panic he expected to claw its way through him, to drive him all the way back to the Old Mother, never came. There was nothing except a feeling of peace, of contentment that this beautiful woman was his. That he was hers.

He couldn't understand how he'd managed to get so lucky, but he wasn't going to waste any more time questioning it.

"I love me, too."

Hannah hit him in the arm.

"I mean you, I love you!" He laughed.

"I love you, too."

CHAPTER SIXTY-SEVEN

"So you don't get to choose who you fall in love with?" Alice's expression was sober.

"Well, no," Byrne said. "I mean I do. You smell wonderful, but it doesn't mean I'm instantly in love with you."

She let out a grateful sigh. "That's good. I—I'm not so good with relationships. This mate thing is already enough pressure."

A psychic sense of smell? How did that even work? But she couldn't deny that she'd never been this attracted to a guy before.

"And, I just want to say that I liked our kiss before," Byrne went on, his deep voice filling the room. "But I'm not sure that I can be fully intimate, not soon."

A multitude of thoughts darted through her mind, each one worse than the next. "Are you gay? And does the scent thing mean that you have to try and be with me? Or don't you find me attractive?"

Way not to sound desperate, Alice.

"No!" Then quieter, "No."

Her stomach dropped all the way to the basement. "You don't find me attractive?"

He glowered at her, his beautiful mouth forming into a hard line. "Are you nuts? You're sexy as anything."

"Really?"

"Really."

While she still didn't believe him one hundred percent, relief surged through her. She wanted to kiss him again, so much. To touch him. Just be near him. "Then...?"

"You know how Hannah said she has a special ability?"

"Absorbing peoples' memories." Alice couldn't keep the skepticism from her voice.

"Right. Well, it's true. She can."

For some reason, she believed him. Well, believed that he believed it.

"And there are others out there too, like her."

"Other people who can absorb memories?"

"No, people who can read thoughts, people who can move things with their minds. Your friend Talan is one of them."

Alice laughed, she couldn't help it.

"I mean it," Byrne said. "Everyone who has eyes with colors other than brown, yellow or purple has a special talent."

"But that's—"

"True."

Sure, there weren't many people she'd met with colored eyes, but she knew a handful. And she'd known Tal her entire life. She seriously doubted that her best friend would be able to keep a secret that big from her.

"There would be some scientific literature on this, if it was real," she said. "It wouldn't be a secret."

"It's a secret because the people with the talents want it to be one. They don't want other people to know. The only reason I can remember is because I have a natural mental shield that prevents my memory from being wiped."

"Okay, say that I believe this — which I don't — what does this have to do with you?"

Byrne settled back into her couch, shifting the cushion on his lap awkwardly. "One hundred years ago, I was kidnapped by weres. They also took my sister, Ruby, and so I didn't put up too much of a fight. They said they'd kill her if I didn't go peaceably."

The blood drained from Alice's face. She might not believe him about the special-mind-powers business, but this she just knew was true.

"They sold me to a group of humans who had colored eyes.

They're called the Graced. They wanted to experiment on me, to learn the full extent of were abilities. They stuck me in a cell, and for one hundred years, I never left that room." His eyes were hard and glittering, his jaw clenched, but his words were even and carefully spoken.

Horror had lodged itself within her chest, and was spreading further through her body with every word he uttered.

"For the most part, they just tortured me with silver and left me to it. But then the last two generations of Graceds came. They were evil bitches. They decided that they wanted to create the ultimate race: an immortal Graced. No one knew that there was already one — no, two — out there. And so they drugged me with aphrodisiacs, and then they...used...me."

His voice broke on these last words, and Alice threw herself at him, hugging him. He didn't move for a precious few seconds, but when she went to pull back, his strong arms wrapped around her.

"So it's not you, it's me. I just don't know if I'm ready."

Alice disentangled herself from him, and pulled her dress down a little to reveal her pale scar. "When I was fourteen, my mother was stabbed to death, and my brother was kidnapped. I interrupted the killer, and I got stabbed. I was lucky to survive, but now...now I worry that everyone who loves me is going to leave. And that I'm going to be left alone. Again.

"So while I can't possibly know how you feel, I do know that I want to take this slow. I think you're incredibly sexy, and you must have so much courage and will to have survived what you did. But to me, you're just a man who smells like cookies. A man I want to get to know better. But slowly."

He grinned then, and it was brilliant, but there was a bitter edge to it. "Please don't tell anyone what I told you."

Alice placed a light kiss on his cheek. "Never."

"I'm just a man who smells like cookies?"

A smile bloomed across her cheeks. "And I'm a woman who smells like chocolate and sin."

Chapter Sixty-Eight

Hannah woke to Fin's arms around her and the smell of verbena and lemon. It was a novel experience, and something that she secretly reveled in. She didn't want to move, but sunlight was streaming through the stables and the human assistants would be up and about soon, tending to the animals' needs. Just because vampires preferred a nocturnal lifestyle, it didn't mean that the animals they relied on did as well.

As quietly as she could, she extracted herself from Fin's warmth. He grumbled something in protest and she smiled down at him. A human. A ladies' man. Someone prettier than they had a right to be. None of those things would have made her list of 'perfect partner' — if she'd ever dared to even produce such a list. But it was funny how she couldn't picture wanting anything different about Fin.

Aside from his mortality.

It was already difficult enough to know that Rena would not survive being Chosen or Bitten; that the baby she'd saved would surely die long before she would. Eventually she would have to convince him that Choosing him was a risk they should take together.

Enough!

Stop being a ninny. You have a beautiful baby, you have Fin, Byrne and even your mother. And a new brother and sister.

Although, if she were honest with herself, she was in two minds how she felt about that last part. Dante was painfully remote, and Misty had a flighty air about her. Neither sibling appeared to share any personality traits with her, and they certainly didn't suffer her affliction. Then again, no one else ever had, not as far as she was aware.

Fin opened his eyes, his Hazel gaze immediately seeking hers. He gave her a sheepish grin. "Morning."

"Hey."

Propping himself up on his elbows, he gave her a naughty wink. "You snore."

Hannah drew herself upright, glowered at him. "I do not!"

"You're right, you don't." Laughing, he sat up.

"Fin!"

"What? Byrne isn't here for me to bother, so you're going to have to suffer, I'm afraid."

She groaned. Surely the man could go five minutes without needing to be a pain in someone's ass? Then his words registered. "Where is Byrne?" she asked, thinking back to the were's abrupt departure the night before.

"No idea." Fin shrugged. "I imagine he'll return soon. Sometimes crowds bother him."

She could understand that. Crowds certainly bothered her, and there had been far too many people in attendance last night. It had been bad enough that her brother had been there, but then there'd been his husband, his Chosen, his Chosen's fiancé, her sister, and oh, his mother-in-law. *Then* his dinner guests had arrived, which included the city coroner, a mathematics professor and Dante's other sister. Hannah's half-sister.

It gave her a headache just from trying to remember it all.

A stable hand appeared in the doorway, bobbing into a slight bow when he spotted them in the wagon. Strangely, he wasn't too surprised to see them there. Maybe he was used to people sleeping in wagon beds?

"I need to give the stables a clean, milord, my lady."

"Sure." Hannah climbed out the wagon, giving the young boy a wide berth. Fin followed suit, running his hands through his blond hair.

"It's a nice day for a walk," the lad said. "No one else will be up yet."

She could take a hint: get out the stables because they had work to do. Hannah nodded at the boy while Fin tucked his shirt in. Once he was dressed with some semblance of order, he extended an arm to her, all gallant hero. "Shall we walk?"

She smiled in response. "Sure."

The lad waved a hand. "There's a gate in the back of the garden."

Arm in arm, they headed into the neighboring courtyard. Just being able to walk next to someone — and while touching them — was astonishing. Hannah knew that part of her affection for Fin was born out of a desire to simply be with someone, anyone, but would she have acted on those impulses if that someone *hadn't* been Fin?

She doubted it. Byrne supposedly had a mental shield and she hadn't even tried touching him, even though he was handsome.

They wandered through the formal garden, the scent of honeysuckle heavy in the air. Breathing in deeply, Hannah took in the little allotment, an oasis of green and calm, before heading out the small gate. The alley behind had a cobblestone road, and bluestone buildings either side.

Fin paused by the gate, letting his arm drop. "Should we grab Rena?"

"She might still be asleep. You said that Elle and Lady Beatrice were caring for her?"

Fin nodded, with a half-smile. "I might have over-emphasized Elle's role in that care, to get Emmie moving. I had a feeling if Elle caught her out of bed sparks might fly. But Lady Beatrice was quite happy to babysit."

Taking a few steps down the alley, Fin right behind her, she looked up at the pale blue sky. It was going to be a cool day, but a clear one. Maybe she and Fin could wander to the market, and he could grab something for Rena? She wouldn't be able to touch the baby while she wore it, but that would be okay. Perhaps she should get some knickknacks to practice her ability on — to try and strengthen her mental shield?

A scent of blood and pomade wafted through the air; there must be some vampires nearby. Something whistled through the air beside her, and as she stopped to sniff, she was shoved to the ground, hard, her knees cracking against the cobbles. She collapsed on her front, the wind rushing out of her lungs.

Fin had thrown himself on top of her, pressing her down to the ground. Air finally found its way into her lungs and she gasped it in great gulps. Then it hit her; her cheek was pressed to the stone street, but no memories were rushing in.

She smiled with delight, and turned to tell Fin but was stopped by the sound of something *thunking* into flesh.

Fin yelled.

Panicking, Hannah fought to get out from under him, but he was pushing her back down, shielding her with his body.

Fin had been shot.

With a crossbow bolt.

She wanted to vomit. To cry. To scream. She could smell his blood as it dripped onto her. Fueled by adrenalin and panic, she rolled Fin onto his side. "Fin!"

He was breathing, his face pale and pinched with pain, but he was breathing. The bolt had torn right through his back, the tip emerging from his chest. Hannah looked around, seeking their attacker. There was someone on a roof near them. Then a draft rushed through the alley, blowing her hair around her face, obscuring her vision. She had to go after the coward who'd shot at them, but she had to see to Fin, too. Grabbing him by the shoulders, she dragged him back toward the gate, toward safety.

He had to be okay.

He just had to be.

CHAPTER SIXTY-NINE

Byrne had fallen asleep on the couch. He barely fit, his huge frame curled up awkwardly. Alice looked over at him, still surprised he was in her house; that he'd sought her out. But she wasn't going to second-guess their situation too much.

Well, she'd attempt not to.

After they had talked for hours, Byrne had nodded off. But Alice had been too keyed up for slumber. His story hurt her heart. And it had made her edgy. Humans with colored eyes having special abilities. People pretending to be something they weren't. Aunt Zara implying that Ashok might have been the one to hurt their mother, to hurt her.

Could her brother really have been the one to stab her, to murder their mother?

No. Alice didn't want to believe it.

But there was a killer on the loose, and she couldn't ignore the fact that there was an element to these murders that spoke to her. Something had been niggling at the back of her mind, ever since they found the countess. She'd had a powdery substance on her body — as had the first victim — which looked like snuff, although it was much finer than what Alice normally encountered. Which meant it was no doubt more expensive. Then there was the fact that the last body had been found dumped within the chrysanthemum podium...the killer had to be someone with access to the palace.

Someone with a grudge against vampires.

That could be one of any hundreds of palace workers, although the staff within the palace were mostly vampire. But here was the thing; snuff wasn't cheap, not for humans. Especially not the kind of snuff she'd found on the bodies, so it was unlikely that a servant would have access to it. At least, not enough where they could just leave it on corpses. And why would someone want to kill aristo vampires? The only thing the victims had in common was court. They were all members.

Could the dead vampires have been competitors? Were they were murdered to consolidate power?

And who in the palace would need to kill to keep their position? It had to be someone already in court. Elle had said she was looking into the aristo human families, but they wouldn't need to worry about strengthening their power. They already had it. But then there was the snuff issue: there was only one human Alice could think of that met all those criteria and who'd she'd seen use snuff at the palace.

She needed to talk to Elle.

Chapter Seventy

"Fuck."

He quickly grabbed another bolt from the backpack by his feet and took aim. He'd missed the first two shots: that stupid memory-stealing leech had been shoved out of the way at the last minute. The arrow had found its mark, but on the wrong target.

Third time's the charm.

For some reason, he'd expected the woman to look haggard, deranged. Which was stupid, he admitted to himself, and he wasn't foolish particularly often. Well, killing that countess might have been a bad idea. But anyway, it didn't matter what she looked like. No matter that she was young and pretty, with dark hair. She'd be dead soon. He aimed the crossbow, finger on the trigger.

Something thumped onto the rooftop behind him. A tingle ran down his spine, and slowly he turned around.

A vampire stood there, her long red hair blowing in the slight breeze that had ruined his first shot. He knew who she was, his brain screaming that he had to run, that she was far too dangerous — but he couldn't stop the words that growled from him.

"Fuck off, I'm busy."

The duchess gave a tittering laugh, her violet eyes all kinds of crazy. "I can see that." She smiled. "But then, I'm about to be pretty busy myself." That grin broadened, showing her fangs, which were longer and sharper than any he'd ever seen before. Bringing the crossbow up fast, he shot at her, should have hit her, but she *moved*. Before the thrum of the bow string had died, she had him by the throat, her strong hand choking him.

He scrabbled at her wrist. How could this be happening?

Chapter Seventy-One

Fin waved his hands at Hannah ineffectually as she dragged him to safety. "Let me go," he panted. "Get away. They were aiming at you."

"No." She was still pulling him back when someone dropped down near them. She threw herself in front of him; she wouldn't let them hurt Fin again. Even if it meant touching someone, killing someone. They would *not* harm him again.

"Hannah!"

It was her mother. Dressed all in black, she stood before them, the stench of blood thick in the air around her. In her right hand, she held a head, her fingers wrapped in curly brown hair.

The body was nowhere in sight.

"Mother?"

"I was on my way to check on you when I heard you yell." Her violet eyes flashed. "Sorry I wasn't quick enough to stop Fin from getting hurt."

Getting hurt? He had been shot through his chest! Who knew what kind of damage had been done? He was more than just *hurt*.

She cradled his head. "Fin?"

He gave her a weak grin. "It's okay, I'll be fine."

"I'd say he won't be fine," Tatiana said, staring at him critically.

"Mother!"

"He's been shot close to the heart. The technology isn't available to save him anymore."

Tears trickled down Hannah's cheeks. He was *dying*. How could he be dying? They were going to the market...

"It's okay, Hannah. I did a good thing. I saved you." He raised a hand, wiping away one of her tears.

No. It *wasn't* okay.

Hannah looked pleadingly at her mother. "Choose him!"

Tatiana shook her head slowly. "I can't do it."

Shock numbed her. Her mother was probably the most powerful vampire in existence — and she *couldn't do it*?

"Of course you can!" Hannah yelled. "You're one of the first vampires! Choose him!"

Blood was puddling under the head. "He is half-Graced. If I Choose him, he could have direct access to my mind. And I'm old, sweetheart. If you think it's bad when you accidentally pick up a few memories, his mind will be crushed by mine. If you want a drooling vampire husk, then yes, I can do it. But if you want *Fin*, then I can't. My personality will overwhelm him."

Hannah thought quickly. "Dante—"

"He already has one Chosen, who is half-Graced. I don't know if his mind could handle a second."

Hannah's thoughts raced. She couldn't Choose Fin herself, she was only part vampire, and he was Graced. It might not take... There had to be someone. Misty—?

Byrne burst into the alley then, followed by a human. Alice, that was it. She was a type of doctor. In an instant he took in the situation and then dropped to his knees before Fin. He grabbed the shaft of the bolt, and her human's face went white. Fin's eyes rolled back in his head and he stopped moving.

"*Fin!*" Hannah screamed.

"Don't pull it out." Alice held a hand out. "Don't!"

Byrne jerked back, letting go of the bolt.

"If you pull it out, the blood loss will be severe — he'll die."

Hannah's thoughts whirled. What about the child, Emmie? Surely she could heal something like this. But it would mean exposing her talents to everyone else.

Was Fin more important than the girl's secret?

Hannah knew the answer.

"Someone get the gir—"

Tatiana spoke over her. "We need someone to Choose him."

Alice shook her head. "That's a wooden bolt. It's right next to his heart. He'll die when he wakes." She turned to Byrne. "You could Bite him."

"What?"

"A friend of mine was seriously wounded a while ago. The only way to save her was to Choose her. It healed her injuries. But Choosing won't work in this instance. The only option is to Bite."

"But he's unconscious," Byrne said. "He can't say no if—"

"That's why you have to do it now."

Hannah knew Byrne was right, Fin should have a choice, but seeing him lie there, blood spreading across his shirt...

Hannah nodded. "Do it."

"Hannah—"

Hannah's voice emerged as a growl. "Do it, Byrne!"

"Fuck." But Byrne was pulling off his shirt, exposing a rock-hard chest puckered with the kind of scars that could only come from silver. There were so many, Hannah thought...he'd had to have been tortured.

"I do not want you in my fucking head, Fin," he said. "But I owe you. After this, we're even. You hear me?"

But Fin was still out cold.

Byrne's canines lengthened and sharpened, his jaw changing shape, becoming something half human, half animal. Then he bit down on Fin's arm, drawing the human's blood into his mouth, swallowing great gulps. Hannah had never seen anyone Bitten before; it was much the same process as being Chosen.

Byrne let go of Fin's arm, his fingers turning into a claw, and he slashed his own wrist. Shoving it against Fin's lips, Byrne dripped blood into his mouth. Fin didn't swallow at first, and crimson trickles leaked down his cheek. Alice reached over and massaged Fin's throat.

Hannah's whole focus was on Fin. *"Please."*

Fin swallowed.

Before long, Byrne pulled away. Hannah opened her mouth to protest, but Byrne shook his head. "Enough for now. We need to move him. Then tomorrow, we give it another go."

Chapter Seventy-Two

A shiver wracked Byrne's body.

He'd been on the way to Greystoke townhouse, walking fast with Alice — she'd needed to talk to Elle urgently — his mind strangely at peace. It wasn't until he'd first caught Alice's rich scent that he'd understood how bitter and angry he'd been. Surviving, that's all he'd been doing since Fin freed him. He hadn't really been *living*.

Then his thoughts had fled as he'd smelled it: Fin's blood.

Even though bears had the greatest sense of smell in the animal kingdom — far better than a vampire's — it was usually difficult to pick out the individual markers of human blood. But Byrne had gotten a bit too familiar with Fin's lately; the human was a magnet for trouble. Wondering what kind of grief he'd managed to get himself into this time, Byrne had started to run, Alice following closely behind him. At least this time, there wouldn't be a mob of villagers trying to beat the shit out of him. Knowing Fin, he wouldn't be able to get himself out of whatever scrape he'd gotten himself into, and Hannah wouldn't be able to help him.

Now the taste of Fin's blood lingered on his tongue, and he winced. He wasn't used to the coppery tang of human blood; weres tended to eat steaks or drink animal blood if they needed it.

And he couldn't believe what he'd started. Biting Fin. It hadn't ever been something the two of them had discussed. Fin had been happy to have a mortal life, and Byrne had never thought to offer.

Did that make him an asshole?

Then again, until he'd seen that vampire guard Elle, he hadn't thought that Graceds could get through the change, not even Hazels.

"We need a stretcher," Alice said. She had two fingers pressed to Fin's wrist, checking his pulse. She was counting under her breath, her brow furrowed, and Byrne's heart swelled within his chest at the idea of someone like her being meant for someone like him.

She was perfect.

They'd spent the whole night talking, getting to know one another, until he'd passed out. While he couldn't say he was in love with her — love took longer than a night, at least for him — he was definitely infatuated. It didn't hurt that she was beautiful and had enough curves that it should be illegal. Plus, she was super smart and kind. How she wasn't in a relationship already was beyond him. But he wasn't about to look a gift horse in the mouth.

Alice nodded at him and he stood up. Fin was still breathing, which meant he had a chance. It wasn't until the third blood transfer that they'd know whether or not he'd make it. While Biting or Choosing someone when they were hurt wasn't common, it did happen. And he'd heard of people surviving the transformation with worse injuries. He just didn't know if Fin's being half-Graced would matter.

Byrne walked over to the gate, his legs shaky. As he pressed the iron handle down, the gate jerked open. He took a step back, surprised. Elle was on the other side, her hair wild and loose, and her clothes thrown on haphazardly. She took one look at the scene, concentration creasing her brow, then nodded to herself. "Dante is going to bring a stretcher."

He stared at her. "Dante knows that someone needs a stretcher?"

"His hearing is quite exceptional — I should know, I inherited a good portion of his strength when he Chose me. But in this case, no." She tapped the side of her head. "Sometimes this comes in handy, too."

"You mean it's real?" Alice said. "People really can read minds?"

On one level, Byrne was faintly insulted that she hadn't believed him, but then Alice was a doctor. She'd need to see something to believe it.

Elle rounded on Byrne, placing her fists on her hips. "You *told* her?"

He held his hands up and backed into the alley. He was in no condition to deal with a pissed-off vampire after sharing his blood with Fin. Biting someone would weaken him for at least the three days the blood transfer took.

"It might be beneficial that she knows," Tatiana said.

All eyes turned on the duchess. Then Elle blurted, "Whose head is that?"

Byrne frowned as he took in the head. He didn't recognize the human, but that didn't mean much. He was new to town, and the last time he'd been in Pinton, this man wouldn't have even been a glint in his grandfather's eye.

Alice was leaning forward, a frown of concentration on her face. Then she gasped, her hand covering her mouth. "I was right."

Elle stood next to Byrne, Fin prone at their feet. Hannah sat next to him, slumped, her hands running over his hair. Crystal tears streaked down her cheeks. Glancing down, he saw the human was still breathing. Two more blood transfers and then three horrible days. That's how long it would take before Byrne would know if his pain-in-the-ass best friend was going to live or die.

"Do you know this human?" Tatiana's voice was cold and directed at Alice. Her eyes were almost reptilian as they stared down at Byrne's mate.

Stepping forward, Byrne placed a hand on Alice's shoulder. She startled, then gave him a weak smile.

"I thought this morning that I might have worked out the identity of a serial killer that has been stalking Pinton's vampires,"

Alice said. "But there were still so many things I needed to confirm. It was why I was coming here."

"You worked out who the killer was?" Elle asked. She took a step closer to the head and whistled. "King Jo is going to be pissed."

"It was all about the snuff," Alice said.

"Snuff?" Byrne asked.

"Killer? You mean you knew this man was after *my daughter*?" Tatiana's voice was low, deadly.

"No. I mean, I thought he might be the killer, but I had no idea he was after Hannah. He's the king's lover."

Tatiana's face went blank. "I just killed the King of Pinton's lover."

"This is going to be a nightmare. You really think this is the serial killer?" Elle ran a hand over her face.

Shuddering, Alice nodded. "But we need to search his rooms. Check for more evidence. I don't know why he was targeting Hannah. And this is a completely different modus operandi."

Tatiana waved the head. "He tried to kill my daughter. He shot her mate in the chest."

"Can you prove that?" Elle asked.

"The rest of his body is up there with the crossbow." With her free hand, Tatiana pointed at a nearby rooftop. Which was still a good twenty-five yards straight up. How had she gotten here so quickly?

Then Byrne wondered how much of the body was left in one piece, considering she was carrying his head around like a reticule. Man, what kind of a family had Hannah come from?

"I could take you there?" Tatiana said.

Elle looked up. "Uh—"

"I don't think that will be necessary," Byrne quickly interjected.

Then the gate banged open and Dante stood there, hauling a stretcher. He paused in the gateway, staring at the scene in front of him. "Why does Hannah's boyfriend have a crossbow bolt in him?"

"Long story." Byrne sighed.

Dante nodded. "Then whose head is that? Wait. Is that *Lance*?"

"Lance?"

"The king's lover."

"I just don't understand why he'd do something like this," Alice said. "He was in a position of power that few could match..."

Sudden movement caught his eye; Hannah lunging toward her mother. Understanding dawned, and Byrne threw himself forward, to grab her as she stretched her hand out to touch the dead man's head.

Tatiana didn't move, her mouth agape, stunned. Byrne's hand came down on Hannah's shoulder seconds after she touched Lance. But it was too late. She collapsed in a heap next to Fin, her limbs twitching on the ground.

Byrne let go. Now he didn't know if he'd made matters worse. "Fuck."

Tatiana threw the head on the ground, and it hit the cobbles with a horrible wet sound. "You touched her!"

"I tried to stop her!"

But that didn't stop Tatiana from advancing on him. "Now she will have two minds to deal with!"

Elle's voice was quiet, but it stopped their argument cold. "No, she won't."

"What?" Tatiana snapped.

Elle's face was pinched, as if in pain. "My ability with telepathy is new — it only came on after Dante Chose me — but I can't read the bear's mind. So if her ability doesn't work on people with shields, which I suspect is the case, then his touching her won't matter."

"Thank fuck," Byrne muttered. He'd figured he'd be fine, but with Tatiana looking at him like that...he was glad it hadn't just been a theory.

But Elle's eyes dropped to the head, then flicked to Alice, Tatiana and Byrne. "But I got a sense of what happened to her when she touched that head. It *hurts*. It's like her whole mind is being overridden by someone else's. Like her personality is temporarily erased. The fact that she has survived that happening to her, over and over again, is fucking amazing. But—"

Tatiana's face was white, and Byrne's fists were clenched. Were they at risk of losing both Hannah *and* Fin?

"But what?" Tatiana snapped.

"But this was completely overpowering. I don't know if it was because she didn't put any shields up when she touched him. But at the moment, I don't get a read of Hannah at all. It's all just jumbled memories of *him*."

They stood there in silence. Dante holding the stretcher. Byrne with Fin's blood on his tongue. Tatiana covered in gore. Alice on her knees, checking Fin's pulse. And Fin, Fin lying there weakly breathing, and fighting the greatest battle he'd ever had to face. The one to stay alive.

Then Alice broke the silence, her face wan and set. "So she just touched him, and now she has some of his memories?"

Tatiana shook her head. "She absorbed every memory that he has retained over his entire life. By the time she wakes up, she will know everything there is to know about him."

Elle didn't say it, but by the look on her face, the use of 'by the time' should probably have been replaced with 'if.'

CHAPTER SEVENTY-THREE

Hannah couldn't tell where her mind began or ended. She was a sea of rage and bitterness, of delusion and narcissism. And it was overwhelming. How had she managed to lose herself so completely?

He called himself the Gardener.

I am the Gardener. I am making the world a better place.

Floating within her own mind, she caught hold of that thought, to see where it took her.

♦

Lance couldn't have that woman touching the corpse of his latest victim. If he'd known that the stupid bitch was in town, he would have waited. Waited until she'd left, or waited until she'd been killed.

He'd never heard of someone with such talents before.

While a large part of him was skeptical of her ability, he couldn't take the chance that the crazy rumor was true, and that she would reveal his secrets. It wouldn't be a problem, if the guards or the king could see how valuable his work was. But sadly, they didn't. At least, not yet.

He'd gone too far, killing that countess. That's what seemed to have stirred up the hornet's nest; but she'd been the epitome of what was wrong with their society. She'd been born into her social position, but Lance had had to work his entire life to gain his. Everything he'd done since he turned eighteen had been about rising to a role of power. It was something he deserved, and had been denied through sheer bad luck.

Sure, he'd done some things that other humans didn't like; as if he cared about those pathetic bloodbags. They were nothing to him.

And it wasn't like he had anyone to answer to.

Not anymore.

Now, all he had to do was eliminate this stupid vampire, and he would be free to carry on his work. Oh, he might have to pause for a while, but he could continue his work unimpeded, once he was Chosen. He just had to ensure that happened.

He chuckled to himself; he couldn't believe how easy this had been to orchestrate. A piece of gold — it was funny how low some people's prices were — and the stable boy had been more than happy to tell the vampire that she had to leave the stable so he could work, not that he normally started mucking the building out for another couple of hours. It hadn't taken much more prompting to get the boy to suggest the morning was ripe for a walk, and that she should use the rear garden gate.

Lance wondered why she was staying in the stables, but he wasn't about to pass up the opportunity that offered. He had a collapsible crossbow in his satchel, ready and waiting...

And then she emerged. He aimed the bow, and pulled the trigger, but the bolt's flight wasn't true. Cursing, he slipped another in. This time, he corrected for the slight breeze. Releasing the trigger, he knew his aim was good, but a man — the vampire's companion — darted out in front of her, shoving her to the ground.

"Fuck." He slipped a third quarrel in place, aimed the crossbow, finger on the trigger.

Something thumped onto the rooftop behind him. A tingle ran down his spine, and slowly he turned around.

A vampire stood there, her long red hair blowing in the slight breeze that had ruined his first shot. He knew who she was, his brain screaming that he had to run, that she was far too dangerous — but he couldn't stop the words that growled from him.

"Fuck off, I'm busy."

The duchess gave a tittering laugh, her violet eyes all kinds of crazy. "I can see that." She smiled. "But then, I'm about to be pretty busy myself." That grin broadened, showing her fangs, which were longer and sharper than any he'd ever seen before. Bringing the crossbow up fast, he shot at her, should have hit her, but she moved. *Before the thrum of the bow string had died, she had him by the throat, her strong hand choking him.*

He scrabbled at her wrist. How could this be happening?

He'd been so close.

"Why?" he gargled.

"Because that's my daughter, and I've already lost too many babies." And then she grabbed one of his wrists with her free hand, wrenching the bone. A scream built within his chest, but it only emerged as a strangled groan.

♦

Hannah shook herself. She didn't want to follow that memory anymore. But his recollections were still there, still so powerful. Hannah delved deeper into Lance's past.

CHAPTER SEVENTY-FOUR

Fin was propped on his side with a mound of cushions, so that the bolt didn't cause any more damage. The bleeding had slowed considerably since Byrne had done the blood transfer, and Alice admitted to herself that she was itching to get a sample so she could study what was happening under a microscope. But she didn't think anyone else would appreciate that. Well, Dante might, but he wasn't the best person to follow when it came to social etiquette.

Hannah lay on the floor, flat on her back on a somewhat tattered blanket; Alice had been permitted to be here only provided she didn't touch the vampire. If she did, Tatiana would remove her hand, and then possibly her head. To be fair, Tatiana had only threatened the hand thing, but Alice was hedging her bets on that one.

You're focusing on this so you don't have to think about the fact that you thought your brother might be the killer.

It had only been for a wild second, but she'd thought it.

She blamed her aunt. But it didn't stop the shame from pulsing through her.

The City Guard had since confirmed that Lance had been the murderer. They'd found mementos from each of his victims — locks of hair glued to a page with their name — within his room, along with a stash of wooden stakes. The latter alone was highly illegal in the palace.

So she still had no idea what had happened to Ashok. Or who

might have killed her mother.

"How's he doing?" A deep, gravelly voice asked from the doorway.

Butterflies exploded into flight in her stomach. With all the drama that had happened in the last twenty-four hours, and the things she wished hadn't happened, the one thing she didn't regret was Byrne.

"He's alive, which is amazing, considering the bolt is sitting right next to his heart."

"You were right then, he would never would have survived being Chosen," Byrne said, stepping closer to her, a sling around his torso.

Alice shook her head. She'd seen firsthand what wood did to vampire's hearts. Fin's would have stopped the moment the transformation took place.

She gazed at Rena, strapped to Byrne's chest; he shrugged, suddenly self-conscious. "She was fussing, and Lady Beatrice couldn't calm her. Rena's been carried by Fin, Hannah or me ever since she was born. She knows the sound of my heart, and it soothes her."

Alice's own heart skipped a beat.

How could she possibly hope to win this man for herself? Just by smelling nice?

"Do you think Fin will make it?" Byrne asked.

"I'd know a bit more if I could get a sample of his blood, but then again, I'm limited to what I could see happening from it."

"Take one. I'll try anything that will help."

Alice nodded. Her medical bag was back at her place, she'd have to duck home to collect it. Turning to leave, she saw the baron, holding hands with a little girl in the doorway.

"I don't think your sister would want you in here," the human aristo said to the child.

"Just for a moment," the girl replied.

She had bright blue-green eyes, and Alice wondered if that meant she too had a special ability. It was still all so difficult to believe, that there might be people out there with psychic powers.

But she'd seen Hannah collapse from just a touch, and quite often Dante and Elle seemed to be able to tell what the other was thinking, to the point where only half their conversation was verbal.

It just meant that she was going to have a very difficult chat with Tal. While she wasn't meant to know about these powers — she gathered from Byrne that it was all some kind of elaborate secret — she couldn't keep the fact that she *did* know from her best friend.

Who had lied to Alice her entire life.

The little girl darted forward and put her hand on Fin's leg. Her eyes widened, and she nodded to herself. Then, just as the baron stepped into the room to retrieve her, she touched Hannah's leg, too.

Byrne grabbed the girl's arm, and gently but firmly pulled her away. "No!"

"It's okay, I can touch Hannah."

"*Emmie*," the baron chided.

"I'm coming." The little girl looked at Byrne's hand and he let her go. She nodded at him, rather regally for such a small child.

Small? Alice thought. The girl was only a foot and a bit shorter than she was.

Pausing on the threshold, the girl said, "I think they will be fine. Provided Hannah's mind fights off whatever is happening to her. And the baby's okay, too."

Byrne nodded, rubbing Rena's back with a big hand. As the baron escorted the child away down the hall, Alice could hear him scolding her quietly. She seemed to take it in her stride, reaching up and clasping his free hand again.

"So what next?" Alice asked.

"I had better Bite Fin again," Byrne said. "Then we wait."

♦

Hannah thought she could hear voices nearby, but she wasn't sure what was real and what was in her head. Lance's mind kept creeping in against hers, but she was fighting it. If she could just unravel his secret shame, she might be able to take control over his memories.

Already she'd learnt that he was the king's lover and had been hoping to be Chosen by the king himself. He'd been so delusional. He'd thought the king loved him. He thought everyone admired him. And those who didn't, well, he just removed them from the picture.

But before he could do that, he'd had to prove to them that they wanted *him* and that he was ultimately more powerful than them. Hence the method behind his murders.

No one can know.

Lance's voice. In her mind. She focused on it, prying open the memory with all her strength.

And then it was there.

"You are a bad person!" His mother was screaming at him, her blue eyes snapping with rage. And pain.

"You just can't accept me for who I am!" he yelled back.

Lance loved his mother. But he also hated her. How dare she tell him how to think, what to feel. So what, he didn't care about other people. He couldn't see what the issue was.

"I know what you did," she said.

He froze.

"I know you took that girl, that you wanted to kill her, but it was only because I came home and caught you that you let her go. You need to stop. You can't hurt people."

"You're wrong, I can do whatever I want."

His mother marched toward the front door. "I'll stop you! I'll get the guards."

The city guards. That bunch of jackasses?

But they might try and stop him.

Leaping forward, he lashed out with his fist. It struck his mother in the side of the head, and she collapsed to the floor with a startled yelp. The sound was so good, that he hit her again. And again.

But what he really wanted was to feel what it was like to hurt her. Really hurt her.

Dragging her into her bathroom, he threw her unconscious body on the tiled floor. Then running into his room, he pulled out the knives he'd carefully hidden there. Picking his favorite — the one with serrated edges — he hurried back to his mother. She was awake, groggy and disoriented. The rush of power was intoxicating. This woman had plagued his entire life. Always telling him how he wasn't good enough.

Bringing the knife down, the feel of it parting the flesh of his mother's chest, it was indescribable. But he had to do it again, and again. Blood sprayed over him, over the floor, the walls. He couldn't stop. He didn't want to stop. Not until the blood emerged sluggishly from her wounds. Staggering upright, he stared at her body, and a laugh worked its way up his throat.

He'd killed her.

She could no longer tell him what to do.

Lance had to get out of there.

Quickly, he threw his belongings together. He couldn't come back here. So he went to the one person who understood him. Who'd help him. Shelter him.

Ashok.

But his best friend hadn't protected him. The blood on his clothing, his story of victory...Ashok hadn't understood, and his mother had overheard their conversation. And so it had all happened again.

And then Ashok's sister had stumbled into the room. Hiding in the shadows, he watched as she tried to take in what was happening. She hadn't seen Ashok's body on the floor at his feet. His friend wasn't dead, no. Lance had plans for him.

"Mom?" her voice came out strangled, weak. Then, "Ashok?"

She stepped further into the room. He couldn't risk her seeing him, and so he brought the knife down. It didn't feel anywhere near as sweet as when he had stabbed his mother, or Ashok and his bitch parent. But it still felt good. He wanted to make sure she was dead but he heard voices yelling in the room next door. He could get caught.

And so he ran, dragging his former friend's unconscious body with him.

♦

Hannah jerked upright. She was in a small room, lying on a tattered blanket next to—

"Fin!"

Scrambling toward him, she held his pale face between her hands. He was breathing. By the blood, he was still breathing. Resting her forehead against his, she was just grateful he was still alive.

"Welcome back. We thought we'd almost lost you, too."

Byrne stood in the doorway, Rena strapped to his chest. "How long was I out?"

"Three days."

"*Three days?*" Shock held her rooted to the spot.

Byrne nodded. "I did the last Bite this morning. We now have to wait three more days until we know if Fin makes it. But he's alive so far, and that's the best we can hope for. Dante said when he tried to Choose fully Graced people, they died instantly on the third transfer."

For some reason, that was comforting, even though it shouldn't be.

"We need to get a message to the king," Hannah said.

"Which one?" Byrne asked.

"The King of Pinton."

"Why?"

"Because I saw something in Lance's memories, something that can't wait."

"I'll call a messenger," Byrne said, and headed out of the room.

Hannah hoped it wasn't already too late. And in the next few days, she was going to have to talk to Byrne's human friend, Alice. She'd recognized the girl's face from Lance's memories. He'd been responsible for so much death.

Turning back to Fin, she pressed a kiss to his still lips. "Three days."

CHAPTER SEVENTY-FIVE

"You want me to do *what*?"

Alice was in the morgue, examining a sample of Fin's blood.

"The king has asked for you to pay him a visit," Misty said, her lavender eyes hard like flints. "With your medical bag, and some surgical equipment."

Alice wasn't sure what she'd done to annoy the vampire, but she didn't particularly care, either. Maybe Misty and Tal were having problems. Alice wouldn't know. She hadn't had time for *that* conversation yet. Or any conversation for that matter.

"Surgical equipment?"

"Whatever you would need for surgery."

"What kind of surgery?"

Misty propped a hand on one hip. "Are you going to stand there and repeat everything I have to say, or will you get moving?"

"But I have to meet Byrne in fifteen minutes."

The viscountess considered for a moment. "Bring him with you."

Right.

And so that was how Alice found herself heading to the Crystal Palace, bag full of surgical gear, werebear and vampire in tow. What had happened to her old, uncomplicated life?

◆

"How can you tell if someone has been subject to wood poisoning?" the king asked.

"Excuse me?" Alice said. "Your Majesty."

She stood with Misty, Byrne, and the other were, Clay, in the king's bedchamber. The room was so opulent her brain had just given up processing it all properly. Gold here, silver there, tapestries, woven mats, delicate pieces of furniture and antiques so old and rare she didn't even know what they could be worth. The king himself was seated in a chair next to a small table, inlaid with a mother-of-pearl mosaic.

"If a vampire were to have been fed, say, sawdust, how could you tell?"

"Why would a vampire willingly eat sawdust?"

"Say it wasn't willingly."

Misty took an angry step forward, a glass jar of white powder in one hand. "Lance fed the king sawdust. We found his supply."

"Hannah saw him do it," Byrne rumbled.

Alice took the container from Misty. Her hand shook as she removed the lid and dipped a finger in the contents. It was so finely ground the king wouldn't have noticed it in his food. But that raised another question.

"Why were you eating food anyway, Your Majesty?"

"To be social," the king said. "Lance preferred I did it. To make him feel more welcome in my home. Because sharing my bed wasn't enough!" He thrust himself up from his chair, but his face paled and he fell back into his seat.

That wasn't a good sign.

"The only way to tell for sure would be to inspect the heart," Alice said.

"But I ate the wood — wouldn't it be my stomach?" the king said.

"If your body could process and get rid of the allergen — the wood — then you'd be okay. But if it got into your blood stream...it would entirely depend on how much had made it to your heart."

The king looked at Misty, then Alice. "Do it then. Look at my heart."

"But—"

"I can gather what is involved. I need to know the state of my health."

"Why me?" Alice blurted.

King Johan stared at her for so long that she thought he might not answer. Then he sighed. "You are the leading expert on vampire physiology in this kingdom, aside from the head of medicine at the university. And I do not want another vampire knowing about this. No other human doctor has the same amount of hands-on experience as you do regarding wood reactions in vampires. Is this not correct?"

Alice wanted to say no, it wasn't. But that would be lying. She'd just performed four autopsies on vampires. More than any other doctor probably had in their lifetimes.

"Will you do this service for your kingdom?" the king asked.

Alice nodded. What other choice did she have?

Byrne and Clay had to hold the king down. He'd been laid out on a beautiful gold-lined table, inlaid with mother-of-pearl. The carpeted floors were never going to be the same after this. It didn't help matters that he hadn't wanted an anesthetic — but then, she didn't know if it would even *work* on a vampire. It was hit-and-miss with most human patients. Plus, she didn't have to bother with it normally because her patients were dead when they were operated on.

Normally, cutting open a person's chest and prying their ribs apart didn't bother her. But when the patient was alive, and conscious? Well, that was an entirely different story. She used a scalpel to cut open the king's chest, and winced when he grunted around the leather he was biting on. It was going to get worse. Alice used a set of retractors to hold the skin open, and then broke several of his ribs. The king moaned and his fangs protruded past his lips, cutting into the flesh of his chin. Twin rivulets of blood ran down his neck.

Looking into her monarch's ribcage, Alice stared at his beating heart. She wished Dante was there, because his eyesight would pick up on any damage much better than hers could. But the fact she could see damage at all? That was bad.

Nodding, Alice began bending the ribs back into place — they had already started to heal. "Just rip them off," Clay said.

Alice choked on her saliva. "What?"

"They'll grow back. If you put them back, they'll heal again, but will be loose in the meantime and could cause more damage if they break off. Just snap them off."

She couldn't do it.

With a hiss, Misty darted forward and broke the ribs clean through. The king screamed, and then fainted.

Alice made quick work of stitching him back up. He was conscious again by the end of it, but at least he'd had a few moments rest. She pulled off her gloves and looked around for a bin.

"Here." Clay shoved a waste basket at her. It was entirely made of gold. She dumped the gloves in it and turned to the king.

"Would you like the others to hear what I've got to say?"

His intense purple gaze met hers and then he barked, "Out. Except Misty." Silently Byrne and Clay left the room. "Make sure they go far enough away," the king added, no doubt mindful of the weres' acute hearing.

Misty walked over to the entry and called out to the guards to escort Byrne and Clay to the gardens. She shut the door, and Alice noticed there were pink dots spattering her pale gown.

They waited for several minutes before Misty nodded for them to speak.

Alice took a deep breath. "I'm sorry, Your Majesty."

"You're sorry?"

"The damage to your heart is extensive. I can see it at a macroscopic level. The tissue is black. And it doesn't seem to be regenerating."

Misty stared at her. "What are you saying?"

"You're dying."

"But, why is it so slow?"

Alice shook her head in frustration. "Usually, wood exposure is sudden and severe, but this has been a slow build up. Because the sawdust was absorbed into your bloodstream, it has been affecting your heart bit by bit; but not slow enough that your heart had time to heal on its own. Exposure to any more wood will cause your heart to fail. "

"Could there be more sawdust in his system?" Misty asked.

Alice nodded.

"I see."

"So do I." The king's sounded tired. Worn.

"I don't think your heart will be able to heal from this much damage. I'm sorry." Alice looked at her feet.

"So I might live, provided I am not exposed to more wood. Which is unlikely."

"Yes." She wished it were otherwise.

Silence fell.

"So what now?" Alice asked.

Misty looked at her. "What do you mean?"

She wished it wasn't so, but..."I presume you'll kill me?"

The king chuckled, then gasped in pain.

"But I know what's wrong with you," Alice said.

"As will everyone else, eventually. I won't kill your for the knowledge. But I expect you to try and work out if there is a way to save me. Now please, go."

Dismissed, Alice grabbed her medical bag. She would clean her equipment back in the morgue. Turning back to the king, she asked, "Do you know why he did this?"

Misty snorted. "He wanted to be Chosen, and Johan kept saying no. We think this was his little revenge. But we don't know if he knew it would kill Johan, or just make him sick."

Knowing some of the things that Lance had done, Alice had a feeling he knew exactly what it would do to the king. But such thoughts were better kept to herself. She left.

CHAPTER SEVENTY-SIX

It was the third day since the final transfer.

Hannah had barely left Fin's beside, except for when she'd needed to attend to nature or bathe. She even drank her cup of pig's blood next to him. She didn't particularly enjoy the taste, but she needed blood now more than ever, perhaps because she was still recovering from touching Lance's corpse.

She'd been out for three whole days.

She'd missed Fin being Bitten. She hadn't been there for Rena. If it hadn't been for Byrne, they would have been screwed. Fin thought he was a failure; it was her who'd let down everyone around her. But she'd had to know what had caused Lance to try to kill her, to almost kill Fin.

And now she did.

It was because he was a deranged sociopath.

She figured his mother had known what he was early on — her having Blue eyes, and all — but he hadn't been aware that his mother was Graced. And so he'd just seen her as a condescending and demanding woman. Not as an empath who could literally feel her son's monstrous nature.

And a monster he'd been.

Even Hannah's mother wasn't that bad. Oh, she done lots of horrible things in her life, Hannah knew, but she didn't kill just for fun. She did it to defend what was hers. And maybe sometimes to prove a point. But her mother *was* a psychopath who'd been born in a lab so long ago that it might as well be a myth; at least that's what it was to everyone else.

"How's he going?" Byrne asked, coming into the room. The conversation felt far too familiar. It had been repeated in some form or another ever since Byrne had done the final Bite.

"Alive. But still out of it." Hannah was holding onto one of Fin's hands. Touching him anchored her, and she hoped that it did the same to him. That he'd fight to stay with her, and Rena.

"It should be any time now. Once he's awake, we can take out the bolt."

Hannah nodded. She'd been waiting nervously since she woke, listening to his heartbeat to make sure he was still with them, that he was still—

There was no sound from within his chest.

Hannah strained to hear the next beat, convinced that she must have just missed it.

Nothing.

"*Fin!*"

Panic boiled through her, she couldn't lose him. Not now. Not after almost making it.

Byrne rushed forward, shoving her aside. He lifted Fin's head, retracting his lips, peering intently into Fin's mouth. Then, with a sigh, he sat back on his heels next to the bed. "It's okay."

"Okay?" Hannah cried. "His heart's stopped!"

Byrne put a hand on hers. "Give it a few more seconds."

She stared down at the were's hand, his skin dark against hers, but there was no press of his memories into her mind.

So he *did* have a mental shield.

And then it happened.

Thump.

Thump.

Thump.

Tears coursed down her cheeks as she grabbed Fin's arm. He was alive!

He'd stayed with her.

"Why did it stop?" she asked, once she'd counted two hundred heartbeats. Two hundred and fifty.

"His heart was the final organ to change. It had to stop for that to happen. It's why the stupid leeches are called the living dead."

"Huh. I'm a stupid leech, you know."

"Nah, you're a smart one."

Hannah chuckled, but the sound was watery.

And then the most amazing thing happened.

Fin opened his eyes.

♦

Everything was too loud, and too bright. And people were blathering crap in his head. Byrne was sitting next to him, Hannah on his right. She was crying.

"Why are you crying?" Fin asked.

"This is going to hurt," Byrne said. And then razor-sharp agony sliced through his chest.

Fin's back bowed. "Mother fucker!"

"All fixed," Byrne said with a grin, holding up a crossbow bolt.

What the fuck was he doing with that?

"Couldn't you have warned him?" Hannah demanded.

"And have him go into a panic attack about it? No." Byrne shook his head.

The pain was already fading. And Fin was hungry. Like, really hungry. For a steak. The bloodier the better. Which was odd. He liked his meat well done.

A memory flashed through his mind. Someone shooting at Hannah, him pushing her out of the way. Pain exploding through every inch of his body.

How was he alive? He shouldn't be...

Turning a narrowed gaze onto Byrne, he then shifted his attention to the arrow.

"Byrne, did you—"

He couldn't even form the words in his mind.

'How am I going to tell him?'

"Tell me what?" Fin demanded, staring at his best friend. The bastard.

'Shit, is he hearing my thoughts?'

Fin shoved himself up, wincing in anticipation of the pain in his ribs, from the crossbow bolt. But nothing hurt. He felt fan-fucking-tastic.

"You fucking Bit me!" He couldn't believe it. "I could have died, you moron!"

"You were dying anyway," Byrne snapped.

"Maybe I would have liked to die a hero."

"Oh, come on. Die a hero? Are you listening to yourself?"

"Don't be a jackass."

"A jackass?"

"You Bit me!" But Fin's voice had gained an air of wonder.

Byrne grinned. "Sure did."

"And I survived."

"Sure did." And then Byrne was hugging him. And he was hugging Byrne. And holding out a hand to Hannah, who leapt on them both.

"So you can touch Byrne?" Fin asked, looking around the bear's shoulder.

"Yep!" Hannah said.

"You touch her and I'll kill you," Fin growled at the were.

Literally growled.

"Byrne's dating someone now," Hannah said in a whisper that wasn't really a whisper.

'She's awesome.' And then in his head, Fin got a picture of the coroner. Being Bitten by Byrne had given him, what? A mental link? Kick-started his telepathy?

"Whoa, Byrne. I'd hold onto these thoughts." Then Fin grinned. He could torment Byrne from a distance now. Awesome. "This is gonna be great!"

Byrne groaned. "My worst nightmare has come to pass."

"Now, more importantly," Fin said. "Did I get any more handsome? I mean, I know it's hard for that to be imaginable. But did I?"

Byrne took a swipe at his head. "No, you're still ugly."

Hannah laughed. "As handsome as ever, although your eyes are different."

Fin's breath hitched. "Different bad or different good?"

Hannah leaned in close. "Well, they're yellow with Green flecks. I don't mind them, but then, I'm a little biased."

'I'm out,' Byrne thought, got up and left the room.

"Finally, I thought he'd never go," Fin whispered. Hannah laughed. He'd never get tired of hearing that sound. He focused hard on tuning out everything else; the sounds, the smells, and the random thoughts. There was only one thing he wanted to be thinking about right now, and her name was Hannah.

CHAPTER SEVENTY-SEVEN

Byrne wandered the Greystoke garden.

Fin and Hannah were off doing gross shit somewhere, and Hannah's mother was spending 'quality time' with her son. That just left the Baron, Anton's mother, Clay and Elle to deal with. Thankfully, Elle had the day off and so she and Clay had gone out. The aristos were being aristos somewhere.

Byrne intended to spend the afternoon visiting Alice. She was at work at the moment, and then having lunch with her friend, Talan. They hadn't talked since Alice learned of the Graced, or since Talan had told her off for showing a little bit of interest in Byrne.

That left Byrne with some time on his own. Which was good, because so much had happened in the last few days. He'd met his mate. He'd Bitten his second human — the first one was long dead — and he'd got a telepathic link to the one person in the world who probably shouldn't have access to his mind, and would abuse the privilege horribly.

But such is life. He couldn't let the asshole die.

Byrne smelled a human approaching. He nodded at the fellow.

"Sir, there are two people here to see you," the servant announced. "They claim to be relatives of yours. I've put them in the Rose room."

Relatives of his? Here? In Pinton? He seriously doubted it.

Heading inside, and then into the Rose room, Byrne was hit with the scent of honey and apples. He stopped on the threshold of the room and stared at its two occupants. One was a tall woman with dark skin, closely cropped black hair and a protruding midriff. Next to her was a towering were, with long striped hair and the scent of mint and cat clinging to him.

"Ruby?"

"Byrne!" The woman threw herself at him, and wrapped strong arms around him.

His younger sister.

Byrne could feel tears trickling down his neck. Hers, his? He didn't know.

Byrne unwound her arms from his neck, pushing her away slightly so he could look at her. "Ruby."

She grinned through her tears. "Byrne, we finally found you!"

The huge weretiger raised a dark eyebrow. "We?"

"Fine, you technically found him first. Only because you were in that inn!"

"What inn?"

"When you were in Skarva," Ruby said quickly. "Cade was on his way home when he thought he spotted someone who looked like you. He'd never seen you before, so he came home and grabbed me. I went back to the inn and picked up your scent. And here we are."

"You two are mates?" Byrne asked, stunned. Clay had said she'd mated to a tiger, but he hadn't quite believed it. Ruby hadn't really believed in fate; he didn't think she would have agreed to a mating, as a matter of course.

"And expecting our first cub," the other were said. He closed the distance between him and Ruby in a couple quick strides and wrapped an arm around her shoulders.

"Well, cubs. There's two heartbeats."

A grin widened on Byrne's face, but then guilt crashed through him. He'd missed all this. This past three years, he'd been off gallivanting around the countryside and they'd obviously been looking for him. He'd had no idea.

"How long have you been searching for me? How did you even know I was alive?" Byrne asked, sitting down on one of the sturdier chairs in the room.

Ruby sat too, cupping her hands around her rounded belly. "Ever since Cade broke me out of the camp."

Byrne sat silent for a moment. "From what-now?"

"They took me when they took you, except they couldn't find a buyer for me. And so they kept me in a cage. Until Cade freed me." She gave her mate a bright smile.

"They took you?" Byrne roared, coming to his feet.

Ruby nodded, her eyes sad.

"They said they'd leave you alone if I went with them. It was the only reason I did...the only reason I didn't try and get away." Byrne had thought he was saving his sister. Instead, she'd been shoved in a similar kind of torment to him. If he could kill the fuckers again, he would.

"Only for a short while," Ruby said. "Not as long as you. But we never stopped looking. Cade helped me."

The were grinned. "I was just making sure she wouldn't just ditch me. She didn't like the idea of a weretiger mate. Not at the start."

"He wore me down."

"And saved your life." A gentle look passed between them.

"That too."

There were so many questions Byrne wanted to ask. How was Gina? She was pregnant the last time he'd seen her. And her mate, Mark. But where could he start?

"Ruby, I'm sorry I didn't come home."

Maybe that would do.

Leaning forward, she stared at him, her yellow eyes bright. "I saw that room where they kept you. I knew you'd need time to get over that. But I couldn't let you have too long. I had to see for myself you survived."

And then they were hugging again.

A wolf whistle pierced the air. Fin and Hannah were watching them, Rena held in Fin's arms. Behind them, the baron and Emmie.

"Wait until I tell Alice you were hugging another woman," Fin said.

Byrne growled. "This is my sister, you idiot."

Fin sighed dramatically. "Well, why didn't you tell me she was so good-looking?"

Good to see some things never changed.

Hannah elbowed Fin in the side, hard. "Oomph."

Byrne rolled his eyes. "I guess you had to meet each other sooner or later. Ruby, Cade, this is Fin. And his girlfriend, Hannah. And Lord Greystoke and Miss Emmie."

Ruby and Cade extended their hands, and everyone but Hannah shook them. Emmie's eyes widened when she took Ruby's hand, and then she looked at Cade. She pointed at Ruby's bump. "Huh. There's one tiger and one bear in there."

Ruby's mouth dropped open. "*What?*"

"I guess," Emmie said quickly. "I'm *guessing* there's one of each."

Cade looked at the little girl closely before thunking down on the seat. The chair groaned in protest, but held his weight.

But Ruby was smiling. "One of each! They will be able to shift."

Emmie slowly backed away. "Please don't tell anyone I said that."

"It's okay, we won't." Ruby's smile just kept getting wider. "But thank you!"

"Gee, glad we don't have to worry about that," Fin said with a laugh.

Emmie looked confused. "But the baby."

"Yeah, but Rena's already born, we know what we're in for. I mean, imagine it. *Twins.*"

Emmie was shaking her head. "Not that baby. *Hannah's* baby. The one in her stomach."

Fin paled. And then he dropped to the floor like a sack of potatoes.

Hannah crouched next to him.

"He fainted!" Emmie snorted, looking down her nose at the new were. "He'll be fine." And with that, the little girl swept from the room.

Hannah gently slapped Fin in the face, and he awoke flailing. "You hit me."

"You fainted."

He put a hand to his head. "Did I?"

"It was pretty funny," Cade said. Byrne had a feeling he might like the guy, even though he dared to touch his sister.

Fin's face was etched with lines of disbelief. "I thought Emmie said Hannah was pregnant."

Byrne laughed. "She did."

"Pregnant." Hannah was shaking her head.

Meanwhile, Fin was glaring at her. "I *told* you it was a risk. But no, Fin. I'm a vampire, Fin. It's fine, Fin."

"I am a vampire. You were human."

"And you're pregnant! And it's not my fault."

"Takes two to tango."

Byrne clapped his hands, breaking up the argument. "So, I see congratulations are in order."

Fin's expression turned thoughtful. "I guess I am that good. Being able to impregnate a vampire first go."

Hannah hit him. "I just thought you said it wasn't your fault."

"Hey, you jumped my bones. But credit where credit's due."

Then Hannah leaned down toward him. "We're having a baby."

And Fin smiled, an expression so tender Byrne had to look away. "I heard."

"You okay?"

"Better than okay." A pause. "But we're totally going to name it Finlay."

Ah, this was going to be fun.

Epilogue

Faith Castle was dreaming. It happened quite frequently, so she didn't think too much of it, except this was a dream about Fin, the twin brother she hadn't seen in a decade. She'd been trying to track him down over the years, but he was slippery as an eel, and tended to sneak away whenever she got close.

He was lying in a bed on his side, propped up with pillows. His chest was pierced with some kind of arrow. She couldn't see any other details in the room, it was gray and indistinct. But she knew Fin was dying.

No!

It's just a dream, she told herself, *it doesn't mean anything.*

Then the pain hit. It screamed through her mind, paralyzing her. This wasn't a dream, it was real.

And then the agony simply stopped. Just...stopped. And a space of her mind that she'd never known existed *died*.

Screaming, Faith tumbled from her bed, hit the floor in the room with a thump. Tangled in her bedsheets, she flailed against the floorboards. Squinting, Faith looked down at her hand clutching the sheets to her chest, pain radiating from her heart and mind.

The door swung open, and her sister, Marcia, stood there, backlit by the weak morning sunlight. Marcia knew better than to approach Faith without warning — Faith kept a dagger under her pillow and a sword beneath her bed.

"Faith, what is it?" Marica's Blue eyes were filled with concern, her gaze taking in her sister's disheveled state.

Faith was never disheveled.

"It's Fin," Faith whispered. She cast her mind out, roaming. Her telepathic range was immense. She tried to latch onto the small part of her brother that she could detect. His natural shield prevented her from seeing his thoughts, but they'd shared a womb, and the shape of his mind was as familiar as her own.

There was nothing there.

"What about him?" Marcia asked, coming closer. The floorboards squeaked in protest.

"He's dead." Faith's voice was hollow.

And then, as if nothing had happened, Fin was there. That small presence within her mind, back again.

Faith searched within herself. Had her mind been playing tricks on her? No, it hadn't. He'd *died*.

"Faith!" Marcia must have detected her swinging emotions. Devastation to elation and then confusion.

Looking over at her sister, she frowned. "He died, but now he's alive again."

"How is that even possible?"

Untangling herself from her bedsheets, Faith stood, her feet bare against the cold wooden floor of her room. Enough of this cat and mouse game. She'd had it. "I don't know, but I plan on finding out."

ACKNOWLEDGMENTS

I am so pleased to be able to share *Bitten* with you all. Creating a book is a very personal journey for an author, but we have help. I'd like to thank my husband for his support; my eagle-eyed editor, Pete Kempshall; my wonderful beta readers — Stephanie Gunn, Liz Grzyb, and Joanne Danton; and my writing buddies, you know who you are. Also, a special thanks goes out to Dr. Brendan Carson, who kindly offered me his medical knowledge when I began developing vampire physiology and had to perform imaginary autopsies.

Amanda Pillar is an award-winning editor and author who lives in Victoria, Australia, with her husband and two cats.

Amanda is the author of the Graced series, and has had numerous short stories published. She has co-edited six fiction anthologies and solo-edited two: *Bloodstones* and *Bloodlines*, published by Ticonderoga Publications.

In her day job, she works as an archaeologist.